PINK

BETHANY-KRIS

Published by Bethany-Kris

www.bethanykris.com

ISBN: 978-1-989658-20-8

Editor: Eli Peters

Cover Design © Black Widow Designs

This is a work of fiction. Names, characters, places, organizations, corporations, locales and so forth are a product of the author's imagination, or if real, used fictitiously. Any resemblance to a person, living or dead, is entirely coincidental.

For all my loves.

CONTENTS

ONE

"MR. ARSOV, would you be a dear and let me steal you for just five minutes?"

Lev hadn't even turned the key in the deadbolt to latch the lock on his apartment door when the building's manager came up behind him. He swore the old woman, Martha Mae, who *looked* like a strong gust of wind would make her bones rattle, kept a day planner right beside her door to track his schedule.

Because he couldn't tell her no—the old girl knew it, too. She reminded him of a grandmother he never had, for fuck's sake. What kind of an asshole would he be to refuse help to a senior citizen managing a sixty-unit building mostly by herself? The actual landlord—a company, not a real person—did very little for the tenants in their part of Harlem despite the fact that the city had been on the company's ass for a few years now about the heating, lighting, and code issues.

To no avail, clearly.

One only needed to give the hallway he currently stood in a good glance to see the truth staring them right in the face. Water stains on the ceiling. Lights that flickered. Worn carpeting and holes in the walls where exposed wires and pipes ran between units.

The place wasn't great. Sometimes, he took more cold showers in a month than he wanted to. Often, his one-bedroom apartment wasn't worth the rent he paid to keep it every month. It kept him off the streets, though.

That's all Lev needed considering the streets had been a real fucking reality for him just a few short years earlier when he finally hit eighteen, and the foster care system that he grew up inside decided ... fuck him. Out on his ass he went with the same garbage bag of clothes and personal items that he'd hauled between homes for the better part of his entire teenage life. He only entered the system because

1

his father passed away in a drive-by shooting in the Bronx when he was two months shy of his thirteenth birthday, and his mother was ... well, who knew?

Life had not been kind to Lev Arsov—he still struggled to get by because education had been a secondary thought in his mind when surviving needed to come first. It kicked him in the ass now when all he could manage to get for job opportunities were ones that included back-breaking manual labor or severely underpaid positions in the back of kitchens washing dishes and hauling garbage.

He did those for a while. Until he landed something a bit better—and dangerous—through the connections he made while proving he was the kind of employee that would do what he was told, keep his head down, and his mouth shut about the things he saw while he did it. In a place like New York City, where corruption was everywhere, he was appreciated by certain individuals. Even if those individuals were criminals. He figured ... whatever kept the flickering lights on and the shitty roof over his head, right?

"Well, could I be a bother and steal you to help me?" Martha Mae asked again.

Plastering a smile on his face, Lev turned the key in the lock and kept a tight hold on the backpack hanging over his shoulder. Spinning to face the woman who peeked out around the doorjamb of her apartment unit at the very end of the basement floor, she was only a head taller than the goddamn doorknob. In her usual get-up for the evenings, from the rollers in her white hair to the pink, fleece nightdress, her smile welcomed him. Her large, glassy blue eyes always held a bit of hesitation, though.

Like she knew he wouldn't say no. But she still wondered if he might.

"She holed up there again?" he asked.

Martha Mae sighed. "I tried—I *really* did."

He was sure she did. It wouldn't be the first time. It wasn't exactly like the old woman was equipped to handle the newest situation that landed in her hands in the form of a truant granddaughter dealing with some serious issues. The kind of things her grandmother certainly couldn't manage on her own.

But that was the system. It fucked everybody six ways to Sunday. The only thing the system afforded Lev was the skill of survival, and the knowledge that he could and would do whatever he needed to do at the end of the day.

Was he supposed to be thankful?

He wasn't.

Lev resisted the urge to check his watch if only because he didn't want Martha Mae to feel as though she was burdening him when he knew her sad reality. Nobody else would help her today—certainly not another tenant. She did her very best to *not* call the cops on her granddaughter because that almost always never ended well for anybody involved, and it was just yet another strike against a troubled teenager that needed help more than she needed the law. Nonetheless, he'd known the time before he left his apartment, and he was quite aware of the minutes passing him by now.

And the fact he was going to be late for work. On a very important night when he really couldn't afford to be late if the warning his boss gave him the evening before was any indication. It was a thirty-minute bus trip from his place in Harlem to the bar in the Kitchen where he worked, but shit

...

Martha Mae's worry showed on her forehead where the wrinkles were more apparent than ever when she said, "She stopped answering my calls through the door twenty minutes ago."

Well, Jesus ...

Lev spun on his booted heels and headed for the old lady. "Why didn't you start with that, woman?"

She tittered and waved her small, frail hands to usher him inside her apartment as she replied, "I will next time."

Right.

Next time.

There was always next time.

• • •

Lev shouldered through the group of young men lingering

in the back hallway of the bar to where the crowd began to spread out nearer his boss's office at the far rear. His task was made quicker by the fact he towered higher than most of the men waiting in the space as he topped out at six and a half feet tall with shoulders that could fill a doorway easily, and a demeanor that screamed he wasn't to be fucked with. It was hard to miss him coming into a place, all things considered.

And life had taught him to make sure everybody knew he wasn't easy prey before anything else. Made things a hell of a lot simpler for him, honestly.

His main job at the bar was keeping a drink in every hand that could buy one. It was his side hustle when the fights came up that kept him motivated enough to run six miles every morning and to use the gym across from the bar where a lot of the underground fighters in Hell's Kitchen liked to train. Usually, after his work was done in the early mornings because it was the only point he had the time to do so.

Everyone in the hallway separated like the sea had parted to let Lev through when he moved down the hallway toward his boss's office. Except for the guy at the end who didn't look old enough to even stand inside the back of the damn bar. Right in the middle of the hallway, he crossed his arms at Lev's approach. He never understood his boss's need to have open fight nights where *anyone* could put their name in for a bid to fight when all it did was invite the stupidest fucks off the streets who only needed cash and nothing more.

Then again ... wasn't that what all of them needed?

He sure did.

"Move your ass," Lev told the guy as he approached. "Before I move you."

Stupid didn't move.

In fact, he folded his arms and held his ground.

Because he was *stupid*.

"Hey, asshole, I was here—"

"Shut that hole in your fucking face before I fill it with my fist, yeah? You're going to move, and if you're really smart— but I doubt you are—you'll head out of here entirely. You're about forty pounds underweight, and they'll use you as filler tonight between the main fights. You know what happens to the *filler* in the ring, kid?"

At least this time, the guy had the decency to give Lev a second look. Which meant he had to tip his head all the way back to stare up at the man towering over him wearing dark-wash, ripped jeans and a black leather jacket that had seen better days but a hell of a lot of nights just like these. Stupid also had the nerve to swallow—a good sign of the fear he really didn't want to be showing in a place like *Nickie's*.

Fed by the underground, corrupted by a variance of organized crime figures that regularly made their way through the door for meetings, entertainment, or whatever else Lev's boss could offer, and controlled by a code this young man couldn't possibly understand ... shit, he was doing this boy a favor.

Bending down, Lev came eye to eye with the kid and uttered, "They'll put you in there with a guy like me just to teach your stupid ass a lesson. Need money? Here's not the place you want to find it. *Move.*"

Who knew what did it?

Maybe Lev's words.

Maybe the gleam in his eye.

Either way, the kid's gaze darted between Lev and the line of waiting men that had backed up all the way out to the floor where the ring was being set up for the fights that should have already started. Stupid didn't need to be told again before he grabbed the backpack from the ground and scooted around Lev without a look over his shoulder.

Letting out an annoyed breath, he straightened up, fixing his jacket as he did so and headed for the opened office door where he knew Nickie was probably playing the little king behind his desk. As he did on every fight night. He enjoyed this chaos.

This shitshow.

Not even bothering to enter the office, Lev remained in the doorway where his large presence was more than enough to catch the attention of the man chatting on the phone behind the desk. Nickie didn't bother to pull his legs down where he had them hooked at the ankles on the corner of the desk, nor did he hang up the phone when he looked Lev's way.

"You're late," the guy barked.

Lev lifted one shoulder. "Shit came up."

Like a teenager with a cutting problem.

He didn't mention that.

"Told you tonight was a big one, didn't I?"

"Looks to me like the place isn't even open yet. Technically still on time."

Nickie sighed, muttering something to whoever was on the other end of the phone before he slammed down the receiver hard enough to make the lamp next to it jump. He pointed a finger at Lev as he pulled his feet down from the desk to straighten up in his chair. "I shouldn't let you fight tonight— lately, you've been fucking off."

No, just ... distracted.

Nickie didn't care, though.

"I could use the extra cash," Lev said.

Not that he wanted to admit it.

Nickie arched a brow at the doorway Lev filled up and waved a hand as if gesturing to the line of people in the hallway that he couldn't even see. "So could they."

"They don't guarantee you wins, though."

That had his boss pausing.

"I need you serving directly from the bar to the front tables—"

"Who's gonna be sitting in them?"

Nickie grinned. "Now you're asking the right questions."

Yeah, that was the thing about this place. One who was lucky enough to work here on a nightly basis—like Lev—and not just pick up extra work on fight nights learned quickly that everything was done with a purpose. And if he was serving the front tables, it was for a good damn reason.

"Marcello will be in tonight."

Shit.

There was only one Marcello that regularly used *Nickie's* as a place of business. Andino Marcello. Infamous mafia Capo. Raging asshole on his good days. Particular and demanding and *difficult* in every possible fucking way.

He also liked Lev. Or the way he made his drinks.

Why?

Lev didn't have the first damn clue.

Nickie laughed huskily, reaching for the two fingers of whiskey and ice sitting on the edge of the desk with condensation dribbling down the glass. "Now you get it—the big boy will be in the house tonight, Lev. He's bringing in an associate to do some ... business. You know, while they enjoy the fights and all. You're the only bartender I have on hand that he'll even consider allowing to mix his drinks, so you're gonna be handling him and his guys until told otherwise. Got it?"

"Can I fight later?" he asked.

He could really use that extra cash. A grand for stepping into the ring whether he won or lost—up to five-k if he pulled a win with enough bets on him. With only a handful of fights throughout the night, he *really* wanted to be on the docket. What little savings he had was already basically gone, and this place certainly didn't pay enough to make his ends meet. The fights helped to make it through the drier spells, so to speak.

"Depends," his boss eventually replied.

"On what?"

Nickie shook his glass with a smirk. "On if your name gets pulled, Lev, like everybody else."

Fuck.

Usually, he had a little pull given he worked behind the bar. Not tonight, apparently. He couldn't say he was surprised considering the situation Nickie had with a guy like Andino Marcello promising to show his face at the fights.

With an associate.

It was good for *Nickie's* in the world of the underground. Bad for Lev when his chances of getting his name pulled to fight were about as good as the rest of the fucks lined up waiting outside Nickie's office.

"But hey," his boss called when Lev turned to leave.

He didn't bother to turn around. "What?"

"Pay is triple tonight. You earned it, kid."

Kid.

Maybe he was just a kid compared to Nickie's middle-age

crisis that he was trying to hide with the gold rings on his fingers and the new Porsche parked in the back. Lev held back from scoffing—he felt so far from a kid at twenty-four. That was a lifetime ago, and though life hadn't been easy then ... it was different. Sometimes, that was the part he missed the most.

Nickie didn't give him the chance to think on it for long before he added, "Says something when Marcello calls ahead and the first thing he asks about is you, doesn't it?"

Did it?

Lev couldn't really say.

Or he didn't want to.

"I just mix his drinks when he's here, boss."

He could *feel* Nickie's eyes burning into his broad back. To be honest, his boss wasn't all that different than Andino Marcello in the grand scheme, really. A different breed of *bad*; with less money and influence, sure, but still dangerous.

Or rather, he *could* be.

When it counted.

"Keep it to serving drinks, huh?"

Nickie's murmur felt loaded.

Lev only nodded. Only one of those two men were currently signing his paychecks, after all. That's really what mattered to him at the end of the day.

What else needed said?

Apparently, Nickie thought more.

"Careful making friends with the likes of him," his boss warned at his back before Lev could stroll back into the hallway, "because men like Andino Marcello only keep people around for as long as they benefit him. You won't like what happens when you no longer do."

He would remember it if only because he thought that was a pretty straightforward way of doing business regardless if he was just serving a man's drinks or not. So long as he did his job well, he still had one to do.

Wasn't that the whole point?

TWO

"ANGE MODELING wants to sign me to work with the French designer, Pierre Missioux."

"*What?*"

The screech came from two different, very distinct voices. One echoed from the phone she had sat on the small table next to her twin-size bed where she hadn't even bothered to fix the sheets that morning before leaving. Her *mother*. Who was also now crying. The other came from her friend who suddenly slid into her bedroom doorway with eyes as wide as her own, she was sure.

"Oh, my *God*," her mother cried.

"Are you serious?" her friend asked.

Gigi wasn't sure who to answer first. Instead, she checked the screen of the laptop one more time—she'd only intended to order her and Cassie, her roommate, Chinese. Even though the salt would probably make her bloated enough that it would show on her measurements tomorrow. She figured, might as well check her emails since she hadn't even had the chance to do that during her very busy day.

Not that it was anything unusual.

"Gi?" Cassie urged, daring to step forward in the doorway but not coming all the way into the room.

She didn't answer her friend back. Or her mother, still crying, on the phone. It almost seemed like she had floated out of her own body for a second. The shock was overwhelming when the last thing she expected to see marked as a *Top Priority* email when she brought up the tab was the one from her agency about the Paris offer. Just a few seconds ago, the only thing on her mind had been greasy noodles and the ache in her legs and soles of her feet.

In the world of modeling, a day of go-sees in a city like New York could be absolute hell. It wasn't so bad when it was only one or two appointments but that wasn't usually how it worked. Typically, Gigi's entire day ended up filled by her mother agency, MGNT Modeling, with go-sees from one side of the city to the other with barely any time in between for a break. Well, come the end of it, every single part of her five-foot-eleven, one hundred-twenty-eight-pound body felt it.

And all she wanted was her *bed*.

Maybe a glass of wine.

Not that she was legal to drink at twenty years old, but that certainly didn't stop her roommate—who was a year younger than her—from somehow managing to keep their fridge and freezer stocked with all the liquor they might want or need. A lot like the benzo bars in the bathroom, or the coke her roommate liked to indulge in on the weekends.

Those weren't really her things.

Kind of came with the territory, though.

Models were expected to be a lot of things. Most importantly at this stage in Gigi's fledgling career, *available*. Pleasant. Ready at a moment's fucking notice. Her weight couldn't—or rather, shouldn't—fluctuate more than a pound or two as though it really made a difference on her tall, slender frame. She couldn't cut her hair or change the style from the shoulder-length, loose dark blonde waves her mother agency settled on as the *best look* to showcase what they considered to be her ... strangely beautiful features.

Sure, strangely beautiful was one way to put it. Growing up, the only thing she wished she could do was hide the freckles that always showed through her makeup no matter how much she tried to put on. She begged her mother to have the gap between her two front teeth fixed because no matter what, the full, round bow of her upper lip always showed it off regardless of what she did to hide it. Kids teased that her vivid green eyes, always wide, made her an *alien* because no one else had that color but her. Add in the flat, wide slope of her nose and eyebrows that were darker than the hair on her head, and well ... there was never a lack of jokes where her looks were concerned.

Funny how the same features that she was once teased about were now the things that everyone promised would someday put her under the brightest of lights all across the globe. *The right person needs to see that face of yours,* her mother, Kimie, used to tell her, and still did, *and they'll find their muse, Gigi Rey Parker. Don't you ever stop showing it off.*

Part of her felt like she was living her mother's dream for her just as much as her own. Especially because her mother left her own budding modeling career to keep and raise the baby she became pregnant with at just twenty-one, and *alone* seeing as how her father had never been in the picture, well … she didn't want to let her mom down, either. Even if at first, her mom hadn't wanted her to model at all.

That was how, barely six months past her seventeenth birthday, Gigi found herself leaving her small New Jersey town for New York City. Where she then signed the rights to her future over to MGNT Modeling without truly understanding what it meant. Everyone else said she was beautiful—that she was going to be a *star*.

So much so, that she wanted it, too.

Three years later with an entire portfolio in hand, a few small runway shows under her belt, and a handful of magazine shoots, and she wasn't any closer to seeing those bright lights than she had been when she first showed up in New York.

The whispers from other models in the agency—it was hard to make friends outside of the modeling circle when every day revolved around *making it*—were starting to creep into Gigi's own thoughts. Especially when she made it back to her Brooklyn apartment that she shared with her roommate because the day was over, and the only thing she had were the thoughts in her head screaming at her. *You're too old. If you haven't made it yet, you won't. Maybe you're just … not what people are looking for, Gi. I mean, look at you.* Not that she ever voiced it out loud or said a word to anyone about those self-doubts and fears.

If she did, they won.

Instead, she kept on keeping on.

Go-sees.

Castings.

Whatever she was told to do, she did it.

Maybe that was why, as her roommate and for all purposes, best friend, squealed in Gigi's bedroom doorway at the news she had just shared, all she felt was a sense of surrealism. She somehow managed to float back down to earth, her body becoming hers again as she nodded to the unspoken question coming from Cassie as the girl opened her arms high and wide like she was saying *this is it, Gigi.*

Her mother echoed the silent sentiment. "You did it, baby girl! This is your break, Gi. I'm so proud of you."

Should she cry?

Breathe?

Gigi didn't know.

"They'll want me to fly out to Paris soon, maybe a few days, or a couple weeks," she said, voice faint. "That's like ... not very long to prep and—"

"Who *cares*? It's Pierre Missioux," Cassie crowed, throwing her head back in laughter as she crossed the room. Gigi didn't even get the chance to respond to that before her friend wrapped her in a hug that ached as much as it felt like a congratulations. "The biggest haute couture designer in *Paris.* Do you know what that means, Gigi?"

Sort of.

Yes.

No ...

"You have to celebrate," her mother said on the phone.

"*Yes.* That's what we're doing."

"But—"

Cassie cut her hand through the air as she took a step back from Gigi, offering no room for argument when she pointed at the phone and said, "Even Kimie said so."

The words came out sing-song.

Gigi wanted to laugh.

And cry.

"Celebrate," she heard her mother say. "You earned this."

"And who knows when you'll have time to do anything after next week? Did you reply to MGNT's email yet?"

Gigi shook her head and finally sat down on the edge of her bed with the laptop still balanced between her hands. If she let it go, then her roommate would see how hard she had been working to hide the trembling in her fingers.

The *nerves*.

All that excitement.

What happens now?

Gigi glanced up.

Cassie stood waiting with hands on her hips and a wide smile at the ready. "*Definitely* celebrating. I'll call Matty—he'll know a good place."

How could she say no?

Gigi was still trying to catch up with everything else. Her entire life was about to change.

• • •

Gigi's idea of a celebration did not include ending up at a dingy bar hosting illegal fights in the middle of Hell's Kitchen but after slamming back a few of her favorite drinks—compliments of her friend's boyfriend, no ID needed—it all looked a little better. Alcohol had that effect on people.

"See that guy over there," she heard Matty holler over the rising noise in the bar, "black suit, sitting by the big dude with dreads."

He nodded—didn't point, she noticed—across the room from their current position. In the dimly lit bar, a makeshift boxing ring had been set up right in the middle of the scuffed, hardwood floor. Closest to the ring where two men were currently doing their best to beat the hell out of each other, tables filled with a melting pot of different people enjoyed the scene in front of them. More than once, she had noticed money passing hands from different men who approached the tables and then left as quickly as they came. And without much fanfare, either.

Was it all that much of a shock there was illegal bets going on?

Not really.

She also noticed the fact that the people closest to the ring were served first, and were also the patrons who the servers returned to far more often than they did anyone else in the bar.

The guy Cassie's boyfriend pointed to, however, didn't sit at a table like the rest did. Instead, he was one of the only people, other than the guest beside him, who sat in leather, high-back chairs with a small table in the middle for drinks that were regularly refilled before the glasses even had a chance to be emptied. He wore a suit, his cold expression didn't change, and he rarely took his dark gaze away from the ring even when the man beside him became more and more animated the longer they spoke.

Cassie nodded, sipping on the gin and tonic the server in a skin-tight dress had brought over earlier when they'd finally managed to gain the woman's attention on her fifth stroll by their table. "Yeah, what about him?"

"Mafia."

Her friend's eyes went wide. "*Really*?"

Matty nodded, grinning. "Yeah, friend of a friend knows the guy. Comes from the Marcellos. Trying to get on their radar is crazy hard. We're a fucking blip but not for long, baby."

Gigi did her best not to roll her eyes at the way her friend seemed to soak up every single word that came out of her boyfriend's mouth. He was a big talker who liked to flex and name drop, but she didn't think that he understood very much of what he spoke about at the end of the day.

Still, her friend liked it.

The *bad boy*.

Late-night calls; vague details about where he had been and what he'd been doing while he was there; the *money*. When he had it, that was.

More than once, Cassie had attempted to get Gigi hooked up with one of Matty's friends. A *guy from the crew*, she liked to say. Hell fucking no. Her life was already a spectacularly busy mess without adding something like a guy with shady business into it, too.

She wasn't that hard up for dick, either.

"What's his name?" Cassie asked.

"Andino—"

"I'm gonna head to the bar and just order another drink," Gigi said, pushing up from the uncomfortable wooden chair at their corner table. "Because I've waved at that girl five times, and the last time she even looked at me."

But still didn't make her way over. It wasn't like the server could pretend she hadn't seen Gigi that time. No doubt, the black romper and leather jacket she had on that matched the three-inch pumps on her feet didn't scream the same kind of wealth as the suits and dresses of the patrons closer to the ring. And that was exactly why the girls working the floor selectively chose who they wanted to serve at any given time.

Bitches.

"Oh, bring me back another of these," Cassie said, waving her half-full glass of gin and tonic.

"They won't bother IDing you."

She passed Matty a look, but he was more concerned with ogling the guy in the black suit across the room that, for whatever reason, he seemed to have a fucking hard-on about. If the guy really was *mafia*, as he'd said, then she didn't understand why he would even want to mess with that kind of trouble.

Matty was bad news, sure.

Not *that* kind of bad news.

Whatever.

It wasn't Gigi's business.

"Sure, thanks for the info," she muttered, stepping away from the table. If they cared or noticed that she left, well she couldn't say because she didn't bother to glance back over her shoulder.

The phone in her clutch burned a hole in her mind as she made her way through an overcrowded floor to get to the far end of the bar. She managed to find one stool that wasn't full. All it took was one good look at the three girls and one guy working the crowd gathering at the bar for drinks to know it was going to be a while before she would get her drinks. Not to mention, the constant stream of servers that returned with trays full of empties and ready for refills.

Instead, her mind drifted back to the phone as she waited to be noticed and served. She wasn't going to throw up her hands and shout at the bartenders who were already moving as fast as they possibly could like everyone else was doing.

Besides, wasn't there enough noise in the place without her adding to it?

She thought so.

Gigi resisted the urge to pull out the phone just to check the email about Paris one more time—like she hadn't already done it fifty times since leaving the apartment. As if the email might suddenly disappear, and the dream that had just been placed into her hands would go up in smoke all because she decided to read the email again.

Still ...

It was there.

Real.

Actually happening.

Soon, she would be on a plane to Paris, contracted to a satellite agency while working exclusively as a model for a major designer that for whatever reason ... picked her. She had so many questions. Starting with *why* and ending with *how*.

Right then, all she could do was smile.

"Has anybody ever told you that your face should be on magazines?"

Gigi's head popped up as a laugh burst from her lips. The man that had been working with the girls further down the bar approached her spot at the end, passing by at least twenty other people who gestured with a bit more ferocity at his blatant disregard for their shouts and demands. The white tee he wore stretched across the broad bands of muscle that made up an expansive chest. Rolled up at the sleeves, the fabric tightened to show off the way his strong arms and golden skin, dusted with dark hair, glinted under the pot lights that made up the backdrop of the bar when he placed them in front of her spot on the shiny top.

Black hair, shaved down to a well-groomed buzz, had a blue tint and only added to the sea-color of the stare that flicked over her features and then chanced a glance down at the low dip in the front of her romper. The man had no shame that he was checking her out, but she didn't really mind all that much, either.

He wasn't hard on the eyes.

16

It didn't hurt to look at him.

Not at all.

And since he seemed content to drink in a good gulp of her, she did the same for him. Standing at least six and a half feet tall behind the bar, he towered higher than even the shelves of liquor behind him. Strong lines made up a face that didn't have a hint of boyishness anywhere—not in the scruff that dotted a jaw and cheeks carved from stone. He was all man, all over. A thick brow quirked up when her stare slammed back into his, and a sexy grin stretched his thin lips wide to show off the white teeth that made up his smile.

And *God.*

What a fucking smile it was.

"Well, have they?" he asked.

Gigi had enough sense to swallow before she spoke, lest her next words come out in a girlish rush of hormones and stupidity. It wasn't often a man could make her tongue-tied, and certainly not by only his approach.

But here she was.

Suddenly, this celebration was looking *way* better.

"It's not the first time I've heard that line, actually," she replied.

A laugh burst from his mouth, and *yes,* she somehow managed to feel that sound all over her body. The noise of the bar began to disappear all around her as the good-looking bartender with a body that looked more suitable to be in the ring than behind the bar leaned in. Edging a bit closer to her, he used his free hand to toss a yellow-checkered bar rag over his broad shoulder.

The action had her swallowing.

Again.

Because she'd noticed his fingers. Their length, the roughness of the digits like he used them a lot, and then their proximity to her when he dared to point one at her.

"But the better question," he said, "is whether you've ever actually been on a magazine, hmm? Something familiar about that face."

"Really? Because everyone likes to say they've never seen one like it."

Those blue eyes of his blinked.

Then, he smirked.

"Maybe that's it—never seen anything like it."

It also wasn't the first time she had been told that line, either. Except there was something about the way he said it and how his tone *dipped* at the end. Like his gaze roving down her throat when his tongue peeked out to lick along the seam of his bottom lip.

"Hey, are you gonna get us a fucking drink or—"

The bartender held up one large hand to the left, his palm stopping all of two inches away from the face of a beefy guy leaning across the bar top. "I'm only mixing for front tables tonight—fuck off to the other side of the bar before I move you there."

Gigi grinned.

He hadn't taken his eyes off her.

"I'm Gigi," she said.

He opened his mouth to reply, but the announcer standing at the DJ's booth just a few feet away from the boxing ring stopped him from saying anything at all when the man's voice filled the speaker. His attention drifted to the man as he straightened up to his full height, allowing him to easily stare over the crowd of people.

"Next fight—*Lev Arsov versus Draven Kinley.* Ten minutes to start—one ten-minute round. Betting begins now."

His gaze came back to her, sharper and sexier than ever. This time, that grin of his was a little more sinful and tempting.

But also dangerous.

"Looks like I'm up next."

Gigi's head snapped to the side, and she was sure her face reflected the shock radiating through her gut in that moment. He was just a bartender, right? "What?"

He winked. "Lev Arsov—that's me. Stick around, Gigi. See what happens next."

And what might that be?

THREE

SOMETHING WAS up.

Lev knew it the second he stepped inside the ring to fight. Not because he recognized the name of his opponent or even saw the guy before he was in the ring himself. No, he knew something was up because Nickie, who always stuck to the shadows during the fights, made his way to Lev's side as he neared the ring.

Just long enough to lean in and say, "Andino wanted me to let you know he'd make it worth your while to end it in a knockout within three minutes."

Then, his boss was gone.

Just like that, Nickie slipped back into the crowd while Lev was left searching for the back of his boss's head or any other sign of the man. He found none as he slipped under the ropes. His gaze scanned the front tables and soon he landed on the man who had apparently sent the message to him in the first place.

Andino.

The mafia Capo sat cool and unbothered in his leather chair; his guest beside him wore a grin as he tried to gain his companion's attention. Andino simply sipped on a glass of whiskey Lev had poured for him twenty minutes earlier. He shook his head at whatever his companion said to his right, but those cold, dark eyes of his nailed straight into Lev.

Rarely did the man speak to him.

Not when he served his drinks.

Not when he tipped.

Never.

Right then, however, Andino tipped his glass in Lev's direction and then nodded subtly. Just as fast, his attention finally swung to the man at his side, and he rejoined a conversation that he clearly had no interest in entertaining in the first place.

Yeah.

Something was definitely up.

"Fight starts in two minutes!"

Thing was, Lev didn't have time to consider it.

The rules were always clear—fighters undressed and readied in front of the crowd to prevent any underhanded business happening. Like someone trying to bring a weapon into the ring. It wasn't always the perfect fail-safe, but it certainly helped to keep the fights cleaner.

If there was such a thing in underground fights.

Since Lev typically just walked right into the ring off the floor, without someone in his corner, it was unusual for him to find a pair of big green eyes staring at him from the outside of the ropes. Gigi, that was.

Seemed the woman was going to stick around. She didn't look sure if that was a good idea or not. Settling on keeping his worn jeans on, Lev ignored the calls from the crowd when he pulled his shirt off and tossed it into the corner where the rest of his items lay forgotten in a pile. Shoes, socks; even his wallet.

Over the ropes, Gigi leaned closer to him with her pink lips pursed as a nervous smile started to flit over her mouth. He suddenly had the strangest regret—that he hadn't tried to get a kiss from her when he approached her at the bar. He didn't really know why he went up to her in the first place when he was only supposed to be worried about making sure Andino Marcello's—and his guest's—glass never emptied.

That was a lie.

He did know.

Her face.

She was the most beautiful creature he'd ever seen in his life and by no conscious choice of his own, he found himself standing in front of her with the lamest line right on the tip of his tongue. He'd not been able to appreciate her height, or the way her legs looked in heels and how her romper stretched over the curves and dips of her body until they walked up to the ring and *damn* ... it was a shame. But shit, if all went well, maybe later he would get a little more time to properly appreciate the woman. Those vibrant green eyes of hers made the freckles stand out even more on the bridge of her nose and across her cheeks. When she smiled, dark lashes fanned over her cheeks and her imperfect smile made her look *heaven-sent*.

How could he not approach?

Take a shot?

"Do you do this often?" she asked him over the loud crowd.

By the sounds of it, his opponent had finally stepped into the ring behind him. Lev didn't even bother checking over his shoulder. Instead, he put all his attention on the gorgeous face of a woman who was clearly trying to hide her worry.

"All the time," he lied.

Sort of.

He did fight often enough—still not a regular thing, though. He wasn't concerned either way.

Gigi's stare traveled over Lev's shoulder at whatever was waiting for him at the other side. "At least you're taller than him, I guess? I have no idea how any of this works."

That made him laugh.

Height?

She was worried about size? Clearly, no, she didn't know how any of this kind of thing worked, and he seriously doubted she expected her night to end up like this with a man she had just met. A man who, despite being *behind* the bar, hadn't even offered her a drink. But if there was anything Lev had learned in his lifetime it was that when shit just worked and it felt right, it was better to go with it.

What would it hurt?

This chick felt the same.

Not even considering his choice, because all he wanted to do was wipe that worry from her pretty face, Lev leaned over the ropes and pressed a bruising kiss against those plush, silken lips of hers. He didn't even think about it—just did it. His tongue swept out to take a taste, and she answered it back with a shuddering breath that stuttered with her surprise. The sweet heat of her mouth only made him want more.

It was a good incentive. After all, he wouldn't be tasting that again tonight if he didn't walk out of this ring with a clear head. Everything he did had a purpose.

As fast as it had happened, he pulled back.

Still wide-eyed, she let out a soft laugh.

"Guess I'm sticking around," she said.

Lev winked. "Hope so, woman. I might want to do that again."

"You better."

Well, then ...

Lev turned to finally face his opponent.

Like he thought, he didn't recognize the bull of a man stripping down to boxer-briefs on the other side of the makeshift ring. Three minutes. That's what Andino wanted, huh? The whys didn't really matter—cash in his hand at the end of the night did.

Lev sized up the guy.

He could make Andino's demand happen in two.

$$\bullet \ \bullet \ \bullet$$

Lev got that knockout with ten seconds to spare.

Yeah.

He'd been counting.

It was easy, all things considered. Southpaws like him were rare in a ring, and a lot of fighters who stepped up against him didn't even know he was one until it was too damn late. One of the few benefits of fighting occasionally instead of making it a regular thing like some of these guys did. The second his opponent's head hit the floor and the guy's eyes remained closed, Lev's bruised fists raised high. He stepped back from the prone body. *Keep it clean.* He never liked a win to be questioned.

It cut into his money.

Simple as that.

As the ropes of the makeshift ring bit into his tense back muscles, he felt the small hands that wrapped around his arms and slid down to the crook of his elbows. As though with her strength and touch alone, she might be able to hold him right there, and he wouldn't go forward into the middle of the ring again as men started to climb into the space with the fighters.

Except those men didn't come near him.

They all went for the one on the floor.

"Are you okay?" he heard Gigi ask in his ear.

Her breath tickled the back of his neck. The distinct scent of her perfume—a burnt pineapple and vanilla mixture— soaked into his lungs with every heavy heave of his chest. Shit, yeah, he'd put a hell of a lot of his power into two minutes to get the knockout done. More than he usually would. Had he let the guy play with him for any longer than a few minutes and then tried to get the fight finished, it might not have been as easy to end.

"Yeah, I'm good," he assured, still watching the men check the guy and attempt to wake him up. It wasn't working, and Lev had to consider if that last punch he landed to the guy's temple had unfortunately finished the job for good.

In these fights, that shit happened. It was always cleaned up—no hard feelings when it went down. Still, it didn't feel great all the same.

What was his name again?

The announcer said it.

Then, the ref.

Didn't matter, Lev decided.

What was done was done.

Those soft hands of Gigi's traveled around the large bands of muscles in Lev's arms that jumped at every single one of her touches. She didn't seem to mind the sweat dotting his spine when her fingertips made silky lines down to the dimples in his lower back, and despite the roar of the bar and the chaos all around him, the only thing he found himself thinking about all of the sudden was how those hands of hers might feel wrapped around his cock.

Fucking hell.

"*Lev!*"

His head snapped to the left until his gaze nailed into the familiar man approaching the side of the ring. The strands of Gigi's wavy dark blonde hair fell over his shoulder when she flattened her chest against his back and leaned over a bit to see who was calling for him. She seemed content to be there and frankly, he also didn't want to move.

Andino Marcello pointed a finger at him from outside of the ring, a pleased smile curving the man's usually stone-cold features. It was almost unsettling to see him grin but at the same time, it felt *true*. "I knew I was right—a pleasure doing business with you tonight. Thank you for saving me a lot of money. Nickie will have your bonus ready in the back before you leave. Take care of me, I take care of you. You get me?"

What?

He didn't get the chance to ask. As fast as Andino had left his seat, and the companion he brought along, the man turned on his shined Italian loafers and headed back into the crowd.

"Who is that?" he heard Gigi ask behind him.

"Winner—Lev Arsov!"

The man who acted as the ref for the fights stopped him from answering—not that he particularly knew *how* exactly he would answer her question. He didn't know anything at all about Andino Marcello except the most important thing.

Don't fuck with him.

Lev's wrist found its way into the ref's hand before being lifted high to a still-roaring crowd inside the bar. It looked like the guys in black were finally beginning to get his opponent to come around where he rested on the floor. He, however, was too busy watching Andino retreat into the crowd.

And the man waiting for him.

His companion from earlier.

Except now, the guy didn't look pleased. He certainly wasn't as friendly as he had been earlier with Andino when the one man offered a hand to shake, but it was left hanging between them. The two men eyed one another before Andino's companion's gaze traveled to the ring, stopping on Lev for only a second before drifting to the man being helped up from the mat.

His lips moved. The words silent to Lev from his position, yet clear all the same. He didn't have to hear them to know what the guy said.

"You said *fair*, Andino."

In response, Andino only shrugged.

Then, he walked away.

Men in suits, situated in different spots within the bar, moved to follow Andino. Probably the same people who had come in with him. Lev's attention was still on the guy Andino had left behind, and the growing rage that darkened his features as the fighter who had lost against Lev was pulled from the ring, clearly dazed, confused, and not in a very good state.

The guy tipped his head to the side, taking in the scene. Then, he lifted two fingers and placed them at the bottom of his throat. Who the order had been given to, Lev didn't know. He knew what it meant, though, and the way the guy turned to leave in the opposite direction of Andino, well, he thought the intention was clear.

Lev could have left it alone. Maybe he should have. Gigi's hands were still soft. His cock was still hard. Soon, he could celebrate the win, possibly even buried in a new, tight pussy.

Wouldn't that be fucking *pure*?

Words lingered in the back of his mind.

Take care of me, I take care of you.

The ref had barely released Lev's wrist before he pushed away from Gigi behind the ropes. Slipping under the designated wall of the ring, he didn't care about the shouts behind him as he headed in the direction Andino had gone earlier.

Already, the warning came from his mouth.

"*Marcello!*"

There were certain things people who occasionally dabbled in the criminal world *didn't* do. Ever, if they could help it. One was draw unneeded attention to themselves. Another was draw any sort of attention to a man like Andino, but especially when he might have been doing business that he didn't want on anyone else's radar.

Lev smashed both of those unspoken rules with one call of Andino's name.

Near the side exit of the bar where Andino was taking a coat being held out to him by a man waiting in a black suit, he turned at the call of his name. He must have recognized Lev's voice because he looked his way, that same cold gaze nailing into him with an intensity that hadn't diminished at all.

He put his fingers up to his throat and cocked his head to the side. A clear indication of the trouble that might be waiting to follow him.

Apparently, it didn't matter. Or Lev's warning just came too late.

Gunfire exploded in the bar.

The last thing Lev saw before he turned to run for the woman he'd left behind at the makeshift ring was the splatter of blood and brain matter of Andino's man that painted the exit door.

Well ...

That was unfortunate.

FOUR

"WELL?"

Lev did his very best to keep the chuckle forming to himself. He didn't think the woman standing across from him on the quiet sidewalk would appreciate his humor at her current state. Even in her distress, hugging her arms tight to her middle to keep the leather jacket closed to the cool wind sweeping through the city's streets, Gigi looked like something that had just walked out of a fucking magazine. She truly was the most beautiful thing he had ever seen in his life, and he wouldn't even try to deny that fact.

Ever.

"Go ahead," he said with a wave of his hands.

If she heard the lingering amusement at her anxious glare, she didn't show it. Instead, she let out a laugh, colored with her tension, as she watched the cab that had just dropped them off in front of an unfamiliar apartment building—to him; the place was apparently hers—only thirty seconds before.

He expected the questions, or shit, even her *anger*, to burst out of her at racing speed. Considering the way she'd barely managed to hold it in on the drive to the address she gave to cab driver, it wouldn't be a surprise. She only stopped asking questions in the cab because every time she opened her mouth, he made a sharp noise to quiet her, and the cabbie watched them in the rearview mirror.

Lev knew how a night like tonight worked—or rather, how he should react to it if he wanted to keep his job and paycheck. *You saw nothing, know nothing, and got fucking nothing to say.* It wouldn't be the first, or last, time he was told those words. Frankly, he found that was the easiest way to deal with shit like the mob making a scene.

Especially at Nickie's.

Thankfully, Gigi got the hint quickly enough to stop talking about the bar shooting until they were finally alone. Although, he had to give her credit where it was due. She hadn't questioned him at the bar right after the shooting started. His hands found her small waist, and she didn't fight him at all when he shoved her toward the doors.

Yep.

He didn't wait for the guns to stop firing before he got them both the hell out of there. He certainly didn't wait around for the fucking cops to get called, either. Despite how shitty his life could be at times, he did actually like being alive. He found to stay that way, it was good policy to get as far away from people shooting guns as quickly as he could.

Chances were, Lev was also out his winnings for the fight. Not that it really mattered in the grander scheme of things. What did was the fact he'd gotten Gigi out of the place safe and sound, didn't have a mark on himself but for the bruised mouth from the fight, and they managed to make it a block away from the bar before he heard any sirens.

Then, he hailed a cab.

Gigi followed, and here they now stood. All it took was him opening the cab's back door and saying, "Give him your address—least I can do is get you home safely."

He hadn't given her the chance to argue or ask questions. The shock of the entire evening and the way it so quickly changed from one violent scene to a far worse one in seconds was enough to quiet even him. He didn't wonder why she moved on autopilot when he took control.

Now, though?

Girl was ready to blow.

Finally, Gigi let out a breath of air and with it came a high-pitch noise he couldn't quite place. "Thanks, I guess?"

It took Lev a second.

Then, he laughed deeply.

"Not exactly what I expected," he returned, "but okay."

One of her hands flicked a wave in his direction when she muttered, "I'm not sure I should ask what happened back there. I don't think I want to know."

"Good policy because you don't, right?"

Gigi's gaze darted from the darkness of the street and

straight into Lev's stare in an instant. "What?"

"*Know*," he clarified. "You don't know what happened—or why, for that matter. Wrong place, wrong time that's all."

"My friend and her boyfriend were—"

"Chances are, they got out of there the same way we did. Best thing you can do in a place like Nickie's when bad shit goes down. Stay gone until the dust clears, and otherwise, make sure everybody knows you don't know *anything*."

Gigi hadn't looked away from him. Lev hoped she got the point he was trying to make without outright saying it. The way her shoulders dropped a bit said she did, but the audible swallow and sniff she made before glancing away from him had that thing in his chest twisting a bit.

Forgot you were there, he thought.

His heart, he meant.

"But do you?" she asked.

The ground had become more interesting than him, apparently.

"Do I, what?"

"Know what all that was about?"

"No," he answered honestly. "And I've learned it's better not to."

"You were talking to that guy—um, the mafia guy, right?"

That had Lev stepping forward before his brain had even caught up to what his body decided to do. Not because he didn't like that Gigi knew something about Andino Marcello, but rather, he was concerned that she did. It was better she didn't.

"How do you even know how who he is?"

Gigi's stare swung back up to meet his, and she lifted one black, leather-clad shoulder. "My friend's boyfriend ... shady as fuck, but he says he knows people, you know? He was just running off at the mouth, probably."

Probably.

It would be best if the guy never spoke of Andino again but especially not in a way that suggested he knew who the man was on any personal level. That was the fastest way to find an early grave on these streets.

Gigi raised a brow, giving Lev a curious look from where

she stood under the stream of light from the streetlamp overhead. "But you *did* talk to him. I saw. And then that guy got shot and—"

"But I don't know why, and I plan to keep it that way. Bad enough the cops will probably be knocking on my door tomorrow for a statement considering I work at the damn bar, and Nickie will have to hand out names of employees. It's a double-edged sword. You don't want a problem with the cops, but you don't want to make a problem with the people who started shit tonight, either. You know what I mean?"

It took Gigi a second to reply.

Lev understood the need.

"Yeah," she finally uttered. "I guess I do."

"That's what matters."

And that she was safe.

Besides, it wasn't like Lev was a saint or anything, but he did have a fucking conscience and some semblance of a moral compass despite what his life might suggest. Earlier his intentions with Gigi had only been to try to have a quick fuck with the girl that looked like his wettest goddamn dreams. Making sure she got home really was the absolute least he could do.

With a wave at the apartment building, Lev said, "I'm sure you don't need me to walk you to your door, but if you want, I'll wait until you're inside. It's been a fucked up night and all. No need to make it worse."

Taking a peek over her shoulder, Gigi let out a soft laugh. "*Funny.*"

"What is?"

She didn't look back at him right away. An approaching couple walking a dog that looked more like a rat didn't move sideways as they passed Lev, making him take a couple of steps forward to avoid crushing their little rat-dog on the way by. It also put him far closer to Gigi, and it wasn't lost on him how she had to tip her head up just a bit when she did finally turn back around to face him on the street.

The girl was all legs.

Tall as fuck, and he loved it.

She still had to look up at him. It kind of made him want to get his hands on the smooth column of her throat while she stared up at him, and he could see every inch of her face when he leaned down to kiss her. The way her gaze followed his oncoming lips that promised a taste of something wicked and good. Would she close her eyes this time, or leave the green orbs wide open for him to drown in?

Either way ...

He liked it all.

"I said *funny*," Gigi said, the heat in her tone unmistakable to his ears on the quiet street, "because this was not how I thought the night was going to end. I thought ... well, the way you seemed at the bar and then you kissed me—"

"My lamest line ever. Had to take a shot, didn't I? At least I got a kiss—that was worth everything."

It wasn't a lie.

He could still taste her. No doubt, there were more parts of her that he would give his left nut to get a taste of, too, but he couldn't afford to focus on that right now. Life had a way of laughing at Lev whenever it could. Including right now.

"Because you did, right?" she asked, her teeth nibbling on the edge of her bottom lip as she spoke. "You wanted to."

He grinned.

It was almost cute how she wouldn't say it.

Or couldn't.

"Yeah," Lev said, his stare drifting down to the lipstick stain on her mouth and how her tongue ran along the seam of her rounded upper lip. "I was just trying to take you down—see if you'd let me fuck you. No hard feelings, though."

Her cheeks pinked at his lack of shame and how easily he let the words slip out. Despite the heat in her color that suggested she didn't know what to do with what he just said, she still didn't look away from him. Not for a second. He was probably more attracted to that than anything else.

"Guess my game just wasn't on tonight," Lev added with a wink.

"It was. Still is."

Her words were a breath, then. Barely there at all.

Yet, he heard every single word and felt them, too. Especially the way they thickened his throat *and* cock at the same fucking time in two entirely different ways. He was all too aware of the fact they were standing on a public sidewalk, but he'd be a damn liar if he tried to say that made a difference to the fact, he'd probably fuck her right there if she asked.

All he had to do was *look* at her. The sight of her was worth the charge he'd catch for doing it.

"It's almost three in the morning," she told him, "I should really just get some sleep, but my roommate probably didn't come home. I'm not sure I'd sleep anyway after tonight and you're already here ..."

Lev flashed his teeth in a grin. "Girl, if you ask me to go into that building ... you'll be lucky if we get to your apartment before I take another taste of you. That's just facts. I need you to know it."

What she did to him, that was. How he didn't seem to have any sense of control. It wasn't that he disliked it, but it wasn't something Lev was used to, either. It only felt fair to give her a warning.

Gigi shrugged, suddenly all unashamed and a little more brazen than before. There was something enthralling about a woman finding something she liked and then deciding she was going to take it. It just so happened to be that she would like to have him, and he was very much willing to give her what she wanted.

All nine and a half inches.

His tongue and fingers, too.

Wherever the fuck she wanted them.

"Well, *try*." Gigi flashed a sexy smile that had his stomach clenching, and his rock-hard dick jerking against the constraints of his boxer-briefs and denim jeans. "I still have to live here. For a little while, anyway."

What did that mean?

Lev didn't care to ask because, in the next second, Gigi closed the bit of distance between them and lifted to the tips of her toes to press a kiss to his lips. It was nothing like the kiss back at the bar. Her intent was so much clearer with the way her tongue struck out to tease his parting lips and in how fast she pulled away.

Turning to the building, she peered back at him to ask, "Coming?"

There was only one appropriate response.

"Oh, we both will."

• • •

Lev hadn't lied when he said they wouldn't make it inside Gigi's apartment before he took another taste of her. He did, at least, *try* to keep his hands to himself as they climbed the three flights to the hallway where her apartment was located at the far end.

She tested his self-control the entire way by reaching back to let the tips of her fingers dance over the skin of his wrist, or his jaw ... wherever she could touch. Every bat of her lashes and each teasing smile tossed over her leather-clad shoulder had him inching closer until he was pressed against her back while she fumbled through her bag to find the keys for the door.

That's when he took his chance.

The hallway was quiet, after all. It was nearly three—she said it, not him. Who was up at this time of night?

Just them, by the looks of it.

Lev would have told Gigi that he'd noticed keys sticking out of the side pocket on the bag, while she was busy fumbling inside the main compartment. The nape of her neck looked too delicate to bother with all of that. She'd pushed her wavy hair over her shoulder on their way up the second flight of stairs. He found himself staring at the little daisy tattoo that had been hidden there and wondered what it might taste like.

He decided to find out.

That first gasp that fell from her lips when his mouth found her nape was heroin to his senses. A wash of heat straight to his veins that shot down to his cock in an instant to make him ache in the best fucking way. Because all too soon, he knew, the heat he would have wrapped around his cock would be better than what he was being teased with right now. A little kiss was not enough; the next time his tongue joined in, licking at inked skin. She whimpered, and her hand moved a little faster inside the bag.

Lev couldn't help but chuckle.

The keys were still in the side pocket.

"What are you—*fuck*, yes," she breathed out when one of his hands slipped down the loose front of her romper. He couldn't do much to get more access to the skin of her shoulders with the leather jacket tight to her form, so he went with something else.

Something better.

Gigi's giggles quickly melted into a low moan. His palm dipped under the stretchy lace of her bra. He squeezed her breast, and then the other, until he felt her nipples harden into peaks. She finally found the keys in the side pocket with a low *fuck* falling from her lips as his fingers found the same soft lace beneath the toned expanse of her stomach. He hadn't stopped kissing the back of her neck, but his lips moved to the spot behind her ear when his hands went lower.

Under lace.

Between slightly widened thighs.

"God, yeah, *so fucking wet*," he praised. "I can't wait to get a taste of *this* ... you're gonna love that, won't you? Do you want me to eat you, too? Get my tongue up in that tight pussy for a little taste?"

"*Yes.*"

Her voice was a lot like her pussy.

Hot and *soft*.

"Love it when a pussy's bare," Lev told her, letting his hand and finger explore a part of her he hadn't yet gotten to see. *Soon*, his spiraling thoughts rushed to soothe. He'd see her and taste her soon, and he couldn't fucking wait. And she was smooth—waxed, it felt like. He loved pussy in all forms but waxed was his favorite because there was no fucking way to be closer than with nothing between him and cunt but *skin*.

Exactly what he liked.

"Just … *oh, my God* … let me get this door—*Lev*," she gasped as two of his fingers swept between her slit a second time.

"Nobody's stopping you, babe. Open it up."

Her hands trembled.

Those keys made so much fucking noise.

And so did she while he toyed with her clit, rubbing fast, wet circles using her arousal and the pads of his fingers to get her shaking by the time she had gotten the keys into the lock. The way she couldn't help but widen her legs a little more for him while she pushed her tight ass into his groin to feel that cock waiting for her … Lev was done for.

He wasn't even getting this girl into a bed. Whatever flat surface was closest, well, it would have to do.

Gigi grabbed the knob with one hand, but her other slammed to the door when her head dropped forward. She tipped her head to the side when his mouth grazed over her cheek, daring to take a kiss from his mouth. He swallowed her next moan, hiding it from whoever might be listening in the neighboring apartments, as she came shaking like the prettiest leaf he'd ever seen.

He might have even turned her around right then and there to lift her against the outside of the apartment door, but laughter echoing from the stairwell at the other end of the hallway had him changing his mind just as fast. Apparently, they weren't the only ones up at this late hour.

Gigi, still drowning in her orgasm, turned at the sound of the laughter, but Lev was there to whisk her worries away with a burning kiss. She spun to put her back to the door that he opened for them before they slipped inside. The war of their tongues dancing together urged the chaos of his hands exploring her body.

Or rather, getting *to* her body.

Gigi's back hit the door after he kicked it closed. He couldn't get the leather jacket down her arms fast enough, but she didn't seem to mind his roughness. If anything, she urged him on for more, twisting into his hands and arching her body against his. He found the underside of her throat tasted like salt and sweetness—a complex he couldn't quite get enough of to be satisfied.

It reminded him of sin.

Of *sex*.

He wasn't the only one rushing. Her idle hands could only stay still at her sides for so long before she began to help him along. He pulled her romper down over the soft curve of her shoulders and past the lace of her bralette to pool at her waist while she undid the button on his jeans to get better access to what she clearly wanted.

And once she did ...

"*Fuck*," he groaned against another one of her kisses.

She found him hard and thick, her palm warm and silken against the skin of his dick. Yet, even in the firmness of her strokes, he felt the way her fingers trembled.

"God, you're ... *big*," she whispered.

"Yeah, I'm proportionate, babe. Lucky you." Lev laughed, the husky echo bursting from his lips between his next moan of her name. "And you'll love it—every fucking inch of it. I'll let you take me slowly at first. Let you feel the way I stretch you open while I fill you up. That's the best part, you know? That first time you let me get inside your pussy. *Let me*."

Her consent came in the way her hands covered his where he'd fisted the material of her romper at her waist. She shoved his hands lower, letting him pull the fabric down her body until she had to step out of the clothing altogether.

Lev could finally appreciate the black lace set she wore—how it smoothed over the swells and dips of her curves; the way she looked like sin poured into something delicate; the color even complimented the golden sheen of her skin.

Before the night was over, he was going to have that skin blushing all over. Pink from his hands. Marked from his teeth and kisses. She'd be hot all over, damp with sweat, and ready for him to have another taste after he'd been lucky enough to be inside her.

"Look at you," he praised. "So fucking perfect. You're beautiful."

That shy heat came back to her cheeks.

He didn't understand why.

"Don't people tell you how beautiful you are?"

Gigi lifted one shoulder. "All the time."

"But you—"

"Not like you do, though. Not like they mean it. Not like it means something *more*."

Shame, that. Well, he certainly fucking did mean it. He wouldn't waste one more second to show her just how true he thought it was, either.

His hand landed to her waist and squeezed tight when he asked, "Where's your bedroom?"

"Last door on the left in the hallway at the back."

That's all he needed to know. In a second, he had her pulled away from the door. Tall as could be, it didn't matter because the girl still felt like a bag of feathers when he lifted her from the floor. She fell half over his shoulder, her laughter ringing out in the darkened apartment as he headed through the kitchen where the front door opened up to.

He noticed the stack of photos on the table—headshots, it looked like—but he was too focused on the way her ass wiggled. His palm cracked down hard, sending her next round of giggles melting into a low moan. He didn't even bother waiting to get to the bedroom before he started pulling those panties of hers off, his mouth landing a wet, hard kiss to her hip followed by his teeth nipping into the same spot.

He found the bedroom. And then dropped her to her back on the bed.

Shameless, Gigi stayed just like, that, too. On her back, legs opened for him, and already teasing him again. Her hands dipped between her thighs, and she worked two fingers into her pussy as he pulled his shirt off.

"Come on," she urged, her grin trembling as her hips rocked into her own hand.

"Fuck, you look good. The hottest damn thing I've ever seen."

After he'd grabbed the foil packet from the back pocket of his jeans—he only kept one condom on hand just to be safe, so he was going to have to make this last for himself—his pants and boxer-briefs followed the same path. He took one step toward the bed, and then another. Her gaze followed his every movement. His steps. Then, his hand fisting his cock while he watched her before he stopped just long enough to open the condom and slide the latex down.

She reached for him when he climbed between her opened thighs. Her fingers, still wet from her pussy, found his length again but only long enough to guide his cock where they both needed it to be.

Soft warmth met the head of his cock when he settled against her slit. His palm opened up to her stomach, fingers splaying wide over the expanse of her skin, so he could hold her to the bed while he filled her full.

"I wanna feel every squirm; hear every goddamn sound that comes out of you while I fuck you. Do you hear me?"

She dragged in a shaky breath, nodding. "Yeah—it's all yours tonight."

All his.

He liked the sound of that.

Probably too much.

It didn't matter.

All he wanted now was to fuck. So did she, and so he gave her exactly what he promised. He took his time pushing forward, each small flex of his hips letting his cock split her open and fill her full a little more. Until those wiggles came, and her head tipped back against the pillow because she wanted more.

"*Oh, my God.*"

"Yeah," he murmured, "pray to me. I wanna hear that, too."

Hovering high so that he could watch the way his cock, slick with her, disappeared into her cunt. Pinning her down meant she couldn't do much, but she *tried*. Her hips rocked, urging him on and silently asking for more, but *no*. One inch at a fucking time. Until he was settled all the way deep and every single muscle inside her pussy clung to each ridge of his cock, and he couldn't breathe from how tight she was.

Their heavy breaths matched in weight, her chest rising when his fell with an exhale. His shoulders ached from the control it took to stay still for just a second so that she could feel him like that.

Full of him.

"*Please* ... I just need, please—"

He was wrong. She was most beautiful when she begged. It also took what remained of his control and shattered it. Part of him wanted to hold her legs open as wide as he could get them while he pounded as deep as he could get. Another part of him wanted to see just how much of him she was willing to take.

How hard would she fuck *him*?

He went with the latter.

All it took was the slip of his arm under her back, and a roll of his weight to the side for their positions to be changed. It took Gigi all of two seconds to realize she was the one on top, and he didn't regret the change for a second.

How could he?

On top of him, tits pushed out as she circled her hips into him *harder* and *faster* with each twist of her body, it was intoxicating. The sight of her was like taking a long drink of the best liquor, and the buzz was immediate. Grabbing a fistful of her ass with each hand to drag her into every rise of his hips as he met her rhythm, he knew he'd leave marks behind. She would feel him for days after this. It only made him hotter.

For tonight, he got to own this girl. Have every part of her. She was all his. He was already fucking delirious from it.

And shit ...

They had just started.

It was going to be a good night.

FIVE

THE LAST person Lev expected to find waiting outside his apartment building two days after the bar shooting was Andino Marcello. Yet, there the man waited while he leaned against a black Mercedes Benz as he worked on lighting up a thick cigar.

In his tailored suit, with a watch on his wrist that glittered in the early morning light every time he moved his arm, the man looked entirely out of place. He certainly didn't look like he belonged in the parking lot of a low-income apartment building, all things considered.

Shit, his vehicle alone was probably worth more than the rest of the rust buckets combined in the parking lot of the building. Lev suspected it wasn't very often that the man left his proverbial golden towers to come and visit the people of Harlem.

Not that any of it seemed to bother Andino.

"You usually this late to get around in the mornings?" Andino asked when Lev approached. He didn't have a reason to suspect Andino had come there to find *him*, specifically, but at the same time ... who the fuck else would he be there for? "Not sure I like that very much."

"What difference does my schedule make to you?"

Andino smirked, that cigar in the corner of his mouth bouncing dangerously with his next chuckle. "Oh, you've got one of those, huh?"

Lev came to a stop just three feet in front of Andino's vehicle. "One of what?"

"An attitude. Curb it a bit, could you?"

He wasn't the type to get defensive, and he was pretty damn sure Andino wasn't the kind of man who appreciated that shit either, but Lev had a line. He really hated it when people crossed it without even thinking about it.

His entire life had been people talking around or down to

him like he wasn't half the human being they were. Either because he was a kid, at the time, didn't have as much money or education as them, or whatever the case may be. He was too old and didn't have the same patience for that shit as he used to, and he was just fine with letting Andino know that, too.

"Is there something you want?" he asked Andino. "Because if all you want to do here is make comments about my mood, I have better places to be and things to do when I get there."

That had Andino pausing.

Just long enough to laugh it off.

"There was something about you that I liked," the guy admitted. "That first time I walked into Nickie's, I mean. Not sure what it was—maybe because you didn't call me *sir* like every other stupid fuck does."

Lev cleared his throat, uncomfortable with the admittance. He wasn't exactly sure it was a good thing to be liked by a man like Andino Marcello knowing what he did about the business of the mafia and whatnot. It seemed a bit dangerous to be liked by someone who spent his days making money by whatever means he could—from selling drugs to murder.

And yet, here the two of them were.

Talking.

"Thought people called a Capo their *Skip*," Lev returned.

Andino grinned. "Some do. Semantics."

That was said with an easy wave of his hand, like it didn't matter at all. Lev had a good feeling it did, in fact, matter to men like Andino what he was called by his subordinates. He wasn't about to argue the point of it, however.

What difference did it make?

"And I liked the way you served my whiskey," Andino added, lifting one blazer covered shoulder as if it was another flippant comment that didn't matter much at all. "Three ice cubes, two fingers of liquor, and without any fucking small talk to annoy the hell out of me. So, every time I came around, I made sure Nickie knew it had better be you that served my drinks. No excuses."

"That's ... it?"

Andino arched a brow as he pulled the cigar from his

mouth. Eyeing the burning red coal at the tip, he showed his teeth when he murmured, "Yeah, that was it. Sometimes, that is all it takes. You never gave a fuck about the politics of my business or even who I was, and I like that about you. See, whenever a Marcello walks into a place, everybody thinks they're entitled to the reasons *why*. Why are we there—why does it even fucking matter? I just want someone who does their goddamn job, Lev. The way I tell them to without needing to be told a second time."

It wasn't the first time Andino used his name. It still felt important that the man knew it in the first place.

"Nothing more and nothing less," the man added after a brief pause. "You get what I'm saying?"

He was starting to think he might.

Maybe.

"Forgive me for asking why right now," Lev said, choosing each word carefully because he might really like to make it out of the parking lot alive, "but why are you here?"

Because really, wasn't that the important thing?

That cigar in Andino's hand curled with smoke when the man dropped his arm to his side. Pushing away from the hood of the Benz, he peered off to the side where Lev noticed another man stood waiting, dressed in all black, about twenty feet away.

"Another man of mine," Andino informed, "he drives like shit, but he knows how to handle a gun and really, that's what I need at the moment. I seem to be down a man considering the one that got his brains blown out at Nickie's a couple of nights ago. Hard to find good, loyal guys in this business so it's always a rough go for a while when you need to replace one."

"About that—what happened at Nickie's, I mean."

Andino's sharp gaze swung back to Lev, silencing him immediately. "More *whys*?"

Well ...

"Something happened, and it kind of felt like I might have had something to do with it without actually knowing about it," Lev replied, keeping his tone as respectful as he could manage. "I might like to know what it was, Andino."

The other man nodded. "Fair point."

"Are you going to tell me?"

"Well, no. I *wasn't*. Business, you know?"

"Not really, no."

Andino laughed under his breath and shook a finger at Lev. Like a loaded gun would be pointed at his face, he wondered if he overstepped a line. The grin curving Andino's lips said all was fine.

For now.

"To simplify it down—my guest at the fights had a fighter that he wanted me to invest in. Nickie is a small fish in the underground fighting world, as I'm sure you've heard."

"I pay less attention to things I hear and more to what I see, actually."

A finger wagged at him again.

"See, another reason to like you, Lev," Andino replied without malice. "Nonetheless, I may or may not be dipping my toes into that side of things, and my potential business partner thought his fighter would be the one for me to drop a few million into over the next few months."

"The fighter—"

"You knocked out in less than three minutes, yes," Andino interjected with a chuckle. "And you don't even fight for a living. You just ... have a way about you in the ring. I noticed. Anyway, my guest felt a bit put out by my dealings on the side that night with picking the fighter his man went up against. A small dispute, really."

Lev's brow lifted high. "You call a man getting shot in the head a small dispute?"

"Wasn't my head, was it?"

He suspected that, in a nutshell, was Andino's outlook on a lot of things. Maybe it had to being a man in his position, Lev couldn't be sure. And he had zero intention of asking.

"You didn't answer my question," Lev pointed out. "Why you're *here*, I mean. Seems to me that the only reason a man like you would be around these parts of the city to talk to someone like me would be to make sure I don't talk at all."

Dark eyes surveyed him. Lev stayed tall and firm.

He lived for pressure.

Always had.

"You wouldn't be wrong on any other day," Andino returned, "but no, that's not why I'm here. Are you in a rush? From what I understand, Nickie's place is closed for the next couple of days so the police can finish their … investigation. If that's what one wants to call that travesty. They were paid off before the night was out—it's all details now. That is where you work, yes? What exactly do you have to do today if work is out of the question?"

Lev shrugged. "Whatever I want. Whether or not my business is important to *your* business doesn't really matter, does it? I'm not on your time clock, Andino."

The man grinned. "But you could be."

Uh …

"What?"

Andino resumed his previous position leaning against the Benz, and the cigar found its way back into his mouth. "See, I'm currently in need of a new enforcer." He flicked a wrist at the word, muttering, "Titles aren't important—a *bodyguard*."

It should have said something to Lev that Andino had bodyguards in the first place. Or enforcers, whatever the fuck he wanted to call the job. The guy was nearly as tall and large as Lev in size. He seriously doubted Andino was a coward or unable to handle himself. And yet, he still needed protection.

A bit worrisome, honestly.

"One I like," Andino continued, clearly oblivious to Lev's distraction, "that knows how to do as he's told, makes an impression just by standing there, and is willing to *learn*. Loyalty is what counts the most with me at the end of the day. I've already built what one might call a *rapport* with you, meaning I like you well enough. You certainly make an impression with your size. And I'm sure you could learn the rest over time. Ten-k a month. You do what I say, you're on my time from the moment you open your eyes until you close them at night, and you don't give me any fucking attitude in between. How's that sound?"

Lev took a second.

Blinked a few times.

Probably looked like a fucking idiot.

"You're offering me a job?"

Andino made a noise under his breath. "Undoubtedly better than whatever you're doing now—in all aspects, I presume."

"You don't know that. I'm not concerned about being arrested or murdered at my current job."

The man still leaning on the car gave him a look. "You sure about that? I mean, the other night and all ..."

Well ...

Fuck.

He had a point.

"I thought your business was for Italians only?" Lev asked. "In case you missed my last name, I'm—"

"Russian on your father's side. Ukrainian on your mother's, from what I was able to find on her. My sympathies for your losses. It must have been hard to grow up without parents in a system like the one we have. People often wonder why some find themselves in hard situations. I tend to find the answers are very clear when someone looks hard enough. Don't you?"

Oh, good.

Now he was looking into Lev.

"Where you come from matters little to me," Andino explained, sighing heavily. "We're not talking about turning you into a made man. I just want to sign your paychecks, okay?"

Was it okay?

Lev didn't know.

"Are you actually giving me a choice with this job offer," he asked, measuring each word, "or are you telling me what I'll be doing, Andino?"

That made the other man pause.

Not for long, though.

"You can't force loyalty," Andino eventually said. "I know that better than anyone."

That said a lot.

Lev respected it, even.

And still ...

"I need time to think about it. No offense."

Lev figured he should tack that onto the end just because. The money Andino offered a month just for the position of a bodyguard was more than Lev made in a half of a year. He had the distinct feeling he'd earn every fucking penny of it, too.

How could he not?

It was the mafia.

Andino nodded. "No offense taken. I'd think long and hard about it, too. Enjoy your day, Lev Arsov. I'm sure we'll be seeing each other again. You'll find me in Manhattan—can't miss my restaurant—when you're ready to give me your answer."

Pushing off the car, Andino whistled low under his breath, and the man across the parking lot came jogging over like a puppy ready to do tricks for his master. Lev said and did nothing until the black Benz backed out of the apartment parking lot. And even once the car was gone, he still didn't move. He had a lot to think about now.

There was a lot to consider.

• • •

"No fights or cops tonight?"

Lev tensed at the familiar voice, but quickly smiled when he turned away from the liquor shelves to face the woman waiting on the other side of the bar. The last person he expected to see on his first night back working at Nickie's was Gigi. He wouldn't have been surprised if the woman tucked her tail and ran as far as she could away from this place after what happened.

Yet, there she stood.

Lips painted red.

Dark blonde hair high in a messy pony.

As sexy as ever.

His gaze traveled down what he could see of her body, admiring the way the shiny black material of her mini skirt hugged her hips and the patch of toned stomach she showed off with her pink crop top. He popped the gum in his mouth.

It didn't hurt him a bit to look at her, and frankly, she didn't seem bothered by his perusal, either. Unfortunately, he couldn't see much beyond where the skirt fell mid-thigh because of the damn bar in his line of sight.

Shame, that.

"Hey, yourself. Now, I know you've got better places to be than here. Don't try to tell me different."

She tossed a small purse to the bar top and took a seat on one of the stools. "Might have been in the neighborhood and noticed that the police tape had been taken off the front door. Or maybe I just wanted to come and say hi—you didn't leave your number. Actually, you left before I even got up."

"Wasn't that the point?"

They had a night.

Some fun.

Lev found things like that were easier when a clean break was made at the end. Just because the two of them could make each other smile, he liked the way she looked, and they worked in bed together didn't mean very much. They didn't know one another. They weren't even friends and most of the time, it was better that way.

At the same time, he knew he wasn't being one hundred percent honest with himself, either. Leaning a little over the bar, he gave her a smile when he said, "Truth is, I got up early, was going to order some breakfast and wake you up, convince you to jump in the shower with me, but then I got a call."

Her tongue peeked out to wet her lips.

A dangerous thing because it only sent memories flooding through his mind in the best and worst way possible.

"That so?"

"My boss—about the shooting. The cops were hounding him about employees. Someone mentioned my name, so they were already rabid about finding me for a statement. Anyway, I thought maybe it was better if I didn't linger anyway. You didn't ask me to stay, and I didn't want to assume I should."

"You're right, I didn't." Gigi grinned. "And maybe I'm lying."

That had his attention.

Lev stepped closer to the bar, tossing the rag over his shoulder. "About what?"

She waved a finger in between them, replying simply, "I *was* in the neighborhood—I did see the tape was gone. But maybe I purposely came this way to check and decided to come in and see where things went from there."

Oh, really?

"What things?" he asked, a grin starting to form.

"*Things*," she teased, offering nothing else.

Her teasing was what found them in bed together in the first damn place, whether she realized it or not. Had the woman not gotten enough their first night? He didn't usually go back for seconds, but shit ... Gigi was exactly the kind of woman he wouldn't mind breaking his usual rules for. It wasn't like he could afford anything more than fun with her, but it didn't hurt anybody if that's all they were both looking for.

Right?

She hadn't answered him yet.

Lev didn't miss it.

Placing both hands to the bar, he leaned across the top and closed what distance was between them. The scent of his mint gum filled the inch of air between them and while her head was still tipped down, he watched those full, round lips of hers form a smile that showed off the space between her two front teeth. All at once, she glanced up, and those green eyes of her—the same color of fresh, new grass in the spring—met his.

"Guess what?" she asked.

He arched a brow. "What?"

"My face is going to be in magazines."

That had him blinking.

But only for a second.

"It should be—it's the most beautiful I've ever seen."

It wasn't a lie.

Gigi laughed. "That's what you have to say?"

Lev shrugged. "It's all that should be said."

Peering to the side, Gigi took in the quiet bar and the

obvious change in scenery since her last time there a few days prior. Andino hadn't been wrong. The cops quickly finished their investigation of the shooting, gave Nickie the green light to open for business again, and that was that. They didn't talk about what happened. The employees knew better.

Including Lev.

"Doesn't even look like anything happened," Gigi whispered.

"That's the point."

She drew in a quick breath that stuttered on the inhale. Lev knew that feeling all too well—how the violence of the world could be so *strange*. How it could set one person off-balance, yet it wasn't even a blip on someone else's radar. He'd never been fully in that world, but his connections and work put him in a place where he toed the line and saw more than he wanted to.

One foot in, and one out.

Nothing was ever simple.

"So, magazines, huh?" he asked, wanting to make her smile again.

She did.

It was fucking *brilliant*.

"I signed a contract today," she told him, her eyes glittering with joy and pride.

Fuck, he could practically feel it radiating off her. One part of him wanted to ask all the questions drifting through his mind. What kind of contract? *What magazine?* Was that what she did for a living—modeling?

Lev asked nothing.

He hadn't forgotten, after all. If all he could offer was fun, then he didn't want her to think he was willing to give anything else by making her think he cared. Oh, he *did* care. He just couldn't let it matter.

Look at his life.

This wasn't a place made for two.

Gigi drummed her fingernails to the bar top, drawing his attention down. Filed into an almond shape, she had painted them in soft pink that faded into white tips. "I just thought

..."
...

"What?"

"I wanted to celebrate. For some reason, even though I *really* shouldn't be here, this is still where I came. It's not like I'm going to be around much longer, and I don't really want to linger, but I do want to celebrate." He opened his mouth to respond, not even sure what he would say, but she rushed to interject with a laugh and a quiet, "Stupid, I know. And you're working so—"

She had started to push up from the stool. Lev's heart about jumped from his chest at the very idea she might leave because, for whatever reason, he had a feeling he wasn't going to see her again. He couldn't have that even though every part of him screamed that he was being stupid by thinking whatever interest he had in this woman could go beyond the four walls of a bedroom. His mouth worked before his brain could stop it.

"Do you want a drink?" he asked.

She hesitated, glancing between the bottles on the wall behind him and then at his mouth. Did she want to kiss him? *Hell*, he'd love another taste of her. Another bite. A nibble. A single fucking *lick*. He'd tasted the salt from her skin for days after. Heard her moans in his dreams. The image of her spread wide for him on a bed was the only thing letting him beat one out in the shower every morning.

Fucking her had been a dream. Yeah, he would definitely do it again.

If she wanted ...

"I'm not even twenty-one," she admitted. "Just turned twenty a couple of months ago. Probably shouldn't be drinking. Don't you ask for ID?"

"Usually."

The bar was *trying* to stay above board for a bit. Just long enough that the attention died down and the reporters stopped coming around to ask if the place was mob-connected. Lev knew the rules and what he should do.

It also seemed like this woman—still a stranger to him, really—could make him break every rule with nothing more than a smile and a flick of those green eyes.

Goddammit.

He kind of liked it.

"Pick your poison, Gigi. Whatever you want in the bar—it's on the house. All yours."

Her grin grew wider.

Sexier.

"Anything I want?" she asked.

He nodded.

She winked. "Let's start with a whiskey sour. Then I think I'll move onto you."

Well ...

He was just fine with that.

SIX

"SORRY," LEV said at Gigi's left, noticing the hole in the wall of the basement-level stairwell inside the Harlem apartment building. "It's new—just showed up one morning last week. The building isn't that great, but it does what I need it to, and it's safe for the most part. Just old and falling the fuck apart."

She heard how the tone of his voice changed; it was the same way he spoke back at the bar after last call when Gigi mentioned if they were going home together, it would have to be to his place. Her roommate was back at hers, after all, and Cassie was too nosy for her liking on the rare occasion that Gigi even mentioned a guy, let alone brought one home.

They passed one apartment on the right before coming to a stop at the second apartment on the left side. His place, apparently, if the keys he pulled out of the back pocket of his jeans could be trusted.

"Hey," she said, leaning her back against the peeling yellow wallpaper on the hallway wall. He didn't look at her, instead focusing his effort on sticking the key into the deadbolt on the door. She couldn't have that so she poked him in the shoulder just because. "*Hey*."

Those ice-blue eyes of his—cold only in color because his gaze always felt so warm when it landed on her—turned her way. The grin that curled his lips up at the edges was the sexiest thing she had ever seen. The heat growing deep in her belly was made worse when that intense stare of his dropped down the length of her bare legs to the strappy black heels that crisscrossed up over her ankles before tying into bows at the back of her mid-calf. He was such a leg man.

Then, his gaze snapped back up to hers without warning when he asked, "Did you just *poke* me?"

"I said *hey* first."

Without warning, Lev pushed away from the door, leaving the keys hanging from the lock, and stepped up to Gigi. In a blink, his legs pushed between hers while his hands landed on either side of her head against the wall. Her mini skirt inched higher on her hips when his body flattened against hers. That gorgeous mouth of his hovered above hers, making her edgy and needy all at the same fucking time. The fresh, crisp scent of his cologne—with notes of the sea and smoke—pulled into her lungs with every breath she dragged in.

The sudden rush of lust that flooded her veins was only aided by the way he stared at her like he was ready to fuck her right where she stood; as though she was some prize he could claim with his cock or hands or mouth. Any and all of it, she was up for it. With him? Why not?

Look at him.

"What is it with us and hallways?" she asked, hearing the tremor of want racing through her voice like the way her heartbeat thundered at the pulse in her throat. "We're always ending up in one."

"Do we?"

"Oh, you forgot what you did to me right *outside* my door in the hallway?"

Lev laughed a dark sound that dripped over her senses like warm, dark chocolate. "Sweetheart ... Gigi, I didn't forget a second that I spent with you. That would be impossible."

And just like that, he took her breath away.

He didn't have to try.

"You're something else," she told him. "Something special, maybe."

Lev shook his head. "I don't think so. Look around—here I am, twenty-four, stuck in a place like this, working for a guy like Nickie ... taking home some random girl because it's all I have time for."

Gigi arched a brow. "Does twice make it *random*?"

That made him pause.

"You know I can't do anything more than this, right? If you came around tonight looking for me because you think I'm in a place to offer you anything more than a night, Gigi ... I can't. I'm not even in a place where I'm doing a great job of taking care of myself."

"I'm not asking for more."

She couldn't.

Her life was in upheaval, too. Maybe in a different way than his, sure. That didn't change her circumstances or that she couldn't afford to get involved with Lev on a deeper level than they currently were together. She didn't mind his honesty, and if anything, appreciated it.

"And *hey*," she said, leaning in close so that her lips brushed his as she spoke, "I don't mind the building. Or the man I came here with tonight. Don't worry about it. My mom told me once that it doesn't really matter where you are or have been because it's all about where you're gonna be someday. I try to keep it in mind. You should, too."

Lev made a noise in the back of his throat. "That's quite a dream to believe in."

"It's a dream that happened to me. Why couldn't it happen to you?"

Something in her words spurred him to crush his mouth against hers in a bruising kiss that yanked the breath from her lungs. Those hands of his left the wall to find her jaw and his warm palms slipped down to cup her throat, too. Pushing her head to tilt back against the wall, that kiss and those teeth of his traveled down her throat, pulling moans from her chest with every inch he tasted.

And each time, she pulled him closer and pushed into him. Before she knew it, the two of them were acting like a pair of teenagers in yet another apartment building hallway. They couldn't get close enough. Couldn't touch enough. *Couldn't get enough.* Without shame, she widened her legs again to get his grinding hips closer to her aching center.

Fuck.

All of her ached.

"Are we going inside yet?" she gasped when his kiss trailed over her earlobe, and his pleased hum had her pussy clenching and likely *soaked*. His hands slipped up under her crop top, and the deep *yes* that came out of his mouth when he found her tits bare of any bra had her whimpering, knowing how this was going to end. With a good, *hard* fuck. Exactly what she wanted, too. "*Inside*, remember?"

She had to remind him.

Or else *she* was going to forget.

His hands flattened to her rib cage when another of his hard kisses landed on her mouth. Her tongue sought his, lips parting to take him in and find that taste of him, too. She adored the way he kissed her. It overwhelmed her senses in a way that made her forget about the rest of the world around them.

"Lev," she breathed against his next, softer kiss, "Inside. *Now*."

Before they caught a charge together. It was like she couldn't control herself with him, and he didn't even bother to try, either.

"Can't wait to get you stripped and on your fucking back in my—"

"Could I help the two of you with something tonight?"

At the new voice, Gigi's back slammed hard against the wall. Lev, on the other hand, chuckled at the raspy tone coming from behind him to the left. His stormy blue gaze caught hers, and he winked before murmuring low, "Building manager—sweet lady; I help her out sometimes."

Then, louder and over his shoulder, he said, "No help needed here, Martha Mae. We were just—"

"Taking that inside, according to the young lady. So, go right along and do that, Lev. You know the hallways of this apartment building aren't the place for extra curricular activities ... or whatever you were just promising to do to that pretty young woman."

"*Yep*. Going inside right now."

Those words squeaked from Gigi. Every single one of them.

Lev's laughter chased her inside his apartment that *she* opened up after slipping out from under his arm. She hadn't even bothered to give the woman—older, by the sound of her voice—a look before she went, either.

What would be the point? She would only get to see Gigi turn as red as a tomato. She simply saved them both the embarrassment. Or just herself.

It all worked.

• • •

"You're not allowed to touch me in hallways anymore," Gigi told the smirking man who helped her out of the jacket. She continued her rant, only *slightly* meaning it as he hung her jacket and his own on waiting hooks next to the door. "That settles it. That woman probably thinks I'm a whore or something."

Gigi's declaration was responded to with a hearty laugh and a hard smack to her ass—which he punctuated with a firm grab—before Lev passed by her in the entry of his apartment. It wasn't a big place. The front door walked into a small kitchen with only a couple of feet of counter space beside an old stove. Just beyond the open concept kitchen with a small table that only toted one chair was a living room with a couch and recliner.

That's where Lev headed.

He paid no mind to the flatscreen on the wall that flickered with whatever channel he must have left it on before leaving his place. Underneath the TV was probably the most *bachelor* thing about the entire apartment. A gaming system with a decent stack of games next to the console and controllers.

Lev dropped into the waiting recliner that he spun to face her, a wicked grin tugging at the edges of his sexy mouth when he said, "Who the hell cares?"

"What?"

"Who cares what someone else thinks? *Fuck*, I forgot how good your legs looked there for a minute." A low grunt, pleased and deep, echoed from Lev as he tipped his head to the side, and his gaze took a slow trek down her body. "We didn't come here to chat about the building manager."

Like she needed a reminder.

Just his stare alone was enough to make her hot and trembling. He sealed the deal when his tongue peeked out to wet the edge of his lip. She had already had him once—she knew what came next and she wanted that.

A lot.

"You could at least *pretend* to apologize," she muttered. Half-heartedly.

Because honestly, she couldn't look at Lev and *not* think about sex. So even as she tried to keep some semblance of seriousness to their conversation, she was already getting lost in his hungry stare from across the room.

"For *what?*"

"You nearly flashed my ... *everything* ... to the old lady down the—"

"She doesn't like it when you call her old. *Also* ..."

Lev leaned forward in the recliner, pointing a single finger at her with one eyebrow cocked higher than the other. Every part of this man screamed cocky and *confidently so*. Like he had a reason to be, he knew it, and he didn't mind letting everyone else in on the secret to. She liked that about him too damn much. Not many men could pull it off, but he could.

"What?" she asked the longer he left his statement hanging.

"She couldn't see anything, so I have nothing to apologize for. I like that red, by the way. Now let me *take it off.*"

Gigi's skin flushed with heat, instantly knowing what Lev meant by *red*. Her mini skirt had ridden high enough on her thighs that now she *was* flashing someone. Him. Not that he seemed to mind in the slightest.

"Keep the heels on," he murmured, leaning back in the recliner. "And I'll take the panties off myself. Everything else can go. *Strip.*"

There was something about the way the low demand crossed the room to reach Gigi's spot that had her drawing in a quick breath. Then again, it could have been the fact that he gave her a little nod that spurred her on to do exactly as he asked.

Her crop top went first. Then, she tugged the skirt down, too. In nothing but the red silk panties that she'd been allowed to keep from a shoot a couple of months earlier and the strappy heels, Gigi edged forward, stepping around the table and chair until she stopped a couple of feet away from Lev.

"Not fair," she told him, "only you're getting a show."

Lev grinned, a gleam lighting up his eye as he glanced up to meet her stare. With his hand laying against his jaw with one finger resting against his cheek, he arched a brow suggestively. "My bad, but see ... now you're just as I wanted you."

"For?"

"*This.*"

He leaned forward again, only this time his hands found her body. One dipped between her thighs, his palm flattening to her sex overtop the silk panties, while his other grabbed her waist. She had no control when he yanked her forward all at once. His thumb stroked her clit through the soft fabric before his mouth replaced the digit. She lifted her leg to rest on his thigh and sighed at the access that gave him to her center.

Her fingers clutched at the top of his head, the buzz of his haircut tickling against her palms when his tongue worked its way under her panties. With the help of his fingers moving the silk aside, of course.

Problem was, as soon as he was eating at her cunt, and his fingers filled her full at the same time, Gigi was lost to sensation. How three of his fingers stuffed up her pussy was enough to make her knees weak. The way he took his time teasing with his tongue between lapping at his fingers to taste them coming out of her and then back to her clit with a faster pace that had her dragging in fast breaths.

He didn't talk.

Didn't say a damn thing.

He just ate her pussy like it was his last meal, and he'd never been more grateful for it. The pleased, throaty hum that vibrated from his mouth to her sex had her rocking her hips into him to get more of *that*. It was only when she started to shake with an oncoming orgasm that he finally stared up, lips wet with her and blue eyes stormy with desire, and he watched her break all apart for him.

No doubt, just as he wanted.

Her loud shout of his name when her knees finally buckled from the crushing wave of her bliss bounced off the walls of

the quiet apartment. The flickering light of the TV almost
made Gigi feel like everything slowed down when Lev lifted
from the chair, his hands traveling over her shaking form to
keep her standing but also explore.

Calloused palms.

A warm touch.

He was a comfort to her senses.

And *sin.*

All at once.

She didn't know how to deal with that.

That was fine—Lev didn't plan to make her think very
much about anything at all except him, apparently. He was
so very good at that. She barely even noticed them moving
from the living room to his bedroom because she was too
focused on the way his hands worked over her body, and his
kiss drowned her in need on the way.

When the backs of her knees hit the edge of a mattress, his
kiss broke from hers for him to murmur, *"Ass high,* babe."

She did exactly that but not before watching the sight of
him drag the T-shirt over his head with one arm pulling at
the material from his back. His chest really was a work of art.
Defined bands of muscles that flexed with every movement,
and the dark dusting of hair that trailed from his chest all the
way down past the waistline of the boxer-briefs peeking out
the top of his jeans.

Soon, that chest was leaning over her back and pressing
her into the bed. His mouth found the back of her neck while
one of his hands fisted the hair at her nape, gathering it all in
a tight bunch.

"Higher," he said into her ear.

Her ass pulled as high as he wanted her to be when he
slipped an arm under her stomach and dragged her upward.
The roughness as he yanked the silk from her body and down
her legs was enough to have her whining. She was lost in him
again. Lost in the way his hands left her hair to stroke her
cheek with a soft touch before two of his fingers pushed past
her parted lips. She found the taste of herself there—tart and
heavy on her tongue in the best way. Grinding her ass into
the erection straining through his jeans, she felt only one

thing.

Need.

So much of it, she was going to explode.

Surely.

"Stay still," she heard him say as he pulled his fingers from her wet mouth. "This is my favorite part."

The zipper rattle had her shivering but with one of his palms flat to her back, he kept her upper half low to the bed. Denim shuffled and a wrapper crackled. That palm of his lifted from her back when the blunt head of his cock pressed into her tight slit.

His favorite part was watching his cock fill her inch by inch while his hands grabbed tight to her ass and hips to spread her wide while he did it. His fingers ached from how deep they dug into her muscles but *God* ... it felt so fucking good, too.

He was still big enough to make her squirm.

To have her clawing at the bed while he made her wait to be stretched to the brim and dying for him to just *fuck her.* All his praises and the way his tone choked with huskiness had her whimpering into his bedsheets as she clutched at anything to keep her grounded.

Every single one of his *look at you* and *take that cock, baby* wrapped her tighter and tighter until she was a coil ready to break. And when he did finally start pounding into her, Gigi was already flying.

So fucking high.

This man was a drug.

One hit wasn't enough.

• • •

"You know, when you ask a woman to stay the night," Gigi muttered against the warmth of Lev's shoulder in his bed, "she shouldn't have to wake up to someone pounding on your door at ..." She lifted her head just enough to see the digital clock on the bedside table flashing with a time that surprised even her. "How is it only *six*?"

On another day, a six AM morning wouldn't be that early

for Gigi, but it was when she had half a dozen drinks the night before, and then spent several hours riding a cock she was sure to feel for a week.

God.

She did appreciate the size of Lev's dick, though.

No lies there.

The wall of muscled, warm man beside her shifted with a groan. His arm stretched out before he grabbed the clock and yanked it closer like he was trying to distinguish the time through the darkness of the bedroom. Like he couldn't see it perfectly fine—same as her.

"Go answer your door," she said in a laugh.

"Kind of don't want to move."

"Me, either, but it's not my apartment, so ..."

She left the obvious unsaid.

Lev groaned.

Fuck him for it, too.

It only made her wet.

Again.

The knocking continued, however.

Actually, it got louder.

"Persistent *fuckers*," he grumbled, kicking off the fluffy duvet. Which unfortunately only took the blanket away from her. She gave him a fake glare from the pillow she'd claimed as hers to use for the night, but all he offered her back was a simpering shrug before he tossed the blanket back over her form. "At least it was only someone knocking that woke you up—your snoring kept me up past three."

Gigi gasped, the sound distinct and sharp in the quiet apartment. "*Lies.* I do not snore!"

He headed for the open bedroom doorway, grabbing a pair of sweatpants from a laundry basket near the door. Over his shoulder, he tossed back, "You do ... but I didn't mind."

Warmth filled her body all the way down to the tips of her toes and fingers. She could feel the heat in her cheeks, too, but she muffled her embarrassed laughter into the pillow. Honestly, she couldn't be that ashamed that he'd heard her snoring in her sleep.

Shit, he had her spread wide.

Tasted *every* part of her.

Saw her at her most raw.

What did it matter if she snored?

"Probably the building manager," she heard him say, his voice drifting further away.

A memory flooded through her sleepy mind without warning. That was right—he mentioned helping the old woman who managed the building and tenants for the landlord when he could. She hadn't gotten a good look at the lady the night before when she poked her head out of her door to ask if they needed anything the night before, but she did remember Lev speaking warmly to and *about* her.

Rolling to her back in the comfortable queen-size bed, Gigi revealed in every delicious ache that woke her up with each movement she made. From the way, her toes cracked when she flexed her feet, to the way she could still feel Lev's hands bending her body to his will while pounding into her deep and hard until she moaned her way through another orgasm.

Sleep had come so easily after that.

Too easy, maybe.

She had a good mind to see if she might be able to get the man up for another round—maybe they could put his shower to use, seeing as how she still felt the remnants from their fucking the night before. Not that she was complaining.

The voices that filtered into the bedroom stopped her thoughts right in their tracks. Any and all consideration of sex flew right out the window just like that.

Shame.

"Lev Arthur Arsov?" she heard asked.

"That's me."

"Officer Ritchie, Mr. Arsov. Sorry to bother you this early in the morning but considering we just got the information of your address this morning, and the circumstances, we really didn't think you would want us to wait to find you. And this is my partner—"

"Is this about the fucking bar?" she heard Lev ask. "Because I already talked to the cops that came in to interview Nickie's employees. I was told that was it; I wouldn't be needed for any further statements. A bit early for you to be knocking on my door for shit that's already done and over with, yeah?"

A throat cleared.

The silence stretched on.

"Mr. Arsov, we're not here about ... that incident."

The officer continued stumbling around whatever he was trying to spit out while Lev barked a bit more of his morning attitude onto the man. All the while, Gigi couldn't ignore the nosy side of her personality that urged her to get out of bed and closer to the conversation happening on the other side of the apartment. She at least had a good enough mind to bring the duvet from the bed, wrapping it around her naked body like a makeshift dress to cover the bits she didn't want police officers to see.

Outside the bedroom, she leaned out the end of the short hallway to peer around the corner. Her presence wasn't missed by the two officers standing just outside the apartment's front door with their hands resting in the pockets of their chest vests. Even Lev glanced over his shoulder at her, and while she might have admired the definition in his naked, toned back and how the muscles flexed as he turned to look at her ... she was more concerned with the matching frowns the officers wore.

"There a problem?" she asked.

The taller of the two officers smiled but quickly put his attention back on Lev. "Mr. Arsov, I think you should accompany us down to the station so that we can explain this situation further ... in private. It's a delicate matter."

"Am I going to find myself under arrest when I get there?"

The shorter of the two officers chuckled. "No, sir."

"Well—"

"It's all right, Lev," Gigi spoke up. "I can see myself out."

He only nodded, but otherwise, said nothing. She really didn't need him to. The entire strange situation spoke volumes all on its own.

First, a bar shooting. This time, cops showed up in the morning. As much as she liked sleeping with Lev, she had to admit ... the guy seemed to find trouble. By the looks of it, far more often than he probably should.

Maybe she should be grateful that her flight to Paris was only a few short days away. At least in Europe, thoughts of this man wouldn't follow her day in and day out ... or chase her all the way to a dive bar to see him one more time.

Right?

What was done was done.

That's what she had to tell herself.

SEVEN

THE COPS that showed up at Lev's apartment hadn't lied. Their reason for being there had absolutely nothing to do with the shooting at the bar despite the fact he couldn't think of a single thing else for their presence.

Certainly not *the* reason.

The blue-eyed, six-month-old reason currently being held across the police station in the arms of a social worker, that was. Even from thirty feet away, he'd known it was her when the woman brought the baby girl in through the front doors. Not because the police officer he waited with said so, but rather ... a part of him felt it.

His heart kickstarted.

Blood rushed in his ears.

Space got smaller.

From all the way across the room, he knew that baby was his. *His* daughter—a child made from his blood. Her big blue eyes, wide-eyed despite the early morning hour, peered all around with the wonder and curiosity only a baby could have.

"Six months old," the officers had explained shortly after they arrived at the station and got him sat down on the other side of one of their desks. For a moment, he thought the two of them were about to play a game of good cop, bad cop with him. It wouldn't be the first time and at that point, Lev was still convinced they brought him there about the shooting. *God.* He was such a fucking idiot. "Her mother had a rough time after her birth according to the grandmother. She voluntarily entered a facility three months ago ... she struggled with addiction and mental health before and after the baby was born, but it got worse after Arely arrived. Unfortunately, she came out of the seventy-two-hour hold and was found identified a week later after a fatal overdose."

They'd shown him a picture.

Of the mother.

And the child that was apparently his.

Sitting in that hard chair, with officers across from him that seemed to both watch his every move and stare at him with a sympathy he'd never been offered before, Lev didn't know what to do. He was struck glancing between the two pictures on the desk.

One of a newborn wrapped in a pink blanket.

The other, of a woman he remembered too well though her disappearance in his life hadn't even been a blip on his radar. Dawn Marks was just ... a chick he slept with occasionally and nothing more, really. He hadn't the time for anything else, and she never suggested she wanted more from him over the ten or so months that they'd been friends.

"Was she just a hook-up or—"

He understood the officer's curiosity and didn't blame the man for it. "And a friend who lived in the building. I didn't know she ... had any issues. Not like what you're saying. She didn't let on to me. We just had fun when she came to drink at the bar. I mean, we were basically going to the same place when we went home, you know? It was a week after she moved out of the building before I even knew that she was gone. It wasn't like we were close. I didn't get offended that she hadn't said goodbye."

But *fuck*.

He was mad right then.

So goddamn mad.

That was his *kid*. She got pregnant with his kid, said nothing, and then left ... just gave his baby to someone else to take care of when she couldn't do it. He tried to sympathize with the situation she must have been faced with and the way she probably felt at the time. Hopeless. Agonized. At the very end of her rope, clearly.

Maybe she thought he wouldn't help.

Or that he wouldn't want the child.

"Arely, you said?" he remembered asking.

Although which officer he asked, he couldn't say. By then, the room had closed all around him and the whooshing in his ears was far worse.

Arely Dawn Marks, they explained. That was what her mother named her just before she signed custody of the barely week-old baby—at the time—over to her mother. The pregnancy hadn't been easy, according to the information the police had and what his daughter's grandmother explained.

And then her grandmother got sick. To the point that she couldn't care for a six-month-old that was starting to move and explore more than she ever had before. The late nights were hard enough, but add in a baby starting to explore and do what babies did, and well … it was too much for her to handle.

"At least," the kinder of the two officers told him shortly before his child arrived at the police station, "her mother had enough understanding of her situation to let the child's grandmother know who the father was if she needed to find you. All she had was a name and a bar. When the grandmother handed the baby over to social services, it took them a couple of weeks to find you."

"And here you are."

"Here we are, Mr. Arsov."

That was that.

Then, his baby arrived with the social worker. Just like that, Lev no longer cared to talk about the details because as soon as he laid eyes on her, he knew she was his. And without a doubt, with no question, he had suddenly never wanted anything more in his life than his child. To hold her because he was sure she was scared—things kept changing for her, right? She was only six months old. She had to be scared.

That *killed* him inside.

Because he could have made that better.

Months ago.

Of course, he heard the officer's warnings that there was still a possibility the baby girl wasn't his as he stood from the chair and headed for the woman holding his child. He understood when they said a DNA test would have to be done, but the grandmother was clear that Dawn Marks had been adamant about the identity of the father.

Him.

She had eyes *so blue.* So blue he drowned in them. Because they were his.

His eyes.

Her stare matched his, and it was the first and most prominent thing in his mind as he reached to take her from the woman without even asking if he could. Frankly, he didn't think he should have to ask—she was *his.* She belonged with him.

The social worker did hand Arely over. She kept hold of the pink and white checkered diaper bag that, thankfully, seemed quite full of ... *things.*

Holy shit.

What did babies even need? She probably wasn't being breastfed, so what did he feed her?

All those worries drifted away when he had the baby girl in his arms, and his much larger form swallowed her whole. The room became less crowded and loud, and the beats of his own heart started to overtake that anxious rushing in his ears.

She stared up at him.

Pretty blue.

"Hey," Lev whispered, all too aware of the people watching him but not caring at all what they saw. "Hey, baby girl. I'm your daddy—yeah, I am."

"Well, we'll have to—"

"It'll only take a couple of days for the DNA test to come back," the officer was quick to interject before the social worker could finish whatever she was going to say. "But we're fairly certain and ... they do say girls take after their dads, don't they?"

Lev didn't know.

He didn't know anything about babies.

But he knew this child was his.

"Arely Dawn," he murmured, rubbing the pad of his thumb over her rosy, chubby cheek. It made her smile. *He* made her smile, and then she laughed, too. "Who's the prettiest girl in the whole wide world? It's *you,* yes it is ... hey, my girl."

Her little fingers wrapped tightly around his thumb, and

she smiled even wider. He swore to fucking God his heart came right out of his chest and landed in her tiny, chubby hands. The pale yellow flowers on her long-sleeve shirt matched the color of the soft pants someone had dressed her in. And the flower on the headband keeping the dark curls out of her eyes.

Weren't most babies bald?

Not his, apparently.

She had a whole crown of dark curls—the same as his, if he let the mess grow out. It looked so much cuter on her.

"Her foster family will be happy to have you visit up until the point when we can prove paternity as well as you can provide proof to show you're capable of taking care of the baby. I'm sure we can speed up the process considering the circumstances and—"

All at once, Lev tightened his hold on Arely, turned his entire body away from the woman he'd just taken his child from, and made *no* effort to hide the venom in his voice when he said, "You're not taking her from me. I just got her. She's mine. *Look at her*. She's my child."

He'd already missed six whole months. He wouldn't miss one more fucking day. That was a promise.

The social worker blinked, her helpless, silent stare passing between him, the baby in his arms, and the officers standing in a very quiet police station.

"She's *mine*," he said again, the words thicker in his throat because they had to understand. *They just had to.* "She belongs with me—whatever I need to do, I'll do it. But can't she stay with me now?"

He dared them to tell him no. Most of all, he wanted any of them to look at the baby in his arms now happily chewing on the string of the hoodie he had pulled on before leaving the apartment to be decent, and tell him she shouldn't be with him.

Her *father*.

"Please," he said quietly, "let her come home with me."

He didn't have the things she needed. He knew that. Couldn't he figure it out? So, she needed a place to sleep. Okay, done. *Somehow.*

What did it matter?

She could sleep in his fucking arms, and he wouldn't close his eyes if that's what it took.

And then, the officer who had been the one to break the news, spoke up quickly to say, "We'll figure it out. I'm sure ... we can figure something out, can't we?"

That made his whole day better.

The baby girl in his arms, though?

She suddenly became his entire life in seconds and although he had only been holding her for minutes, and knew of her existence for an hour, he didn't want to remember what it was like before he knew she was there.

"*Brrrr,*" the baby babbled, drool wetting her pink lips as she smiled wide when his attention came back to her. "Babababababa."

She had two teeth on the bottom that she showed off with her unrestrained laughter when he blew kisses. Not once did he consider that he was twenty-four and struggling to survive when all he had to take care of was himself. Not once did he think *you didn't even want kids, Lev.* She was there now. In his arms. *His.*

Everything changed for Lev just like that. Nothing would be the same now.

He was fine with that.

EIGHT

ONE DAY turned into two and it felt like Lev hadn't even blinked before it happened. He quickly realized that when it came to babies, time was irrelevant. It all bled together. From one bottle to the next—the last dirty diaper to the subsequent fifteen that followed. Not that he complained; the only person his daughter could currently count on to love and take care of her the way she needed and deserved was him, after all.

He planned to do the job well.

Perfectly, in fact.

Whatever she needed.

It was also why he didn't complain when the social worker promised—and did—to show up at his apartment twice a day until the DNA results were back in. That first check-in hadn't gone spectacularly well. Mostly because the woman found a hundred different things wrong with his apartment, starting with the fact it was only a one-bedroom and she didn't think it was appropriate for Arely to sleep in the same room as her father.

A man.

Lev wanted to rage.

Her suggestion was *gross*.

And yet, he knew that wouldn't do him any fucking good. So he shut his mouth, forced a smile on his face, and lied his ass off. As far as she thought, he would be moving into a larger apartment in a better neighborhood, closer to his work.

All lies.

Sort of.

But whatever.

His kid was with him.

"Babababa!"

From his position behind the small kitchen counter, Lev

had a full view into the living room where Arely currently played in the Pack 'N Play that also acted as her bed for the moment. He watched his happy baby girl throw the handful of colorful blocks onto the brown carpet that had seen far better days. It wasn't like moving would be a bad thing—at least then he wouldn't feel like his kid was just rolling in irremovable dirt every time he put her on the floor.

The past two days hadn't been easy. She cried to communicate. He didn't understand what any of those cries meant, but he was learning one at a time.

Oh, and what was sleep?

Those two teeth? They were turning into four—she had more coming on the top, and it made nighttime particularly long and hard. He had to quickly learn how to change a diaper, something he'd never done before, and make bottles out of powder and water he boiled to make sure it was clean and without contaminants.

Like fuck was his daughter drinking from the *tap*. Especially not the taps in this goddamn shithole.

All the while, Lev still had to handle the demands of the social worker—including finding a pediatrician, proof of his employment, the new apartment, and any childcare. She said he would have ample opportunity to do all of those things and that he shouldn't worry about doing it as quickly as he could, but it didn't feel that way to him.

He saw her judgment at the state of his place *and* when he explained his job, not to mention his income. He wasn't stupid enough to think the social worker thought he was in any way capable of taking care of a baby, but he would be.

He had to be.

It certainly helped that the courts favored biological parents having custody of their children if there wasn't a reason for them not to ... and so far, Lev was proving to be capable. At the very least.

"*Brrrrrbrrrbrrr*," Arely babbled from the living room. Followed by more blocks dropping on the floor and her loud laughter. Then, "Babababa!"

Along with the Pack 'N Play, a handful of age-appropriate toys, and enough clothes to do the baby for a week, she didn't have much else. The diaper bag that came with her held a single can of powder formula that was already half gone and diapers that would be used up by that evening, likely.

He needed to buy more.

She needed a lot more.

Right then, however, he was trying to deal with yet another one of his problems. His work, that was.

"Nickie here," came the voice through the speaker pressed to Lev's ear.

He took a second, dragged in a breath for yet another battle he was sure to face with this phone call. Considering the way his boss acted the night before when he called in, without much of an explanation as to why to be fair, he didn't expect this time to go much better. Although now, he was willing to at least tell Nickie *why* he needed one more day before he could get back to work at the bar.

"Hey, Nickie," Lev said. "It's Lev. I'm calling in again tonight, but I was hoping if it was early, you would be able to get someone to cover my shift at the bar. I'll be back in tomorrow night; I just need tonight to get some shit in order that I'm trying to handle. I know—"

And that was all he got out.

"That's twice—two times too many. Don't bother coming in at all."

Lev blinked, unsure he had even heard his boss correctly. "What?"

"You heard what I said. You're a decent guy, and I appreciate that, but I don't have time to chase your ass about coming into work. Nor do I give a fuck when I've got a handful of resumes on my desk on any given day to replace you with. You don't want to come into work? Fine. Someone else will. Don't bother coming in at all. Not tomorrow. Or anytime. You got me?"

"I've kind of got a situation going on here, man."

And now more than ever, he needed a fucking job. Regardless of how much said job paid, he just needed one to satisfy the damn social worker.

"Oh, really?" Nickie asked, not sounding at all interested.

"Yeah, just found out I have a—"

Kid, he was about to say.

Nickie didn't give him the chance. "Couldn't give a single fuck, Lev."

Click.

It took him ten entire seconds to realize the asshole had hung up the phone on him. In that time, Arely had also decided to start screaming her little lungs out because she had run out of blocks to throw out of her Pack 'N Play. He couldn't decide whether to laugh or cry himself because in the next breath, a knock sounded on his apartment door.

"Give Daddy one second," he called to the crying baby. Then, to himself, he muttered, "Swear to God if it's that bitch upstairs again ..."

She spent the entire evening before beating her broom on the floor because Arely wasn't quiet enough for her liking. The *cunt.*

He didn't use that word lightly.

It's what she was, though.

"*Babababababa!*"

Arely's angry babbling mixed in with her cries which did nothing to help Lev's already frayed nerves when he yanked open the apartment door with a sharp, "*What?*"

The teenager waiting on the other side with a scowl was not who he expected to be standing there. Nessa, the troubled granddaughter of the building manager, pursed her lips and folded her arms over her chest as she stared up at him. Bigger men than this teenage girl had cowered at the sight of Lev looming over them.

She just *glared.*

"That's *not* how you greet somebody," she told him. "Could at least be polite."

Lev drew in a deep breath, his patience already long fucking gone. "And what would you know about being polite, huh? You spend your days skipping school and calling your grandmother a bitch. Hypocrisy isn't a good look on anybody, kid."

Nessa sniffed and then glanced away down the hall. "Yeah, *well ...*"

The screeching from the baby inside the apartment picked

up a notch, making Lev straighten a bit in the doorway and
Nessa flinch.

"Jesus—she's got good lungs, doesn't she?"

"It only gets louder from here. Welcome to birth control.
Best kind there is. Wanna babysit?"

He was joking.

Mostly.

Lev didn't think this teenager was in *any* way capable of
taking care of a baby when she barely managed to make it
day to day in her own circumstance. And yet, when that joke
of an offer slipped past his lips, a spark of joy came to
Nessa's eyes when she met his stare again.

"Could I? I will, if you need somebody. I like kids. I looked
after my little brother, Mikey—well, until they took him away
from Mom."

Wait ...

"You have a brother?"

Her grandmother never mentioned another grandchild.

She shrugged. "Yeah, he'll be three next month. If I don't
get anymore write-ups, I can go to his birthday party to visit.
Or that's what the social worker told Nan. Oh, yeah ... that's
why I'm here."

Lev blinked.

It felt like he was doing that a lot lately.

Nessa continued like he wasn't standing there staring at
her stupidly. "Nan wanted me to let you know the apartment
in Brooklyn came through—the landlord told her you could
move in like Friday as long as you've got the deposit and first
month's rent."

Shit, that soon?

He could do that in the physical sense. It wasn't like he had
that much shit in his one-bedroom apartment. If he could
borrow a friend's vehicle, he could have it all moved in a trip
or two.

It was the financial side of things that made him pause. In
his head, he did the math. It added up to a lot more money
than he had now considering how much he needed to pull
out of his paltry savings to get what Arely needed over the
coming days.

The baby continued crying.

Nessa tilted her body to the side and looked past him in the doorway. "You sure she's okay?"

"She's mad. She threw out all her blocks. It's a thing she does."

"Huh."

An idea had started to form in Lev's head. He needed money, and fast. He also needed to pull everything together before the social worker decided his time had run out to do so. It wasn't like he had very many people he could go to for help, but there was *one* man who had given him an offer he'd been willing to refuse, even if he did say he would think about it.

Well, now he was really thinking about it.

Andino Marcello, that was.

If the guy could afford to pay Lev ten-k a month to be a bodyguard, then what else might he be able to help him with? Especially if he did want him as an employee.

Time to find out.

"Hey," Lev said, gaining the teenager's attention again, "is your grandmother busy? You wanna earn twenty bucks?"

Nessa snapped the gum in her mouth. "Why?"

"I do need someone to keep an eye on her tonight. If you're capable, then cool. *With* supervision."

She rolled her eyes. "I'm not gonna hurt her or something."

"But you hurt yourself sometimes."

That quieted the girl.

"I'm doing better."

"Are you?"

With dark, honest eyes, she peered up at him still unafraid. "Trying to."

Good to know.

And yet ... "Let's go chat with your grandmother."

• • •

"Let him in, Petey."

Andino hadn't lied when he said finding his restaurant in Manhattan would be rather easy. All Lev did was make a call

76

to a friend who knew somebody else that had the name of the business in question where the mafia Capo spent many of his days. Mind, it was made very clear to Lev that asking about the availability or current whereabouts of a man like Andino Marcello was a dangerous thing to do.

Well, what choice did he have?

Lev took the risk.

The girl at the entrance podium gave him a look but pointed in the direction of a private dining room when he asked where he might find Andino, if the guy was around. She didn't even say a word to him while she did it, either. He didn't bother to appreciate the fine dining or the rich decor of the place as he headed for the section where he would find Andino. Tiled floors squeaked under the heels of his boots and the noise of the busy restaurant surrounded him but none of that really mattered.

He was here for one thing.

That was it.

A six-foot wall of muscle met him at the doorway of the private dining section. He had to tip his head up to meet Lev's gaze as he was taller than the man standing guard, but he had to give the guy credit. He didn't look frightened of the larger man asking about his boss.

"He did say let me in, right?" Lev asked when the guy didn't move.

"Did he?"

"Could move *you*," he returned, smirking a bit. "If that's what you want. Let me know."

His amusement wasn't shared.

Clearly.

Meathead—Petey, that was—grunted under his breath. "And who the fuck are *you*?"

Lev didn't mind educating him. It was a good lesson for everyone to learn.

From within the dining section, a sigh echoed. "As fun as this pissing contest is, I have a busy day ahead of me, so ..."

"You have dinner with your mother," meathead muttered under his breath.

"Heard that, Petey."

"Sorry, boss."

Just like that, Petey stepped to the side to let Lev pass. The second he was inside the private dining section, Andino had already stood from the table in the middle where he had what looked to be his lunch and work spread across the top. Between the steak, potatoes, and a half-eaten cheesecake rested open folders and scattered papers. He didn't bother to clean up the mess as Lev approached.

Nor did he offer his hand to shake.

Or even a smile.

"Lev," Andino greeted. "I didn't think I would be seeing you again so soon. Have you thought about my offer, then?"

"I have."

"And?"

He gestured to the seat at the table. "Can I?"

"More power to you. The comfort of others isn't usually my concern, but you're welcome to it all the same."

Lev sat and so did Andino.

"I have conditions," he said after a beat of silence.

Across the table, the man in a suit that seemed tailored to fit his form perfectly in every way arched a brow and chuckled. He didn't look away from the watch on his wrist—a Rolex, Lev knew. The rather large face and emblem on the item gave the brand away easily enough. He bet that watch cost an easy few grand, not to mention the suit the man wore.

"It's not a ... democracy ... when you work for me," Andino said, finally glancing up with a devilish grin. "You don't get a vote or a say on very much. You get an order, and you follow it. That's how it works."

"How often do you approach people to work with you—like you did for me, I mean? "

Andino drew in a careful breath before replying calmly, "*For* me, not with. No one works with me. It's not that kind of employment, Lev."

Right.

He wouldn't soon forget it.

"My main question remains the same."

And unanswered, he added silently.

Andino shook his head and lifted one shoulder to shrug. "Rarely. Associates usually come from the inside of my business, you understand? Someone vouched for by someone else. It's what's acceptable in this life of ours. The standard for made men. Not that I expect you to understand much about that. I'm not looking for someone like me, however. I'm not fond of that—I like to pick my men. Makes a difference."

"Does it?"

"Yes, I tend to want to kill them less when I choose someone to be on my books."

Well, then ...

Lev appreciated his honesty. At the same time, he still had conditions. He had to now. Things had changed since Andino approached him.

"What does that mean?" Lev asked. "To be ... *on the books.*"

"Paid," Andino replied simply.

"Legally?"

A dark laugh answered him back.

Lev figured that said everything.

It was also problem number one. He figured before this conversation went any further with Andino, he needed to just lay his entire situation out on the table. That way, the man across from him knew where Lev stood, and they could either move forward or not.

Pulling out his phone, Lev unlocked the device and turned the screen around for Andino to see the new picture that took up the entire background.

Arely.

And her big smile.

"My daughter," Lev said.

It still wasn't official.

It didn't matter to him.

He knew.

"I just got custody of her two days ago—cops showed up at my door. Guess her mom figured I couldn't be a dad and didn't think to tell me. Not sure what good it did. She didn't want to be a mom either, apparently. So, to keep her, I need a few things. Like a stable job that pays the fucking bills but also isn't going to get me thrown in jail."

Andino cleared his throat, his gaze never moving from the screen. "Can't promise *that*. Nature of the business, you know?"

"Not particularly."

"Yeah, well ... I can make it look legal. Cash can come from legal sources, if that's what you're asking from me. On paper, it'll be legit."

"But—"

Andino's gaze slammed into his with a weight he wasn't sure that he could carry. It silenced Lev instantly. "But it isn't what's on paper that counts. And a lot of good it'll do for you to keep her if you end up in a grave somewhere because you're working with me. Have you considered that? The only reason I offered you the job was because a guy got his brains blown out for being my enforcer."

Lev sucked in a deep breath.

It didn't steady him.

"Maybe he didn't do his job right, then."

"Perhaps," Andino returned. "Matter of semantics and I don't speak ill of the dead, you know?"

Neither did Lev.

Still ... "Keeping you alive keeps me alive here, right?"

"And paid," Andino murmured. "It's a win-win, really. You can start next week if you want." His stare drifted back to the phone that Lev had yet to lower from view. "Cute kid—are you gonna want weekends off?"

"Just some heads up about hours, maybe. So I can work out—"

"Childcare, yeah. Figured. You better be worth the effort here, Lev. I don't usually bend to help someone else. Not my style. Never gets me very far."

Lev laughed under his breath. "Then why are you?"

Andino leaned back in the chair and folded his arms across his broad chest, eyeing the man across the table from him with a severe expression. Like he was considering his reply. "I don't know ... I just liked you. I don't like very many people."

Was that a good thing?

Lev figured … they were about to find out.

"Next week, then?" he asked.

Andino nodded. "Have your phone number plugged into Petey's phone before you leave. Don't show up wearing what you are. That'll never fly with people I work with. Slacks and dress shirts—blazers daily. I can do with or without a tie. That's the least of my fucking concerns."

"I don't think I even own a—"

"*Petey!*"

As fast as Andino shouted the man's name, the meathead popped his face in the doorway. "Yeah, boss?"

"Call Richard for me. Let him know he'll have a guest at his shop tomorrow afternoon—say one-ish—for fittings. Put it all on my tab." Then to Lev, Andino said, "Consider it an investment you'll return to me as soon as you're capable, but there's not a deadline on it. Lower Manhattan. It's a bit of a trip for you from Harlem but make sure you're there. Petey has the address. That work for you?"

Jesus Christ.

"I'll make it work," Lev replied.

"Good. That's what I want to hear. Now, excuse me. I have some work to finish."

Clearly dismissed but also feeling like he might have just won a battle somehow, Lev didn't question the order from the man across the table. He stood from the chair and without a goodbye, headed out of the private section. He stopped just long enough to hand over the info Petey needed and to get the address of the shop in Manhattan that he *would* be at the next day. On the way out of the restaurant, his phone beeped with a text.

Pulling it up, his smile grew wide at the picture waiting for him from a number he'd only recently plugged into his phone.

From Nessa.

The shot of a smiling, drooling Arely with a face messy from some red sauce had his heart kickstarting all over again. Before he could reply, however, his phone rang. He didn't recognize the number, but he picked it up the same way he always did any call.

"Lev Arsov here—what's up?"

"Mr. Arsov. Officer Doucette here. I know we had an appointment for you to come in tomorrow and get the results of the DNA test, but my partner said ... well, fuck it." The man laughed. "We know you were really wanting this—she's all yours, man. One hundred percent yours. We'll make the calls and fax everything over to the social worker's office. Congrats. It's a girl."

He didn't need that call to know. It still put him on top of the world. For once in his life, Lev was fucking *winning*.

In every single way.

NINE

"HOW ARE you still not packed? You leave *tomorrow*. If you're waiting for me to help, I can't. Matty's coming to pick me up for dinner—cute little Italian place. I'd say you could come but ... wouldn't want you to show up to Paris with an extra couple of pounds, right?"

Gigi did her best to ignore the nagging of her roommate. It was easier said than done. Her silence and turned back did nothing to curb Cassie's constant stream of bitching. She wasn't sure what changed between them. Or *when*. Maybe when the girl realized Paris and the famous fashion designer who wanted to work with Gigi was a real thing that would happen.

Not just a possibility, no.

An actual thing.

Something Cassie wasn't doing and might never have the chance to do. The business of modeling was not an easy one—in fact, Gigi thought it was probably one of the most deprecating and difficult careers one could choose to step into because *everything* was judged, compared, and then rated. And the scales differed for everyone.

Beauty to one was ugliness to another.

Fame was fleeting.

Nothing was easy.

And very little felt real in a world where everyone was airbrushed to perfection constantly; where everyone had a part to play and a mask they put on because whenever the cameras turned on, so did the models being photographed.

Simple as that.

It was something Gigi had tried to keep in mind in the years since she decided this was the path she wanted to follow. Her mother also reminded her regularly that there was a good chance for some people, Gigi was just a steppingstone to something else. Someone they could use on the way to their own top, so to speak. She hadn't believed that to be the case with people she considered friends; how silly of her.

Turns out ... that's what Cassie thought she was, too.

Or, that's how it felt lately.

"Are you ignoring me?" Cassie asked.

She had kept talking.

Gigi just didn't care.

"No," she lied, bringing up the browser on her laptop. It made it far easier to pretend like she was doing something more important than having a conversation with her jealous, soon-to-be ex-roommate when her back was turned, and the computer was in front of her. "Just busy. Have a good dinner, though. Say hi to Matty."

"Why? Not like he'll say it back."

Well ...

Cassie wasn't even trying to be nice now.

Neither would Gigi, then.

Tossing a cool smile over her shoulder, Gigi replied, "Then don't tell him shit. I don't care. Did you need anything else? Because I am actually trying to do something here and—"

"Don't know why you bother. The agency will have everything ready for you when you arrive. There'll even be a driver at the airport. Right now, you're their next big meal ticket, and they know it. What are you looking up—how to speak *French*? Little late for that. Learn as you go, I guess. I hear they have apps for that, anyway."

What?

It didn't even matter.

Gigi decided right then and there that she wasn't even going to bother and *try* to decipher the multitude of Cassie's current issues. It could be boiled down to the fact that the girl was jealous, felt like she was being left behind in Gigi's current success and was lashing out by using her words. She thought it would hurt.

It didn't.

Not that much.

And it just went to show that Gigi shouldn't waste her good vibes and energy—at this very best time in her life—on someone who only wanted to bring her down.

"Actually yeah," Cassie said, "there is one other thing. I almost forgot."

Gigi did her best not to sigh.

And failed.

Still, she turned away from the laptop and spun around in the chair just enough to face her roommate. Maybe if she let the girl get it out, she could go back to *trying* to get a hold of the man from the bar. Lev, that was. Although she had been fine to let their hook-ups be *just* that and nothing else ... she couldn't deny there was something.

A connection.

Maybe a friendship.

She didn't know but she also didn't like the idea of leaving the country, for God knew how long, without at least giving the guy a proper goodbye. It wasn't like they had the chance to do that when the cops showed up at his apartment and all. She certainly hadn't found the time to make a trip all the way to Harlem—or the bar where Lev worked—to say goodbye in person when her days had been filled with last-minute appointments to set things up and meetings with her mother agency.

It never stopped. It wasn't about to get better; she knew. Not once she landed in Paris. Gigi wouldn't complain, though. This was the chance of a lifetime. She *had* to take it.

"The lease on this place," Cassie said.

Gigi arched a brow and rested an arm over the back of chair. "What about it?"

"It's got another six months and—"

"You said Matty was moving in."

"But *your* name is still on the lease and that means you're responsible for half the rent. Even if you're off living your best life in Paris."

It was petty.

Rather stupid.

Gigi decided ... fuck it. If this was the game Cassie wanted to play during her last night in this apartment with her old friend, then so be it. She could be just as nasty.

Fair was fair, right?

"I'll talk to my agent—I'm sure MGNT will handle it."

Just like that, Cassie's face drained of color, and her pleased grin faded into a thin, grim line.

"Well, okay," Cassie muttered, glancing away.

"Have a good time with Matty."

Not bothering to waste any more energy on Cassie— besides, the whole situation was kind of sad—Gigi turned back to the laptop and the browser she had brought up. The second her fingers hit the keys to start typing in the search bar, Cassie's sigh echoed behind her. Thankfully, she heard the girl's footsteps receded into the hallway outside the bedroom. She put her attention back on the computer screen.

Nickie's Bar, she typed into the search engine. Considering the time was later in the day, it really was a last-ditch effort on Gigi's part to say goodbye to a man she'd only recently met. She still had to finish packing, tomorrow was an early run to the airport, and then it was goodbye New York. She didn't have Lev's phone number, but she did know where he worked and hell ... it couldn't hurt to try.

It wasn't like she owed him shit—he hadn't made it seem like he expected anything, either. A part of her still just wanted to.

The bar's information came up as the top result with a photograph of the front, address, and ... *yes*, she thought. A phone number, too. A little before dinnertime was probably a bit early for a bartender to be working on a Thursday, but maybe she could get *his* number—or even a time when he would be working later to call back.

Gigi grabbed her cell before she could think better of it and plugged in the number to call. It rang four times before someone picked up.

"Nickie's," a gruff voice said into the speaker.

"Hi, this is Gigi Parker," she replied, knowing how silly her request was going to sound but determined to get it out anyway. "I'm hoping I might be able to get a hold of one of your bartenders—Lev Arsov? He's a friend, and I'm heading out of town. I wanted to—"

"Lev doesn't work here anymore, sweetheart. Can't help

you."

"But—"

"Can't fucking help you."

Each word was enunciated a little stronger than the last. Then a click echoed in the speaker before the dial tone sounded.

He hung up on her.

Asshole.

What could she do now?

• • •

"Miss Gigi, I really don't think we have time—"

"It'll only take a couple of minutes," Gigi replied, already pushing open the rear passenger door of the black town car sent by the agency to ensure she made it to the airport on time.

Ha.

She was really pushing that now. Besides, those damn flights never took off on time, and she was sure she had at least a half-hour of cushion to make this work.

"We only have an hour, *and* you need to go through security!"

"Just two minutes!"

She headed for the familiar apartment building waiting across the street as the driver called out behind her, "It'll take that long for you to … get inside!"

Oh, well.

It was too late now.

She was already halfway there.

Over the night as she finished packing her bags, Gigi decided she did have one last chance to say goodbye to Lev before flying out of the country. Going to him—or his place, rather. Was it a long shot?

Probably.

If he'd recently quit, or lost, his job then he was likely out trying to get another. She really was going through more effort than was needed to see the man one more time considering their time together had been mostly spent in bed, but it felt right.

Like she should at least try. After all, he *did* say they would meet up again.

Right?

Gigi climbed the cement stairs at the front entrance of the building and expected she would have to buzz in. Instead, she found the front door to the place propped open by a plastic crate filled with bricks. Giving it, and the stack of packing boxes inside the entrance hallway near the mailboxes, a look she sent up a silent thanks to whoever was looking out for her that day. Probably saved her some time.

She didn't waste time, since she couldn't afford to, and headed straight down the steps to the basement level of apartments. Again, another plastic crate filled with bricks held the metal fire-safety door open down there. Another three packing boxes, stacked one on top of the other, waited a few feet inside the hallway. Right beside the apartment door she knew to be Lev's.

The door to the apartment was open, but Gigi didn't have to go inside to see what was going on from where she stood out in the hallway. The place was mostly empty. All the way back, she could see ... nothing.

No furniture.

No people.

No Lev.

"Hey, you need something?"

Gigi spun on her heel at the unfamiliar, *young* voice. In the doorway of the apartment down the hall that she'd passed on her way to Lev's stood a black-haired, dark-eyed girl that looked no older than sixteen or seventeen, if that. In her arms, sitting on her hip, was a curly-haired, babbling baby with the biggest, bluest eyes she had ever seen.

Cute kid, she thought.

"Uh, I was just looking for—"

"Lev? He moved out today. Just missed him. He's got a little bit of stuff left to take to his new place, though, if you wanna wait."

Dammit.

So much for luck.

"I have to head out, actually. Could you let—"

"Nessa, come help me reach this bowl!"

The teenager glanced over her shoulder at the voice calling from within the apartment. As she stepped back into the shadows of the doorway, grabbing the door to close it as she went, the girl said, "Sorry, gotta go. He'll be back in like an hour."

She shut the door before Gigi could explain that wouldn't do any good. And now, those two minutes were up.

Paris was waiting.

TEN

"WELL, YOU look like shit."

Lev sighed and seriously considered closing the apartment door right in Nessa's face. Except he couldn't because the girl was *really* helping him out on the weekends by coming over to babysit Arely when he got one of those calls. The random calls from Andino that simply offered a time, address, and that was that. He was expected to show up, dressed appropriately, remain quiet unless told otherwise, and look like he was ready to kill someone.

All things he could do.

And did.

Despite his concern about the teenager having some personal issues to handle, he swore this kid loved his daughter as much as he did. Whenever the two girls were in the same room together, the smiles and laughter didn't stop. Even Nessa's grandmother mentioned the baby was doing something good for the girl.

If she kept showing up and doing the right things, then Lev didn't see the issue with letting her babysit unattended when her grandmother couldn't be there to supervise. Especially if it was only supposed to be for a couple of hours.

Like today.

"Thanks," he grumbled.

Nessa shrugged. "Long night?"

Well ...

Yes and no.

Single fatherhood was not for the faint of heart or the weak. Frankly, though ... babies were a hell of a thing. Just when he thought he had everything down pat, like there was nothing he couldn't handle when it came to his six-month-old daughter, she seemed to take that as a challenge.

God, he loved his kid.

He was still tired.

So fucking tired.

"Don't worry about me," Lev said, stepping back from the door to let Nessa enter his new apartment. The place was bigger, cleaner, and brighter than the old one. Two bedrooms plus a nice little veranda that the social worker just had to bitch about because she apparently thought he planned to let his kid play out there unattended.

Even though Arely couldn't even pull herself up to stand yet.

The place also had a rather large closet that could act as a small office or for something else. He planned to use it as a toy room for Arely when she started showing interest in literally anything other than colorful blocks and the pots she could pull out of the cupboard.

"Where's Arely?"

"Finally down for a nap. Let her sleep for *at least* an hour before you wake her up. I swear to God," he muttered at the teenager's back when she headed down the hallway with a wave over her shoulder. As though she wasn't hearing him at all. She probably wasn't. "She's grumpy when she doesn't have her afternoon nap, Nessa!"

"Yeah, yeah."

Knowing he was already running behind and couldn't afford to be late when Andino called him in with lots of time to be early, Lev decided this was one of those battles he just didn't want to pick today. Besides, a grumpy Arely wasn't really so bad.

Just ... moody.

He'd let her pull out the pots again. That would make her happy.

"You good?" he asked.

"Yep," came the reply.

Perfect.

It was time to move his ass, then.

Stepping out of the apartment, he headed down the hall to the laundry room at the end. It just so happened that this building had a laundry room on each floor which made shit so much easier for him. Something else he hadn't realized about babies? They made *a lot* of laundry. It was basically constant. He found himself doing a load a day, at the least. Usually of clothing that smelled like baby puke or formula or ... another diaper blowout. Those happened way more than he wanted to admit.

This load, however, was his.

Or rather, for his dress shirts. Because despite getting fitted for suits that Andino's tailor had explained would need to be dry-cleaned when required, the dress shirts only needed a quick cycle in hot water with stain remover and detergent. Twenty or thirty minutes in the dryer, depending on the number of shirts, on medium heat and he was good to go.

Wrinkle-free.

At least, some shit was simple.

Or so he thought.

"What in the *fuck*?"

Lev knew something was *very* wrong with his load of shirts the second he opened the top of the washer. His cursing became more and more severe as he pulled the hot shirts from the washer to inspect. What should have been white was now *pink*. It didn't take him very long to figure out why exactly that was, either.

The offending garment that came out in his next handful explained everything. The deep red panties that he recognized instantly. The same ones he'd pulled off Gigi the last night they spent together at his place. He hadn't realized she left them behind, and when packing up his place, he probably didn't even notice when he shoved them into a box.

"Jesus *Christ*," he muttered, clenching the panties in his fist in the same manner he had when he practically ripped them off the woman.

Yeah.

Couldn't forget that.

Or her.

His mind had just been ... preoccupied lately with other things. More important things, and he was sure she would understand that if the two of them ever met up again. Not that he figured they would.

Nessa had been helping unpack his boxes the last couple

weeks while she babysat—maybe she shoved the panties into the hamper with his shirts thinking something like that shouldn't be washed with the baby's clothes. She wouldn't be wrong considering the tag said to wash with *like items* but in *cold water*.

Fuck.

Fuck, fuck … fuck!

Sometimes, there was no better word.

And Lev didn't have time to fix his mistake when he still needed a dry, clean shirt to wear under his black blazer for work. None of his t-shirts would work because God forbid, he take the blazer off and there not be a button-down underneath.

That shit didn't fly with Andino. It took him very little time working with the man to know the guy was particular. About literally *everything*.

"Screw it," Lev ground out, his jaw aching from how hard he'd been clenching his teeth. He shoved the shirts—and hell, even the panties—into the dryer before putting coins in the slot to turn it on. In twenty minutes when he was out of the shower, he would have clean button-downs.

They would just be pink.

Perfect.

● ● ●

"Cutting it really close, man," Petey said when he opened the rear door of the Manhattan restaurant for Lev to slip inside. "Boss was asking where the fuck you were—*not good*."

Right.

Like Lev needed a reminder.

"Well, here I am. Move."

If the other enforcer had an issue with Lev's attitude, he didn't show it. Then again, Lev realized quite early on in his work with Andino that when it came to the other men he employed … well, they only understood one fucking language at the end of the day.

The promise of violence.

As long as Lev behaved the way he looked—large, intimidating, and not in the damn mood for anybody's shit— then everyone else acted accordingly. If he had a problem, then he said so. Did somebody want beef? He was down for it.

It couldn't hurt Andino's business. That was the main rule to keep in mind on the daily grind as he worked alongside men who had been doing this very thing for years while he'd only agreed to step into it a couple of short weeks ago.

Lev still wouldn't take anybody's shit. He couldn't afford to, but especially not with guys like Petey. They wouldn't let him forget it if he did. Simple as that.

"What the fuck is up with *that*?" Petey asked when Lev passed him by in the doorway.

"What?"

"Your shirt, man. It's ... *pink*."

Goddammit.

He should have known better than to think no one would mention his bright pink button-down under the black blazer that was his new standard. Most of the guys preferred white or black dress shirts, including Andino although he rarely wore anything but silk. That Lev seriously doubted the man ever had to wash because *he* had been sent on a dry cleaner's trip twice since he started working for the Capo.

"*Shut up*. Don't say a word." When Petey opened his mouth, Lev pointed a single finger in the man's face as one more warning when he said, "Not a single fucking one."

"But—"

"Fuck off, Petey, or you'll eat my fucking fist after we're done here."

That shut the guy up.

Thankfully.

Lev liked to follow through on his threats, after all. He found that was the best motivator to ensure everybody knew where he stood when he made the next one.

Not surprisingly, Petey didn't follow Lev into the private dining section of the restaurant where Andino liked to hold his business meetings. Not that Lev knew what was happening—or if it *was* a business meeting today—because he'd simply been told to show up, and Andino rarely offered any information about his dealings. All that information, Lev learned by keeping silent and listening while he worked.

Nonetheless, Petey headed for the front of the business where he would likely wait for ... whatever. Or whoever. It's what Andino liked for him to do.

Lev, on the other hand, went into where his boss waited. Andino didn't even bother to glance up at his arrival, more interested in the cute brunette currently pouring what looked to be whiskey into a lowball glass.

"Less ice next time," Andino told the girl.

"Sure," she replied with a smile.

She headed out of the section and gave Lev a nod on her way by that he returned in kind. While some of the people he had to work with being a man of Andino's constantly got on his nerves, the more normal ones weren't so bad.

"New girl?" he asked Andino when the chick was gone.

"Moved her over from another restaurant—people liked her there, and she didn't shy away from my attitude. All good things, yeah? She was wasting her time over there when she can make far more in this place, and it's a better fit. Studying ... something. Anyway, she needs the money. I figured what did it hurt?"

Huh.

As much as Andino seemed like an asshole to most—and he *was*, let's be real—there was also a side of the man that ... was considerate of those around him. He didn't show it in truly obvious ways, but when someone paid attention to what was beyond the cold, gruff exterior, they could find the softer soul of a man who did have a heart that cared.

Sometimes.

"Is the vehicle I provided for you to use to travel not suitable, or ...?" Andino peered up from the open folder on the table to meet Lev's gaze, unbothered and chilled. "Because you're very close to being late today and that would have promised you didn't get another call to work, Lev."

"The Jeep works just fine. Thank you, again."

Really.

It was another *investment*, as Andino called it. The Jeep

Wrangler had to set the guy back several tens of thousands of dollars, all of which Lev was expected to repay at some unknown time, and he hadn't known what to say when the keys were handed over. Andino quickly fixed that by telling him to say *thank you* and nothing fucking more. Especially not *no*.

So, he didn't.

Andino smirked and gave a little shake of his head. "See, you think you're being smart by avoiding my unspoken question, but I'm not stupid, am I?"

Lev sighed. "No, boss. Just ... traffic. Other shit. I'm here— won't be late ever, you have my word."

A noise of consideration echoed from across the room but otherwise, Andino offered nothing else. That was until he took another look at Lev.

"Is your shirt ... pink?"

Fucking hell.

Lev held in his irritation. "Yep."

"Why?"

"Laundry error."

"That's unfortunate," Andino said in a chuckle.

"Tell me about it."

His boss didn't have the opportunity to say more on the shirt topic because footsteps approached from behind followed by a loud, "*Andino!* Your uncle always knows how to make a trip to New York worth it when I get to do my business with you."

Lev didn't even bother to glance over his shoulder before he stepped aside to let the approaching men pass him by without any issue on his part. Really, he tried not to be a bother at all when Andino did business—simply a presence people understood was always there. Either because they couldn't look away once they did notice him, or because he was impressionable in size and one tended to notice those things.

Otherwise, he didn't invite attention or conversation. Not by joining or pretending like he might or even that he wanted to be—people seemed to get the hint. Andino liked that just fine. So did Lev.

"DeLuca," Andino replied, his tone as kind as Lev had ever heard it when he spoke to another human inside the walls of this restaurant. Or outside of it, for that matter.

Chicago.

DeLuca.

It sounded familiar to Lev as he sized up the guy who greeted Andino in the middle of the room. It wasn't often he witnessed Andino actually *stand* and shake someone's hand because he always seemed to like to let people know they weren't even worth his time to get up and say hello. Not this man, though.

He stood up for him.

They offered hands at the same time to shake, too.

"And we both know," Andino said, grinning, "the only reason I entertain your business is that you're one of the very few people in Chicago that my father gives a fuck about, Theo. How's the wife?"

"Beautiful."

"Good to hear it."

"Speaking of Gio, how is he?" the man asked Andino. "Been a while since I sat down for dinner with him."

"Sends his regards to his old friend but he's busy with my mother this weekend, so we won't be seeing him while you're here."

"Shame." Then, the man named Theo turned a bit on his heels to face Lev standing against the wall. While he hadn't moved to acknowledge the newcomer or the two men who followed him into the room and took posts at both sides, not interfering with his position at all, the man from Chicago clearly took note of him. "And this is—he's new, isn't he?"

"He is," Andino said.

"You have a name?" Theo asked Lev.

"He has a job to do," Andino replied before Lev could say anything. "And we have business to discuss, right?"

Theo gave Lev a second look, as though he were giving him the chance to deny Andino and tell him his name. He didn't. Instead, he stared the man in the eye and shrugged, offering no words at all.

If the man who signed his check said he didn't have a

name to give, then he didn't have a fucking name. Simple as that.

"Next time, Mr. ..." Theo trailed off, giving him another look though his gaze lingered on the pop of color under his blazer. He gave a grin and a light laugh, "Mr. Pink—yeah, that'll work for now. Next time, though, you'll have to tell me your name."

Lev couldn't help but give a sigh. Mostly because laughter echoed around the room. He even heard Petey's muffled laughter from outside the space. Some days, these guys could be real pricks. He had to admit, though ...

He kind of respected it.

Pretty typical.

Another day at work.

Even if now, typical meant everything had changed.

ELEVEN

After

Five years later ...

IF LIFE guaranteed anything, it was that all things changed with time. It was the one thing Lev clung to at the most difficult points when he became a single dad overnight. Before his daughter, life was just another daily task that he had to get through. Figure out how to survive it—to make sure ends would meet, catch the next bus, and sleep a few hours every night. He hadn't been living much more beyond that.

Well, the sleep thing hadn't changed much. He still didn't sleep enough.

Speaking of which ...

Despite his eyes being peeled wide, he hadn't bothered to shut his alarm off, and he didn't reach over to stop it when it did start beeping loudly.

Why?

"How many days left now, Daddy?"

The alarm wasn't really for him. His internal clock was a bitch—he woke up at five every morning regardless of the weekday. He blamed it on the fact that it was the only time he could spare a workout between his duties as a parent and his job for Andino Marcello as the man's closest and most trusted enforcer.

His kid, though?

That alarm was Arely's way of knowing it was time to start the day. The *only* way Lev learned to make the days work with his kid was by getting her on an easy schedule that worked for both of them, didn't overstimulate her with too many demands, and still allowed for a little bit of wiggle room.

That six-thirty AM alarm started the day.

For her, anyway.

"How many? *How many, Daddy?*"

His angel's rapid-fire repeat questions followed the patter of her bare feet against the hardwood of their home. A home he'd only been able to buy two years before because he saved *every fucking penny* he could. Every single one. Whatever money he had to pay back to Andino, he did. He got them on their feet; steady and healthy and *great*. The cushion in his savings account and the educational fund for his daughter was something he knew wouldn't be possible if not for the ten-k that Andino dropped into his account at the end of each month.

But it wasn't enough.

Lev wanted more—needed his kid to have more.

He could have quit years ago; maybe after the first shoot out where a bullet nicked his arm and after stitches at a bribed doctor's office, he went home to put his daughter to sleep. Or even when he became totally debt-free for the first time in his fucking life.

Except he didn't.

And it wasn't all about the money, either.

He'd come to learn that because he treated his boss well, Andino afforded him the same respect. In every aspect.

But when he was at home?

Off the clock?

None of that mattered.

"Well? Huh? *How many days?*"

Lev pretended to be asleep until he couldn't anymore because Arely had climbed up on the large king-size bed. He liked to call her a spider because those long arms and legs of hers could grab onto anything or anyone, and she wasn't getting off. Just like a little spider on its web or crawling up the wall.

He wasn't the exception to the rule.

A grunt of disapproval burst from Lev, and his eyes popped open when a little knee came *far* too close to his groin as his daughter jumped from the empty side of the bed to him. It wouldn't be the first time that particular hell happened when she woke him up, but she was getting better about being careful.

Big blue eyes met his and dark curls fell in a curtain when Arely leaned over him. She blocked out what sunlight there was from the windows. Her toothy smile was more than enough to brighten up the morning and was an image he'd carry with him for the rest of the day.

In fact, it was the thing that got him through the day. More than anyone around him actually knew because that was the thing ...

Other than his boss, *no one* knew Lev had a kid. Out there working for Andino, he became someone else because he had been afforded that luxury. All by accident, really. He didn't have to be, Lev Arsov, a single father doing what he had to do to make sure his child never wanted for a thing in her lifetime. They didn't know about her at all ... which meant there wasn't a soul out there that could hurt her because of him.

No, when he left his home ... he became someone else entirely.

"You tell me," he said, grinning.

Arely's gaze tipped up, and her pink lips pursed in her consideration. "Ah, I *forgot*."

His laughter rung out in the bedroom. "Really?"

"Twenty-two?"

"Little more, kid."

She sighed. "Don't know, Daddy. How many?"

This little game between them had been ongoing for months now. About three, actually. From the point that Arely learned she was going to start kindergarten in the fall, she started counting down the days to her first day of *big girl* school. Well, that's what they were calling it to differentiate between her current education at daycare and what she would start in the fall. It was also how she learned to count to twenty, and then thirty ... forty. Day after day, they sat down and counted the days.

She couldn't wait.

He loved watching her learn.

"Time to count again, I guess," he told his girl.

She didn't pout.

Didn't even complain.

Pushing up from the bed, Lev grabbed his charging phone from the side table and dropped it into his daughter's waiting hands. In her striped yellow—her favorite color—pajamas, she unlocked the phone using his four-digit key and quickly toggled to the waiting calendar.

"Start here," he told her. "It's Monday today—the twenty-first."

"Okay, Daddy." Her firm nod punctuated her words before her finger started tapping on the days following the current one on the digital calendar. "One, two, three ..."

And so, their day had begun.

Like so many others.

With Arely distracted, Lev took the chance to slip into the walk-in closet attached to the master bedroom of the townhouse. Had someone told him years ago that he'd end up living in a neighborhood in Manhattan with bedroom windows that overlooked the Hudson River, he would have laughed in their face.

Yet, here he was.

The joke was on him.

Sort of.

"Ten, eleven, twelve," Arely's child-like tone echoed to his spot in the bathroom where he'd moved after grabbing the waiting garment bag he'd readied the night before. "Thirteen, fourteen, fifteen ..."

Inside the bag waited a blazer, slacks, and a pressed, black button-down shirt. And his daughter's yellow summer dress and white knee-high stockings that she preferred over tights that, on more than one occasion, had caused bathroom accidents. The *only* thing that could send his five-and-a-half-year-old into a tantrum now.

Not that he blamed her.

Nobody wanted to piss themselves.

Her counting continued past thirty as Lev made quick work of getting dressed and doing his business in the bathroom.

"Fifty-five, Daddy," Arely said when he strolled back into the bedroom, mostly dressed and ready to start his day. He still had to button up his shirt and throw on a blazer, but that shit could wait. He tossed her dress and stockings to the bed. "Fifty-five more days to kindergarten."

How many kindergarteners were counting past fifty by the time they started school? Not very many. He was *damn* proud of his girl.

Kneeling at the edge of the bed, he met her big smile with his own. No, the last few years hadn't been easy. Not on him, or her, he was sure. Even if she never showed it or asked for anything more than what he provided. She was happy, yes, and so was he. Sometimes, though, he wondered if this little girl of his might be missing out on something more.

Like a mom.

Or ... anything.

He didn't know.

She never said.

Lev was kind of scared to ask.

"Better tell Nessa that when you get to daycare," he told her. "She *really* wants to be there, so we can't let her forget the date."

"I will," his daughter replied, "*promise.*"

Not that Nessa would—like him, the date was marked in her phone. Because despite how much work Lev had done to raise his daughter alone, there had been people who helped. She was one of those, and if there was anybody else in the world who loved his kid as much as he did, it was Nessa.

Arely hadn't just saved him when she came into his life so unexpectedly. She also gave a troubled teen a place to focus her energy—and a reason to keep doing better. Nessa did exactly that, too. Now, she was studying to get her degree in early childhood education while working at the same daycare that Arely attended five days a week.

Picking up the yellow dress, Lev asked, "Ready to get this day started?"

Arely flung the phone across the bedspread. "Let's do this!"

That was his kid.

Always down.

So long as he was there.

• • •

While some shit changed as time passed, other things never did. One of those happened to be the fact that Andino Marcello handled business and started his workday at the same place no matter what.

At his restaurant in Manhattan.

La Vita Bella.

And because that's where his boss showed up every single morning, that's also where Lev was expected to be considering where Andino went, so did he. Even if that meant a trip to the West Coast for the weekend, or a flight to Chicago for a dinner with the Outfit boss on a Wednesday evening just because.

Sure, Andino had other enforcers—he simply preferred Lev.

"*Pink*—my man!" The guy, a face Lev recognized but couldn't place with a name, stood from the dining table filled with people he didn't know or care about, to greet him with a slap to his shoulder. He offered the guy a grin and nod, but it wasn't enough to indicate he needed to keep moving to the rear of the busy business to find his boss. The man kept talking. "How're things? Been what, a couple of months since I last saw you, huh?"

"Something like that. Glad to see you're well. I'm on my way to the back—"

"No, sit down. Have a drink. Is Andino around? I'm sure he won't mind."

Why did people still think he wanted to be sociable? Lev was just here to work.

Oh, and the nickname?

Yeah, that shit stuck. Of course, it quickly became shortened from *Mr.* Pink to just plain old Pink. Lev thought the tried and true philosophy of ignoring anyone who said it would work, but it didn't. *Shocker.*

All it took was one man—Theo DeLuca, infamous front boss for the Chicago mob—saying it for it to catch like fucking wildfire. By the time Theo left that day? Everybody called him Pink from that moment forward. Well, everybody who didn't know him outside of work, anyway. Working with Andino, however ... he wasn't sure that was such a bad thing. Really, he honestly hadn't thought the nickname would stick.

But it did.

For years.

Lev had come to accept it; he just didn't use it. People introduced him with the moniker—they said it before he even had the chance to correct them. He made the choice not to offer something else because it worked.

Here, he was Pink. At home, where it mattered, he was a little girl's daddy. She didn't give a fuck what people called him, anyway. So, why should he?

"Pass on the drink," Lev told the guy, removing the hand that was still on his shoulder. "Try not to mix pleasure and business, you know?"

"Of course. Tell your boss I said hello."

The man with the familiar face in a suit that said he could at least afford to eat in the restaurant took a seat back at the table, but Lev was already halfway across the main floor. He had zero plans to tell Andino shit about the guy—if he was really *that* important, the boss would already be out on the floor talking to him.

It was that simple.

Lev passed through the kitchen without issue. The head chef throwing orders actually moved out of the way for *him* which wasn't anything new. He didn't fuck with their work, and they never bothered him about his. Things just worked easier when that was the case. For everyone involved.

"You got a request for lunch, Pink?" the chef threw at his retreating back.

Over his shoulder, Lev replied, "Whatever the boss is having. I'm not picky."

"Got it—*Rickie*, put it on the fucking board!"

"Yes, chef, right away."

There was a time when Lev used to show up at this place before the doors even opened. For a time, he even waited at Andino's front door before the man was awake so that he was ready to pick him up.

But years passed.

Some shit changed ... like it did.

For one, Andino Marcello no longer held only a Capo position in his family's organization. A year back, he'd taken over completely, got married, and they started to do things differently. The more men Andino needed to feel safe and handle business, the more he delegated Lev to be a personal enforcer that spent his days at the boss's side unless told otherwise.

There was something to be said about the trust Andino put in him. Lev wasn't ignorant, or disrespectful for that matter, enough to not see it and understand what it meant. He had keys to the man's home. To his *cars*. Access codes to businesses, warehouses ... personal garages.

And more.

At some point, the job changed.

He did more than just watch Andino's back. It was the most important part of his job, yeah, but in a world where his boss depended on cash flow and violence to keep people loyal ... Lev wasn't quite the same. He offered his loyalty because, well, Andino was his friend.

One of the few he did have.

"Fucking hell ... where you been?" Andino asked when Lev finally came to stand in the doorway of his office. "Petey's been calling—"

"Tell his spoiled ass to shut the fuck up. I'm not doing shit for him today when I ran for him all last week to make things easier on him."

Someone else making comments like that about a newly minted Capo in *la famiglia* and Andino would have put a bullet between their eyes. For Lev?

The man just *laughed*.

"Busy morning?" Andino asked when the amusement faded.

Lev shrugged. "She had to show me *all the things* she did last week. I didn't pick her up on Friday last week, so, you know. Took an extra twenty minutes. My bad."

It was always just *her* when it came to Arely during his

work hours. Andino never seemed to mind, and he hadn't
ever offered information about Lev's personal life to anyone.
Yet another reason why he trusted his boss inexplicably, even
if he was just a well-dressed criminal sitting atop an empire
that ran the city of New York like a fucking machine.

"What's the plan, anyway?" Lev asked.

"Business, Pink. What else?"

He sighed. "Yes, but *what*? It seems like it's always
changing lately. I never do the same thing twice anymore."

"Are you complaining?"

"Not until it gets me thrown behind bars."

Andino chuckled and reached for the wooden box at the
corner of his desk where he liked to keep his cigars. "Come
in, close the door, and take a seat. This is going to be a good
one."

"Oh?"

A pointed look at the still-open door had Lev rolling his
eyes. Shouldering his large presence into the small office, he
slammed the door behind him. He took a seat at one of the
two high-back chairs sitting across from Andino's desk.
While he settled in to get the details of his next job—because
clearly he wouldn't be handling Andino directly this week—
his boss worked on clipping, then lighting, his cigar.

"Don't tell Haven I'm smoking these, she'll ... make a
whole scene," Andino muttered.

"Should quit. Bad for your health."

"So are mouthy men and phone calls that send my blood
pressure up but here we are. I've had to deal with both today.
Might as well add some fucking tar to my lungs while I'm at
it."

"You know she can smell it on you, right?"

Andino grumbled under his breath, eyeing the cigar in his
hand. "Yeah, I just blame it on you, so ..."

"Fuck you."

"Is what it is, Pink. We all gotta do what we gotta do to
make shit work."

"Speaking of work," he hinted.

"Right." Andino nodded and reclined back in his chair in a
way that spoke of comfort. Truth was, Lev knew that only

meant his boss was restless and considering things. He glanced down at the empty space beside his desk where a dog would usually be sitting looking like the meanest thing to have ever graced his presence. "He likes being with her in the daytime, you know? I kind of miss his growling ass."

Snaps, he meant.

His pit bull rescue.

Another one of Lev's duties whenever the dog accompanied his boss.

"Anyway," Andino said, waving a hand and making cigar smoke scatter in the air. "Your face isn't recognizable to certain individuals whom the Marcellos have connections to outside the city, and I need that benefit of anonymity for something. It'll be happening in the coming weeks, I don't have an exact date yet. I will, though. Soon."

"Which is what?"

"A meeting. Specifically, a meeting between a businessman—you'll get all the info you need in time to know who he is—from California and a guy I know of here who has ties to ... things I don't want my name, business, or family attached to in any way. Yes, I'm being vague. For good reason."

Sucking air through his teeth, Lev considered his boss's words. "What do you want me to find out? That's why you're going to send me in, right? You want a fly on the wall."

It wouldn't be the first time.

Andino's smirk only confirmed it.

He pointed a finger at Lev, nodding as he replied, "Good catch. I want to know if the man from Cali plans on doing business with the people he's supposed to be meeting here. Some shit I can turn cheek to, others ... not so much. I've let them do their business if it doesn't touch mine, and they keep it out of the city, for the most part, but a partner of mine getting involved? I'll have to cut ties. And if that is what they're meeting to do, then I'll have to flex a bit."

Lev thought about that. "Meaning what, exactly?"

"Get them out of my fucking city entirely. They won't be doing business here at all. Not even a meeting."

That was a big move. A lot of the time, it was easier on the mafia to let people move and do their business as they saw fit so long as it didn't cause a problem. Because problems that came from anything illegal almost always ended in a lot of bloodshed. Yet, that never bothered Andino, Lev knew. The man would, and did, do what he had to do to make sure his city was exactly as he wanted it to be.

This wouldn't be an exception.

Whatever it was.

"What kind of business are they doing that you don't want to touch, even if it only means through a third-party involvement?"

Andino's dark eyes drifted to Lev, and his grin faded away. "Don't worry—you'll know it when you hear it ... if you hear it. That's what I need to find out, Pink. If it's even happening at all. I try not to get ahead of myself in business. Facts first. Action second."

Right.

Lev would remember it.

TWELVE

"GIGI!"

   "Miss Rey, could we get a picture!"

   "Gigi, over here!"

   "Gigi!"

   "Give us a smile, sweetheart!"

   "Welcome home!"

   "Gigi!"

   "Look this way, Gigi!"

   "Gigi!"

   She never thought there would come a time when she became tired of hearing her own name, but here it was. It was far worse whenever she made a trip to the states because America was nothing like Europe when it came to celebrities, the rich and famous, or just a recognizable face.

   Overseas, Gigi could do whatever she wanted without much bother even though one couldn't turn a corner in a major city without seeing her face on a billboard or in the magazine stands on a cover. Stateside, paparazzi made a game out of chasing anyone with a little bit of clout. Even leaving a hotel for a coffee down the street became a game of cat and mouse if it wasn't a well-planned endeavor.

   Here, she couldn't even use her real last name—and sometimes, her agent even booked her rooms under the names of her assistant or someone else on the team—just to give them a bit of legroom to breathe.

   Although she ignored the fucking *hoard* of paparazzi, and their constantly flashing cameras on the way up the stairs to the entrance of the Manhattan Hilton, she did stop at the sight of the teenage girl standing just behind awaiting security. One of three security guards on her team for this trip to New York that would last a couple of months. Between the upcoming shows that she would be walking in for Fashion Week, the campaigns she had to do, and trying to just ... see her mom and visit with old friends, it was going to be busy. She needed her entire team to make it work.

Not that it was anything new.

She had come to learn in the five and a half years since she took that deal for Paris that to most of the people in her circle, all she was to them was *money*. Success. A way to survive and thrive. Every contract she signed to sell her beauty and fantasy for another campaign paid a lot of people, not just her. If she had to guess how many of the people in her team actually gave a shit about her on a personal level, and how many were only there for what she could give ... it was probably fifty-fifty.

Just to make it fair.

Hell, even the designer who made her face a household name in Europe in the first year of working with him didn't care much about who she was—just what she could give to *him*. He called her his muse but made her a doll that moved and behaved at his demand and will. She hadn't even been able to keep her name the way she wanted it under his contract. Gone was Gigi Rey Parker, the girl from a small New Jersey town. In her place came the untouchable, unobtainable beauty of *Gigi Rey*.

Who was Gigi Rey?

It didn't matter.

Because nobody could be her. Or that was the slogan her agency liked to sell.

But who was she to complain? Wasn't this what she signed up for?

The security guard already had the door open and ready for her; she could have walked right in past the waiting teen, but the magazine clutched in the girl's hands that she held at her chest, cover facing out so Gigi could see it, made her stop.

It was her face.

Her latest cover—she stopped keeping count after the first hundred.

GIGI REY, the cover read under her tilted face. With her lips set into a pout, wet hair and mused, and smudged makeup, it looked like she had just gotten out of a pool. *THE*

MUSE OF THE LAST HALF DECADE SPEAKS ON WHAT IT'S LIKE TO DO WHAT SHE'S DONE IN JUST FIVE AND A HALF YEARS.

In smaller print under the headline and her name read in quotes, taken from her own words, *"I'm only trying to find happiness—don't expect me to provide yours."*

It was the only message she cared to be heard in that particular interview, and she knew the second the interview and shoot finals passed through her agency for approval because every member of her team let her know it.

She didn't care then.

Didn't care now.

A lot of questions were pretty standard—what was it like working with the famous Paris fashion designer who launched her fledgling modeling career into supermodel stardom; how she dealt with it all; and now her rising fame in the states, too. She hadn't needed to do that shoot before she left her estate home in Milan to travel to New York. In fact, her agent didn't even want to pass the offer along to her manager so that she would know about it. People didn't really like for Gigi to talk on record if they couldn't edit and censor everything.

She had to be the fantasy, right?

Sell herself, the lifestyle … the product.

Whatever.

Soon, things would change. Her expiring contract said so, and because of that, she felt free to speak her mind more often now than ever before even if it meant a renewal might not be on the table with her mother agency.

It was a risk she was willing to take.

For girls like the one standing beside the security guard with a magazine featuring Gigi's face on the front clutched at her chest like it was a lifeline. Because she didn't want those girls who idolized her like she was some God to think that this was all normal or sunshine and roses.

Because a lot of the time, it wasn't.

It was lonely.

Hard.

She sacrificed *everything*.

"Gigi, come on," her assistant called, already inside the hotel.

She waved a hand, not even bothering to give Kayla more. If anybody understood her need to stop and speak with fans—like this girl who probably did everything she could to be outside of this hotel today to even get a glimpse of Gigi arriving—it was Kayla. Because a lot of the time, it was her handling all of Gigi's social media accounts and interacting under her name and brand. Not because Gigi didn't want to, but because she couldn't.

Sometimes, the agency didn't want her on it. Other times, it was what was best for her mental health. Social media was a lot of lies—a lot of perfection airbrushed to the point of insanity with staged locations and friends and *bullshit*. It got tiring.

"*Oh, my God*—hi!" the girl with the magazine rushed to say when she realized Gigi was coming her way. "You don't have to sign anything I just wanted to see you and—"

"It's okay," Gigi interjected, already seeing the tears well up in the girl's eyes. "What's your name?"

"Lia. I'm from Brooklyn. I *really* love you. You inspired me to smile more."

Lia did just that.

The small gap between her two front teeth had Gigi smiling to show off her own—a feature that despite the designer who controlled her life for two years wanted to change, she held her ground and refused with the threat of breaching contract. They let it go. Eventually.

"I wanna be just like you," Lia said, handing over the magazine when Gigi pulled a mini-Sharpie marker from the back pocket of her jeans. She always kept one on hand. It was good policy in her business.

The comment made her pause.

She still signed the magazine, and then handed it to the teenager with another smile, but it wasn't as big this time. "Hey," she said, meeting the girl's gaze, "don't aspire to be me—I'm already here. Show them all *you*. I promise you'll be happier that way."

Lia glanced down at the magazine and the small print

under the headline of Gigi's name and the article title. Her words in quotes had never really been meant for her team but everybody. Anyone who looked to Gigi as the one thing that made them happy and expected her to always be that for them.

That wasn't real life.

Magazine her wasn't *her*.

"Thank you," Lia said.

"You are *so welcome*. Love ya, kid."

That was punctuated by her making the peace sign. Something that had become synonymous with her, not the brand or the agency or the clothes or the pictures. Just *Gigi*. The cheeky *love ya, kid* and her two fingers spread wide when she put them high. On a runway, she could make that peace sign, and the whole crowd would give it back. Her comments on socials were flooded with that emoji.

Peace.

Happiness.

Love.

She lived it for the public but hoped that someday she might truly find it.

• • •

"Almost there," Kayla said to Gigi's right in the back of the town car. The car *and* driver, provided by the agency to keep her safe and allow her to travel within the city while she was there for the next couple of months, was just another thing she had learned to deal with. Rarely was she given the opportunity or ability to do things alone now. Even driving, whether it was for work or pleasure, was a task given to someone else. "Another five minutes."

"Perfect."

But it wasn't.

She hadn't even bothered to open her eyes at Kayla's declaration to see where they currently were in New York City. Manhattan, that was for certain. But where, exactly, she couldn't say because she just didn't give a shit. That, and the pounding headache starting to form behind her eyes because

Riccardo Delavange, owner and designer of the largest lingerie brand in the world, decided his entire office building needed to have the *brightest* white walls she had ever seen. Complimented, of course, by floor-to-ceiling windows in every fucking room.

Lights, Gigi could deal with.

She learned how.

"They were pleased with your measurements for the fitting—one good thing."

Gigi hummed a noise under her breath, daring to crack open her eyes. The bright daylight was made slightly more bearable by the dark, tinted windows in the rear of the car. It did nothing for the glare coming in from the front, though. She much preferred for her driver to use the SUV with the divider between the front and back seats so that she could pretend like she was alone. Even if she wasn't.

Too much natural light and white color, however, was something her brain just couldn't seem to handle without giving her a raging fucking migraine. But she kept her mouth shut over the period of the two-hour fitting at the Delavange offices because she was the model headlining the show, and if her waist deviated more than an inch, according to the asshole in charge, then it would throw off the balance of the huge angel wings she would be wearing to open and then close the show.

A back piece that weighed thirty pounds and was three feet taller than she was in the six-inch heels she would be wearing down the runway for Fashion Week. While the wings would go on over her arms and shoulders, a belt had also been made to fit around her waist, too. But to not take away from the fantasy, according to the team, she couldn't afford to put on weight because then they would have to add to the belt.

A bunch of bullshit, really.

It was also her life in a nutshell.

"You okay?" Kayla asked. "This next appointment is just ... are you sure you don't want me to get you something? I can get it by—"

"No, I'm good."

"Gigi, don't be a hero."

"Kayla, I'm *fine*."

To prove it, she even opened her eyes and turned her head on the leather headrest to look her assistant in the face as she smiled. Gigi dared *anyone* to see her smile and tell her it was fake. She could sell the lie like nobody knew.

"You sure?" her pixie-like, red-headed assistant asked.

Gigi shrugged. "Does it matter? Another normal day in paradise, babe."

Kayla sighed. "Yeah, I know, Gi."

A normal day in Gigi's life didn't look very normal at all. She could easily go straight from a four-hour flight to a six-hour shoot or a fitting for some upcoming event, and from there, an interview or a meeting with any number of people. She had quickly learned that despite the fact everything revolved around *her* being there for those events, she was just a piece of the puzzle that other people moved from point A to point B to make it all work.

Her presence made money.

Simple as that.

To make it easier, she just followed directions. She accepted that her assistant had a better grasp of her daily schedule than she did. Time was cash but also, the only way she could covet any of that time for herself was to get through the mountain of responsibilities that came with her career as efficiently—and always with a smile—as possible.

It was exhausting.

In the business, it didn't take very long for a model to realize there were plenty of people waiting in the shadows to step forward and provide whatever was needed to keep someone at the top of their game. Cocaine was a favorite of a lot of models—it kept them way up but also thin as fuck which was a *must*. Except the drug use didn't just stop at keeping someone awake and smiling for shoots and runways in their world.

No, it was everywhere. At the parties. In to-go tumblers full of iced coffee. Backstage between outfit changes.

Gigi learned fast that almost every model she knew was just medicating to get through it; to be happy or whatever they needed it for that day. Molly. Liquor. Pills. It didn't matter what it was ... nobody put it in their body because they wanted to get *high* ... they just did it because if they didn't, then life was a lot more difficult to deal with.

Except her.

She wasn't perfect—she had dabbled a lot with different drugs in the first couple of years after moving to Paris. It was almost a cultural thing inside the modeling world. Expected, even. Oh, she didn't want to sit on a tiny swing while she hung thirty feet in the air over a pool because she just spent twelve hours on a red-eye flight coming back from a brand trip?

Here, she was told by a former handler, *take this pill. Your day will get a whole lot better.*

And it had.

It also came to an end eventually.

If someone didn't keep medicating to stay happy or able to function, then they stopped being any of things or able to do anything altogether. That terrified Gigi because she watched all around her as her peers fell into those same traps again and again.

"What is the next appointment today, anyway?" Gigi asked.

That question sent Kayla's brown gaze dropping to the phone in her hand. "Uh ... Marla told me you knew about this. Something special for the agency—they have that campaign coming up with the major league baseball team?"

"The New York Revvers, yeah. So, what does that have to do with today?"

Because that campaign wasn't even going to be shot for another month or more. She would show up, a rack of clothes would be waiting for her to wear and change through the process of the shoot, and then her check was signed over. She might do one or two media things if they asked it of her, but that was usually it.

"Marla said she explained this," Kalya muttered. "Listen—"

What did her agent have to do with shit?

"What's the appointment?"

"Lunch with Jensen Todrey."

Why did that name ring a bell?

"The owner of the Revvers?"

Kayla gave her a look. "Yeah."

"Since when do I do *lunch* with baseball team's owner just because I'm a model in an upcoming campaign?"

A heavy exhale answered that.

"Marla said—"

"*Fuck* Marla," Gigi snapped although she instantly regretted it when Kayla flinched at her burst of anger. "Sorry—it's not you. I know, you just ... do what you're told."

"I really thought you knew."

"So, what, did he like ... get the lawyers to sneak some shit in the contract, or what?"

"Kinda seemed like he talked directly to Marla. I don't know, she was down for it. Said it was standard at your level in the game. And she's not wrong. Look at Tara Franco's social feed for the last year. The girl has been around the globe on the arms of some of the richest men in the world. *No* isn't a word people with money usually hear, Gi. *You* know that better than anyone."

She did, but ... "*I'm* not for sale, though."

Kayla cocked her head to the side a bit, and then asked softly, "But aren't you ... in a way? Think about it, Gi. They've been selling the fantasy of you for years. Surprise, someone's decided to tell them to put their money where their mouth is."

Gigi didn't believe that.

She couldn't.

"So ... lunch?" she asked.

Kayla shrugged. "Guess so."

"What, is he expecting to talk about the campaign or—"

"From what I know, he's having a business meeting. You're just going to be there with him for it."

Oh, really?

Perfect.

Just like arm candy.

• • •

Plastering a smile on her face because of habit and nothing more, Gigi had a harder time keeping her composure under control as she was directed to the table in a semi-private section of the restaurant that she hadn't even bothered to catch the name of on the way in. She was only doing this *lunch date* with the Revver's team owner because she didn't have enough time to rip Marla a new asshole about it and get it canceled.

She would, though.

"Here we are," the girl who had greeted her at the entrance said. "Mr. Todrey and ... guest. Miss Gigi Rey. I will be right back with a menu for you."

Gigi gave a little laugh, not even bothering to greet the men who had stood from the table yet. "Don't bother. I don't eat in front of others."

It was a lie. Not the first time she told it, either.

It also wasn't uncommon in her business for models to use that exact excuse to get out of eating a meal they knew would fuck up their diet or otherwise. So, if any of these people had any familiarity with her line of work, it wouldn't be an unusual statement. She just didn't care to eat with these men when she hadn't agreed to lunch in the first place.

"Sure," the woman replied. "A drink, then?"

"Yeah, why not? Whatever's on the top shelf for wine today—bring the bottle. On the tab, of course. I'm not paying for this lunch, right?"

That time, she did look to the men at the table. Only one she recognized, the black-haired man in his early forties standing on the left. The shorter of the two with brown eyes that locked on hers and didn't let go. He smiled—charming and warm—with a nod.

"Of course, you're not paying. Top-shelf wine, please."

"Cabernet, if possible," Gigi added with a wave of her fingers.

"Right away."

Just like that, the woman left.

Gigi hadn't bothered to ask her name, and she didn't regret the choice, either. Too many people passed through her life daily to be on a first-name basis with them. She was willing to do the same for the other man waiting at the table beside Jensen, if only because he was just here for a business meeting as Kayla had explained, but the baseball team owner had different plans about their introduction.

"Marco, this is—"

"Gigi Rey," the taller, *younger*, blond man said. He had to be mid-thirties. By all standards, *handsome*. But so was his counterpart, and the wealthy usually did carry an aura about of some unobtainable standard. Whether it was beauty or success or otherwise, those around them tended to sense it. Gigi was no exception and this man radiated it. "I know exactly who she is, *Jensen*."

"Yes, well—"

"Do you know what she brings with her? *Attention*. Media. Publicity. I don't think she can even walk down the fucking street without someone recognizing her face today. How fast do you think it would take before paps were chasing her down the block, Jensen?"

"I wanted to show you what I was capable of, and here she is. We should sit down and continue to discuss our possible arrangement, don't you think?" Jensen asked.

The two men shared a look. The man named Marco, however, was clearly more agitated than Jensen Todrey in that moment. Evident by the clenching of his fists at his sides and the vein starting to pop out in his forehead.

Well ...

It looked like Gigi wasn't the only one displeased about this lunch.

Good.

"There a problem?" Gigi asked. Then, to Marco, she said with a smile, "And anywhere from ten to twenty minutes depending on how close a paparazzo is to my location. A fan tags me in a story, and they're already on their way, trust that. Less outside of the states, but here it's ... life."

It was also why, despite feeling like America was home, Gigi preferred living out of the country while her notoriety was high. It was just easier to manage the expectations of her fame that way. Not that she thought these men cared at all about those details.

Marco gave Jensen a *very* pointed look. "There you are."

"Listen, it's a delicate thing, I know. But *she's here.*"

"I can see that."

"What does that tell you?"

The blond man sighed, and he gave Gigi another glance. Despite their well-dressed appearance, both men in their suits with groomed hair swept back in tidy styles, and the fact she knew this had been all set up so it should be safe, something seemed off. The lunch hadn't even begun yet, but already she could tell something wasn't right.

"Excuse us," Jensen said with a chuckle, dragging Gigi from her thoughts in an instant. He stuck out a hand, and out of habit, she did the same. The second his hand found hers, he stepped closer and brought her fingers up to his lips for a quick kiss that she hadn't wanted at all. "Thank you for agreeing to this lunch."

I didn't, she thought.

A small part of her screamed to *keep quiet.*

"Sit," Jensen added quickly, "and I'm sure your wine will be here any moment. Don't mind us ... we're just discussing the benefit of our businesses and how they might work better together."

"How do I factor into that, exactly?"

Because wasn't that what this felt like?

Jensen laughed and released her hand. "Don't worry about that, Gigi Rey. Just keep smiling. It's worth a lot more than you realize."

What did that mean?

She took the seat pulled out for her and with the two men facing her, it put their backs to the half partition wall that separated their semi-private section from the main floor. She might have paid attention to whatever Marco was currently saying to Jensen at the table, but it was the flash of blue eyes just beyond the partition that held her attention.

Every bit of it.

It was him.

Those eyes.

She'd know them anywhere.

He'd turned around so all she could see was the back of his

head, and the way his buzz cut faded from skin to black hair from the nape of his neck upward. But then, he turned to his left, glancing over his shoulder once more and looked right at her.

The facial hair was new.

It was her first thought.

Not a bad look on him, though.

It had been five and a half years since she laid eyes on him, heard his voice, or spent a night in his bed. Yet, she never forgot it. Or him. Not for one single fucking second. How could she when he had been the last person who really knew her—without even knowing her at all—before she became *this*? That short time, those nights she spent with him ... he didn't know it, couldn't possibly, but it meant the world to her.

For a moment in time before she became *Gigi Rey*, she was just a woman having fun with a man who told her she was beautiful. And she went back to those nights with him in her memories more often than was probably healthy.

There he was.

In that restaurant.

Looking right at her.

Lev Arsov.

THIRTEEN

THE NEXT time Lev saw Gigi's face after she left his apartment in those early hours of a morning five and a half years earlier? He'd been trailing Andino down Fifth Avenue on a sunny afternoon, and there she was on his left ...

Plastered across a glossy magazine, the freckles splattered across the bridge of her nose and under her wide eyes drawing the gazer's eye to the unique *rawness* of her natural beauty. Other than black mascara on her lashes, the rest of her face was bare of makeup and in grayscale, she stared outward from the page at the passersby on the street.

At *him.*

He didn't remember what the headline of that magazine was, and he hadn't even bought it to read the article or see why she had been put on the cover. Shit, he hadn't even managed to look at it for more than ten seconds before he had to continue following Andino that day to make sure the man stayed safe in his stomping grounds.

Not that it made a difference.

It wouldn't be the last time Lev got a glimpse of Gigi's modeling career from a distance. He didn't really *follow* her in the sense that he sought information out about what she was doing, but occasionally something would drop into his lap to fill in the pieces.

The chance of a lifetime had been handed to her, and the girl took it. Lev had known that day in the bar her face was made to be revered by as many people as possible and had settled himself with the fact that he'd been lucky enough to meet Gigi Parker before the rest of the world knew her as Gigi Rey.

He didn't, however, expect to find Gigi sitting at the business lunch between two men who were currently discussing trafficking women into New York for the baseball games that drew in hundreds of thousands of people every season.

Trafficking.

Yep.

Lev managed to move his seat from one side of the table after Gigi's arrival so that his back no longer faced the men behind the semi-private partition wall. He'd been satisfied before to listen to their conversation through a speaker in his ear and the amplification device he'd stuck on the table that simply looked like a small fidget toy. That changed when the circumstances of Gigi's presence became apparent.

Nobody noticed he moved, though.

Lev could see them *all* now.

Including her. She used her hair, a shoulder-length blonde body wave that flowed around her face down to the faded pink at the tips, as a shield between herself and the men at the table. Tipping her head down or to the side was just enough to offer her gaze privacy as she typed on a phone.

It appeared that Marco, from Cali, and his private jetliner corporation, would be of great benefit to Jensen Todrey's plans to have a thousand working girls available and on-call for the next baseball season. And there would be a girl for *every* taste; young or old, rich or poor.

"Look what I provided for viewing today," Jensen explained, his words carefully chosen to not draw the attention of the woman at the table that he was discussing *her*. "Everyone has a price. If it is here, they will come. We're looking at an easy half a billion for the season if it's run well. And you can help with some of the ... travel aspects."

"And the ..." Marco glanced Gigi's way, his tone dropping lower when he asked, "What about the *product*?"

"Handled. We're just tying up loose ends which is why you're here. I was told you've done this before ... on a smaller scale, correct?"

"I have, but it's a delicate endeavor."

Yeah, Lev fucking bet.

He filed away the information that Andino's business partner had been working with human traffickers before this meeting. The circumstances of those deals and business wouldn't matter much to his boss except for the fact that it was going on at all. He could make his choices about what to do with the man from there.

All the while, Gigi sat sipping wine and scrolling through her phone, oblivious to the fact she could *be* one of those girls. Lev figured that out fast enough, and he blamed her ignorance on the fact she just wasn't *listening*. Because it seemed like between her distraction at having seen him and not wanting to be there at all, she just zoned out.

He hadn't.

The warning bells were ringing.

Way too damn loud.

Fucking ... *trafficking*. Skin trafficking.

That was what Andino hadn't wanted to say. The thing he wanted Lev to confirm for him about his business partner in Cali and the *mysterious* man he'd be meeting with during his recent stay in New York. Turns out, the fucker wasn't very mysterious at all once Lev laid eyes on the prick. Anybody with any knowledge of the highly successful New York Major League Baseball team, the Revvers, knew their *disgustingly* rich owner that made a game out of showing off his wealth every season that people flooded the city to watch the games.

He had a hand in the pocket of all the right people.

The mayor.

A senator.

Even the Russian crime family in Little Odessa that Andino refused to fuck with for the same reason he didn't want his business partner from Cali messing with this dude. Their heavy hand in the trafficking of humans could be a difficult pill to swallow when the reality of it was presented at your feet in the form of money made off the backs of broken and abused women and children.

Because apparently, though it was no business of Lev's as his only job was to handle Andino's safety and needs, there were criminals with a moral code. Some did have lines they would not cross. This was one of the Marcello *famiglia's* lines.

He could have pointed out how the criminal activity Andino *did* make his money through hurt innocent people all the time, but Lev opted to remind himself that again, it was not his business. He wasn't *in* Andino's work, after all. That was not his concern.

Of course.

And maybe he was just fooling himself, too. They all had choices to make; they all had to survive. Even if that meant in the end, he chose to be the lesser of two evils.

"Could you excuse me for a moment?"

The question at the table across the room had Lev glancing that way when he lifted the cup of coffee in front of him for another fake drink. He wasn't putting that sludge in his mouth. For such a boujee fucking place, their coffee was trash.

"Absolutely—washrooms are through the hallway past that corner there," Jensen said as he stood from the table when Gigi did the same.

He offered his hand to help her out from around the chair and table, but she was quick to do it herself without letting him lay a finger on her. Part of Lev liked that *way* too much but not for just the obvious reason. The guy was clearly a fucking problem—and *dangerous*. But the possessive claw digging into his chest at the sight of another man eyeing Gigi like she was a *thing* he bought and provided for the lunch was enough to turn Lev into a psycho.

Because shit, wasn't that what the guy basically said?

Unfortunately, to get to the washrooms, Gigi did have to pass Lev's table. He did his best not to stare at her as she passed because the men at the table were still watching her go, and he certainly didn't want to draw attention to himself.

She peeked at him, though.

Quick, and fleeting.

Green eyes so bright it *ached*.

So, yeah ...

Maybe he looked, too.

But not for long.

The second she was around the corner and down the hall heading for the washrooms, the conversation at the table picked up again between Jensen and Andino's partner from Cali.

"*God*, she really is fucking something, huh?" Jensen asked.

"Cost me a quarter of a million to get those legs walking in here today. And that was for an *hour*—a *lunch*, man. Imagine how much somebody would lay down to get a taste of what's between her thighs."

A fire lit in Lev's chest.

He remained still.

"Thirty percent of your cut—that's what I want."

Jensen dragged in a heavy breath, leaning back in his chair to survey the windows a few feet away from their table. "So, you're in? It's gonna be great."

"Definitely in ... unless circumstances change. And what about *her*, hmm? You're not telling me you seriously just brought her here for lunch. You're not even going to take a shot?"

"I may. Or I might just pay for it at a later date."

Yeah.

Lev figured he got what he needed. For the Andino side of things, anyway.

He *should* have paid his tab and left the restaurant. Instead, he dropped a hundred-dollar bill on the table, grabbed his jacket and device on the table, and then headed for the hallway leading to the bathrooms.

He had to warn Gigi.

At the very least.

• • •

Lev hadn't meant to *run into* Gigi as he rounded the corner at the end of the hallway when she came out of the bathroom, but he still did. Her quiet *ompf* muffled against his chest, and the cell phone she'd been staring down at fell from her hands to skid across the floor.

With a chuckle, Lev bent down to pick up the phone that landed screen up, saying, "Shit, sorry about that. Hope I didn't scare you."

"*Give me that.*"

"What?"

The high squeak in her voice said she was embarrassed, and it had Lev instinctively glancing down at the screen of the phone in his hands. Instantly, he understood why she didn't want him to have her phone.

A stream of text messages stared back at him.

HE IS HERE, the first one read.

From Gigi, it looked like.

Someone else asked, *Who?*

Him. The fucking guy!

What guy?

THE GUY, MOM. From before Paris! That was Gigi's last message. To her mother, apparently. About him, if he were to guess considering the phone beeped with the next message that popped up at the bottom of the blue and white thread of texts that simply read, *Oh, you mean that guy—Lev, right? Say hi!*

"Hi to your mom, I guess," Lev said, not even bothering to hide his growing smile as he handed the phone over to a fuming Gigi. "You told her about me? Was I ... that special or something?"

"It was a ... *time*," she managed to spit out. "Just a strange time between then and now and ... yeah." Then, the red in her cheeks heated up to whole other level while she did her very best to avoid his attempt at eye-contact. "Stop asking questions!"

Lev's hands popped high, palms up. "Okay. No more questions, then."

Her easy blush was kind of cute, though. Good to see that hadn't changed about her.

"I was going to ask what you're doing in New York. Every article I ever see says you live in—"

"Milan, yeah." Gigi's gaze darted to his, and a small smile formed on her pretty lips. "Bought a property there a little while back. I'm in New York for work. Fashion Week in September. Some campaigns before that. Never ends."

"I knew I was right about you."

Her light laughter had the fire in his chest easing as he admired the way she wasn't ashamed to grin wide in her happiness. He wondered if the beauty that was presented about her and her life in the magazines was the truth sometimes. It had to be a lonely life to constantly be watched

128

and seen but not really *known*.

"Did you follow me back here?" she asked.

Unconcerned about letting her know the truth, he nodded. "Yeah—they're bad news, you know? Those men you're here with today, I mean. I'm not sure what you were told about today, but—"

"Nothing until I was here. This was all set up around me; I was given a time to show up. That's how things work in my business sometimes. My time is money, as I'm often told."

"Really."

It wasn't even a question.

Just a heavy understanding.

One he didn't like at all.

Gigi raised one brow. "What did you mean by that—bad news?"

"*Them*. Their business. Whatever Jensen Todrey thinks he might be able to get from you. It's all bad news. Without details, he could cause you a lot of problems. Word to the wise—keep away from him, and anything he wants you to do, as much as you can."

She cleared her throat, shifting from foot to foot and hugging the bomber jacket she'd thrown over a short, flowy dress tighter to her form. "I don't think my agency would put me in any danger, Lev."

"Don't be so sure."

He wasn't going to give her all the information he learned today. Not because he couldn't ... but because he wasn't sure that it was safe to do. Hopefully, if she stayed away from Jensen, then that would be that.

Right?

The buzzing of a phone in Lev's pocket reminded him that he still had a boss to report back to and *soon*. Probably tomorrow because he needed to grab his daughter after daycare, too, and he was running out of time to beat the worst of traffic if he lingered too long.

"I gotta run," Lev told her, "but don't trust them, Gigi. *Please*."

He'd use the exit at the end of the hall to head out of the business and then just round the back and side of the building to where he left his Jeep parked with a meter running.

Before he had the chance to say goodbye, Gigi asked, "Could I see you again? I'm going to be in the city for a while, and if you have time I would love to catch up."

He should have told her no.

She already had traffickers too close.

Did she really need a mob enforcer around, too?

Lev's heart raced to speak before his brain could explain why it might be a bad idea—all because looking at her gave him a sense of nostalgia that he had never felt before. She looked at him differently than most people did; she saw a man she had known from a time before.

And that time came before he was this man.

Pink.

So yeah, he should have said no.

Instead, he said, "Yeah, there's a bar I like where we could meet up in the next couple of days ... it's private, and you probably need that, right?"

Gigi laughed. "More than you know. I'll still have to sneak there to not be noticed. I mean, if you don't want your picture splashed on every social media gossip site basically within hours. Or you might get a day, if you're lucky."

Well ...

At least she was honest.

He appreciated that.

• • •

"Well, I don't know, John," Andino said into the phone receiver pressed between his ear and his shoulder. With his feet propped across the edge of the desk, shoes hooked at the ankles, the man varied his attention between his call and the ruddy-colored dog at his side letting him play with the tips of his ears. "Well, I'm saying because if you think someone's skimming off the top of it, we'll have to get on it now—you hear what I'm saying?"

Feeling comfortable enough to think he could afford to be distracted considering his boss's current conversation with his cousin, another major figure in the New York criminal underworld, Lev went a little deeper into his thoughts. Straight back to the other afternoon when it felt like he walked right into his fucking past.

He had needed to *switch off* after doing his job for Andino and having his moment with Gigi. Arely was waiting for him to pick her up from daycare with the small scoop of strawberry gelato from the little place down the street like he promised. He went from mob boss's most trusted man to a little girl's daddy in the span of ten goddamn blocks.

Because he was a *dad* now. Somebody's father. Somehow, he was going to have to explain that to Gigi.

And even though he had done what he always did for his little girl the day before, that didn't mean his night was made any easier. Stuck between memories of a few days in his past and the concerns about the present, he bounced back and forth from irritation to infatuation all in one fucking blow.

He wasn't any better today.

"And what do you have for me, huh?" Andino asked, his voice an echo in the back of Lev's racing thoughts.

He didn't answer back, thinking the man was still talking to his cousin. John was decent—another man he occasionally worked for under Andino's discretion or demand. He just didn't care to entertain their business when he had his own to consider.

Which was Gigi ... and the fact he would be seeing her again.

Soon.

"*Pink*—did you check the fuck out on me or what?"

The grumbly growl of a dog—his response to the anger in his master's tone—had Lev coming out of the haze that was his mind in a flash. It didn't take him very long to realize he'd checked out for too damn long.

"Sorry," he muttered, straightening up a bit in the chair. "Got some shit on my mind, that's all. Your Cali partner is doing exactly what you thought he was doing. *Exactly*, and then some. This isn't his first rodeo into it, even. And as for the other side of the equation—that fuck's been doing it seasonally. Someone else is providing the meat of the operation."

All his words were carefully chosen. A lesson Andino had taught him long ago. The code only men in their life could truly appreciate, and it was almost an art. To explain a situation without ever using words that named criminals or their acts. The paranoia about wires was still a very real thing for some people.

Lev was one of those.

Andino nodded, clearly understanding what he said. "Good to know—I'll be dealing with that, then. Back to you, though. It's not your kid, right?"

"I'm sorry?"

"Whatever had you checked out there. Arely's good, isn't she?"

"Yeah, man. The best."

"Good. I know you try to keep ... all of this away from her, Pink. I respect your right to do that, but I wonder if you realize that the longer you're in this life, the harder it is to get out."

He hadn't, actually.

And it wasn't something he wanted to consider at that very moment, either. Didn't he already have enough to handle that weighed down his shoulders?

"I'm not talking about getting out," Lev said, chuckling. "Never even crossed my mind."

It wasn't a lie. Because even if he had his issues, moral or otherwise, with Andino's business and even his own for the man, at the end of the day it was all pretty simple for Lev. These men took care of him because he took care of them.

"Right, well ... back to business, then." Andino leaned back in his chair, hooking his ankles over the edge of his desk again. This time, Snaps licked at the side of his master's hand where it sat along the armrest. "I'll handle things. You, however, keep your head down and your phone on. I'll call. Or John will. Stay out of trouble and let me work. Got it?"

"Always do, boss."

"And shave that fucking beard you've got going on. I hate when I have to listen to made men bitch about how the boss's *personal* enforcer," Andino grumbled, even going as far as

132

to make air quotes, "won't follow the fucking rules of us Italians."

Lev tipped his head back, and then took a moment to run his fingers through the beard he'd spent a good couple of months growing out. He kept it neat—trimmed short—by a barber downtown. The only man he trusted to put a blade to his throat. He rather liked the look.

Humming under his breath, Lev shook his head and then said, "Nah."

"Ah, for fuck's sake, *Pink*."

"I'm not Italian, Andino, I don't follow those rules," Lev said, standing from the seat and giving his boss a grin. He was still going to be him even in their world and yeah, he'd shave his face. When he was good and fucking ready to. Not because he was told. "And you knew that when you asked me to be here doing this, right? Wasn't an issue then; you get to be the big shot boss that tells them all to fuck off when it is now."

Andino sighed. "The only good part about being the boss."

"Is it?"

"What?"

"The only good part."

That made the other man pause but only for a second. For whatever private reason Andino came up with in his head, he smirked when he finally replied, "No, it's not."

FOURTEEN

"DADDY?"

Lev did his best to smother the smile at yet another interruption from Arely during their nightly story time. It was the exact reason why what should be a half-hour of reading easily turned into an hour. Sometimes more, depending on which book they picked up. He encouraged the questions, though. He never even suggested she should just keep quiet and let him read to her.

Why would he?

That wasn't how she learned.

"Yes, dove?"

At his side in the twin bed, that he mostly filled, Arely peered up at him from underneath her pink duvet with yellow flowers. Her favorite color was still bright yellow. The sunniest, *happiest* of all the colors. He thought it was appropriate seeing as how she was also the brightest ray of sunshine in his entire life.

"Where's mine?" she asked, her small brow knitting together at the question.

"Your what?"

"My mommy—like the ducky mommy. Where's mine?"

Lev blinked, the ache that stabbed into his chest all at once coming on without warning and with no mercy. It hurt like a bitch, but he didn't show it to his daughter. She was still staring up at him, after all, patiently waiting for his answer like she did with all her questions. Unlike him, she didn't seem to be pained by the missing, important piece in her life.

It was just an unknown to her. Something she needed an answer for. *God above* ... Lev wished it was that simple for him.

"In heaven," he settled on saying. "Remember when we talked about that at the church fair?"

Not that he wanted to have that conversation last summer

when they were only supposed to be enjoying the day provided to neighborhood kids by a Catholic church they sometimes attended. The nun who asked where Arely's mom was didn't get the hint to quit asking until Lev outright said the woman was in a grave.

That led to a whole conversation with his kid because she really didn't understand what *dead* meant. It was that point when he also realized Arely had never known she was missing something in her life until someone else pointed it out.

"Well, *yeah*," Arely said, shaking her head with a small smile starting to form on her sweet face. "I know but ... Mackenna has *two* daddies, right?"

Lev's brow lifted on its own accord at that statement because even he—forever a statue, unfeeling and unbothered in the worst of circumstances—wasn't quite sure what to make of that statement from his five-year-old. Where was she going to go with this conversation next? Because he didn't know how to tell her, but there wouldn't be two dads in this house—Lev just didn't swing that way; more power to the people who did.

"She does have two dads," he replied, "but you won't."

"Why?"

Oh, God.

"Are we reading about ducks or are we—"

"If Mackenna can have two daddies," his daughter interjected, as serious as ever while she rolled over to her stomach in the bed and propped her chin in her palms, "then how come I can't even have one mommy?"

Kids, man.

They really did say the craziest shit.

"You *did* have a mom," Lev said, folding the book closed and setting it on his lap. If they were going to talk about this, then he figured it was better to give Arely his full attention instead of just trying to distract her with another topic altogether. "Her name was Dawn Marks, and no matter where she is right now, she will *always* be your mother."

"Like my name, right?"

Lev grinned and palmed the top of his daughter's curly

head with his hand. "Right, just like your name—Arely Dawn Marks."

"*Arsov.*"

Yep.

Marks-Arsov, actually. He had it added with the hyphen as soon as he could and didn't regret it for a single second.

Then, Lev tickled Arely's cheek with the tips of two fingers. She squealed her giggles, falling into the pink and yellow print of her bed coverings. Until she quieted again and stared up at him with those big blue eyes that matched his own.

She still had questions.

He knew it.

Lev just didn't know how to answer them. Maybe someday he would. Or shit, maybe someday she could even have what she was missing in the form of a woman in her life who gave her that motherly love and affection she so clearly needed.

Just not today.

Unfortunately.

"I know some people have two daddies or mommies ... or some kids even live with their mom and their dad lives somewhere else. Or whatever," he muttered, rubbing a hand down his newly clean-shaven jaw. Arely complained his beard was *scratchy* when he gave her kisses after picking her up from daycare, and that was that. He shaved it off while they handled their nightly routine. Andino would be pleased. "And then there's people like us, you know? No matter what, we're still a family. Even if ours doesn't look like somebody else's."

Arely's lips pursed in her thoughts before she sighed and nodded once. "Okay."

"Really, *okay*?"

"Yeah, Daddy. More duckies?"

Lev picked up the book again, feeling like he dodged a bullet the whole time. How much longer was he going to be able to dodge it before one finally landed? "Yeah, dove, let's read more about the duckies."

• • •

"How's Martha Mae?"

Nessa shrugged as she placed her messenger bag to the kitchen counter. "Still smiling. She finally agreed to let me move her out of that shitty apartment building."

Lev nodded and continued drying the pile of dishes he'd finished washing shortly before Nessa arrived. He had a dishwasher to do the job but the many years of working behind a bar taught him that there was something therapeutic about handwashing dishes. Maybe it was the time it gave him to think, who knew?

Whatever it was, he liked it.

"Into *your* place?" he asked, turning back to the cupboards to place the cup in its spot. "Or somewhere else?"

"My place. She decided that was better than the home social services was suggesting because of her age."

Lev swore under his breath. "I can already imagine how that flew over for her."

"Yeah, not well."

The young woman's tired laughter told him all he needed to know about her current situation with her ailing, *aging* grandmother. Martha Mae didn't want to admit that she could no longer live unassisted ... not to mention, the apartment building in Harlem that she managed for the better part of twenty years had recently been sold to the city for some housing project.

It all spelled the same thing.

Martha had to move.

She didn't want to.

"So ..." Nessa drawled out the word slowly, the amusement in her tone clear even though Lev wasn't facing her to see it. "Are you not going to tell me why you asked me to babysit tonight? I can't remember the last time you wanted me to look after Arely at night."

"Three months ago. A Wednesday night."

"Right ... because you had to run across town for something for your boss. But it's Friday and you're wearing a button-down and pressed slacks." The squeak of the stool he used for Arely to eat breakfast at the island in the mornings echoed, giving away the fact that Nessa had leaned up from the chair. "And you're wearing those loafers you say pinch your toes."

"I talk a lot under my breath, don't I?"

"Yes."

"You should stop listening."

Nessa snorted. "Unlikely. Are you going on a date? Because when you're not working, you live in sweats. And you didn't say you were working tonight."

"*Nosy.*"

"And?" She offered that as if it wasn't a problem. "But is it—a date, I mean?"

Lev's shoulders tightened when she asked the question a second time, but it was his silence that had Nessa cooing out a loud *ohhhhh*.

"It is," she said.

"I'm meeting an old friend," he said. "It's not a date."

"Who?"

"A *friend*."

"A nameless friend?"

"Nessa—"

"When was the last time you even went out on a date? All you do is *work*. And take care of your kid, too. Can't take that away from you."

She had a point, but still... "It's not a date."

"I think it might be just based on ... you right now."

Lev tossed the drying rag to the counter and pinched the bridge of his nose while he mentally willed away the irritation. "Jesus Christ."

Turning around so he could tell Nessa to mind her own damn business, Lev ended up just staring at the grinning woman on the other side of the kitchen island. It was the gleam of expectation in her eyes that stopped him from being an asshole.

"Are you nervous?" she asked.

"It's really not a date."

She gave him a second look. "Are you sure? You even shaved, Lev."

Fucking hell.

"We didn't say it was a date. We're just meeting up while

she's in town for work."

None of that was a lie. It took a few days before Gigi sent him a text saying she could finally slip away to meet up without a whole media circus following along, but tonight was the night.

"*Ohhhh*, it's a *she*."

"What in the fuck is that supposed to mean?"

Nessa grinned and glanced upward as she replied, "I'm just saying."

"Fuck you."

"No thanks. You're ... kind of like my older brother. I'm not really into that."

"Am I?"

"What?"

"Like your older brother?"

Nessa nodded. "I mean, yeah. Who knew what ditch I would have died in if Nan didn't have you just down the hall to help me when she needed it? And I guess you were the first guy who showed me there were men who *would* show up, so to speak. You didn't owe me shit. You weren't my family. I wasn't your responsibility, but you just kept showing up."

He didn't know what to say to that. She seemed to be okay with his silence.

"You're a good guy, you know?" Nessa asked, shrugging under her tweed coat with buckles on the shoulders. "That's all I'm trying to say."

Was he?

Sometimes, he had to wonder ...

"And if it's not a date," Nessa said, sliding off the stool with a sly smile, "then why do I smell *Creed*? Because you only wear that when you want to have a good time."

His cologne, she meant.

Rare.

Expensive as fuck.

And she wasn't wrong.

"It's not a date," he said, pointing at her retreating back while her laughter echoed in the townhouse. "It's *not*."

But goddammit it ... a part of Lev wished it was.

Gigi was still the woman of his wettest dreams, and she had been a feature in all of them for the last five and a half years. That also meant nothing in their current circumstances. A lot had changed.

For both.

. . .

It *wasn't* a date. Telling himself that fact when Gigi walked into the quiet bar looking like sex on smooth, long, fishnet-covered legs, however, was easier said than done. Her high-waisted, leather mini skirt fell mid-thigh, and the fishnet tights disappeared into her ankle boots with sharp stiletto heels that clicked on the hardwood floors. What really turned heads—literally *everybody* in that bar couldn't help but stare when she came in—was the top she wore.

Lev didn't know what to call Gigi's top. Made up of leather panels at the side, and mesh and buckles up the front, it hugged her curves and hid very little of her body. It did the *best* thing for her tits, though. She almost looked like a *Domme* that had walked off the set of some erotic film. His cock couldn't handle it considering he had to adjust his position on the barstool to relieve the pressure growing in his pants—what was a little discomfort, anyway?

Apparently, his brain didn't know what to do with the sight of Gigi, either. The damn thing decided it didn't want to work when he tried to stop staring, just like everybody else was doing, but failed miserably. Sometimes, life still liked to have a good laugh at his expense.

Fuck it.

She *should* be stared at.

The woman was a work of art. Carved from God himself, surely. Sculptors had spent decades attempting to showcase the perfection of female beauty, but Gigi *defined* it. From the sexuality that she oozed to the softness in her aura. It was in the way she walked, her stride and the sway of her hips graceful and sexy with every step, and in the sweet smile she offered the man who actually turned on his chair as she walked past him to watch her go. She was perfect in every way. At least, that hadn't changed even if she was way out of his fucking league.

Yeah.

How could he not stare?

"Close your mouth, bro. You'll catch flies like that."

Lev glared sideways at the bartender who had offered that comment from behind the bar where he was currently wiping out a wine glass. "Fuck off somewhere, why don't you?"

The guy—Joey was his name—widened his arms like he was silently saying *come on, man, give me a break here.* "Do you know who she *is*? Wait, is she coming to see you—do you know her?"

The second time he turned to the bartender, Lev didn't even bother to hide the warning in his voice when he muttered, "Get *gone.* Now."

"Fine. *Fuck.* What's stuck up your ass tonight, Pink?"

Maybe he should have picked a different bar. One that he didn't frequent, even if the place was basically a hole-in-the-wall inside the city and quiet for the most part.

"Who's Pink?"

Jesus Christ.

The bartender's gaze drifted to Lev's right, widening like his gaping mouth as he tried to form words. All it took was Lev pointing a single finger and muttering, "Whiskey sour, thanks."

"Right ... right, I'll get right on it."

"Great."

Without missing a beat, Lev spun around to step off the stool and greet Gigi by reaching for her with both hands. She replied in kind, her soft fingers curling around his wrists and then dancing up his arms before he pulled her in for a hug. She still had that note of vanilla in her perfume, but now the floral undertones felt more suited to this woman she embodied. And yes, when he had her curves flush against his harder lines, he absolutely knew just how much of a woman she was.

He took a small step back to once again admire the very sight of her while not letting her go, so that he could keep her close. The mesh and buckled top with the leather side panels showcased her plump breasts but was tight enough to keep any accidental flashes from happening. There wasn't another soul on the earth who could pull that top off, but Gigi looked amazing in it.

"Nobody. Pink is nobody," he told Gigi, his palm skimming the bare skin of her mid-back where her shirt and skirt didn't quite meet. *God*, what he would give to have his hands *under* her fucking clothes. "That's not important, you are. You look ... *shit*, you didn't have to get this done up for me, Gigi."

"Didn't I? You like the top? One of a kind."

"You know, I would have guessed that."

Her smile widened before she pulled him in for another tight hug. Their laughter melted into the rest of the bar and for a second it really did feel like two friends just catching up. In his ear, she whispered, "And look, no paps."

Lev laughed and as he began to pull away, he couldn't help but drop a quick kiss to Gigi's cheek before he let her go from his hold. *Mostly*. The urge to keep touching her was a little too much when she was this close and so, he kept one hand lingering on her wrist, but she didn't seem to mind.

"Managed it, did you?" he asked.

She shrugged, her smile as much of a tease as her outfit. Everything about this woman was a goddamn tease to his senses. "Wasn't easy—even had to get my assistant in on it because I'm not supposed to be outside of the hotel without security nearby."

That statement had Lev glancing over her shoulder to the front windows of the bar that overlooked the busy, but dark city street just beyond the sidewalk. It wasn't like he expected to see men in black suits with comms in their ears standing there, but ... well, she certainly made it sound that way.

"Nobody followed me," she promised, clearly noticing his stare. "No security, no paparazzi ... hopefully no fans, but sometimes that happens so if it does, just let me say hi, do my thing, and don't answer anybody's questions because they *will* try to get literally anything they can out of you. Fair warning."

Lev's attention went back to her in an instant. "Oh, no

worries on that. I wouldn't mind if you did need to bring somebody, by the way. It's probably a normal thing for you, right?"

"Regular ... not something I'd call *normal*."

"Point taken. Wanna sit down?"

Her brilliant, gorgeous smile was back just like that. "Yeah, let's sit. Nice place. Not my usual style, but ... it serves the purpose for keeping me out of sight, right?"

Lev's laughter came out dark and husky as he reclaimed his stool, and she took the one on his right. "Sorry, would you have preferred a club?"

She peered his way, and her dark lashes fanned wide with black mascara distracted him from the bartender's approach with the whiskey sour he'd ordered for Gigi. "I preferred to catch up with *you*, Lev. I didn't care where we did it."

Right.

He would keep that in mind.

"And you remembered, too."

"What's that?" he asked.

Gigi winked and pointed at the glass the bartender set on top of a white, monogrammed napkin in front of her. "Whiskey sour. My drink of choice."

A pointed look from Lev sent the bartender spinning around to head for someone else down the bar when the man opened his mouth like he was going to say something to the woman next to him. Gigi's light laugh might have embarrassed him for being so possessive over her time and presence but *fuck it* ... he wasn't going to apologize for it.

"I think he knows who you are," Lev said, palming the beer on the bar that he'd been nursing long before Gigi arrived. "And I didn't forget anything about you, Gigi. Not a single damn thing."

Chancing a look at the woman on his right, Lev found her nibbling on her bottom lip while her striking green eyes lowered to appreciate the tailored fit of his white button-down and how he'd rolled the sleeves up his forearms.

Painted a dusty rose color, her plush mouth threw him back in time without any warning. He could still remember the way her lips felt against his skin. How she kissed him *hungrily.* All the sounds that mouth of hers could make for him.

Not a date, he told himself. *This isn't a date, Lev.*

But she sure looked like it.

"Although to be fair to the bartender," Lev added in a murmur, "he wasn't the only man in this place that couldn't stop staring at you. I think every single man in here—"

"But I was only looking at you, right?"

"At, or *for?*"

Gigi wet her lips, and drummed her black-painted, stiletto fingernails to the glass in front of her. "Could it be both?"

"I thought you wanted to catch up?"

Unashamed and brazen, her sexy smile turned on him when she replied, "I do ... maybe more than I should. Part of me thinks we never really finished what we started, Lev."

"I didn't know we started anything."

"We wouldn't be sitting in this bar if we hadn't."

Well ...

Lev barked out a hard laugh. A shitty attempt to hide the fact that her words and their frank truth slammed into his chest like a wrecking ball. "All right, let's catch up." He spun sideways on the stool, facing her entirely with the beer firm in his palm. He tipped the bottle up for a sip, fully enjoying the way she watched his throat bob with every swallow. Setting it back to the bar but not turning back in his seat, he said, "Tell me all about Gigi Rey, sweetheart."

Gigi rolled her twinkling eyes and waved a hand high. "Her? She's nobody."

"Never heard a worse lie."

That had them both laughing. Hard and without care about who was watching. And fuck him ... he forgot how beautiful she was when she let go like that.

So, yeah.

Maybe they did need to catch up.

FIFTEEN

THEIR CONVERSATION and drinks at the bar quickly moved to the single dartboard that sat alone and unused twenty feet behind an equally lonely-looking pool table. She didn't mind the change in scenery as less people watched them, and the bartender had finally quit trying to jump in on their chat.

"Why *Gigi Rey* anyway?" Lev asked.

Trying to balance the dart in her hand the same way Lev had done when it was his turn to take shots at the board ten feet away on the wall, Gigi shrugged. "I was told it looked better on a cover than Gigi Rey Parker."

She took her shot.

And failed *terribly*.

The damn dart didn't even hit the multicolored board but rather, the wall underneath it. She flinched at the sight of the silver dart sticking out of the wall almost haplessly, nearly ready to tumble to the floor but managing to somehow hang on.

In a way, it felt like a shitty euphemism for her current life. She was just like that dart being thrown by hands that had no idea what to do with her and sometimes she stuck in and held on, and other times she crashed and burned.

"That was ... bad," Lev said behind her, chuckling.

She might have felt some kind of way for his teasing about her horrible dart skills, but he wasn't wrong. Also, she had forgotten just how much the sound of his voice was like a drug to her senses. Made of all bass, his deep tenor could easily make the rest of the quiet bar disappear around them when he talked.

She liked that just fine.

"So, they just *picked* your name?" he asked.

Gigi rested her hands to her waist, still annoyed at how bad she was at this game while she surveyed the dart that was nowhere near where it needed to be. "Like most everything else, yeah. I mean, I'm at a level now where I can push back. It helps too that the agency knows my renewal is coming up, so they're more likely to please me than piss me off. But mostly, I signed away any right to refuse what my agency chooses for me to do or look like. Even this hair, you know?"

To make a point, she flipped a hand through the loose waves of her dark blonde hair with the faded pink tips.

"What about it? It's cute, babe. Very … *you*."

She preened.

Compliments in her business were a dime a dozen. Being on magazine covers and in front of millions daily either by way of social media or whatever the case may be, Gigi had become a little numb to people praising her beauty and surface style. Because that's all it ever was … the things on the *outside*.

Lev's compliments didn't feel the same. She wanted *more* just like the first time they met. He always left her wanting more in one way or another.

"Thanks," she said, "but this hair cost me a fifty-thousand-dollar fine for violating a body modification clause in my contract and nearly cost me my upcoming walk for Fashion Week."

"What kind of bullshit is that?" His entire frame turned her way, and his intense blue stare locked onto hers with a fire she hadn't expected. He looked so irritated that she almost couldn't even admire how gorgeous he was in his pressed, black slacks that hugged a narrow waist and muscular hips. Sweet Jesus, the man hadn't changed a bit. He was still sex poured into the form of a man. "They tell you what you can or can't do to your body—even your *hair*?"

"I mean, yeah?" She hadn't meant for that to come out like a question, and yet it still did. "It's basically how this works. They tell me who to be, where to go, and what to do when I get there."

"Like the restaurant?"

Gigi let out a slow breath and a dry laugh. "Yeah, like *that* shit. I guess Jensen had been chasing my agency for the last

146

six months to have a *moment* with me. That's what the
agency tried to call it when I went crazy over a conference
call. I was then told *it's not unusual, Gigi, models do this all
the time.* Not me."

"That guy is—"

"Dangerous, I know." She folded her arms over her chest,
adding, "I heard it from you. You didn't say why."

"I shouldn't have to. He just is; leave it at that. Some things
are better left unsaid. But really, *normal*?" he asked, giving
her a look.

"Does it sound strange to you?"

"Entirely fucking weird, yes. Sorry to say it, but it does. A
little."

"It's the business. I'm used to it."

"I see you kept the hair, though."

Gigi flashed her teeth in a wicked smile. "Yeah, well ... it
was that or they cut three inches off the bottom to get rid of
the pink. I can't work a high bob, or a pixie cut, and nobody
was shaving this head, right?"

"Why'd you do it in the first place?"

That wasn't an easy answer. Or maybe it was, and she just
didn't want to say it.

"Well ..."

Lev reached for the beer he'd sat on a nearby table and
tipped it up for a drink while he waited for her to continue.
She liked that he didn't push her; everything, even their
conversations, was always on *her* terms and time. It was so
unlike every man she had ever dated in the last five and a
half years, although there hadn't been that many. And she
wasn't even dating Lev.

It just ... was a glaring difference she couldn't ignore.

"I wanted some kind of control," she finally admitted,
grabbing her own glass as well and then downing what
remained in the bottom just because it felt appropriate.
"Something to say *fuck you* without saying it. I wish I could
explain to you how pissed off my manager and agent was the
day I posted the pink hair. Not because I did it, but because it
was my most-liked post all year with the highest *positive*
engagement. There was no way they could do anything to me

beyond the fine because they couldn't spin it to the public, right?"

Lev laughed huskily, the pride clear when he replied, "So that passive-aggressive *fuck you* worked, then."

"Basically. To an extent. And now all my private appointments have to pass from my assistant through the agency and management to make sure I don't pull another *Gigi*. Or that's what they're calling it."

Lev made a noise under his breath that didn't come off as happy. "Sounds ..."

She passed him a look.

Lev made a noise under his breath and shook his head.

"Say it," she told him. "I already know."

"You know what, let's just get back to darts instead."

She nodded. "That's fair."

Stepping up beside her for his next turn, Lev didn't even wait for Gigi to head forward and pull her dart from the wall. According to him, no one really used the dartboard in the bar anyway, so they were just fooling around. There weren't even enough darts to have a proper game, he explained. She didn't know anything about darts, to begin with.

Except that she liked watching Lev play it. Gigi was a sucker for a man with nice arms, and he certainly had those. She didn't mind taking a step back, so she could enjoy the way his arms looked flexing in the rolled-up sleeves of his white button-down ... or admire his back when he considered his shot. She was such a sucker for a good back on man.

She hadn't even asked if he had someone in his life—like maybe a girlfriend, or a wife. A part of her didn't care to know but another part just knew he wasn't that kind of guy. He wouldn't be here flirting with her and looking at her the way he did if he had someone waiting for him at home. It didn't seem like Lev's style.

"Got a nice view back there?" he asked.

Gigi grinned, entirely unashamed when he peeked over his shoulder. That cocked brow and his knowing smirk were enough to make a heat bloom in her belly. A warm shot of lust traveled lower and lower until she was shifting in her ankle boots to relieve the new ache that started between her thighs.

It didn't help.

At all.

"I mean, it'll do," Gigi replied, tampering the neediness trying to fight its way out of her mouth.

That had Lev gawking at her. "*It'll do?*"

She couldn't help but throw her head back and laugh.

Lev's loud sigh echoed before he told her, "Save your pride, then, woman. I won't fault you for it. Laugh it up."

She sure did.

That was the great thing about this man—he knew how to take a joke. That hadn't changed, and they could still make each other laugh without barely any effort at all.

He was kind of perfect.

And that's terrifying, her heart whispered.

Gigi ignored it.

Lev adjusted his stance one more time before lifting his arm and taking his shot. Of course, his dart hit the target that he intended for it to. He tossed her a smug wink before heading for the board to grab his dart—and hers still stuck in the stupid wall.

"And hey, about what I said," Gigi told him, smiling a little brighter when he was in front of her again.

"You said a lot of things."

"Yeah, but I mean about the modeling. All the control. That nonsense."

"What about it?" Lev asked, lifting a single brow.

"Don't let it bother you; I sure don't." Before he could open his mouth and say something else, she was quick to add, "Back when I first started and my career blew up, I didn't have a choice. They were making me, you know? Except they didn't realize that they were also putting me in a position where I could fight for myself, too. I'm doing that more often. I'm looking out for me now."

"What you're saying is ... you got smarter than them."

She tipped her head to the right and lifted her shoulder at the same time. "A girl has to do what she has to do, right?"

Lev wagged a finger at her. "That's right." Lifting the darts higher, he added, "You could just let me show you how to properly throw one of these instead of pretending like you know how."

"Why, so I can stroke your already humongous ego a bit more than it already has been tonight?"

Darts still in hand, Lev flattened the items and his palm to his chest in mock indignation. "How has my ego been stroked, Gigi? Very little of anything on me has been *stroked* by you. At least, not tonight."

Shots fired.

She heard the warning.

And yet, her cheeks still flushed pink when she stuttered out, "You are the *worst*. The absolute worst."

"*Yep.*" He popped the *P* like he was having the most fun of his life, but if she was an honest woman, and she was, this was the greatest time she had in a long while, too. "But seriously, come here ... let me show you. It'll make a difference."

That was how Gigi found herself entirely distracted and not at all paying any attention to Lev's attempt at teaching her the proper way to throw a dart. Why? Because the man figured the best way to teach her was to mold his hard, warm chest and strong thighs against the back of her body while his hands touched *her*.

Oh, not like that.

No.

It all seemed innocent.

She was sure it looked that way to the other patrons in the bar, too. The shivers racing through her body every time his fingers grazed her throat when he showed her how to hold her arm or the proper way to toss the dart forward, however, told an entirely different story. All Gigi needed to do was squirm just a *little* and her ass was even tighter to Lev's groin. His dark hiss in her ear said he knew exactly what she was doing.

And what he had done.

His cologne washed over her senses, and every breath she had to take was measured when she was this close to him. Every touch was a tease. Every word he said became an echo in an ever-growing chamber between the two of them.

"Go ahead," he said in her ear, "try to throw it."

"I wasn't even paying attention."

She felt his lips press against the sensitive skin behind her ear, and the vibration of his chuckles only added to the sinful sensations that danced over her nerve endings. Every single one of her nerves, really.

"Who's the worst *now*?" Lev asked.

Gigi didn't bother to throw the dart.

Instead, she turned in his arms because he didn't seem to want to let her go just yet. She was fine with that because she didn't want him to let go of her yet, either. Face to face, she couldn't look away from the hard lines that made up his handsome face.

"You know what, I'm only a little bit sad you shaved."

Lev grinned slyly. "Oh?"

"Yeah, I was hoping you might have kept it just long enough for me to get your face between my thighs and—"

A dark, harsh noise burst from Lev's lips. The sound was sexy enough to have Gigi shifting in her heels and swallowing the lump that formed in her throat.

"Don't provoke me," he warned, "when we're in public because we know what happens in hallways, right?"

"The situation is a little ... trickier now, I guess. And yet, I bet you could still get your hands up my skirt right now. Do you want to know what I'm wearing under these fishnets, Lev?"

"*Gigi.*"

Her name coming out of his mouth was a prayer. And a *warning.* One she didn't heed.

Lev's hands skimmed around to her back, his fingertips teasing the patch of exposed skin before drifting lower on the leather of her skirt.

"Nothing," she told him.

He grabbed her ass; his palms flexing against her rear almost painfully. Except it didn't hurt at all, and she was two seconds away from telling him to do it again.

"I'm warning you, Gi—"

"I'm wearing nothing under these fishnets."

There was barely a breath between the moment those

words left her lips and the second his mouth slammed against hers. The force of his kiss was enough to send her stumbling back a step, but thank God for this man because he was right there to catch her. Her stiletto nails dragged down between his shoulder blades as his tongue darted between her parted lips to find hers. She answered him back equally, memories and lust flooding her mind and clashing together in the same way their lips and tongues and teeth did in their kiss.

She'd forgotten how his kiss felt all-consuming. How he kissed in the same way he fucked; without control and wholly lost in what he found between them.

That was the part she liked the most. They both drowned together—in each other.

"*Jesus Christ.*" His heavy breaths panted against her trembling lips. She grasped his shoulder, needing to stay steady as she regained her own wind, but used the tip of her index finger to press against his lower lip. His tongue struck out to taste her skin, making Gigi's next inhale hitch hard in her chest. "Killing me, woman."

"I'll certainly let you bury *something*. In me, of course. You wanna check to see if I was telling the truth about the fishnets? You *can*."

"*Fuck.*"

The word burst against her finger at his lip in a hard grunt. The sexiest fucking sound she had ever heard. Those fingers of his raked over her backside and down to the slit in the back of her skirt. One of his hands grabbed the back of her thigh, but the other slipped between the slit in the skirt to explore. He was quick about it, but *God*, she still felt every bit of his soft touch. Especially when his fingertips skimmed along the stretchy strings of the fishnet tights where a panty line *should* have been,

She hadn't lied.

She *was* bare under her skirt.

"You're not lying," he said sounding both turned on and amused. "I don't know what to do with that."

"Fair is fair." She tossed her head back and let out an airy laugh just because. Still, her words were breathless from his proximity alone, and she was sure Lev could hear the quake in her tone when she said, "I had to get you back for that little *stroked* comment, didn't I?"

"Well played, woman. Well fucking played."

It was.

Even she was proud.

His lips grazed her chin, making her quiver everywhere. Even down to the tips of her toes. The blooming warmth crawling through her veins was undeniable. A lot like the want she felt for this man holding her close.

"*Lev.*"

"Hmm?"

Hungry eyes found hers. It took her breath away. For whatever reason, maybe it was the catcall from somewhere behind them, she was reminded of where they were and the fact that *everyone* could probably see Lev's hands slowly working their way up under her skirt. She didn't even want to tell him to stop. Hell, there was something to be said for this man and his ability to bring out the exhibitionist inside her.

She had to, though.

Otherwise, the entire world would see it, too.

"Say it," he murmured, still watching her like a predator might survey the prey he was about to feast on.

Gigi didn't even hesitate to let him know exactly what she wanted. "Come to my hotel tonight. Spend the night with me again. I want you in my bed—I want *you.*"

He licked his lips, and air hissed from his mouth when he gave her ass one last squeeze. "I gotta make a call, then I'm all yours."

That was all she wanted to hear.

SIXTEEN

"HEY, MR. *It's Not A Date*," Nessa said, all too joyfully, in Lev's ear when she finally picked up his call. "What's up?"

"You're a shit. You know that, right?"

Nessa's light laughter crackled in the phone's speakers. "Am I?"

"Entirely."

Truth was, Nessa would get far worse in the next minute after Lev asked for a favor. It wasn't like he didn't deserve it, though.

Leaning his lower back against the sink in the men's washroom, he eyed the *Out of Order* sign on one of two stalls while he chewed over his next words. "Did you have plans tonight or anything—after I got back, I mean?"

"Uh ..."

"Not for me," he rushed to say. *Sort of*, he added silently. "I'm not asking if you wanna do something, I just—"

"It was a date, wasn't it?"

Good God.

Lev swallowed his pride and muttered, grinning to himself, "It *wasn't* ... but it might have turned into that."

"I knew it!"

"You are way too interested in my private life," Lev said in a chuckle. "Which tells me you have none of your own, and you should probably fix that."

"Probably, but who asked you?"

"Nobody, but you didn't have to."

"Mmhmm. I bet. So ..." Nessa drawled out the word like she knew Lev was just biding his time until he finally spit out whatever he called for. "Did you need something?"

"Arely's good, right?"

"Perfect. Still sleeping."

"And you didn't burn down the kitchen trying to cook, did you?"

"Fuck you, Lev."

His laughter matched Nessa's. It was only partly a joke. She had set fire to his stove when she once left a flammable cloth sitting too close to the induction burner. He couldn't let her live it down, either.

"Joking aside," he muttered, scrubbing a hand down his jaw, "would you mind staying later than planned? Maybe until early morning. I'll be home in time to wake Arely up, no worries on that."

He thought for sure Nessa would make another one of her comments. She loved to be right, after all. She also surprised him.

"Lev?"

"Hmm?"

"I'm glad the date is going well—you deserve some fun. All you do is work and take care of your daughter. It won't hurt for you to also enjoy *your* life. And yes, I don't mind staying here until you get back ... whenever that is. Be safe, don't bring home any nasty ST—"

"That's enough of that. Thank you, Nessa."

"I'm just saying!"

"*Bye.*"

Lev hung up on the sound of Nessa's laughter knowing she wouldn't be too offended. Ninety percent of their friendship was made up of them taking cheap shots at one another, anyway. It wasn't like this had been anything new.

Not wanting to leave Gigi alone any longer than he had to, Lev left the men's bathroom to go in search of her. He expected to find her at the table near the dartboard—he promised his phone call wouldn't last long—but instead found her back at the bar. With a phone pressed to her ear as she nodded and then replied to whatever conversation she was having, she passed her empty glass to the bartender. Just as quickly, she turned her back to the man now cleaning her glass, going back to her call.

He did a sweep of the bar.

The few people inside still weren't that interested in the celebrity that was only a few feet away from some of them— excusing the bartender seemingly recognizing Gigi, that was.

Then again, he figured the age group of most of the bar's patrons probably wasn't that *in the know* in regards to famous people. Or they just didn't care.

Gigi noticed Lev's approach and held up one finger while her gaze slid toward the phone she still had pressed to her ear.

"Another drink, man?"

Lev draped an arm around Gigi's waist and shook his head. It seemed like the second he was touching her and back at her side, she only wanted to be closer, moving against him until her body was tight to his. He liked that just fine, too. "No, we're going to head out, I think."

"Ah, okay. Think I could get her autograph before you go, or nah?"

He gave the man a look.

Really?

The bartender shrugged. "Never know if you don't ask, right?"

Well, that was fair.

"Not tonight," Lev said. "But I'll see what I can do for you another time maybe."

That satisfied the man. He shot Lev a nod and a thumbs-up before returning to his task of wiping out glasses.

That was as much of a promise as he could do seeing as how he didn't know where this night, or the days after, would lead him and Gigi. He was, however, quite aware that he would be back at this bar at one point or another, and the bartender wasn't likely to forget Lev's words.

Not only was the place somewhere he frequented for his own enjoyment, but the bar was also mob-owned through a shell company Andino used to launder dirty money until it was clean. Illegal cash was funneled into the business, making it look like the place was more successful than it was, and it basically came out as profit on the other side that Andino paid taxes on. Or that's how the man explained it once.

Lev didn't understand much about that shit. He tried not to ask too many questions because the less he knew about the mafia and its workings, the better it would be for him if the police or FBI ever came knocking with questions for him. It was hard to answer shit you didn't know, right?

"Absolutely, five minutes, then?"

Gigi's question drew his attention back to her. She watched him from the side, those green eyes of hers worthy of drowning in when he stared back at her. The small smile tilting her plump lips upward at the corners had him leaning in to steal a quick kiss.

She didn't seem to mind.

He only wanted more.

Her smile grew into something sexier when his kiss traveled from the side of her mouth to the underside of her jaw. His next kiss came with his tongue flicking out to taste her skin, and then he sucked on the same spot, too.

Just because.

"Okay, thanks," Gigi said on the phone, her free hand fisting into his button-down with enough force to strain the fabric, "*really* appreciate this, Kayla. You're the best."

She hung up the phone but didn't even take the time to explain the call or the reason why before she turned her head into his next kiss. There was no softness in the rushed, bruising hunger of their lips molding together, their tongues tangling with every stroke until he had to pull away for a breath.

Gigi blinked up at him. "You still have no patience."

"That's not the case at all, sweetheart."

"Oh?"

"With you, I just don't have any control."

Her hand laid flat against his stomach, her fingernails raking tender lines overtop the fabric of his shirt and making his muscles clench over and over. *Such a fucking tease.* Her hand could be a little lower; he knew it, so did she.

"I made a deal tonight—had to have a driver bring me here and then back. That's what I was calling about. He'll be here in five minutes. Did you bring your own car?"

"I did."

"Can you leave it or do you want to—"

"Woman, I'll do whatever the hell you want me to do."

That had Gigi beaming. It was the simpering smile she

shot him and the dip of her lashes as she glanced toward the bar's windows that had his blood heating up, though. Not to mention, how hard his fucking cock had become under his slacks.

It was starting to ache.

"It'll be easier to keep out of sight if you come with me, but also ..."

"What?"

Her bottom lip caught under her top teeth. "You'll see. Did you get a hold of whoever—"

"Yeah, all is good. I have to head out early—probably around five for ... work."

His deflection did the job.

"Good," she replied. "So, we're ready to go?"

"Yep. Ready whenever you are. Say the word."

Lying by omission was still a lie. Lev knew that better than anyone. He came here to see Gigi with *every* intention of telling her about his daughter but hadn't quite figured out how exactly to do that. When was he supposed to fit that little tidbit of information in? Between the drinks and darts and flirting? Or how about now, when her hand was drifting down to cup his dick through his slacks? Yeah, he was sure that would go over perfectly fucking well.

"Jesus," he grunted when she grabbed his length firmer and stroked. "Now who's trying to catch us a public indecency charge?"

He caught her wrist and yanked her hand away from his dick before he lost what little control he'd managed to maintain over the evening. Weaving his fingers with hers, Lev brought their connected hands up to press two quick kisses to her knuckles.

She trembled.

He could feel it.

"We should ..." Gigi swallowed hard, her gaze locked on his mouth that moved in for another taste of the skin on her hand. "We should head outside. The faster I can get into a vehicle, the better, you know?"

"Just say what it is, babe."

"Which is?"

"You need to be fucked. You *want* me to fuck you. Say it."

He kissed her knuckle again, but that time, he used his tongue to tease her shaking hand, too. Gigi let out a hard breath, the color flooding her cheeks rushed down her throat in the *prettiest* way. He bet he could get her flushed all over before the night was out.

He looked forward to it.

Meeting his gaze, Gigi said, "Yeah, I want you to fuck me. I've needed you for a while."

Well, then ...

Lev gestured a hand toward the entrance where the quiet, dark street waited for them. "Ladies first, Gigi."

• • •

"Thought you said five minutes?" Lev asked, keeping a tight hold around Gigi's form. Despite it being summer, they were still quickly approaching fall and her top and mini skirt offered little to no protection from the wind that traveled through the streets. At least tucked in his embrace, she was soaking up some of his warmth and her trembling subsided. "We've been out here for at least ten."

"I can call?"

Or they could have just taken his Jeep which was parked behind the damn bar. Lev knew better than to make the offer, though, because as she had already explained, her driver was a necessary evil. At least, for tonight.

He seriously doubted it was just for tonight.

"When was the last time you drove yourself anywhere?" he asked.

Gigi barely thought about it. "Three months ago. My assistant cleared my schedule for a day, so we could drive to the beach. Nobody knew my face. I was cleaning sand out of my ... well, everywhere ... for *days*. I loved it. Every second of it."

Lev's laughter shook them both, but he heard her unspoken words, too. "It gets tiring, then? The fame, I mean."

"Overwhelming. It's hard to take time away when it's all

around you all the time, you know what I mean?"

She tipped her head back, and he stared down at her.

"No," he admitted, "I can't imagine that at all."

Gigi lifted one delicate shoulder. "That's okay. You really don't want to."

How *indifferent* she seemed about her life. Because that was the thing, he knew ... that was her life. Her everyday normal. Lev couldn't help but wonder if she often remembered what it was like before her face became a worldwide phenomenon and if she missed it at all.

He didn't get the chance to ask.

Gigi ripped those thoughts right out of his mind when she closed the distance between them to take a kiss without warning. It didn't last long, far too fleeting for his liking, but it was enough to remind him of exactly what they were doing together.

Again.

Lev pinched Gigi's chin between his forefinger and thumb, keeping her face close to his when he told her, "Do you know how often I've thought about you these past years? You haunted my wet dreams."

Her tongue teased the seam of her lips. "Yeah?"

How could she doubt it?

"*All the fucking time*, woman. But none of my dreams compares to you. My mind couldn't do you justice even when it tried. It's a piss poor comparison, let me say."

Gigi's lashes fluttered with her sweet smile. "I really found a smooth talker with you, huh?"

Lev smirked. "None of it is a lie, though. Nobody tells you, do they?"

"People tell me things all the time, Lev. That's half the problem. Someone is always waiting to tell me something they think I want to hear, but it never feels quite ... right."

Well, he could tell her a few things.

They were *all* right.

"You're kind of amazing ... no, fuck that noise," Lev was quick to say, cutting a hand through the air before it was right back on her ass to squeeze tight. "You *are* fucking amazing. Look at what you've done, huh? I feel like I should be honored to even know your name—to know *you*, does that make sense?"

"You know what's funny?" she asked as a black SUV pulled up right beside them on the street.

"What?"

"It's just … there's this part of me that thinks you know more about me than anyone else who gets to see my life every day does. Or it feels that way, and I'm not sure what to do about it."

The weight of her words hit him hard.

Lev could only reply, "I don't know either."

"Miss Gigi, if you wouldn't mind getting in the vehicle as to not linger—"

"Yes, Gerald, we're coming."

Her words were punctuated by the roll of her eyes that didn't even bother to glance in the direction of the window he had rolled down. Lev's laughter chased them both into the backseat of the SUV where warm, black leather seats waited for them. He might have admired the vehicle and the fancy interior with emblems embroidered into each headrest once the door was shut, and they pulled away from the street.

But he didn't.

Gigi made sure of that.

Her whispered *I want you* was all he heard before she crossed the space between them in the backseat. Her hands *and* face dipped low, locked in on her target of his pants and getting them undone as quickly as fucking possible.

Lev's harsh *shit* cut through the air as his gaze snapped to the front seats. Her deft fingers had already worked the button of his slacks open and got his zipper pulled down. Relief swelled through his chest at the sight of a divider separating the front of the vehicle from the rear, and the fact it was closed.

The feeling was short-lived.

Not that he was complaining when it was instead replaced by Gigi's hand finding his rock-hard cock. As fast as her palm was around his length, stroking him from base to tip with a grip tight enough to take his breath away, her mouth was on him, too.

"*Holy fuck,*" he grunted out, hips jerking upward.

She took him all in, though.

Every fucking inch but for the bit of his cock at the base where her hand stayed firm to squeeze and stroke him in the best way. There was no way he could keep quiet—no way he really wanted to, either. It was then that music started to filter through the speakers of the car, drowning out the low moan of Gigi's name that fell from his lips.

From his lap, she watched him, her eyes wide, expansive, and *pleased*. She looked so fucking sweet like that; happy to be sucking his cock in the backseat of an Escalade like she didn't have anything better to do with her time, nor did she want to.

"Fucking hell, you're going to make me come if you keep that up, Gigi."

She sucked him harder.

Her tongue teased his tip.

Lev slammed his head back in the seat, gritting his teeth while he fisted a handful of her hair and pulled the strands back to keep it from falling into her face. The dusty pink lipstick on her mouth smeared to his dick and at the edge of her mouth. Already, he was ruining the makeup she had clearly taken time to apply to look her best.

And he liked that.

Too much.

There was something primal about taking her beauty and making it *raw*. He wanted to see her like that. *Needed* to watch her swallow his dick, and then the rest of him, too.

"*Look at you,*" he groaned. "God, why are you so fucking perfect?"

Where had she been all his life? Why had he let her go all those years ago without even a goodbye?

Gigi had him coming in *two* blocks. It was probably a record for him, and he might have been ashamed that she made him blow his load so fast ... except he wasn't. It was her, after all.

She swallowed every drop that she drew from his balls. And then let him lick her lips when he asked for a kiss, too. She tasted like him and *liquor*.

Sin and sex.

• • •

Getting inside the hotel where Gigi was staying was not as easy as just walking through the front entrance, apparently. Security had to be called first, and then the decision was made for them to enter the building through a side exit door that could only be opened from the inside. It all happened rather quickly and not one of the security guards even blinked at the sight of Lev exiting the SUV with Gigi, nor did they ask any questions.

"The floor is quiet, and your room has been prepped for the evening, Miss Gigi," was all they were told as they were directed to a private elevator for the penthouse suite. "Don't hesitate to call down if you need anything else. Enjoy your night."

The trip in the elevator didn't last long, but Lev made the most of it all the same. From the moment he had Gigi entirely alone, he was *on her*. He didn't plan on wasting a single second of their time together. And he wanted her to know, every minute of it, that she belonged to him when they were like this.

The possessive thoughts banged around in his head when he backed her against the elevator wall and drove that leather skirt she wore high over her hips, and his hand disappeared between her thighs while his other held her by her throat to keep her firmly against the wall. There, he could tell her all the dirty fucking things he planned to do to here. Like that, he could watch how she struggled to maintain control and finally let it all go for him.

God.

It was a beautiful sight.

It was a fifteen-floor trip.

He had her shaking and begging in *ten*.

"Oh, my *God … oh my—Lev, please.*"

Every one of her breathless pleas only urged him on more. The way she twisted in his hold, her hips rocking against the fingers he filled her with, twisted his need for her into something darker and dangerous.

Dangerous, because he couldn't get enough. Not when she finally came undone for him, head tipped back to the wall with lips parted wide where the camera overhead could see her pleasure, and not when he kissed her as the elevator finally came to a stop, opening to a private entrance for the penthouse suite.

He was sure there were other ways to enter.

He didn't care to ask then.

Gigi watched him, her chest rising high with every breath, as he pulled his hand from between her thighs and lifted the two fingers he'd used to make her come to his mouth. No sense in wasting honey, right?

He sucked the taste of her pussy from his fingers, and then told her, "Next taste is yours, babe, if you ask me nicely. That's a promise."

Not even giving her the chance to respond, Lev yanked Gigi away from the wall and spun them both around to step out of the elevator together. His mouth slammed into hers for another breathless kiss that she answered back *beautifully*. Every flick of her tongue and sweep of her lips felt like war against the fight of his own to maintain dominance. He loved that she fought him, though.

It only made him want to win *more*.

In their haste, their backs found one wall. And then another. Each time, something else was shed. His shirt. Then her top when he finally figured out how to get those damn buckles off. By the time they finally made it to the bedroom at the far end of the suite, Lev realized they had walked through three separate rooms.

The suite was huge.

He didn't care.

The only thing he wanted right then was to be buried balls deep in Gigi Rey Parker. He wanted to hear her screaming his name and feel every inch of her pussy hug his dick when he made her come again and again.

All fucking night.

He hit the light switches on the wall, sending color cascading through the bedroom from all corners. He wanted the lights on for this.

Lev met Gigi where she stood at the edge of the bed. He dragged her in close for one more kiss. Holding her jaw, he took control, demanding with each strike of his tongue against hers until she was shaking, and her lips trembled as his kiss slowed.

"These stay *on*," he said, his fingers curling into the fishnet stockings. With a hard twist, he ripped the thin strings between her thighs, leaving a gap that he knew would work for him. "But get that fucking skirt off, sweetheart."

She rushed to obey when he finally released her from his hold. He didn't waste time, either. As she shimmied out of the leather mini skirt, her gaze stayed locked on him like a missile ready to launch straight into him. When they exploded together, he knew it would be fucking glorious. She was still a work of art—pristine, golden skin dotted with freckles that he could spend hours tracing and memorizing. Curves he wanted to worship until the sun came up. Legs for days that he knew damn well looked a hundred times better wrapped around his head.

But they didn't have time for all of that.

Not tonight.

Someday, he thought.

Why was he already planning for the next round?

When would enough be enough?

It wasn't yet.

That was for sure.

Gigi sat on the edge of the bed, knees pressed together while he finished pulling off his pants, a foil packet already in hand.

"Open up—show me what you've got for me, sweetheart."

She did.

Hell.

Heaven waited there. All pink, and glistening wet when she used two fingers to slide between her slit and show him her bare sex. He bet *soft* and *hot*, too.

"Wider," he urged.

She did, bringing fishnet-covered legs high to rest her heels on the edge of the mattress. "Like that?"

"Just like that, yeah."

Could she hear how tight his throat was by the sound of his voice alone? Did she realize how hard he was going to fuck her just because he could, and she would let him?

Lev didn't think so.

She would soon find out.

He made her wait for it, though. Until he was naked, standing in front of her, and rolling latex down his cock. She reached out to stroke him, but he was quick to catch her wrist in his grasp to stop her. The same hand she'd used to touch herself with.

"I made a promise, didn't I?" he asked huskily.

Gigi swallowed hard, a sly grin starting to grow. "You did."

"*Taste*."

Leaning between her thighs, and hovering over her, Lev had the best view of her body spread out before him while she sucked the taste of her arousal from her slender fingers. Her green orbs darkened with her lust while his cock pulsed from the ache driving him fucking crazy. That need to be inside her was too much to handle.

"You look like you're about to ... eat me whole," she whispered, her lips swollen from his kiss and still wet from her fingers.

"No, I just wanna have you. All of you."

"Take me, then. *Have me*."

He couldn't get on that bed—between her thighs—fast enough. Somehow, he managed to convince his crazy brain that they would have another time to do this. He would get another chance to spend those hours he envisioned relearning every inch of her body again but right then ... he just needed to have her.

With his hands tight to her waist, he moved Gigi back on the bed. Just enough to sit down, and then he was dragging her close again. Her legs hooked over his, and her palms laid flat to the bed behind her for support as he brought her down on his cock. He should have taken her slow—let her get used to his size again and how it felt to be so fucking full of him.

He didn't.

And her deep, broken moan when he yanked her down on

his length said she didn't mind at all. Hell, he would have been happy to hold her like that for a moment. Just to appreciate the sight of her tense, with her tits pushed out for him to bend down to lick and taste, pussy stretched full of him.

But the second he started their rhythm, a hard, fast pace driving into her again and again until he was soaked with her, she was throwing it back just as hard. Riding his every thrust, taking him so fucking well.

"Like that," she gasped. "*Yes*, just like that ..."

His words were lost between the chaos of them and the noise of their fucking. Still, he told her every filthy thing that had crossed his mind from the moment he watched her walk across the floor of the bar.

"Lucky I didn't fuck you right then, Gigi. *Jesus*. How's that cock feel, babe? Who fucks you like this, huh? Who does this for you?"

She didn't have to say it.

Her wide, hooded eyes, quivering lips, and her body in his hands said it all.

No one.

It was *just him.*

Knowing that only twisted the possessive streak Lev already had growing for this strangely beautiful woman into something wicked and primal. He couldn't hold her tight enough, even when she whined from the strength of his grip, and he left red marks from his fingertips behind. The waist band of her fishnet stockings twisted into his fist while his other hand kept her body working hard against his. He couldn't get enough of her into his mouth to satisfy the desire to taste all of her. Every kiss he laid to her skin was followed by his teeth raking over the same spot. Her moans became music to his ears.

She came riding him like that.

And then he got her on her back, spread her wide, shoved her hands over her head and kept her pinned like that until he fucked her through another orgasm that had her quaking.

He just needed more.

Still.

Even after he'd finally reached his own peak, pulling out to yank off the rubber, so he could mark her skin *another* way, too, he hovered above her. Stroking his cock through the aftershocks of an orgasm that left him panting, while she trembled beneath him in the same state and realized ...

It wasn't enough.

This woman was a drug.

Fuck him.

He was still addicted.

SEVENTEEN

HEY, DID you happen to see the pic—
"Daddy, look!"

Lev's brain didn't have the chance to process the rest of Gigi's most recent text because the second his daughter called his name, all of his attention went to her. He quickly found where she stood at the top of a bright red twisty slide in her sky-blue summer dress. With her hand outstretched in front of her, she pointed at something across the park that Lev couldn't quite see from his position on the bench.

The phone in his hand buzzed—likely with another text from Gigi—but he was more concerned with whatever it was that had his daughter's interest. Two days after he left Gigi's hotel *way too early* in the morning, and the only thing the two of them had been able to spare for time with each other was a text here and there.

Arely looked his way, her little brow knotted together. "What are they doing, Daddy?"

"Who?" he asked.

"Them."

Shoving the phone into the pocket of his jeans, Lev stood from the bench and headed for his daughter who was still pointing in the direction of the parking lot. They frequented the park often enough that he was sure Arely could walk the trek on her own from their place to here, but he would never let her do it alone.

Certainly not at her age.

Nonetheless, it was one of her favorite spots to play. Especially on the hot summer days when they had the water play equipment up and running and she could easily cool off while also running her little ass off. It tired her out. She slept a hundred times better.

A win-win in Lev's book.

Plus, the place was open to the public and was one of the

few parks near their home that was maintained and kept rather clean. Or clean enough that he felt okay with letting his kid go batshit with all the other children using the park. Nonetheless, the place didn't have much trouble happening and that's what he liked about it most of all.

Stepping beyond the crushed rock walkway that separated the benches and running trail from the kids' play equipment, Lev finally found what his daughter was talking about. For a split second, confusion drilled down hard in his chest, nearly nailing him in place as he stared across the park into the parking lot.

Or rather, to where the chain link fence separated the two spots. Three people stood there with cameras in hand. Taking photos.

One had a lens longer than he'd ever seen. The more pressing issue was the fact that it looked like their cameras were locked on *his* fucking child. Then, at the sight of him—because he must have been out of their view on the bench—one of the photogs started gesturing his way, and the cameras turned on him.

What the fuck?

"Arely, come here," Lev said, waving one hand at his daughter while keeping an eye on the fuckers across the way.

"Are they taking pictures?"

"Get down from the slide, baby."

"Why?"

Jesus Christ.

He knew how this would go down with his kid. He would tell her five more times to do something, and she would ask why each and every time. It was just their way.

"*Now*, please," he said, getting closer to his daughter with every word. He didn't want to run, especially if those photogs were taking pictures of them, and cause a scene. "Get down—we're leaving."

"But I want to *play!*"

Arely's wail echoed across the park. Lev gritted his teeth at the attention it brought their way from other kids and parents at the park.

Then, a new voice joined in to piss him off even more. As

faint as it fucking was.

"Mr. Arsov—*Pink*—it's Lev, right? Do you have any comment to make about your daughter and her mother? How long have you had custody of Gigi Rey's child? Are you—"

How the fuck did they know his *name*?

And his nickname?

And what in the hell were they talking about Arely being Gigi's kid?

What was going on?

"Two minutes, Mr. Arsov! We just want to ask some questions!"

Great.

Now they were starting to come around the fence.

"Daddy, why are they—"

Holy hell.

Lev's heart had started to race so fast in his chest that he was sure the organ would explode. Fuck not causing a scene. Those few questions were enough to tell Lev this situation was not at all good, and he needed to get him and Arely the fuck out of there as fast as he possibly could.

Now.

"Come here, baby."

Lev didn't allow Arely to argue with him further even though she tried to turn away from his reaching arms. It was pointless. Quickly, he had his daughter in his grasp and in one fell swoop, brought her down from the slide. He didn't let her go, keeping her hooked to his side like a little monkey before he headed back to the bench where he'd left Arely's mini backpack where he kept water and snacks.

Maybe it was his rushed movements or the tone of his voice when he snapped a rude *no fucking comment* at the paps surrounding him in the parking lot where his Jeep was parked, but Arely's grip on him became tighter. Unfortunately, going to their vehicle meant passing the photogs. One even had the audacity to shout questions at his kid. Like the five-and-a-half-year-old would answer the asshole back or knew *anything* about what they asked.

Arely just hugged him tighter.

"Daddy," she whispered.

"It's okay, it's okay," he assured, desperately trying to keep his tone calm as he buckled her into her seat.

As he stepped back and slammed the backdoor to the Jeep shut, another asshole with a camera got a little too close to the rear of his vehicle to ask, "Why has Gigi kept her daughter a secret for all these years?"

"What are you *talking* about?" Lev growled at the man. "She doesn't even know my kid. Did you get that—*my fucking kid*. Not hers." He stepped closer to the man who had his camera up and ready, his fists clenched and twitching to break somebody's face. "Get the fuck out of here before I feed your fucking camera to you, asshole."

By the time Lev got inside the Jeep and turned the engine over, Arely was sniffling in the backseat. Fuck them for making his child cry. That was enough to almost make him turn around, so he could feed that asshole his camera.

His heart broke as Arely asked him *why* again, but he didn't have an answer. He had no idea what was going on.

He'd soon fucking find out.

That was a promise.

• • •

Lev didn't have to wait long to get answers. Between the texts from Gigi on his phone that he had left unread, and the call he got from his boss that in no uncertain terms told him to get his ass to the restaurant, well ... things became painfully clear.

"What is this *shit*?" Andino asked, tossing three magazines to the top of his desk. He pointed a finger at the pictures splashed across the front of one of the gossip tabloids. On that one, it featured a photo of Lev and Gigi standing outside the bar, hugging one another while his face hovered close to hers. It was clear they were being ... intimate. Another picture in the bottom corner showcased Lev walking down the street by their home holding his daughter's hand.

The day before. Literally *yesterday*. That's how fast they put that shit to print. The headline, though? That was the fucking killer.

GIGI REY'S SECRET CHILD.

On another one?

The headline read: *GIGI'S SECRET MAN—PINK, INFAMOUS MOB ENFORCER.*

Holy shit.

It went from bad to worse before Lev had even blinked. He didn't even bother to flip to the magazine on the bottom to see what pictures were splashed across the front or what bullshit headline they plastered on top of it to increase sales.

"*Pink,*" Andino ground out, shaking with his finger still aimed at the magazines across his desk like a gun ready to blow, "you better start fucking talking, man. This is the kind of attention the Marcellos don't need. You know better than this. What is going on?"

"I don't know. I just ..." Lev's hands found the edge of Andino's desk, and he prayed for something to steady him because the ground just wasn't doing it. "I'm sorry, boss."

Andino let out a hard breath. "How long have you been fucking with ... she's like a goddamn *supermodel,* Pink."

He flinched. "I knew her before that ... we just met up again while she was in town. For work, you know? It wasn't supposed to cause any problems. We spent the night together and that was it. I was just at the park with Arely today and photographers showed up out of nowhere asking questions and—"

"*Exactly!*" Andino's roar froze Lev to the spot. "Exactly," his boss ground out again. "Asking *questions.* About you." His finger jabbed down to the word *ENFORCER* in block letters on the tabloid's cover. "About fucking *business.* What in the hell am I supposed to do about this?"

"Call your fucking lawyers and get them on their ass? I don't know! Why are you asking me?"

"*Pink.*"

Lev met Andino's stare and quietly said, "I know this is bad."

"Do you?"

"Yeah, man. But it's also bad for me, you know? And my kid. So I get you're pissed off about your business being out in the public right now, but give me a chance to catch up and take care of my shit first. Okay?"

Andino straightened to his full height at the other side of the desk but said nothing more. It gave Lev the chance to drag in another deep breath, settling his overworked and already frayed nerves a little more.

He'd checked Gigi's texts after getting Arely home and calling Nessa to come and sit with her while he ran into work.

Gigi was pissed. Not just because of the pictures, either. *Obviously.* Everything he hadn't told her ... well, he didn't really need to tell her anymore. It was plastered across the rags, headlining every major gossip blog, and shit, he wouldn't be surprised if something made the damn news.

Her last text?

My team is putting out a statement. We need to talk. ASAP.

Yeah, he bet.

Goddammit.

"Christ, Lev," Andino muttered, falling ungracefully into his office chair with enough force to shake the floor. That wasn't half as shocking as his boss using his *name* instead of simply Pink like he usually did. "You're seriously fucking with that chick?"

"I mean ... yeah?"

"Why is that a question?"

Lev laughed under his breath because what else could he do? "*Look at her*, man. If you were lucky enough to be fucking the woman who was listed as one of the most beautiful women in the world, wouldn't you wonder how it happened too?"

Andino arched a brow, replying, "*Well* ... Listen, happily married man here."

"But?"

"No buts."

Right.

No one could say Andino Marcello was a saint, but they certainly wouldn't ever be able to say the man was unfaithful to his wife, either. He didn't even look at other women in a way that suggested he was interested. It was one of the things Lev respected the most about the man because very little else *was* socially respectable beneath the surface.

"Fucking *gross*," Lev snapped, picking up the one tabloid that called his daughter a *secret*. Just as fast, he tossed it into the trash bin beside the desk. "Just make up shit like that. Come on."

Andino glanced his way with a bit more sympathy. "Really bothers you, huh?"

"Wouldn't it bother you? You know how much effort I put into keeping my daughter safe from ... everything I do. She doesn't even know who *Pink* is, Andino. And now what? Are we going to have people outside our house with cameras every day asking if her father is connected to the mob? What if she goes to daycare and someone runs their mouth? Or shit, what about when she starts kindergarten and—"

"Okay, you're just catastrophizing now. Don't call on trouble that isn't even here yet."

Sure.

That was easy for his boss to say.

Lev found a chair and sat down in the same manner his boss had minutes earlier. Scrubbing a hand down his face and then massaging his temples with the pads of his fingers, he willed away the raging headache starting to form. "We were careful ... she made it clear we had to be. It wasn't supposed to be a problem."

At first, Andino didn't reply.

The silence was fine.

He needed it to think.

"When are you going to tell me?" Andino asked quietly.

Lev glanced up, meeting his boss's stare head-on. "Tell you what?"

"That she was at the meeting I asked you to report on. I know everybody that was there—she was one of them. You didn't mention it when you reported back about it. You didn't think to tell me now that was how you ran back into her if you're being honest about—"

"I *am*. Do you think we could have kept a relationship a secret for this long? Shit, I fucked her two nights ago, and they've already got pictures of my kid in the goddamn rags, Andino!"

"Lower your voice."

Lev checked his attitude.

But *only* because it was Andino.

"I didn't mention her being at the meeting because it didn't matter ... why should it? She was there to show off for Jensen Todrey. A way to show the guy he wanted to do business with what he could do. You know what I mean? I was more worried about her and what that asshole might be trying to pull with her than the fact she might be interesting to you. Forgive my ignorance. I won't make the mistake again."

Andino sighed sharply.

Lev rolled his eyes.

So, maybe his attitude was still there.

"This can't be a problem," Andino said, pointing at the remaining magazines on his desk. "Whatever you do with her from here on out, you make sure it's not a fucking problem, Pink. Especially not one I will have to fix."

"Yeah, I know. I got it."

"I don't want to see you in the tabloids again."

"Well, I can't really—"

"*Try.* And I'll get the goddamn lawyers on their asses, too. Not that I suspect it'll do any good except to maybe get the mafia out of their fucking mouths." Andino shook his head, grumbling under his breath all the while. "Probably the least of my fucking problems now, honestly."

That had Lev's attention. "Why is that?"

Because, to him, this couldn't get worse.

Right?

Andino passed him a look, shrugging. "What are the chances the other men at that meeting won't see these magazines? *Your face.* Her. How long will it take for them to put two and two together and realize I had a man of mine watching their meeting to report back to me, huh? I haven't even handled my associate from Cali yet. This is not good, Pink."

Perfect.

A little more to add to his ever-growing plate.

"I was sporting a beard; let's hope they don't put it together," Lev muttered.

"Lev, be real."

Yeah, this was ... bad.

Lev sunk into the chair; his chest heavier than ever. "She didn't know."

"What?"

"Gigi. She didn't know about ... any of this. The mob. My kid. *Me.*"

"So?"

Lev coughed out a laugh, wishing it could be as easy as him saying *so* like it didn't matter at all. Because it was then that he realized he didn't want those things that he'd kept hidden in his life to be the reason Gigi walked away. She did that once. For a different reason, sure, but he wasn't sure that he wanted the same thing to happen this time.

And that just fucked him up even more.

"I gotta go," Lev said, pushing up from the chair.

Andino grunted with a wave at his desk. "Take that shit with you. And remember what I told you, too. No more problems."

Yeah.

It wasn't like he could forget it.

EIGHTEEN

"PLEASE EXPLAIN to Gigi that we have now hired a *second* team to handle this mess—"

"Please explain to Marla that I couldn't give a *fuck* what they're doing about those lying rags," Gigi tossed over her shoulder to Kayla. Who currently had Marla on the conference phone's speaker so Gigi could hear the conversation while she paced the hotel suite. "And I am allowed to have a life outside of the confines of my contracts. The statement was made by the team—let them do what they want with it."

"Gigi, I don't think you understand how serious—"

That had Gigi swinging around on the spot to glare at the black, triangular phone where it sat in the middle of the large cherry-stained dining table. "Are you for real? Did you really just say that I don't understand how serious this situation is when it's literally *me* they're talking about? *My* private life. I have been in this hotel for *days* now waiting for this to blow over, but I'm the one who doesn't realize how serious this is? Give me a break, Marla. I'm going out of my fucking *mind* about it."

"Well, I ..." Marla sighed, the sound crackling in the speakers as she took a second to regain her usually calm composure. Gigi had a way of making the agent's facade crack faster than anyone else could—or that's what she liked to tell her every time a new issue came up. "Gigi, I know you're upset because your private life was brought into the public spotlight in a way you didn't like ... but you have to understand on that side of things, it's bound to happen. It isn't the first time. Remember the trip to Maui—the pictures?"

Low blow.

That was a dark time in Gigi's modeling career that she would really rather not fucking revisit but of course, now would be the time when her agent brought it up.

"Oh, you mean when my supposed best friend was selling private pictures of me to whoever would snatch them up for a couple of grand a piece? Because apparently, I should have known better then, too. According to you. Can't trust anyone, right?"

"That's not what I—"

"That's exactly what you meant. It's the same thing you told me then, too. If you're trying to suggest *Lev* had us followed, you're delusional. The man wouldn't even know where to begin or how to make that happen."

Or at least, that's what she was hoping. Then again, the rags had brought up a lot of things about Lev's personal life that Gigi didn't know about, either. Like the fact he was apparently connected to the mob. Which made a lot of sense as to why he seemed to have a confident knowledge that Jensen Todrey and his friend at the lunch date were *bad news*.

Because Lev was bad news, too.

Right?

Were there really *good* men when it came to the mob? Except she also felt like she knew a part of Lev, or he showed her a part of him, that wasn't bad at all. She had a hard time connecting the dots in her mind to fit Lev to the man the magazines called *Pink*. How had he even earned a nickname like that? Oh, they had facts. Pictures, too. Even named names.

And somehow, his connection to the Marcello mafia family and the boss running the show was the absolute least of Gigi's concerns.

Why? Oh, yeah.

He had a *kid*. A child. A little girl named Arely. It pissed her off more than anything that the *journalists*—if one wanted to give those jokes of writers that kind of respect— thought not only was it acceptable to publish pieces calling the child hers, but they actually went as far as to *name* Lev's daughter. Her first name only, sure, but still.

How had they even gotten that information? Gigi didn't really wonder. Everything was accessible with the internet.

Why hadn't he told her those things? Why hadn't *he* been the one to tell her? That's what bothered her the most.

It made Gigi think that maybe the feelings she had held on to for years where Lev was concerned weren't shared by him. Why should he tell her anything about his personal life when the only thing they had shared together was a bed, right?

Yeah.

That shit hurt bad. Gigi just didn't want to admit it.

Marla's droning voice pulled Gigi from her depressing thoughts, but it didn't make her feel the slightest bit better to hear what the woman was saying. *Story of my life.*

"It has been suggested we take legal action regarding the false publications and the damage it could have done. We're looking into different routes on that topic. We're also working on damage control elsewhere. What we *really* need right now, Gigi, is for you to remain out of sight and keep your mouth shut unless told otherwise. We may have you do an interview if it gets to that—"

"I won't speak on any of this publicly," Gigi said, drawing her hard line. "Because there are two other people in this equation who were dragged into this by no fault of their own. I am not going to get on a public platform and speak about them like I have the right to. I will *not* do it, Marla."

Another frustrated sigh echoed from the phone. "Well ... can you stay away from the gentleman, otherwise? At least until this blows over."

Gigi made a face, knowing good and well she couldn't promise *that* without it being a total lie. In fact, Lev was set to arrive at the hotel later that day because they had finally managed to pull together sometime to sit down, and he seemed willing to talk.

She was going to give him the chance to clear some things up. Where they went from there, or how it left them at the end of it, she couldn't say yet. They would deal with that when they got to that point.

"Gigi?" Marla pressed on the call.

"Prepare for an onslaught of pictures of him arriving and leaving the hotel. I'm sure they'll be *everywhere* by tomorrow."

"*Gigi!*"

Kayla, Gigi's assistant, snickered into her hand to hide the noise.

"I mean, I could have lied," Gigi replied to her agent. "Is that what you would have preferred?"

"Well, no, but—"

"All you needed was the *no*, Marla. And hey, I just gave you some time to get ahead of the story. You should really be thanking me."

With a wave of her hand in the direction of the phone, Kayla reached over and hit the red button to end the call without warning. At this point, Gigi just didn't care. She had far more important things to handle.

"Don't worry," her assistant said when Gigi turned her back to the room, needing a sense of privacy even if she had finally, *truly* learned that she had none. "In a few days, somebody else will do something that blows up and takes all the attention off you."

Maybe so.

That didn't make this easier.

"Who tipped them off that I was going to be with him that night? We were careful, right? *Extra* careful, Kayla."

Quietly, her assistant replied, "I don't know, Gi."

That was the problem.

Nobody knew anything.

Including *Gigi*.

• • •

Gigi pulled open the hotel's door—the one that guests could use while she had the private elevator access—but the man waiting on the other side was not who she expected it to be. Jensen Todrey screamed casual and confident in his tan, cashmere cable-knit sweater, gray slacks, and matching loafers.

Lifting his attention from the watch on his wrist, the man smiled warmly at Gigi's presence. She couldn't quite say the same as the happiness she had previously felt about who she thought was behind the door quickly melted away. If he noticed, it wasn't apparent.

"Gigi," Jensen greeted, reaching out a hand that cupped her cheek with a soft touch before she could even react. It didn't last long enough for her to tell him to remove his hand, because in the next breath, he dropped his arm back to his side. "You're not busy, are you? I hope I didn't … interrupt."

As he said that, his body tipped to the side slightly right along with his head, like he was trying to get a peek inside the hotel suite behind her. There wasn't anyone in her rooms. Kayla had left a while ago to handle things for Gigi and the agency. A new schedule had to be made for the upcoming appointments and events related to Fashion Week. All things Gigi didn't care to get too involved with beyond showing up like she was told.

She wouldn't say any of that to this man, though.

Instead of answering his question, the first thing out of Gigi's mouth was, "How did you get past the hotel's security … and *mine?*"

Because the three bodyguards that stuck close to her whenever she was on an official outing or working had a room two doors down from her suite and should have been called before *anyone*—but especially this man—was allowed up to see Gigi. That was the rules.

Jensen laughed, waving a hand like it wasn't a big deal. "My name is … recognizable, you could say. I pulled a favor with the hotel manager. And besides, we're friends, right? You don't need to be screening me if I come for a visit."

Her brow lifted. "Everyone gets screened. Even my mother."

Accordingly, if they were on her list of people she approved, then the screening process moved a lot faster. Jensen, however, certainly was not on that list. And as she hadn't heard a thing about or from this man since the day she was made to go on a lunch date with him like a piece of arm candy to show off, she had assumed whatever he wanted from her was over.

Wasn't it?

Apparently not.

It didn't sit well with Gigi.

"Huh."

Gigi kept a tight hold on the edge of the door, refusing to move even an inch in the doorway lest this man think she was inviting him inside. "If you went through the trouble of getting up here to see me today, why didn't you just have a call put through to my room?"

Jensen shrugged, his dark eyes raking over her body and lingering on the low dip of the flowy dress at her chest. She had the strangest urge to fix the delicate, loose material so that it covered her a little better, but she held back. Her body had been put on display more times than she cared to count in a variety of different ways—she wasn't ashamed of her curves or her freckled skin or the way she looked naked in front of the camera. In fact, she kind of loved it. If anything, it taught her how to love herself and she owned that shit.

This man, though?

She didn't want him looking at her at all. Because he did it in such a way that made her feel like he was *appraising* her. Not appreciating. Simply appraising.

"I was going to do that," he said, wagging a finger at her and grinning, "but then you had a little issue this week, didn't you? The magazine articles, I mean."

Gigi cleared her throat but kept her gaze locked on the man still trying to get a peek over her shoulder. "The lies, yes. What about them? Why would that stop you from calling instead of just showing up like this?"

"It is, then?"

"Pardon?"

"*Lies.* You have no connection to Andino Marcello's enforcer ... no secret love child you've kept hidden for the better part of a half of a decade?"

His chuckles and playful expression said he was just making light of the situation, but the sharp way he surveyed her face as he laid out the recent crap from the tabloids told her something else, too. He was fishing for something. What, she didn't know.

Jensen didn't actually wait for Gigi to reply to his question, and instead, he barreled right ahead with, "They did have pictures of the two of you, though. See, that's why I didn't call. I was hoping we might have another lunch ... or you might let me take you out to do something before you get too busy with what you have coming up. But if you're involved with—"

"I'm not in a place to be dating at all," Gigi said, carefully choosing each word she spoke. "I met up with someone I didn't know at a bar and look at what happened. I really can't afford that kind of attention right now with Fashion Week coming up. I would rather every interview I do leading up to my walk is more focused on the designer I'll be wearing and less on who is in my bed at night. If you understand, I mean."

Another dry laugh left the man. "Of course. "

"I'm sorry." Taking one step back into the hotel, Gigi started to close the door, telling Jensen at the same time, "And I'm sure my agent would be happy to deal with anything else you need—she did handle all of that the first time around, right?"

Jensen tipped his chin up, cocking a brow. Clearly, her subtle shot wasn't missed by the man. "She did; even if it didn't work out entirely well."

"Yeah, well, that happens some—"

Ding.

Gigi was too far back in the doorway to see who came out of the elevator when it dinged to say the doors had opened to the floor. Jensen, on the other hand, glanced to the side and just like that, it was as if a blank sheet had fallen over his features, giving nothing away. No recognition, emotion, or otherwise. Footsteps approached from down the hallway, but the man still standing in her doorway simply turned back to her with a smile.

"I guess you were expecting to be busy, hmm?" Jensen nodded her way once and then turned in the same direction of the approaching footsteps like he might leave. "I'll be seeing you, Gigi Rey."

She opened her mouth to say *no*, he wouldn't. Lev passed the man at the same time, keeping her quiet as she watched the two men stare each other down before the one she had been expecting finally looked her way. Without a word, Gigi stepped back from the door and let Lev pass her by to enter the hotel suite.

Jensen only smiled.

She closed the door knowing … this wasn't over.

• • •

"What was he doing here?"

"What?" Gigi asked while she dug through the mini-fridge stocked with her favorite vitamin water.

"*Jensen Todrey*," Lev said, stressing the man's name like it was shit in his mouth. "What the fuck was he doing here?"

Cracking open the cold bottle, Gigi turned to face the man who was still standing near the closed door instead of further inside the hotel room. As if he might need to go back out there and handle something.

Why did she like that idea?

Not the time, Gi.

Right.

"You ask that like I'm supposed to know why he just showed up," Gigi said, "but I don't, and he rubs me all wrong, anyway. I hope he doesn't come back."

That had Lev's attention, making his blue gaze cut from the door to her in an instant. "Why?"

"I don't know … it's just a feeling I get when he's around. He doesn't say anything that screams bad or whatever, but yeah. It's a feeling. Silly, I know—"

"*Not* silly," Lev interjected fast, his tone offering no room for argument. "That's called instinct, babe. That's your mind and body's way of alerting you to the fact shit ain't right. Be it with someone or *something*. You should listen to that, okay?"

Her gaze drifted back to the door, and while Jensen was gone, her nerves still hadn't entirely settled. Even sipping from the cool vitamin water, flavored lightly like sweet strawberries, wasn't enough to make the strange pressure in her chest go away. "He asked about you."

Lev stiffened on the spot, his arms flexing like straining coils when he crossed them over his chest. "Did he now?"

"Named your boss ... or the boss the tabloids say you have. *Mafia*."

"Word to the wise?"

Gigi arched a brow. "Try me."

"Keep all of that out of your mouth unless you don't have a choice, sweetheart. It's better for everybody. *You*, most importantly."

"Should that feel like a threat?"

"No, a warning from someone who knows all too well what happens when you get involved with something you think you understand ... but really know nothing about it at the end of the day. That's all."

"So, you're not going to talk about—"

Lev sighed, his jaw working with a tic like he was chewing over his next words. "That's why we're here, right?"

"Are you?" she asked, holding tighter to the bottle like it might ground her or keep her settled. "Are you here to *really* talk, Lev? Because from what I know, there's a lot of shit you didn't want to talk to me about before. The only reason why you would want to now is because the tabloids didn't give you a choice. Right?"

He stared hard at her from the other side of the room. Gigi didn't move, more than willing to take the intensity of this man if only he *said the right things*. He was so good at that every other time they were together. He did it without effort, and it never felt dishonest. She was trying to give him the chance to do the same thing now.

"Arely, you mean," Lev finally murmured. "My daughter. That's what you really want to ask. So, *ask*, Gigi. Ask me about my kid."

"I don't really know what to ask, I guess. I just—"

"She's five and a half and starts kindergarten in September. Can't fucking wait. We've got a whole countdown going on and everything. I've had custody since she was about six months old." Lev kept talking, but Gigi was doing the math in her head, realizing he gained custody of his child around the time they first met. If he noticed her distraction, he didn't say. "I wasn't trying to hide her from you back then, *or now*. Let me make that clear, okay? I had every intention of telling you about her at the bar—even had a picture of her in an outfit she picked out that day. Thought you'd think it was cute because she was all done up in daisies. Even had daisy barrettes in her hair."

Oh.

Because of the little daisy tattoo on the back of her neck. A simple flower, yes ... but her favorite.

"But you didn't tell me," Gigi said quietly.

She couldn't even hide the hurt in her voice, or how it broke at the end. She *tried* ... God, she did, but it still came out. Because it did fucking hurt that he hadn't thought he could trust her with just the knowledge of his child.

"When was I supposed to fit it in, sweetheart?" Lev asked, opening his arms wide to the room. "You're just ... *fuck*, you show up, and it's like I get so wrapped in you. And then I'm stuck trying to figure out when I should slip in the fact I have a kid. Between the drinks and the darts or the blowjob in the backseat? *When*?"

"Lev—"

"What did you want me to say ... hey, around the same time we met, I found out I had a kid with a chick I used to hook up with, but she didn't even tell me. No, she gave my kid to someone else and then shot herself up with enough drugs to overdose? That would have really helped the mood, huh? *Fucking hell.*"

He had just given her a lot of information, and Gigi decided to absorb it before she spoke again. He didn't mind, simply continued on saying, "Yeah, I wanted to tell you. She's the love of my life—like I didn't even know I wanted kids and then there she was. *Mine.* She's all I had so the second she came into my life, I made sure she was my whole world. Do you think I didn't want to share that with you? She's *important.* Yeah, I wanted you to know how much. I just ... fucked up."

Lev shook his head and dragged a shaking hand down his clean-shaved throat as he muttered, "When I first got her, it was a mess. I didn't even know how to be a dad. I had social services up my ass on every fucking aspect. You remember the old building manager?"

Gigi nodded. "A little."

"She helped me all the time. And her granddaughter, too. It's a lot to explain. Forgive me for not knowing how to do that."

Huh.

"I saw her once," Gigi admitted because she had just realized it herself.

"What?"

"The day I was leaving for Paris; you were moving out of your apartment, but when I stopped to say goodbye, you weren't there. Your place was almost cleared out. Some girl—she came out of the manager's apartment—asked me what I was doing or something ... I can't remember exactly what she said. She was holding a little girl. Black curly hair. Big blue eyes. I thought it was her kid, but it wasn't, was it?"

"That was my Arely, yeah. Nessa helped me a lot. Still does."

My Arely.

It wasn't lost on her how he spoke about his daughter. Or the way he smiled when he said his child was the love of his life. His adoration shined through so much that she could feel it in her own chest.

"Say something," Lev said quietly. "Please."

"Why?"

"What?"

"Why do you want me to say something at all? Does it matter what I think or—"

"I ..." Lev blinked, his arms falling loosely to his sides when he said, "It shouldn't because we weren't doing anything serious, but it doesn't *feel* that way, does it?"

Exactly.

He said what she was scared to.

"Could I meet her? Arely ... would you let me meet her? I mean, I know we'd have to be careful and everything."

"We were careful last time, too, right?"

"*Lev.* We don't even know how they found me."

"*We?*"

"Sorry ... Kayla, she's part of my team. My assistant."

Lev nodded. "Huh."

"Anyway, she helps with planning things like me getting out for a night. We've done it before with no one any wiser. Why would this time be different? I didn't even bring security."

She *was* careful, it went without saying.

He laughed deeply. "Hey, I was kidding. If you want to meet my kid, then, yeah. Of course. We can figure something out. Shit is just really ... complicated outside of these four walls, Gigi. And I can't get into all of that right now."

"But will you someday?"

Lev glanced upward at the ceiling, almost like he was praying, before his attention came back to her and he shrugged. "Someday. I mean, I came here today, didn't I? It's not like I have to be—we don't owe each other anything. Except I'm trying here because ... well, I'm really not sure why."

She thought she might know.

"Us, maybe."

"*Us*? That's fast, babe."

"No ... what I mean is that it's a thing. Or it *could be*. You just said it, Lev. Even if it is in a different way. It still means the same thing."

Her heart kickstarted at the admission; at the fact she had finally said it out loud. She put it into the universe and made it *real*.

Lev shifted from foot to foot, staring at her from where he stood *way too far away* after all of that. In a blink, he changed all of it, striding across the room and making her breaths pick up speed the closer he came. Until one of his hands palmed the side of her throat, and the other pulled her body close to his. One of his arms wrapped her tight. That sinful mouth of his found hers with a slow kiss that set her alight.

Hearts on fire.

But it felt right, too.

So right.

NINETEEN

"THIS IS ... more public than I expected it to be for this," Gigi admitted at Lev's left.

"Oh?"

"I keep expecting someone to pop out with a fucking camera."

Lev laughed and muffled it by pressing a quick kiss to the top of Gigi's head. "Nobody is popping out of anywhere with *anything*, I promise. Not today."

He grinned and stroked her lower back where his hand had been resting from the moment she stepped out of the black SUV and greeted him at his daughter's daycare. The *one* place that, so far, had yet to be picked up by the paps. Or maybe they did know about it, but bylaws kept them at a distance where their presence was made pointless.

Either way, it worked. He promised Gigi she could meet his daughter, and he made sure that happened—or *would*, soon. Today.

She had been right that day in her hotel suite a week earlier when she called him out on everything he *wasn't* saying. They were doing something together even if they hadn't put labels on it.

It didn't matter.

Gigi could become someone important in his life. They were already working on it, after all. His daughter *was* the most important thing in his life. It felt right to, at the very least, allow those two things to meet in a way that was safe and appropriate.

Plus, Lev called in reinforcements for the day. After all, what good was being an enforcer for someone like Andino Marcello if he didn't occasionally pull some weight of his own? Currently, another enforcer of his boss's that he trusted—and liked well enough—was posted to watch his daughter during the day. An extra man came along for today, too, just because Lev asked.

The men would make sure anyone who even looked funny wasn't getting anywhere near close enough to take a picture or ask a question. Never mind someone causing a scene. While he had been concerned about keeping his private life *away* from the mob, when he—and his kid—got splashed across the tabloids, the guys he worked alongside within the Marcello organization didn't even act bothered. Not that he had a kid, or that she'd been kept quiet.

If anything, the guys seemed to understand.

Besides the enforcers, Gigi was accompanied by a bodyguard who didn't even speak to Lev. Not that he gave a fuck. The guy stayed out of the way and that was really all Lev cared about at this point.

Other parents had started to gather at the front walkway of the daycare—that also acted as a pre-k program for kids like Lev's daughter that would be starting school soon—but none of them paid him or Gigi any mind.

Maybe they didn't recognize her given the large, opaque sunglasses she had arrived wearing, alongside a matching black sunhat that kept her face shaded. She kept it simple with skinny jeans, a large tote bag that hung off her bare shoulder, and a strapless top that showed off just a touch of her tummy and gave him access to the soft skin of her lower back.

Beautiful, of course.

He expected nothing less.

Gigi glanced his way. "This is ... okay, right? Like you don't mind—"

"Gigi, we wouldn't be here if I did."

That was that.

She nodded once and smiled. "Yeah?"

"Yeah, babe. No worries."

A lot of shit around their current circumstances might not be normal or average, but some of it still was. Like the fact that they were humans navigating ... whatever this was. *Together.* They both had lives, and she wanted to see his. So, he was showing her.

Or a part of it, anyway.

Happy yells, stomping feet, and childish laughter had Lev dropping his hand from Gigi's lower back as the older kids started to flood out of the daycare's front doors. He stepped forward, sweeping the crowd of kids that were allowed to leave to meet their waiting guardians ahead of the younger children who had to be checked out inside. Soon enough, the bright yellow headband with the large sunflower that Arely chose that morning to go with her matching dress and leggings caught his eye.

She was already coming his way.

Arms wide open.

Smile *huge*.

"Daddy!"

"Hey, baby," Lev greeted, stepping forward and kneeling down to catch his daughter that darted away from the crowd of kids. Her little backpack jumped with every step she took, and her sneakers lit up with pink and white lights along the soles. The high ponytail she asked for that morning swung back and forth, wild black ringlet curls bouncing every which way. Once she was close enough, his girl jumped and landed right into his waiting arms. He hugged her close, feeling her little arms tighten around his neck as her legs hooked around his chest. "How was your day, huh?"

"Good. I got a picture I made."

"I have a picture," he corrected.

Arely rolled her eyes, already sick of the new thing he was trying to do to correct the way she sometimes spoke. "*Same thing.*"

"But one is saying it right and one is—"

"I made a picture, Daddy."

Well ...

She didn't say it the first way.

Or his way.

But she wasn't wrong, either.

"Can't wait to see it," he told her, pressing quick kisses across her grinning, pinked cheek. The tighter she hugged him, the better he felt. It wasn't like he had ever told anyone before, but he missed his kid every second that he wasn't with her. "Love you, kiddo. Missed you."

Arely grinned wide. "Love you, too."

"So, hey ..."

Trailing off, Lev dragged in a deep breath as he started to turn on the walkway to face the woman who had been waiting patiently and *quietly* to meet the little girl he held. Arely wasn't looking for Gigi to be standing there when they turned around, but he was. Something twisted hard in his chest when he found Gigi shifting from foot to foot and chewing on her lower lip while she fidgeted with her manicure.

Like she was *nervous*.

She shouldn't be.

"Somebody wanted to meet you—say hi and stuff," Lev told Arely who was now trying to pull her backpack off while he balanced her in his arms. God, he sounded like a fucking idiot. "She's a friend. I thought she could have supper with us tonight, maybe?"

"Huh?" Arely peered up from her bag, and her gaze landed right on Gigi who had pulled off her sunglasses and smiled hesitantly.

"Hi, Arely. I'm Gigi. Your dad told me so much about you. I wanted to say hello."

From his arms, his daughter quieted. He thought maybe Arely would look to him, like she usually did, for direction but she didn't. Her stare continued to linger on the woman just two feet away before Arely prattled out, "I like your hat."

Gigi's smile bloomed in the best way. "Yeah?"

"Like that show, Daddy. *Miss Poppy*—you know?"

Lev nodded. "Yeah, same kind of hat."

He shot Gigi a wink.

She relaxed a bit.

Setting his girl to the walkway, Lev kept a tight hold on Arely's tiny hand. She stared up at Gigi, her brow knotting like maybe she recognized the face looking back at her. But again, she simply rattled out something random.

As sweet as it was.

"You're *very* pretty," Arely whispered.

Gigi let out a breathless, soft laugh and dropped down to be at eye level with Arely. Reaching out a hand, she brushed

one of Arely's curls back over her shoulder. "And so are you—
I wish I had curls like yours."

"They *always* tangle."

"Yeah?"

Arely shrugged. "But I like 'em."

"Me, too."

His daughter tipped her head back, meeting his smile with
her own when she asked, "Gigi is coming for supper?"

Ah, so she had heard him.

"She is, baby."

"Okay!"

That was that.

Kids, man.

• • •

"Which color do you think would work?"

At Gigi's question, Lev shot a peek over his shoulder to the
girls currently huddled over the pile of items on the table. Or
rather, *Gigi's* things that Arely had managed to convince the
woman to let her play with. Makeup, a bottle of nail polish,
and a few other things that seemed foreign to Lev because he
didn't even know what they were called.

Women.

It wasn't lost on him how comfortable his daughter was
with Gigi, though. Or how easily they bonded over simple,
pretty things. Not to mention, that he *liked* it.

"That one," Arely said, pointing at something with glitter.

"Why?"

"It's *sparkly.*"

"Guess I should have known that, huh?" Gigi asked,
looking Lev's way as though she knew he was watching them.
"Somebody is all about the sparkles."

"And yellow," he added from his spot at the stove. "*Loves*
yellow. You saw her room."

The potatoes he had boiling would go well with the cheesy
chicken currently baking in the oven, and it was one of a
handful of things his kid didn't complain too much about.
Pickiness was a real thing with kids. A real thing he didn't

appreciate when he spent an hour or two cooking just to have Arely look at the food like he'd taken a dump on her plate.

But what could he do?

As he was told, it would pass.

"And pink, too," Arely added, her tone offended. Likely because nobody had asked her. "I like pink!"

"Speaking of *pink* ..." Gigi's amused tone didn't translate to Lev.

Lev cleared his throat, shoulders tensing as he put his attention back on the boiling potatoes. "As in the color or the ... *noun*?"

Because in his life, pink was both.

A color.

And him.

To some people, anyway.

"What?" Arely asked.

"Nothing, baby."

"Hey," Gigi said, the sound of her fingernails tapping a beat to the table echoing in the kitchen, "how about you go find me that singing mirror you told me about, and I will show you how we put this lip gloss on, hmm?"

"*Yes!*"

A chair scraped hard against the floor before pounding feet followed, racing across the floor of his townhouse. Lev still didn't move, even when the creak of a chair sounded, and Gigi approached from behind until she was leaning against the counter beside him.

"Sorry, I didn't mean to put you on the spot. I was just making a joke."

He waved his free hand, muttering, "It's not you asking. It's her."

Setting her chin into her palm, Gigi peered up at him through thick, dark lashes. "What do you mean?"

"All she knows about my work is that her dad looks after an important man named Andino. And that's really it. She doesn't understand that I have a whole moniker and persona when I step out of this house."

"Makes sense."

"Does it? Sometimes, it feels like I'm just lying. Daddy gets to be her hero, right? But what about when she figures out her daddy is really just a paid bodyguard for one of the biggest criminals in North America?"

Gigi let out a *woosh* of air. "You're going that deep?"

He laughed, as weak as it was. "I mean, someday she will."

"*Lev.*"

"Hmm?"

He kept his attention on the boiling pot. It was made more difficult when Gigi reached out to drag the fingernails on her thumb and forefinger across his cheek and up to his jawline.

"Don't those men have kids, too?"

Lev did look at her then, only to find her wide eyes waiting for him to answer expectantly. "I mean, they do. What does that—"

"Do you think their kids understand what they are or do? Do you think their little girls wake up one day and hate their fathers when all they knew was *love*? I mean, I assume they love their kids. Why wouldn't they?"

"People just see criminals, Gigi. And it's ... fair."

"That doesn't change that they're also people who have lives; people they love; *homes* they go to at the end of the day. Because that's the thing, right? All she knows from you is love. Even I can see that. This whole place, this home ... it's just like a little world you've created for you and her. Worry about what you're building *inside* here with her and less about what's out there. I promise, this home and you are what she'll remember the most."

"Did your dad—"

"Never knew him. And that's not okay. Dads are so important to their daughters. More than they realize. You're the first person she is going to look to when she's learning how to let other people—*boys*—treat her, you know?"

Lev blinked, heavy in his chest again. That seemed to be happening a lot lately. "I'll keep it in mind."

"Do," she replied. "It's the only thing that matters."

Without waiting for a reply, she straightened to her full height, leaned in, and gave him a soft kiss on the underside of his jaw as little footsteps echoed from the hallway nearing the kitchen. He turned his head to capture her lips with his own, their kiss slow and steady, building one stroke at a time, until she pulled away first.

Just in time, too.

Her pink cheeks told the truth when Arely ran back into the kitchen with her mirror in hand. The toy was already singing one of the three songs it had prerecorded.

"Found it!"

"Awesome," Gigi said, her voice lighter than before. "You good?"

Lev nodded. "Perfect. And hey?"

"Yeah?"

Too quiet for his kid to hear, he asked, "Are you staying tonight?"

"I mean, I didn't plan—"

"You don't have to, I just wondered."

"I only need to make a call. Kayla can handle the rest."

Lev grinned. "A whole team at your beck and call, huh?"

"It's not always to my benefit."

Well, Lev didn't know much about that.

"Stay tonight," he murmured.

Gigi turned so her back was to the cupboard. Staring down at the floor, she folded her arms over her chest while the noise of Arely climbing back into her chair echoed through the kitchen. "I will. But will it confuse—"

"She's going to be up and gone by seven. Nessa is picking her up for daycare. She works there, too, so it helps when my schedule doesn't always work out for me to take her. I think you can stay in bed until then, right?"

"Well—"

"I can make sure you do," he added, his tone dipping lower.

That pink flush came back to Gigi's cheeks in a flash. It had him laughing, even when her arm swung out and the back of her hand smacked his side.

"You're terrible."

"Hey, I'm just making this even."

"What did I do for it to need to be *even*?" she asked. "And since when are we keeping score?"

"We've always kept score, and you know it. Also, you're

about to introduce my kid to lip gloss. *Sparkly* lip gloss. That is a hell even men like me don't deserve."

Gigi pursed her lips, nodding. "That's fair."

Yep.

• • •

Lev's gaze drifted between the phone in his hand—and the last text his boss sent—and the little girl snoring away in her bed. His mind, however, bounced back and forth like a ping pong ball from one thing to the next.

The question his daughter asked as he put her to bed; the woman down the hall, showering in his master bathroom; the man waiting for a response from him.

"Will Gigi come back to play again?"

Lev hadn't known what to say. So instead of fumbling about like an idiot with the wrong words, he simply told his daughter, "I sure hope so."

Because he did.

And that was terrifying.

He was a man who had spent the majority of his life, but certainly the last few, in a bubble of privacy and protection. Mostly for his kid's sake. Gigi wasn't quite the same when her entire life was focused on being a public figure.

How should they deal with that?

He didn't know.

As for Andino ...

That was a different matter.

Lev stepped out of his daughter's room, closing the door as he went to dull any noise from down the hall, so she would have a decent sleep. Frankly, a hurricane wouldn't wake that kid up, so he wasn't exactly too worried.

He put his attention back on the phone in his hand, and Andino's last text. It simply read *Marco Farginpane is flying in next week from Cali for a sit down with me. His new business partner will apparently also be making an appearance. Your presence was requested. Specifically. Be at the restaurant tomorrow first thing. We have a problem.*

Lev didn't need Andino's last sentence. He already knew

they had problems. Shit, he saw that coming when he ran
into Jensen Todrey at Gigi's hotel suite.

The fucking *asshole*. Something was off with that guy.
Beyond the obvious. Tonight just wasn't the time for him to
deal with it.

Sure thing, boss, Lev typed back.

Andino didn't reply.

That was fine.

Lev's attention went to the last thing he had to deal with
for the evening. The woman who was currently naked and
wet in his shower. No doubt, what remained unsaid between
the two of them about his job for Andino and how it related
to the men she had been having lunch with would soon be all
out in the open.

He *had* to tell her.

It was only fair.

Right then, though, he only had one thing on his mind.
And that was getting as close to Gigi as he possibly could
while he had the chance because it had become apparent that
the private moments they had together were far and few
between.

He wasn't wasting tonight.

Not one second.

Gigi was humming a tune he didn't recognize when he
stepped into the steam-filled bathroom. He didn't surprise
her—couldn't with the antifog glass surrounding the large
shower. She had a perfectly fine view of him coming into the
room and stripping down to join her without even asking.
Just like he had the best view of her soapy breasts, and the
way the suds trailed down over her curves and the length of
her legs.

How this godly creature wanted anything to do with the
likes of him, Lev would never understand. But she did and he
was determined to give her anything she asked.

Or as much as he could.

At that moment, he knew exactly what she wanted. It was
all in her eyes. How she stared at him when her gaze drifted
from the dark hair dusting his chest straight down to his cock
that sprung out from his boxer-briefs, *already hard*, when he

shoved them to the floor. Her throat flexed with a swallow, and that teasing tongue of hers licked at the seam of her lips when he stepped out of the pile of clothes.

Lev entered the shower, the sting of the hot water barely even registering to his senses as he passed right under the heavy spray to get to the woman he wanted. She was already reaching for him, too. The fluffy loofah she'd been using with his bar of soap hit the floor the second his hands found her wrists.

In a breath, he had her against the wall. Pinned with her hands on both sides of her head, her pretty lips parted for his promise of a kiss. He nipped her lip instead, not quite ready to taste her when he hadn't even taken the time to properly admire her wet and supple and smelling like *him*.

That did something to Lev. A *good* kick to the gut, if there was such a thing. The fact she used his soap, despite it being a crisp, *male* scent ... it made his dick harder.

Pulling her hands higher to the wall, he held them both with only one hand. His other explored *her*. Fingertips gliding down her cheek, over her quivering chin, and then to her lips where she parted them to take the digits in to suck.

"Are we doing this?" he asked, voice husky with need but he *had* to maintain that control. For just a second longer. "This—*us*. Are we?"

The pad of his thumb dragged down her bottom lip after he pulled his fingers from her mouth, so she could speak.

"Yeah, Lev. We're doing this."

That drove him crazy, too.

Not that she knew.

Without prompting, she told him, "I'm on the shot. I want *you* tonight. I want you in me ... just you, *bare*."

Oh, he wanted that, too.

More than she understood.

His hand kept its exploration over the curve of her right breast and across her nipple that had hardened into a tight peak. Her soft hiss when his thumb flicked her nipple had him grinning, but the way her stomach clenched when his fingers danced lower to her navel had his mouth watering.

Already, he could hear the way she'd moan. See her in the

throes of her first orgasm of the night. Feel her squeezing the come right out of his dick once he got her on top and let her work his cock how she liked the best in his bed.

"*Nobody* touches you but me," he murmured, his gaze snapping up to meet hers. "Nobody, Gigi. You hear me? I swear to God, I'll fucking kill any man who puts his hands on you the way I do."

If that declaration scared her, she didn't show it. It wasn't a lie, either.

She dragged in a ragged breath, her soapy tits rising and falling heavily. "Then please touch me."

His fingers tapped just above the hood of her clit, the wet sound bouncing off the walls and then drowning in the rushing water. "Here?"

"*There.* Everywhere. Just touch me."

How could he deny her?

Especially looking like she did.

Impossible.

Lev's hand dipped between her widening thighs at the same time he closed the distance between them to get the other thing he knew she wanted. *His kiss.* She moaned a prayer against his lips as his fingers worked to fill her pussy. Two fingers, then three.

"*Wider,*" he urged.

She did, parting those thighs, and her mouth, and even her eyes, too. All of her opened to him, and he found it overwhelming. Her sounds, the way her lips trembled against his with each of his kisses, and even the softness of her pussy grinding into his hand for more.

The speed at which he went from stuffing her full of his fingers to lifting her leg to hook around his hip, so he could fill her with something else shocked even him. He just couldn't wait any longer, the need to be inside her clawing at his chest in the worst goddamn way.

The relief when he slid into her tight cunt was *everything.* That pressure building in his chest exploded in a hard grunt that vibrated along her cheek.

Slick.

Hot.

Satin.

She was heaven.

Fucking her was his salvation.

It had to be.

Nothing felt like this.

"What the fuck are you doing to me, Gigi?"

"*Lev*," she breathed.

"Again. Say my name again. *Sing for me.*"

She did.

The harder he fucked her, the better she sounded. He finally let her hands go from above her head, and she used those fingernails to send him flying even higher when she scored burning lines down his shoulders. Then, he had her lifted against the shower wall, legs spread even wider so he could fuck her deeper. One hand at her throat, and the other leaving a bruise on her thigh from how tight he held her.

As tight as her pussy was around his dick.

Christ.

Every thrust was another shot straight to his heart. Until there was nothing left of him to give, and the only sound ringing in his ears were her soft whispers, soothing and sweet and *oh, so* pleased.

Fuck what waited for him.

He was just fine here.

TWENTY

LEV DECIDED one of the best ways to start a morning was with Gigi riding his dick like it was the last thing she was ever going to do. He vaguely remembered rolling over to see his phone flashing with a text that must have come in over the night while they were sleeping, and after checking it, decided there wasn't much point in going back to sleep when it was five AM, and his kid would be up soon.

Instead, he rolled around to wake Gigi up because why not? Knowing the kind of day he was facing with Andino demanding he come in ASAP, well ... he deserved *this*.

There was nothing quite like staring up at a woman while she worked his cock to get herself off. Gigi made it even better. She fucked a little violent, he learned. Especially when she was the one in control, chasing what she needed.

She was a hell of a sight.

Her messy hair. Lips swollen and pink from his kisses and bites. Skin reddened from his rough hands grabbing and holding her the way she liked the most. The sheen of sweat slicking her flesh tasted like salt and sex on his tongue when she leaned down close enough to allow him a taste of her.

Her hips swirled and lifted on his length, driving him crazy while above, she watched him through hooded eyes with sharp breaths escaping her trembling lips. Her tits bounced with her wild rhythm while strands of her wavy hair stuck to her face. She kept that pace up until he was panting and squeezing her waist so hard that he was sure he was about to snap this fucking woman in two from forcing back his own orgasm.

If she didn't have his fingerprint-shaped bruises left behind when they were done, then what were they even doing together?

"*Jesus Christ, Gigi* ... get it, babe." How was that his voice? His words came out in a growl that vibrated in his chest with every syllable. The things this woman could make him do were unbelievable. She could turn him from a man to an animal eating out of the palm of her hand with nothing more than her pussy. "Come for me, huh? *Give it to me.*"

"*You,*" she replied in a breathless rush, "*you come.*"

No fucking way.

Not before she did.

Lev wasn't about to let that happen, even if he was letting her take a bit of control this time. Her shaking hand laid flat to his chest while her other hovered just above his mouth. He caught the tips of her fingers between his teeth as one of his hands skimmed around her round ass. She was made up of all sorts of conundrums.

A fat ass.

Tiny waist.

The kind of body men would start wars to possess and here he was, *owning hers.*

It was only once he started massaging the tight hole of her ass with the pad of his thumb, stretching her a little bit before pulling back, that he felt her telltale signs. The way her voice broke on his name, how her shoulders started to shake, and then when her pussy clamped down around his cock when she froze on top of him.

His thumb slipped into her ass at the same time she came. *God.*

Yeah.

Best way to spend a morning.

Gigi was still trying to catch her breath, and every sweep of his hands over her slick flesh drew shudders from her trembling body, when he flipped them over. Spreading her legs wide, and shoving her knees high, his fingers wove with hers overtop her head on the pillow as he took her again.

Slower.

Deeper.

He couldn't get enough of her mouth with his kiss—licking the taste of their sex right from her tongue; swallowing her whimpers and moans with his lips and teeth.

Lev was already high.

Ready to blow.

It took nothing but watching her beneath him for his orgasm to come on strong. He kept his cock deep, her body tight to his, as he emptied his balls in hot spurts.

"*Shit*, babe," he muttered, pulling his cock out enough that he could see how her creamy arousal had mixed with his and streaked down his length. "Holy fuck, look at that pussy ..." He let go of one of her hands. Dragging his thumb through the cum soaking his cock, he brought the slickness up to her throbbing clit to stroke soothing circles that had her hips jerking into his touch while his name fell from her lips in a prayer. "Wanna come again, just like this? With my cum all over your cunt, Gigi?"

Twisting in the messy sheets on the bed, her hand fisting the duvet, she whispered, "Oh, God, *please.*"

Every bit of this made him fucking stupid. In the best way.

He could count the number of times he'd dared to fuck a woman without a condom. And one of those had been in a drunken stupor that resulted in the little girl down the hall. Even so, it just wasn't something he made a point to do barring stupid mistakes he couldn't—and wouldn't—take back. Except now that he'd had Gigi bare, he couldn't imagine fucking her any other way.

It was too good.

Too right.

He made sure she came again, and only then did he roll his weight off of her. Gathering Gigi in his arms to tuck her back flat against his chest while their legs tangled together, he buried his face into the sweaty, sweet-smelling skin of her neck.

"You better wake me up like that the next time I spend the night," she murmured against his arm holding her close. "You can't spoil me like that and then not keep it up, Lev."

His dark laughter echoed in the quiet bedroom. "Noted."

The tips of her fingers ghosted over the veins in his arm, sending chills racing through all of his nerve endings. She turned into a kitten after sex ... soft to the touch, quiet and sleepy, and willing to be adored by him in whatever way he wanted.

And he was about to ruin it.

Because of course.

"It's almost six," he murmured in her ear before kissing the spot right underneath. "I have to get up and around. Get a start before Arely wakes up. Things changed last night."

"What things?"

Well, that wasn't an easy answer.

"Work things," he settled on saying. Gigi stiffened in his hold, but he continued talking, deciding now was the best time to just get it all out there. "Jensen Todrey and the other man at the restaurant—Marco, he comes from California— are in the business of trafficking. *Women*, Gigi. They traffic women, and they're planning on bringing in a lot of skin for the upcoming season of baseball games. I was there that day because my boss wanted a fly on the wall, so to speak ... someone who wouldn't be recognized that could report back on what they were planning."

Air left Gigi in a hard woosh. "Like for prostitution?"

"That's secondary to the main problem right now."

"Which is *what*?"

"Well, let's start with the fact that I've been in the tabloids with you and then end on the note that they've called in a meeting with my boss. And me," he added lower.

"Lev—"

"It'll be handled. It always is."

He was kind of banking on that.

Gigi shivered in his arms, saying lowly, "And you knew this last night?"

"Got the message while I was putting Arely to bed."

"You didn't tell me until this morning?"

"I didn't have to tell you at all, Gigi. And sometimes, that's how it has to work. I can't help it."

That was the mafia. Whether he liked it or not, or she did, he was in this business up to his fucking eyeballs. He didn't need to be told the truth because he already knew.

Lev was in this for life now.

"I'll give you a set of keys—spares for my place. I'll have to take off right after Arely leaves this morning. You can see yourself out, yeah? Lock it up and everything?"

Gigi sighed. "Of course, but ..."

"Hmm?"

"The next few weeks are going to be crazy for me with Fashion Week coming up, and I don't know when we'll be able to get five minutes to—"

That's what she was worried about?

Hell.

Lev had Gigi rolled over to face him in a breath, and in the next, he pressed a quick kiss to her lips, quieting her and hopefully her fears when he promised against her mouth, "We'll figure it out. All of it."

It was the best he could do.

• • •

The week leading up to the meeting between Andino and his business partner was spent planning. Lev's least favorite part of work for his boss, really. He liked being told what to do and how he was to do it. *Not* being the one who had to decide things, but he appreciated that he was allowed in on it at all. He knew to men inside Andino's *famiglia*, it was an important distinction that their boss made about his personal enforcer.

So, fuck what Lev thought. His boss wanted him to be involved hands-on with the meeting and the plans, and that's what he did.

Marco Farginpane stepped into the quiet Brooklyn pizzeria—another business owned by the Marcello family— and took in the traditional decor and checkered floor with an eye of disinterest. Andino had made sure the place was closed for the day. There wasn't even a chef in the back to cook, or a girl working the floor to bring them drinks for the meeting.

This was clearly all business.

They weren't here to entertain.

In a tailored suit and shined leather loafers, Marco seemed entirely unbothered that he had just taken a very long flight to New York, and the man he came to meet wasn't even standing to greet him. Andino, that was.

Not that it was anything unusual. In the five and a half

years that Lev had worked for his boss, he could count on one hand the number of people Andino would stand to greet like they were his equal. It wasn't very many. Marco had a very large hand in the business of smuggling drugs—and handled a mass amount of smuggling into and *out of* the country for Andino's organization—it wasn't like the guy was a little fish in the ocean. In Andino's eyes, however, he was just a means to an end and not worth very much when someone else could do the job just as well. Or, that's what he explained to Lev over the past week.

Lev, on the other hand, wasn't sitting at the table in the middle of the restaurant's floor like his boss. No, he stood directly behind Andino, dressed in his usual black button-down and slacks, his leather shoulder holster clearly visible with the Eagle on his left side, and the knife he liked on his right. With his hands folded at his back, he kept his gaze locked on the man at the other side of the room.

And the guy behind him.

Jensen Todrey.

While Marco seemed cool and calm, Jensen wasn't quite the same. His glare leveled on the enforcer behind Andino, recognition flaring in his eyes and growing darker when Lev dared to wink at the asshole.

He didn't know what the Revver's owner wanted with Gigi, but it was something. Definitely. There was a sick part of Lev that took great satisfaction in the fact Jensen wouldn't be getting *shit* from Gigi. Not with Lev in the picture, anyway.

"Andino," Marco said, not *unkindly*. Stepping forward, the man waved at the table, and the two empty chairs opposite to Andino's seat. "Good to see we could at least come together and agree on one thing here."

In front of Lev, Andino tipped his head to the side a bit. "And what is that *thing*, Marco?"

"Your man there, of course. I'm glad to see he's also in attendance here considering you had no problem sticking him like a little rat in a private business meeting between me and an associate. It's good that for this time, he's out in the open where we can all see and know him for what he really is."

That comment made Lev bristle.

All fucking over, too.

As though Andino could sense the tension radiating from Lev, his boss raised a single hand high for him to see. A silent acknowledgment that he should remain still and quiet in his spot. They were far beyond a time when Andino needed to give him actual, verbal orders. He knew what the man wanted with nothing more than a gesture.

Andino chuckled dryly. "I'm sorry—did you demand a meeting with me and then fly all the way here just to insult my personal enforcer, Marco? Because we both could have saved time and finished that business over a phone call. Do you want a seat? Take one. Your ... little friend there, too. Why not?"

"Little," Jensen scoffed. "Like I don't have a name in this city—"

"You have fuck all in this city compared to me," Andino interjected sharply, his finger pointing like a gun at Jensen. "You *are* fuck all in this city standing next to me. And if you think your schemes have flown under the radar of my *famiglia*, try again, Mr. Todrey. Nothing happens in this city without me knowing about it. Have a fucking seat."

Marco gestured a hand toward the table, and Jensen didn't hesitate to step forward and move for the chair on the left. He wasn't kind about yanking the seat out and dropping into it, folding his arms over his chest like a petulant child might when they were being punished.

Lev would have laughed.

It wasn't really his style, though.

Marco followed soon after, albeit with less attitude and a whole lot of indifference. It was only once the two men were seated that Marco looked Lev's way again.

"Is he not good enough to sit with us?"

That time, Lev spoke up before Andino could, replying, "I can't be bothered to lower myself to your level even if it is just to sit at a table together. Keep it in mind."

Marco's cheek twitched at that comment.

Lev simply smiled back.

To the left, Jensen made a disgusted noise as he looked

Lev over. "What on earth she could possibly want with *you*, I don't know. You're glorified *muscle*. A pawn in a game you probably don't even know how to play."

Andino snapped his fingers twice, drawing all eyes back to him when he said, "Speak to my man one more time, and I will have him remove your tongue before you leave this place. Is that clear, Jensen? The only reason you're even here today is I afforded that respect to Marco *because* of our previous business dealings and nothing more. You are a pissant I could have crushed with *one* phone call—understand that."

Clearly tired of the back and forth between the men, Marco folded his arms over his chest and leaned back in the chair. Appearing more relaxed, and perhaps even ready to talk as that's what this entire meeting was supposed to be about, he said to Andino, "And yet you showed me no respect when you slid into my business by having your man spy on my meeting, Marcello. How am I supposed to respond to that? I mean, I know how *you* would respond. Is that what you wanted for me to do?"

"When you come into my city to do business," Andino replied, the arrogance dripping off his every word, "you forfeit your right to privacy when there is even the slightest possibility it might affect my organization or our dealings here. This isn't the first time I've made that clear to men far larger than you, Marco."

"Right, right. How silly of me to think I could come to New York and simply *talk* to a potential business partner without you having something to say about it, hmm?"

"Are you trying to say something, or ...?" Andino trailed off, waving a hand at the man across from him. "Because all I heard in that is, *I do what I want.* And no, you don't when you're on my territory. If I haven't made that clear yet, New York is mine, and I decide what does or does not happen here. Including you, your business, and that stupid fuck right there," he added, pointing at Jensen but still staring at Marco. "Who, by the way, is nothing but clout to add to your resume. We both know it. Why did you want this meeting?"

"I *was* going to ask you to back off and let us resume our

dealings without input, and also discuss the little issue of your man being involved with—"

Andino barked out a laugh, straightening in his chair at the same time. "Like *hell*. Something else we could have done over the fucking phone, Marco."

"How is my involvement with Gigi an issue?" Lev asked.

Because that was the important thing he heard. Whether or not his boss did, well that didn't matter to him.

"Lev," Andino murmured over his shoulder, shooting him a look.

"No, that's something I want to hear, boss."

He spoke to Andino but didn't look away from a grinning Jensen. Two more seconds of that and Lev would rip the expression right from the man's fucking face.

"Keep getting in my way," Jensen told him, "and you and the rest of yours will find out exactly why."

Lev took one step forward.

Andino stood from the table faster than Lev could blink, and a palm met his chest hard. Under his breath, his boss said, "Quite enough ... he's worthless and trying to get a reaction. Nothing more. He can't do *shit*." Then, Andino turned back to the table with the same disinterested expression from before as he told Marco, "Safely assume all business between you and I has ... reached its inevitable end. Also know you're no longer welcome to do any dealings in this city. Should I find out you are doing business here, I will have your body dropped into the harbor with cement in your pockets so that nothing will bring you back to the surface. Even the fish need to be fed, after all. Are we clear?"

Marco tipped his chin up, gaze drifting between Andino and Lev before he finally replied, "I can't say that we are, no. You're ending business for what, your man there? Or because you don't like that I do business elsewhere? Foolishness."

"Wrong answer, Marco."

"So be it. Say hello to your wife for me, Andino. I didn't get that invitation in the mail, unfortunately. I have been keeping up, however."

Andino didn't reply.

Marco didn't seem to mind.

The silence between the four men remained throughout the time it took for Marco and Jensen to stand from the table, and then remove their presence from the restaurant altogether. Even then, the only thing Andino said to Lev was, "Take the rest of the day off. Go get your kid and ... do something. Get your mind off this shit. They're not important."

Lev was still staring at the door. "Do you really believe that?"

"I have to. Until they give me a reason otherwise."

Right.

And so far, all they had were words. What good was that, really?

• • •

The week that followed the meeting with Marco and Jensen was quiet. Strangely so. Normal, even, considering Lev returned to handling his business and life like nothing had happened. Andino kept telling him the silence didn't necessarily mean something was about to happen, or that the assholes were planning an attack, but Lev didn't know if that was actually the case.

History told him differently.

He'd had enough time watching Andino's back to know silence after a meeting like the one they had was nothing more than a waiting game. His boss was simply trying to keep him calm because that was better than the chaos of the opposite.

But who was he to say?

"So, is that a no on meeting up tonight, or—"

Gigi's light laughter filtered through the speakers of his Jeep as he navigated the familiar block leading to his daughter's daycare. It was Arely's last week at the place— technically her pre-k graduation was the week before, but she still was attending for the week to make things a little easier on Lev with work.

"I wish I could, I mean ... if you want to come here between a conference call and my next fitting, then you're more than welcome. It's boring, there's going to be way too many people in the hotel, and yeah," she said lamely.

Lev sighed, drumming his fingers to the steering wheel while his thoughts ran wild. She hadn't been lying when she told him things were about to get a lot busier for her. Even their phone calls were constantly interrupted by someone else on her side. He understood that was just her life, and it was something he had to accept but that didn't mean it wasn't frustrating sometimes when all he wanted to do was sneak her away from the watching world.

Especially because his kid kept asking about her.

"When is Gigi coming back, Daddy?"

"Will she bring more lip gloss?"

Typical girl.

Lev loved it.

"Maybe I will," he settled on saying.

"What?"

"Just show up. Five minutes is better than nothing, right?"

The smile in her tone was clear when she replied, "Yeah, right. Say hey to Arely for me when you pick her up, okay? I've got to jump in the shower before my assistant starts bitching that I'm behind on the schedule again."

Lev chuckled. "Will do. Later, babe."

"Bye."

The call ended with a click, replaced by the rolling beat of a hip-hop song he'd been listening to before Gigi called. Now, his fingers drummed to the beat of the song as he closed in on his daughter's daycare. What would usually be a busy street filled with a line of cars and groups of parents waiting for their kids was ten times worse when Lev pulled up on the side street.

It took him all of two seconds to realize why.

The paps had found his kid's school. They were all over the fucking place—like *flies*. Buzzing and annoying, cameras clicking faster when he stepped out of the Jeep with a scowl that he was sure rivaled the fucking Devil's.

What were they doing here?

Gigi's team put out a statement—they were clear on the fact that Arely was *not* her secret love child hidden from the spotlight. Some media outlets apologized for splashing an innocent child's face across the tabloids without an ounce of consideration. Others doubled down on the bullshit. Nonetheless, they had kept their distance.

Until today, it seemed.

"Lev! A question! Or would you rather Pink?" a man shouted at him as he passed the car the guy was sitting on, using the trunk to steady his tripod.

Lev turned to look at the man, asking, "What do you even know about *Pink*, asshole?"

The paparazzo grinned, swinging his camera to take a picture of Lev when he replied, "What kind of dealings does Gigi Rey have with the mob in New York? Are they funding her career, too?"

What the fuck kind of shit—

Lev reached out and snatched the man's camera before whipping the fucking thing right back into the stupid prick's face. The crunch when the camera fell from the asshole's hands to the ground said something broke. *Whoops.*

"Hey, that lens is three thousand—"

"Fuck you and your camera, man."

He could hear the shutters clicking.

The buzz of all the people talking.

"Daddy! *Daddy!*"

Shit.

Swinging around, Lev was able to see through the gathered crowd that the children had finally been let out. There stood his daughter with her little backpack, her eyes wide and scared as she surveyed the scene in front of her.

Everything else disappeared to Lev but his kid. The only thing that he cared about at that moment was getting Arely the hell out of that mess as fast as he could. He darted and dodged the people and the questions being slung at him, including the demand from one of his daughter's educators for a word, to reach Arely and then to make his way back to the Jeep.

By the time he buckled her in, they had swarmed the vehicle.

"Daddy?" she asked from the backseat when he slid into

the front. "Why do they have cameras? Do they know Gigi, too?"

She must have heard someone say Gigi's name. He didn't answer Arely; he was too busy dialing a number on his phone while he navigated the idiots that had flooded the street.

"Andino here," his boss said, the man's voice echoing through the vehicle.

"We need more than one enforcer with Arely because the one who should have been watching her today was nowhere to be seen when I showed up to a half of a dozen assholes with cameras." Although if he was fair, he hadn't given the guy much of a chance to show himself with how fast Lev was in and out of there. He very well could have been inside the school with Arely as the employees of the daycare were all well aware of the tabloid situation and his daughter's need for a bodyguard currently.

Lev shook those thoughts off, adding to his boss on the phone, "... and probably Gigi, too. Maybe more than one, even."

Even if Gigi did have her own security. Lev didn't care. More couldn't hurt if people were going to play stupid games.

Andino, not even missing a beat, asked, "Why?"

"Paparazzi decided to show back up and ask more questions. About business. *Our* business."

"The lawyers—"

"Clearly, they had a reason to come back and ask more questions, Andino. Right out of the blue, too. Because that's not suspicious at all."

"That's fair."

"Yeah. Looks like your partner, or fucking *Jensen*, decided to feed the paps and get them up my ass at the worst possible place. Arely's daycare. Since they hadn't showed up there once, even the day I had Gigi there *with* men posted, but they did today ... it *really* says something. The pricks."

Or *prick*.

Lev couldn't say whether both Jensen and Marco had a hand in today or only one. He did plan on finding out, though.

Andino cleared his throat roughly. "My apologies."

"Appreciate that."

"Well, nobody needs that mess. Even I wouldn't be that much of an asshole. Where is the enforcer that should have been watching Arely?"

"Didn't see him."

Andino hummed darkly. "Well, I'll find him."

Lev swallowed the lump forming in his throat, slightly happy that Arely was quiet in the back seat but also torn the fuck up inside because she was sniffling. Scared. Sad. It was all the fucking same to him, and he hated that he was partly to blame for it.

"Listen, I have been quiet and private with Gigi after that first shitshow and tried to stay out of trouble like you told me."

"You have, I agree. You can't control the spiral, can you?"

"No, but on the real side of things, I like that girl. So, she might stay around. With that said, she's got important shit coming up. *Big* stuff, Andino."

"Mmm, Fashion Week, huh?" Andino *eh'd* under his breath, adding quickly, "My wife did a whole search and showed me *all the things* when I explained to her the situation about the tabloid mess. Have to love her, don't I?"

Lev couldn't help the tinge of amusement pulling at his chest, but it did very little to help with anything else that he was feeling in that second. "I don't want this shit going on to affect that for her. She's not said much one way or another, but if there's even a chance your friend from Cali or the prick here might do something to her—"

"Pink," Andino interjected, his tone calm but kind.

"You know I wish you'd call me Lev, right?"

A laugh answered that followed by his boss's amused, "I do."

"And yet ..."

"Pink has just stuck for us, you know? You're Pink to us, like it or not. Back to what you were saying, though."

"Yeah?"

"You are my most loyal man, you know that, right? You're not even made—you just *are*. You're also my friend. I've told you this before. I don't have many of those. Running fucking joke in my life. I digress ... you can do whatever you need to handle your situation while we also handle ours. Fair?"

Yeah.

That's all he needed.

"Fair," he replied.

TWENTY-ONE

"MARLA IS planning on flying in because of the latest mess. She'll be here to handle the rest of the PR and whatever else comes up between now and the walk, Gi."

From the pedestal where Gigi stood in nothing but a pair of white cotton panties as a woman moved from one body part to the next with a measuring tape, she winced at her assistant's latest update on the *situation*. Or that's what every member of her team was calling the latest round of lies to get plastered across the media.

"Yeah?" Gigi asked.

"At least this time she didn't waste time ragging you out on the phone?" Kayla asked, shrugging while still staring down at the phone in her hands. "Better for her to be here with the rest of the team than overseas yelling into a speaker, I guess."

That wasn't a consolation to Gigi because one way or another, she would still feel the agency's wrath. Whether it was a forced interview or a social media blackout. *Hell*, someone had even gone as far as to suggest maybe Gigi shouldn't walk in this year's Fashion Week because she had drawn far too much negative attention to herself which was taking away from the major event itself.

As it was, her manager no longer even bothered to call her to overlook statements they were making on her behalf. She hadn't gotten a peek at her social media feeds in far too long to see how her fans had reacted to the latest attempt to connect her career to the mob beyond just her private relationship with Lev, but maybe that was for the better.

She couldn't focus on all of that mess right now. Not when she was set to walk the runway for one of America's top names in fashion in two weeks. Not just *walk*, no, but open and close the show for the brand. It was *too* fucking important. A goal she had been striving to achieve for years and was now finally looking down the barrel of her dream while the rest of the world tried to explode around her.

The thing was ... Gigi had come to a realization of sorts as she moved from one appointment to the next over the last couple of days while final preparations came together for her, the team behind her, and the rest of the models taking part in the same show.

What happened after she hit her goal? Once she achieved *the* dream?

Where did she go from there when she was already at the top? Not having an answer to that question or a clear outlook on what she wanted to do when she also knew her contract with the Paris agency—and her mother agency, too—was coming up for renewal.

What was left other than the next sponsorships, brand deals, and more people telling her what she could and couldn't do?

"Well," the girl who had been taking her measurements said as she took a step back from Gigi, "I think we're just about done. I'll take in the two centimeters on the waist of your garments—your gown for tomorrow night's event is going to need correcting as well. It's not like you to fluctuate, is it?"

Gigi let out a slow breath, asking, "Stress?"

Across the room, Kayla laughed out, "Or lots of good sex."

"Kayla!"

"Sorry, sorry," her assistant said, her palms flying up in surrender. "I couldn't help myself."

Picking up the tablet she had discarded earlier when she started one of the final rounds of Gigi's measurements, the woman said, "Couldn't imagine having *that* much sex."

Well ...

"Maybe you're not having the right kind of sex," Gigi replied.

That comment had the woman's cheeks pinking. Gigi regretted nothing. Lately, there were a lot more people on her team and in her work circles that thought they could speak out of turn about the things they were seeing in the media.

She had news for them.

It was *not* up for discussion. Not unless she brought it up. Otherwise, she didn't have a problem with putting anyone in their place if they needed it. Just like today.

Stumbling over her words, the woman tapped her fingers to the screen of the tablet and quickly said, "Yes, that's about it. Your gown will be sent over to the hotel in lots of time for the event tomorrow. And I was told to ask what you wanted to wear for the afterparty—"

"I won't be attending."

The woman glanced up. Even Kayla looked her way, surprise flitting over her features. Gigi understood the reaction. If there was anything she was known for, it was her enjoyment of what came *after* events and shows. The parties were usually the best. One of the few times she could let loose without fear of reprisal because *everyone* did the same thing. They worked hard, and partied harder.

And yet ...

"I think I might just call it an early night," Gigi lied.

Bullshit.

The truth was she could waste hours at an afterparty watching models get turned up on whatever the latest craze was—probably a new e-pill—or she might be able to get some time with Lev. Considering the extent of their conversations over the last week since a hoard of asshole paparazzi showed up at his kid's daycare had been mostly through text and a couple of late-night phone calls, well ... she needed more.

Wanted more.

She would much rather spend an evening with him, if possible. It was something she was still trying to work out.

"Isn't it required—"

"Optional on Gigi's contract to attend afterparties related to events," Kayla quickly spoke up.

Gigi shot her a thankful smile. "Exactly."

Ding.

The familiar text notification sound for Gigi's phone sent her scrambling off the pedestal to race for the device on the leather sectional a few feet away. Right on top of the silk robe that she quickly shrugged on while activating her phone's home screen and bringing up the most recent text. All the while, Kayla finished the conversation so that she didn't have to.

A missed text from her mother was second on the list, but Gigi would get back to that later. It was the text ribbon at the very top that had her smiling.

From Lev.

Hey, it read, *can you come to the front desk? They won't let me up.*

Gigi typed back: *You're here?*

In less than five seconds, his reply came in. *I did ask where you were, right?*

Yes, he had.

But she didn't think he wanted to know where she was in Manhattan because he planned to just show up. Especially when she had told him she was doing something for work and as far as she knew, he was supposed to be handling business with his boss. Or, that's all he told her with no added detail. Not that it mattered; she wasn't mad about him showing up without warning.

He was *here*. That had her heart sky-high. Lately, it seemed like there was only one thing that could make Gigi feel genuine happiness amidst the craziness of her life.

Lev.

• • •

"Miss Gigi, could I steal you for a picture if you have a minute? We would love to put you on the company's feed to—"

Gigi gave the girl—probably an intern for Delavange, the lingerie company and designer she was getting her final fittings for—an apologetic smile as she passed by her desk that led out into the common area of the building. "Sorry, social media blackout. Even on someone else's."

It was a lie.

She just wasn't getting on socials or putting herself on someone else's feed. No one had told her—*yet*—that she was to stay off the web until told otherwise. She expected another

221

issue like the one from last week and it would happen, though.

"Maybe next time, then," the girl called after her.

Over her shoulder, Gigi smiled. "Maybe! Love ya, kid."

It was her thing.

Her *line*.

And it felt false.

Why?

She didn't know.

Rounding the corner that opened to the main receptionist's desk and the entrance of the Delavange offices, Gigi only saw one man despite the usual, busy movement of many people going about their day and work. Lev, that was.

Turned sideways where he leaned against the receptionist's desk, he wasn't looking her way but toward the front doors. Gigi was only staring at him and the way he filled out the leather jacket and dark-wash jeans. *Fantastically*, by the way. He filled them out fantastically. Right down to the black runners on his feet, one of which he tapped to the floor like he was bored.

Or maybe stuck in his head, thinking.

She was used to seeing him in dressier, more professional clothing. The laid-back style he currently wore was new but also not a bad thing. Not at all.

"Hey," Gigi said when he finally noticed her approach from the side.

Standing to his full height, Lev pushed away from the desk to reach for her. Pulled into his tight hug before she could even get another word out, the crisp notes of his cologne pulled her into an entirely different place. One that felt like soft sheets, warm skin, and his dark tenor whispering wonderful, dirty things in her ear. Lev didn't let her go right away, and she settled into his embrace, all too happy to tip her head back and take the kiss he offered despite the fact she knew people were probably watching.

Let them watch.

Fuck, everybody else already was.

"You could have said you wanted to know where I was because you wanted to stop by—I would have had someone down here to bring you up."

Lev grinned a sexy sight, shrugging his broad shoulders. "I can't stay long. What are you wearing?"

He held her out in his arms just far enough that he could take in the silk robe she had tied tight enough to keep any slips from happening.

"I was having a fitting," she said, trying not to be defensive, but his cocked eyebrow made it *hard*. "And I'm working, getting a fitting. That's what the robe is for; ten minutes ago, I was in nothing but white panties."

That had Lev humming under his breath when he replied with interest, "That so?"

"*Stop.*"

"Just white panties? Are they still on? You wanna ... open that robe up and show me?"

"Oh, my *God*."

"And you're gonna be walking in lingerie, right?"

"*Lev*."

How this man could make her bashful, she didn't know. He managed it, though.

Lev laughed deeply, his arm coming to rest snugly along her lower back when he said, "I'm just giving you a hard time. You make it too easy. And don't worry, I'm not about to cause a scene. Besides, I'm just doing something that should have been done a week ago."

"What?"

"Keep in mind, they're only going to be as close as they need to be until ... well, either you no longer need them or things blow over. Whichever comes first."

She still didn't know what Lev was talking about, but he didn't make her wait to learn. Turning them both to face the entrance doors, her back stayed pressed against his chest when her gaze landed on something—or rather, *someones*—that hadn't been standing outside the office building when she arrived earlier.

Four men.

All in black suits.

They stood with their backs to the doors while they looked out to the busy street ahead of them. From her position, she could see the wires behind each of their right ears. The same kind of spiral wire *her* security team used.

"Four enforcers from the Marcello *famiglia*, posted by Andino Marcello himself," Lev explained quietly. "Mob detail, babe. They are dressed and will act appropriately as to not draw attention or seem out of place with your usual team, but they will not follow the same code of conduct when it comes to dealing with issues as your security will."

She had a ton of questions.

A chill raced through her.

"My team probably won't like—"

"They're not going to have much of a choice, Gigi. I assure you."

"Why do I need more—"

Lev's heavy sigh quieted her, but he soothed away the anxiety starting to climb up her throat when he pressed a warm kiss to the spot behind her right ear. Lingering there, he murmured, "Because nothing is going to ruin these next two weeks for you, and we have enough of a reason to suspect someone might try to do exactly that."

"You mean Jensen Todrey."

"Or someone else. His little friend from Cali, or even the fucks they're working with in the skin trade. Listen, I don't want to get into details, but we're digging into every possible avenue right now. They certainly had the media in a fit again, didn't they?"

"But is that the only reason?"

Lev stiffened a bit behind her. "No."

"What else is there?"

When he didn't answer right away, Gigi turned in his arms. He didn't stop her, and he met her gaze when she faced him again.

"Lev?"

His tongue peeked out to wet the edge of his bottom lip before he muttered, "Last week when the assholes showed up at Arely's daycare, her enforcer was nowhere to be seen. He eventually showed up ... dead in a ditch. The media wasn't the only message we were sent last week. This is extra precaution right now, babe. That's all."

Jesus.

Lev could clearly see the panic Gigi couldn't hide because his hands came up to cup her face and his lips found hers in a slow, sensual kiss. One she couldn't help but answer back, once again lost to him and this strange thing growing between them.

"You focus on your thing," he told her, the words a breath against her mouth, "and let us handle our side, okay?"

"Easier said than done."

"But it *will* be done." Then, Lev gave her another one of those toothy grins she loved so much when he asked, "And hey, what are you doing today, anyway? Or later?"

"Finishing this fitting. A dinner I can't get out of but nothing after. Tomorrow I have an event, but the rest of the evening and night is all mine to do with what I want."

"Yeah?"

His excitement had her laughing. "Yeah."

"So, maybe I could ... take you out?"

Gigi blinked. "Like on a date?"

"Surely we've got enough people around you now to keep any photogs at bay, right?"

"Well, don't hold your breath."

Lev barked out a laugh. "Fair enough. You up for it, though?"

"I am. What about Arely?"

"She keeps asking about you."

Did she?

Why did that make Gigi's heart skip a beat?

"I like her," Gigi admitted.

"She likes you, too." His smile stretched wider. "If you're not doing anything tonight, then maybe me and her could—"

"Come to the hotel. Everything is kind of *everywhere* but hey ... she'll love it."

Lev gave her a look, his brow dipping in confusion. "Do I even want to ask?"

"Probably not."

After all, everything between them up until that point had been by the seat of their pants. They learned on the fly, right? She kind of liked it that way.

• • •

"It's too big!"

"Now, just you wait one second here," Gigi said, working the fabric of the wrap dress around and around Arely's wiggling form. It was *far* too large for the girl, but for whatever reason—she was blaming the shimmery fabric—it was the one dress in the large closet of her hotel room that Arely just couldn't say no to. A few more wraps, and a big bow at the back with the loose ends, and Gigi stepped back to admire her work. "See? *Perfecto!*"

Arely struck a pose with one little hand to her popped hip and another against her cheek as she kissed the air. "Pretty?"

"The *most* pretty."

"*Yes.*" Arely pumped a small fist into the air. "Now we do the walk."

Gigi laughed. "The *cat*walk, yep. Think you're ready to show your dad?"

"He better like it."

"I'm sure he will."

Mostly.

She was sure Lev was gonna *love* the sight of his kid in a three-thousand-dollar dress that Gigi had turned into some hybrid romper. Topped off with bright pink lipstick, some blush, and even a wide-brimmed hat *just because.*

It was her idea to play dress up and model whatever look they came up with. Arely jumped at the chance, especially when she saw the closet full of *things.* Most of which probably wouldn't follow Gigi back to her home in Milan, if that was where she decided to go after her work in New York concluded. At the moment, she didn't know if she was leaving the states ... or if she wanted to.

But that was a topic for another time.

"Wait, can I—the shoes, too!" Arely's excitement came out in a rush as she pointed with all the ferocity she could muster at the sparkly, five-inch peep-toe pumps on the shelf to their left. The shoes had been a gift sent to Gigi from a friend the week before. She hadn't even worn them yet. "I has to have shoes, Gigi."

Gigi held back her smile, not wanting the girl to think she was making light of her seriousness, replying, "Well, obviously."

Unfortunately, the shoes made walking just about entirely impossible for Arely. At least, not without the girl likely rolling her damn ankles. Gigi wasn't going to have that. The quickest way to ruin the fun was by someone getting hurt.

Besides, she was pretty sure if she—even accidentally—hurt Lev's kid, it would be the last time she ever saw the girl. And probably him, too. Maybe she was being a little dramatic but honestly, she wouldn't blame the man. Clearly, it had been him and his kid for a long time. Lev was all Arely had when the rest of the world went away, and it was time to be tucked in at night. Even Gigi could see the absolute love between the two.

She pushed those thoughts aside to handle the overly excited little girl with very expensive shoes in her hand. Leading Arely out of the closet, she waited until they were just inside the suite's bedroom door before taking the shoes back.

"Okay, we'll put these on, but just to strike a pose and show your dad. Then, we've got to take them off, so they don't hurt your feet."

Arely sighed, her big blue eyes rolling at that. "My Auntie Nessa says beauty *is* pain."

Gigi cocked a brow, almost impressed at the five-and-a-half-year-old's confidence, but more concerned than anything. She was sure Nessa—who Gigi had yet to properly meet face to face beyond their first interaction years ago—hadn't meant anything bad by saying the same type of thing that other women had been saying for decades. Thing was, that didn't always make it right.

Kneeling down so the two of them were eye-level, Gigi rubbed away the little smudge of lipstick on Arely's chin. How she even got lipstick there, Gigi didn't know. "Hey, listen ... nothing that makes us beautiful should hurt, you know? If it hurts, then it doesn't feel good. And the best way to be beautiful is to *feel* beautiful inside first."

Arely pursed her lips. "Yeah?"

Gigi shrugged. "Yeah."

"Can I show my daddy now?"

"Absolutely."

She helped Arely into the shoes, and then put her index finger to her lips, silently telling the girl to be quiet as she stepped out of the bedroom. Of course, making sure not to spoil the surprise by closing the door, leaving only a crack left, behind her.

Across the room, Lev was looking over the cart of food that room service had finally brought up. She only ordered it an hour ago. He shot her a curious look, and then the door to the bedroom, too.

"Where's Arely?"

"Coming. Get your phone ready," she told him. "You're gonna want it."

"Why?"

"You'll see."

That was all she was giving him. The rest was better experienced firsthand.

"Well?" Lev asked waving his phone. "Ready whenever you are."

Gigi waved a hand his way. "Patience."

"I'm ready!"

Arely's muffled yell had Gigi laughing before she pulled open the bedroom door. There, already striking her pose and looking as cute as ever, was Arely.

"Next on the runway," Gigi said, tossing Lev a wink and grin, "is Arley Arsov wearing the latest fashion, styled by Gigi Rey Parker."

Arely grinned wide as Lev's laughter coated the room. She heard the camera on his phone click at the same time he said, "What in the fuck is she wearing?"

"It's *pretty*!" Nobody could glare like a little girl staring down her father from the other side of the room. "Right?"

"Beautiful," she assured Arely. "Very *avant-garde*."

Not that the girl would understand what Gigi meant by that. She wasn't even sure Lev had explained to Arely what Gigi did for a living or why there had been photographers following them lately. Would he ever?

"The prettiest," Lev was quick to add. "Obviously."

Without warning, Arely kicked off the shoes. Gigi might have winced another time, knowing damn well the floor probably scuffed the heels. But the way the girl proceeded to strut across the room like she was on a runway had her laughing instead.

Lev, too. The smile he shot her way said he wasn't mad about the outfit, makeup, or anything else. Besides, Arely's smile was worth far more than some scuffed shoes and a wrinkled wrap dress. She had a feeling by the time the night was over, there would be a few more ruined shoes or dresses.

Gigi didn't mind at all.

It was easier to focus on this and making Arely smile instead of the unknowns. Like the dead man Lev had mentioned. *Yeah.* Wasn't like she could forget about that. She could, however, pretend for a little while.

Just like the camera had turned on, she would play her part. Except it wasn't a camera—it was a smiling five-and-a-half-year-old ready to put on her next outfit to show off. Same difference, right?

TWENTY-TWO

"ARE YOU going to do a little strut for me, too?" Lev asked Gigi.

Too low for Arely to hear where she stood in front of a large mirror position directly across from the sitting room's wall of windows. Checking out her poses in the reflection, she shot the mirror a kiss into the air in front of her.

"I *could* put on a little something to—"

The ringing of a phone stopped Gigi from saying anything more, making Lev groan when she tossed him a wink over her shoulder. It certainly wasn't the right time for the two of them to be playing their games together what with his kid there, but he couldn't help himself. Plus, he was keeping it clean.

Mostly.

"Give me a second, that's the conference phone," Gigi explained, heading through the open concept rooms to where a long table sat between the sitting area and the small kitchen on the other side. "The hotel uses it to call me. Same with security. And my team ... yeah."

He laughed under his breath. "Does it ever end?"

"Not really."

Lev couldn't even imagine.

"Daddy, I forgot, look at what Gigi gave me!"

Gigi answered the conference phone at the same time Arely came rushing over to his spot on the white leather sofa. He swore his kid didn't know the meaning of quiet, but he tried to shush her all the same.

"Gigi here," came the sweet voice from across the suite.

In his lap, however, Arely wasn't having any of his efforts to keep her quiet when she shoved a mini backpack—mini for an adult, anyway—into his face. The supple leather of the bag was enough to tell him the backpack was pricey. The logo printed all over the item, including on the hardware of the bag, only confirmed his suspicions.

In her second outfit of the evening, a dress that was probably short as hell on Gigi but fell to the floor on his daughter, combined with a belt to keep it tight to her tiny waist, Arely couldn't be happier. It was not lost on him that, with women, his daughter *really* shined. She found familiarity in feminine things that he couldn't provide.

She looked like every girly girl that ever existed with her curls piled high on her head, and her cheeks pink with a rosy blush. The lipstick had faded from her lips after drinks and snacks, but a stain remained to make her look as though she had been sucking on a popsicle.

"Arely, are you sure Gigi said you could have—"

"Yes," his daughter rushed to interject, grabbing the mini Louis Vuitton backpack right out of his hands to clutch it to her chest. "She did, Daddy. I *promise*. It's mine."

"Oh, really?" he heard Gigi say to his far left.

He wasn't *trying* to listen to her conversation. Especially when he had his kid to handle. Some habits were hard to break, though, and being aware of his surroundings was just one of those.

"Yeah, okay. I'll see what I can do."

"Arely, baby," Lev said, chuckling as Gigi ended the call across the room, "I don't think you understand how much this bag costs and—"

"Five thousand dollars," Gigi said, her approaching footsteps gaining his attention and stare. She'd changed outfits too the second time she disappeared into her hotel suite's massive walk-in closet with his kid to play another round of *Arely the Model*. Although, the cut off shirt and low-hanging sweats were probably more for comfort than style. Even if she did look like sin in it all the same. "It was also a gift from a popular florist in the city that wanted me to shout out her boxed arrangements while I was in town. The bag was ... incentive. Trust me, Arely can keep it. Doesn't she start kindergarten soon?"

"Next week, actually."

"Five more days," Arely put in, grinning a toothy smile. Gigi smiled right back. "See. Let her use it for that."

"Yeah, Daddy. For *school*."

Like he hadn't already bought her a bookbag for school. Not that it mattered because he was clearly losing this battle *terribly*. Lev sighed, giving Gigi a look from the side that had her grinning. "*Killing* me here. What happens when you start them this early on designer shit, huh? Don't worry. I know exactly what happens."

The collection only continued to grow. Because *he* would be expected to buy it.

Gigi shrugged, falling gracefully onto the arm of the couch where she sat with an all too pleased smile. "It's just a little flex. How many other kids are gonna have that kind of backpack their first year?"

"A *flex*." He scoffed. "Right, she's not even a teenager and already *flexing*. Not that it matters. Can't exactly tell her no when you've already given it to her, can I?"

Gigi stuck out her tongue. "Nope."

Arely's fist pumped into the air as she climbed out of her father's lap, her LV bag still clutched close. "*Yes*."

His kid headed back for the mirror.

Gigi, on the other hand, leaned a little closer to him, her pretty lips pouting just a bit. "You're not too mad at me, are you?"

"For that?"

"Well ... It's okay to tell me not to step over a line. Even if I've already jumped over it and didn't even see it, Lev."

Right.

Except she hadn't.

Not really.

Up until that second, Lev had been careful about showing any kind of physical affection toward Gigi while his daughter was in the same vicinity. Arely witnessed nothing more than perhaps his hand on Gigi's back or a hug between the two. Certainly not the slow, languid kiss that he stole from her because she was close enough, and he couldn't find an excuse not to. He hadn't meant for the kiss to last as long as it did, but the way Gigi's lashes fluttered closed and she hummed against his mouth ... well, he took just a few more seconds to enjoy it.

The giggles across the room pulled him back, though. By the time he looked Arely's way, she was watching herself in the mirror again. Clearly pretending as though she hadn't seen a thing. He knew different, but he also felt comfortable enough that if his daughter had an issue with it, she would just say so. After all, she didn't have a problem doing that any other time.

"That was security, by the way," Gigi said, dragging his attention back to her instantly.

"Pardon?"

She waved a hand over her shoulder. "The call. They said a bunch of paps and some fans have gathered at the front and rear of the hotel. Maybe the ones that have the place staked out, put out a call that they saw you arrive or whatever. Anyway, they were wondering if you might wait a little while longer before leaving or—"

"We can't take a side door again or ...?"

A shrug fell from her delicate shoulders. "You could."

"But?"

Gigi's expression turned a little sheepish as her gaze darted from him to the girl in front of the mirror. "Well, I was thinking maybe you would stay for the night."

"Arely—"

"There are three bedrooms in this suite, Lev."

"The paps are gonna catch us leaving one way or the other, won't they? Tonight, tomorrow. *When* really just determines what they might write, doesn't it?"

She reached over to sweep her thumb along the hard line of his jaw. "But is what they might say about us really all that untrue at this point?"

He swallowed hard.

She wasn't wrong.

"Doesn't mean they *should*, Gigi."

"Part of the package, Lev."

"Yeah, I know. I'm supposed to be staying *out* of the spotlight, though. The boss doesn't want it to look like we're attempting to antagonize anyone from outside—or in—town, if you get my drift."

Meaning Jensen or Marco.

She arched a brow, silently questioning. He offered nothing more. He couldn't.

Gigi's life came with strings. So did his.

"Are you staying, then?" she asked softly. "I'll call down and let them know."

Lev knew it wasn't the *best* idea. There were a million reasons why he should say no. He also wanted to stay more than anything. "Yeah, let them know we're staying, babe."

That gained him another one of her brilliant smiles. And a searing kiss. Surely that was worth another round with the tabloids.

Wasn't it?

• • •

It was far too easy for Lev to forget about the outside world when he was watching Gigi work his dick. With her knees pressed into the plush cushion of the chaise, she threw her body back into his cock, riding him reverse-style and giving him the *best* view while she was at it.

"You like that?" she breathed, her words colored with her pleasure as her pace became painfully slow. *God.* "You like that ass, baby?"

"Keep fucking teasing me, and you're going to see what I like, sweetheart."

Hell, her ass was already red from his palms. And the way he'd slapped the round cheeks earlier when he had her bent over the bed with her panties stuffed in her mouth to keep her quiet when she couldn't do it on her own.

"*Yes, please.*"

Lev groaned out his agreement through clenched teeth, determined to hold back his release for as long as he fucking could despite the fact they'd spent the better part of the early morning hours wrapped up in one another. It didn't matter.

It wasn't enough.

Every time they fucked, he just wanted more. He wanted to drag her right back into the bed the second they were finished. If he could keep her naked and wrapped in sheets, then he fucking would but alas ... life was always waiting to catch up.

Like now.

Room service would be there anytime. She had called down for it almost an hour before. Arely would have to be woken up soon, too. Then, they had to worry.

But right then?

Fuck life.

He had two handfuls of Gigi's ass while she backed her soaked pussy into his dick, and he got to watch every second of it. The way she tossed her head back, blonde and pink hair flipping over her shoulders. How a tremor worked its way over her shoulders the slower she fucked him because she too was trying to hold back.

To make this last longer.

Peeking over her shoulder at him, Gigi's teeth dragged over her lower lip before she whispered, "Make me come."

Yes.

Abso-fucking-lutely.

Lev didn't need to be told again, his hands flying to Gigi's waist to keep a better hold on her as he lifted from the chaise. His cock didn't even leave her cunt when he pushed her down to the cushion, her head hanging off the end while she grappled for the edge. She was barely hanging on when his fingers dug into her ass again, spreading her wide as he nailed into her.

The slap of his hips snapping against her pinked backside was music to his ears. Just like her low, keening moans with every thrust she took from him.

And *Christ* ... "You take me so fucking well, Gigi. Your cunt *loves* this cock, doesn't it, babe? Fuck yeah, look at you."

"I can't ... I *can't* ..."

He wasn't sure what she was trying to say, but the spasm that rocked her spine came in time with the clench of her pussy around his dick. The orgasm came on with no warning, and while he might usually slow down a bit to enjoy the feeling of her milking him through it, he just picked up the pace. Pounding into her through broken cries of his name that sent him spiraling closer and closer to his own edge.

He was almost there.

Balls tight.

Back slick with sweat.

Nearly there.

Buuuuzzzzz.

Lev's pace came to a halt all at once as the loud, annoying buzzing continued to resound throughout the room. Gigi's breathless laughter had her pussy contracting around his dick in the best and worst way, pulling a thick sound from his throat that even he didn't recognize.

Except he did know that ache in his balls.

That *pain.*

Fucking blue balls.

"Food's here," she told him. "And if we don't answer the door, they're going to keep hitting the ringer."

"Your security—"

"Probably waiting right there with room service. We have to go out and answer the door."

"*For real?*"

His voice came out too high. Unnaturally so. It only made Gigi laugh again.

"Stop *that*," he growled, his hands flexing hard against her ass. She just grinned into the cushion. "You're being serious, aren't you? I was just about to—"

"Come," she said in a pleased sigh. "I know."

Goddammit.

Buuuuzzzzz.

Buzz. Buzz. Buzzzzzzz.

The more buzzing he heard, the worse his balls ached until he was swallowing a fucking *whimper.* Like a damn boy. It didn't help that Gigi's giggling had his dick jerking inside of her which only made the pain flare all over again.

Buzz.

"They're gonna wake Arely—"

That was all Lev needed to hear. He pulled out from Gigi faster than he thought possible. Her smile was a little more sympathetic as he searched for something decent to wear, wincing with every step. Which just ended up being his slacks from the day before, left unbuttoned, and nothing else because he didn't have time to grab the button-down he'd left in the bathroom with the buzzing seemingly getting *louder*.

It really wasn't.

That was just his crazy mind.

Gigi had managed to pull on a silk robe that she tied tight at the waist as he headed out of the bedroom and back into the main rooms. Passing through the sitting room for the door at the other side, Lev didn't even bother to check the peephole before yanking open the door with a scowl he leveled on—

A woman with a suitcase.

Oh, the security that followed Gigi stood behind the woman, of course. But he was less concerned with them and more concerned with the woman who looked familiar enough for him to know she *had* to be Gigi's—

"Mom," Gigi said, coming to stand next to Lev in the doorway. "We were expecting—"

The green-eyed, blonde-haired woman smiled slightly. Her stare drifted over Lev's naked torso and straight down to where he hadn't bothered to do up his pants. Another time— another woman—and he might have asked if she liked what she saw.

Not this time.

"Someone to dress you?" Gigi's mother asked.

Gigi sighed. "*Mom.*"

"Kidding." Then, she smiled wider at Lev. "Hi. I'm Kimie Parker. And you're the man I keep seeing plastered all over the papers with my daughter—Lev, right?"

His mouth opened to reply.

No sound came out.

Behind Kimie Parker, the security in the middle of the three men explained, "Screened as always, Miss Gigi. We didn't think you would mind her coming to the door without a phone call, however."

"That's fine," Gigi replied.

"Is it?" Lev muttered.

Kimie's gaze turned on Gigi, a little sharper than it had been for Lev when she said, "So, what the tabloids said were true?"

"Well—"

"And you didn't tell me?"

Gigi laughed weakly. "I didn't want you to worry. A lot of it is nothing but lies."

"*Right.*"

"What are you doing here, Mom?"

"You're walking the runway for Fashion Week, and you seriously thought I wouldn't come to watch you? *At home?*"

Beside him, Gigi stared at her mother like she was begging the woman for something he didn't understand.

"Are we going to keep standing here like this or are you inviting me in?" Kimie asked. "I didn't drive here from Jersey to book my own hotel room, Gi. I shouldn't have needed to wait thirty minutes downstairs, either. I'm your mother."

Okay, that was enough of that. Lev stepped back from the door first, but Gigi was quick to follow when he said, "Come on in. We're waiting for food, and then we're going to wake up my daughter to eat. You might as well join, right?"

Kimie *huh'd* under her breath, saying to Gigi as she passed her by beyond the doorway, "He's really got a kid, too, does he? I thought the rags were just reaching with that. Apparently, I should be following the tabloids more often. They clearly know more about your life than I do lately, Gigi."

Ouch.

Gigi said nothing, simply slammed the door behind her mother. The stare she shot him, however, both pleaded and thanked him at the same time. For what, he had no idea.

But damn.

This had been quite the morning. It could only go up from here, right?

Lev hoped so.

● ● ●

"Arely's first day at kindergarten went *spectacularly*," Lev said, laughing. "And you'd be proud of how many pictures I took."

"I liked the one you sent me. Did she pick the outfit, or you?"

"Her."

Gigi grinned, the pride shining through when she replied, "Girl has style, Lev. You should really consider getting her an agent or something."

"You're kidding, right?"

A shrug fell from her shoulders. "Partly."

"Hell no."

Absolutely not, in fact. The time he had spent with Gigi was enough to tell him that the lifestyle she lived was not as glamorous as it seemed from the outside. He couldn't imagine Arely being put in the same position.

Gigi didn't seem offended about it, and instead changed the subject altogether to something they hadn't been given the time to delve into what with their busy days getting in the way. Even this lunch was probably going to get cut short by a meeting he had to have with his boss later while Andino visited his barber on the other side of Manhattan.

"My mother liked you," Gigi said, rolling her glittering eyes. "She wanted me to tell you that she looks forward to spending time with you after Fashion Week is over."

Lev's chin tipped up at the slight bitterness he heard in Gigi's tone. She didn't show it where she sat across from him at the table in the restaurant that he had been able to both get a reservation last minute but also make sure it was private enough for them. Andino's *La Vita Bella*, that was.

She might not show her bitterness, but she didn't have to. Not when he had so clearly heard it.

"Is that an issue or something?"

Gigi's gaze snapped from the windows to his face in an instant. "What, no. I just—"

"There's a pap," Lev interjected before she could explain more on the topic.

Before Gigi could even find the man aiming a lens of a camera out of his car's window, focused on them through the restaurant's large bay windows, one of the enforcers Lev had trailing Gigi came into view with a hand already waving at the guy. As fast as the car had pulled up to the side of the street outside the business, the vehicle sped off with the window still rolled down.

Although now, the enforcer walked away with the camera. That earned a chuckle out of Lev.

"We haven't even gotten our food yet," Gigi muttered, "and already they're showing up. I'm sorry, I know you wanted to have a normal date."

Right.

Well ...

"I wanted to have lunch with you while I could this week," he murmured, reaching across the table to catch her hand with his own. Weaving their fingers together, he lifted her hand to his lips and dotted soft kisses along her silken skin. "I'm still trying to work on that *date* thing, so let's not count this as that. Not yet."

"I mean, at least they're good for getting rid of the assholes. The enforcers, I mean. They don't care about catching a charge for something like my security does. Not sure what they're really *doing*, though."

"Keeping you safe, babe."

"From *what*? Nothing has happened for me to need them. Jensen hasn't shown back up. According to my agent, the campaigns for the Revvers have all been canceled. Not on our end, either. I think it's safe to say whatever you thought might happen because of all that—"

Lev made a dark noise under his breath, stopping her from saying more when he said, "I can't remember what it feels like to think the way you do. "

"How do I think?"

"Normally, I guess."

That had Gigi's brow dipping low. "What does that mean?"

He might have laughed at how she sounded *offended* at the very idea of being called normal. Problem was, this wasn't a laughing matter. In any way. The bigger issue was that Gigi clearly didn't understand how serious the possible issues with Jensen and Marco could actually be for them both. Maybe that was partly his fault.

After all, he hadn't really explained what it was like to be ... the person he was. The man he had been turned into the moment he took a job for Andino Marcello.

Lev sighed when Gigi continued to stare at him, clearly

waiting for an answer to her question. "It means ... before the fucking mob came into my life. Before they turned me into *Pink*, you know? I used to think like you, too. If nothing was happening, then all was good."

Gigi swallowed hard. "Why did you ... did you join, or?"

"I work for Andino. That's it. That's all. Saying I joined implies something that doesn't exist for guys like me in this business."

Mostly.

"But why?" she asked.

Lev shrugged, his thumb stroking the side of her hand because it helped to keep his thoughts from running wild into a past he really didn't want to revisit. "I needed the money and the security for my kid, so I took the job offered to me even knowing it might mean that same job could take me from Arely someday, too. But before all that, I was like you. I had no idea how everything was going to change when I stepped out of my house and became Pink for the mob. Girl, a week? Two or three ... five fucking years, it doesn't make a difference to these men. They'll wait as long as they need to for a vendetta or just goddamn business. Don't think because it's been a quiet week that we're safe. We never are."

Gigi quieted throughout his spiel. Her silence continued long after he was done, too. Lev hadn't meant for his words to hit so heavy, but it was what it was.

"Things were easier then, weren't they?" she finally asked softly. "Before I was this and you became ... *you*. What might have happened if we had a little more time back then?"

He didn't have the answer to that. Still, he smiled for her, saying, "But it might be worth it."

They hadn't gotten that far to know yet.

Gigi shot him the kind of look that would usually have his thoughts darkening with filth, but the server coming their way with plates of food balanced on her arm took his attention instead. Funny how the only things that could get Lev's mind off fucking Gigi was food or his kid. Neither of them said much as the dishes of the restaurant's most famous lasagna were placed down to the table, and they dug in.

It was only when Lev noticed the enforcer walking past the windows again that he told Gigi, "I'm probably gonna have to run before you're done eating. Meet up with the boss—can't keep him waiting or he turns into a raging asshole. The guys will still stick close. You'll be fine."

Gigi arched a brow at that. "You know they're not going to be allowed backstage at the event, right? There's no way, Lev. Even my security gets posted where they're told. The event has its own security and—"

"We'll handle that." Reaching across the table to squeeze her hand, he decided to go back to the conversation they hadn't finished when he said, "And back to your mother."

That had Gigi frowning.

He hated that.

"What's that face for, anyway? Your mom seemed great that morning we spent with her. She was great with Arely and—"

"She is ... I love my mom," Gigi was quick to say. Her eyes said she was telling the truth. But that didn't mean everything was *fine*, either. Those were two different things. "When I first wanted to leave home to come to New York, she hated the idea. Then she was so excited when I went big. She was a model, too. And then I came along so that changed ... anyway, the more time I spent overseas, or the bigger I became, the less I wanted to come back here. I think she noticed that and took it personally. Sometimes we're good. Other times we're—"

"Like the other morning?"

Gigi glanced down at the table, saying, "I mean, yeah. I don't like it, but I haven't exactly had the chance to make it better. It's easier to just get her off the phone than try to argue my way through a conversation about *whatever*. Doesn't matter, I guess."

"Why's that?"

Because he figured she was lucky to even have *one* parent considering he had fucking none. If he did, he would want them around as much as possible. If not for himself, then for his kid. But he also wasn't Gigi.

Setting the fork to the side, Gigi let out a heavy exhale.

"Well, in a few more days it'll be over. I'll have walked the runway. She'll go back to Jersey. And I'll go … wherever I want. I don't want her to think I'm in trouble or that I can't handle this. She doesn't say it, but she worries too much as it is. Another reason why I hate taking her calls."

"Don't do that to your mother. That's not fair."

Across the table, Gigi stiffened. "You don't know—"

"What does she think all the security is for? The enforcers? She must know you don't usually have that many bodyguards on a regular basis."

"She thinks it's because of the tabloids and Fashion Week."

"What are you going to tell her when it's all over and we're gone?" Because that was the thing. Lev had heard the other statement she made—how she was going to go *wherever* when her work here was done. Where did that leave Lev in her plans? Without, apparently. Without *her*. "When you go, what are you going to tell her?"

Or *me*, he wanted to ask.

He held back.

The ache in his heart didn't hold back at all, though. That bitch came in fast, strong, and without a lick of mercy.

On the other side of the table, Gigi stared at him but said nothing. The hurt shined through in her gaze, unashamed and clear for him to feel as well. Maybe she didn't know what to say. Frankly, neither did he. This was not how he expected their lunch to go down.

Immediately, he regretted his words. He wanted to apologize if only because to be fair, they hadn't really discussed anything beyond the next time they could get five minutes together, but the ringing of his phone stopped him from saying anything at all. Not bothering to excuse himself for the call, he pulled the phone out of his pocket and answered it without checking the screen.

The pre-recorded message, the same robotic voice that he'd heard at least five times leading up to the day his daughter started kindergarten as the school sent updates for parents, droned on in his ear. It chilled him to the very fucking bone.

"*Bomb threat at Karter Elementary. Evacuation in*

progress. Police have been notified."

Lev didn't hesitate to leave the table without an explanation. He had already dialed the number to one of two men currently posted outside of his daughter's school. Behind him, Gigi called his name, confusion coating her voice. "Lev, wait!"

He didn't.

He couldn't.

TWENTY-THREE

LEV HAD never felt fear like the absolute terror that racked his body and trembled through his hands as he drove like a madman through city traffic to reach his daughter's elementary school. It wasn't calmed by the phone calls he had with *both* enforcers posted at the school; both of which confirmed there was a threat made to the school, and the evacuation of the children was well in progress. If anything, that only made it worse.

Real.

Was she fine?

Was there an actual bomb?

None of those answers were clear from the enforcers. They weren't allowed in the school. The kids were evacuated to the parking lot across the street, a spot that was predetermined by the district's education officials. The same place he had to go to meet up with his daughter and pick her up. He hated that despite the school preparing parents—and the kids—for events like these, it still happened at all.

And on Arely's *first* week.

Fuck.

She'd been so excited to start school; she counted down each one of the days until the morning of her first. This wasn't how he wanted her to start kindergarten. Not at all.

He blew through every red light and hit fifteen over the limit when he could manage it despite the clogged streets. Probably caught a few radar tickets on the way, too. Lev didn't care about any of that.

The only thing on his mind was his baby.

Arely.

Her name was a mantra in his mind even as his shaking hands reached to answer the call ringing through the Bluetooth in the Jeep. Another two blocks—through worse traffic now, as he bet a lot of the cars ahead of him were probably other parents flooding the pickup spot—and he would have his daughter in his arms.

Where she belonged.

Safe again.

Like she should always be.

Vaguely, he registered Nessa's name crossing the screen of his radio, but he didn't fully connect that it was her until her voice filtered through the speakers, confirming at least *one* thing the enforcers hadn't been able to during their last call. Of which he spent the majority raging at the man for not knowing anything as though he was in any better of a position now.

"It was a prank call," Nessa said, the very first words out of her mouth. Yet, the fear clutching Lev's heart didn't let go of its painfully tight grip in the least. "I was able to find that much out. They're still letting parents check the kids out for the day. Probably because they're terrified, I mean—"

"Who does that kind of shit?"

"Teenagers who want the day off school, maybe."

"Teenagers don't attend *elementary school*, Nessa."

That quieted her. Only for a second.

"Sorry, I was just trying to help," Nessa replied. "I tried to get off work after you called—thought maybe I could make it to the pickup spot first, but my boss is being a bitch."

Lev sighed, scrubbing a hand down his face in an attempt to ease some of the tension coiling through his nervous system. It did little. His tone tempered a bit when he said, "They wouldn't have let you sign her out, anyway. Only her guardian. *Me.* Can't even get her bodyguards—"

"Are you still going to pretend like she has bodyguards because your girlfriend is famous, or is it because of what they were saying about you in those magazines that you were so pissed off about? You know, the ... mafia stuff."

A sharp breath sucked into his lungs, aching the whole way. Despite knowing only a little about the situation with Gigi, Nessa had been kind enough not to push for more information when Lev didn't offer it. Not that the two of them had very much time to chat at all lately.

"I can't really talk about that shit," Lev muttered. "What

matters is that she's safe, anyway."

"Is she?"

"What?"

"A bomb threat was sent to her school today. She has bodyguards, Lev. Is she *really* safe?"

Up until that moment, he hadn't considered that the bomb threat might be related to the issues surrounding Andino's business partner, Marco, and Jensen Todrey. It wasn't like the assholes had done much beyond rile up the media again. But what good did a *fake* bomb threat at an elementary school do?

It didn't make sense.

"Lev?" Nessa urged quietly.

"Yes," he forced out, "she's safe."

Wasn't she?

• • •

The fear holding him hostage didn't settle until Lev had his—*tired and confused*—daughter in his arms. He knew Arely didn't quite know what to make of the day, or the panic that had ensued between kids, parents, and educators at the pickup spot. Instead of chattering on like she usually did when she was overstimulated, his girl was quiet and limp where she laid her head to his shoulder.

She didn't ask questions.

Didn't tell him what happened.

Nothing.

"You wanna get some gelato and pizza for supper?" he asked.

Arely shrugged, one arm tight around his while her other clutched the mini Louis Vuitton backpack from Gigi against her still frame. "Okay."

Part of him wanted to make her talk. Another part knew that if she wanted to say anything about her day and the trauma it caused, then she would, and he shouldn't push. Wasn't that fucking parenthood in a nutshell? The constant struggle between letting a kid do what they needed and *making* them do it because it was what the parent felt was correct.

Lev wasn't sure he had this fatherhood thing nailed down perfectly, but damn if he wasn't trying. All the time. Every day. With no one to tell him he was doing it *right*. Sometimes, that was the hardest part.

"Nessa's gonna come over tonight, too," he said, flexing his arm around Arely's back to hug her closer. Kissing the top of her head, he dragged in her familiar scent—the smell of baby soap lingering on the strands of her hair—and found a little bit of peace.

Not enough, though.

"Okay, Daddy."

That was it.

Just *okay*.

He had a feeling she wasn't okay at all.

Stopping four rows away from the one where he'd left his Jeep parked, Lev set Arely down to her white sneakers on the pavement. Bending down so the two of them were as close to eye-level as he could get, he found sadness staring back at him from his daughter. That was enough to about rip the heart right out of his chest.

"I wanted to finish my picture," Arely muttered, a quivering pout making her watery eyes seem far wider than normal. "I was painting a rainbow. And Trevor *pushed* me, Daddy. He didn't say sorry, either."

Lev's brow raised as a tinge of amusement speared through the heaviness raging within his emotions. "Do you know why I had to come to get you? Why all the kids left school?"

"Mrs. Fitzpats said there was an *emergency*," Arely said, carefully sounding out each syllable of the word as though she had been practicing it.

"That's it?"

Arely lifted her shoulders high, saying nothing more.

Lev let out a shaky exhale that felt like the sweetest relief. At least, he wasn't going to need to have an entire conversation about *bombs* and threats. Not today, anyway. "I love you, baby. I'm sorry your day wasn't a good one. I'll make it better, okay?"

That earned him a small smile.

Better than nothing.

"I know, Daddy," Arely said. "Hey, look." She pointed at somewhere behind him, happiness lighting up her features in a blink. "There's Gigi!"

What?

Snatching his daughter's hand within his own to keep her from darting away from his side, Lev stood and turned to find she was right. A sheepishly smiling Gigi waved a hand as she weaved between a row of parked cars. The line of men in black suits with comms in their ears followed behind at a respectable distance but none of them looked very pleased.

Lev said nothing until Gigi was standing just two feet away. "What are you doing here?"

"I made your guys find out what was going on and then I had my driver bring me here." She offered that information like it should have been obvious. Her next statement explained exactly why that was. "Before you say anything, I know I didn't have to come here. But didn't I? Maybe I didn't answer you the way you wanted me to at the restaurant … or I just wasn't clear because things are a mess right now, and I'm still trying to figure things out, but what's happening with us is important to me, Lev. Even if the things I don't know or understand about you scare the hell out of me. It doesn't matter. Whether it's today or in two days after I walk the runway or a month from now. If this whole thing was the universe's way of giving us a second chance at … *whatever*, us, then I'm not throwing it away. Okay?"

He swallowed hard, acutely aware of his daughter at his side who glanced between him and Gigi with more interest than she had previously shown. Beyond that, his heart thundered so hard in his chest that he was sure the organ was trying to escape. He wasn't sure what this woman was doing to him, or *with* him, a lot of the time, but they kept coming back to the same thing. Them *together*.

"Really shouldn't order the guys around," he said, nodding toward the enforcers currently chatting with her regular team of security. "It confuses them about who's in charge, you know?"

That earned him one of her sweet laughs.

And a beautiful smile.

"That's what you say back to me after I spill my guts?"

Lev grinned and stepped forward, closing the space between them with Arely coming along for the ride. Not that his daughter seemed to mind. Nor did she say a thing—except for her soft giggles—when he slid a hand around the back of Gigi's neck to pull her in for a kiss that set his heart on fire the second their lips melded together in a now-familiar dance. His chest grew tight when he pulled away just enough to rest his forehead against hers, their eyes locking in on one another's like missiles finding the target.

"You made yourself clear," he murmured. "I hear you."

She rubbed her lips together, probably tasting him, and nodded. "Okay. Is everything good here or—"

Lev chuckled dryly, pulling away and then lifting Arely up from the ground to rest on his hip. "Without details because someone—" he nodded to his daughter "—doesn't know the full story, yeah. Prank. Bullshit. Scared the hell out of me for nothing. I sent her enforcers home once I finally got here because I was ready to rip their heads off, and it wasn't even their fault."

He was seriously considering asking Andino if it was possible to *bribe* his daughter's school into allowing Arely's enforcers inside the building while she attended classes. Shit, maybe they could be class helpers. Wouldn't that be fantastic? Sarcasm was his new friend.

"Sorry, but at least it was just a false alarm," Gigi said. Then to Arely, she beamed, saying, "Good to see your daddy let you take your bag. I thought he might hide it on us."

"I would never."

Lies.

He totally considered it.

Arely held the backpack high, as proud as could be. "My teacher made me hang it up on the high hook in class."

Gigi snorted. "I bet."

"Miss Gigi, will you be returning to the hotel with Mr. Arsov, or will you be needing your driver?"

"We're having pizza and gelato," Arely said, bouncing in

her father's hold.

The question from one of the men a few cars down the row had Gigi turning to Lev with an apology already on the tip of her tongue. "I do have to get back to the hotel. I wasn't even supposed to be out today. Kayla canceled my meeting with my agent, so I could have lunch with you. She just got in; I wasn't in the mood. She's supposed to be around later, though, so—"

"It's fine," he told her. "Besides, only a couple more days, right?"

"Right," she replied, "only a couple more days and things will be a lot better. I can walk you to your Jeep?"

"Sure."

The walk to the Jeep didn't take long, but Lev was pleased to see his daughter's earlier sadness drifted away with Gigi there. The two of them chatted on and on while he tried to let them have their moment. After all, it wasn't just about what was happening between him and Gigi, he knew ... something was happening for Arely, too.

The second his vehicle came into view where he parked it at the end of a row, Lev knew something was different. The piece of yellow paper flapping under the windshield wiper caught his attention instantly. Setting Arely down to the ground beside the Jeep, he reached for the paper, already seeing the black words scrawled boldly across the bright background.

His heart stopped.

Ice slipped through his veins.

See how easy that was? Tell your boss, it read. Jensen and Marco were back, it seemed. Who else could it fucking be?

He crumpled the paper in his fist when Gigi called his name, asking, "Everything okay?"

No.

No, it certainly was *not* okay anymore.

In that moment, Lev went straight into survival mode—or rather, his switch flicked on, bringing out the side of him that only knew how to handle *business*. Pink, the enforcer. He shuttered the urge to calm and soothe the concern in Gigi's tone and the worry in his daughter's eyes as she stared up at him where she stood at his side.

Turning to find the closest of Gigi's bodyguards standing just a few feet ahead of the Jeep, he pointed at the man and said, "Take her to the hotel and don't let her leave until you're told otherwise. Do you fucking hear me?"

Gigi's knotted brow dipped lower. "What, why? Lev, I have things to do. I can't be holed up—"

He didn't look away from the enforcer. He couldn't when this could literally mean the difference between life and death if that note meant what he thought it did. "Take her to the hotel and keep her there."

"Daddy?"

"Lev!"

Gigi didn't look at all pleased when he turned on her and asked, "Remember what you said to me here today."

"About what?"

"Us. That it's important. That even if you don't know things and it scares you, it doesn't matter. Remember it. It's going to matter now, but it'll be okay."

A flash of fear replaced her anger. "Will it?"

It had to be.

• • •

Lev didn't go home. Before the sun had even set, he stood on the front porch of his boss's large home in the suburbs. Down on the grass, Arely threw a ball for Snaps, Andino's dog, like the animal didn't frighten her in the least. He should have taken her home, kept their routine, let Nessa handle her for the night, and then went ahead with business as usual.

Something told him not to.

He couldn't keep pretending. There was no way he could continue to separate the parts of his life into categories where one existed within the mafia and the other did not. Others weren't going to let him do it anymore, after all.

So, he would act accordingly.

Starting with his boss.

The home was large enough to be considered a mansion,

and while it wasn't the first time Lev visited the place, he never stayed long enough to impose on his boss or the man's wife. Until now.

Stepping out of the front door, Andino said something Lev couldn't hear over his shoulder, but he did understand the name his boss tacked on the end of his sentence. *Haven.* Andino's wife.

"She said Arely could come in and have a cookie and juice if she wants," Andino said, coming to stand next to Lev on the porch. "Or if *you* want her to, I should say."

He relayed the message to his daughter who quickly headed inside the house with Snaps on her tail.

"I was being stupid, wasn't I?"

"Pardon?"

Lev sighed harshly, shaking his head as he glanced to the side where Andino eyed him speculatively. "Trying to act like I could be two different people. That I could somehow keep her and our life separated from ... everything else."

"The mafia, you mean."

He only shrugged.

Andino replied with silence.

Lev didn't mind.

For a while, the two men stood side by side in their quiet contemplation. Lev didn't need to go over the events of the day with his boss. Andino had already been filled in by the rest of the men that had been there when he found the note that linked the bomb threat to him, specifically. And by that same token, likely the men they were currently having issues with.

Lev didn't know if he wanted to call their threats simple *issues*, anymore. Before, he was fine to believe what his boss told him. That they were nothing. Jensen and Marco could and would do *nothing*. They weren't capable of going against an organization like the Marcello mafia. He wasn't so sure that was the case anymore.

"I want to send Arely out of town with someone safe," Lev said, the first to break the silence. "With someone she knows, or *I* know, if possible." Likely Nessa, although that would have to be worked out considering the girl had a life that didn't revolve around him telling her what to do and when to do it. "The enforcers can go, too."

"That might be an overreaction," Andino replied.

"Is it?" He gave the man a look, sneering when he asked, "If your wife had gotten a note on her car like I did today ... after *everything*, would you call it an overreaction then?"

Andino dragged in a slow breath, his chest rising with the action as he shoved his hands into pockets. "Point taken."

"Exactly. And if you would do it for your wife or kid, then you will do it for mine, too. You and me both know the only reason why I'm even here in the first place is because of Arely. I *stayed* because of you. Because we're—"

"Friends, I know."

Lev swallowed hard. "What are they fucking doing? How do stupid fucks like Jensen and Marco even come up with shit like they pulled today? What's next, huh?"

Andino grunted under his breath. "Yeah, that's the real question. Or the *right* one, for that matter."

Lev didn't like not having the answer.

Not one bit.

"Marco has been attempting to make contact with me over the last week," Andino admitted.

Lev's head snapped to the side, his gaze nailing into his boss like a bullet blowing out of the barrel of a gun. "*What?*"

"Listen, my business is personal, and you're not privy to all of it. I'm not required to discuss or disclose *anything*, Lev."

"From the start, this has been about me and—"

"The moment Marco decided to join in on the skin trade in my territory, I was done with him. I made that clear. I believed his attempts at contact were in the vein of business as that's what he suggested and, in that regard, I had nothing to say. I cut my losses; I won't waste time with a pointless back and forth that will do nothing to fix the reason I walked away from business with him in the first place. I don't engage or entertain that sort of nonsense."

"Is it possible today was retaliation for you ignoring him?"

Andino cleared his throat, rocking on his heels when he replied, "Anything is possible. Let's just get through the next couple of days. Get your woman down the runway *safely*;

make sure Arely is far out of anyone's reach."

"And then what?"

"Well, then we end it all."

Lev's shoulders ached from the weight sitting there when he replied, "And how exactly are we going to do that?"

Andino smirked. "The Marcello way. The *only* way."

That should have been it. Lev *should* have felt satisfied.

For a second, maybe he did. But then his phone started to ring in his pocket. At damn near the same time, so did Andino's. What were the chances of that?

And he knew ...

The day wasn't over.

Not by a long shot.

TWENTY-FOUR

"HAVE YOU called through to the hotel so they know we're on the way back?" the guard driving the SUV asked at the front of the vehicle while he navigated the familiar streets of Manhattan.

The man in the seat next to hers—she was sure his name was Todd, but that was only because someone else said it, not because her mob detail *offered* their names—waved a phone high but didn't look away from the window at the passing buildings. "The last twenty-minute check-in from our guy at the hotel was ten minutes ago. I told him then. He's probably not going to check-in at the next twenty-minute mark when we're practically going to be right there anyway. They'll be ready for us to arrive, no worries."

"Good."

"I would like my phone back," Gigi spoke up.

Neither man acted as if they heard her. Or that they gave a shit about what she wanted. She had learned early on that these men weren't there to feed into what Gigi wanted if they had orders that came from Lev, or their boss who she had never met. They might be protecting her, but she wasn't *running* them or signing their paychecks.

Apparently, that was an important distinction.

"I said, I would like my phone—"

"Once we get you to the hotel," Todd said beside her. "And we get confirmation everything is good ... or not."

"What does that even mean?"

The guy gave her a look, clearly unimpressed. "Means your attitude is getting on my fucking nerves, Gigi. You'll get your phone back when you get it. *Capisce*?"

She jerked back hard into the leather of the seat. "Yeah, okay. I get it."

"Good."

Behind them, another vehicle trailed close with the rest of

Gigi's security team. It had never been more apparent to her than now about just how strange and unusual her life actually was but especially in times like these. Not that there had been many times where she felt like her life was in *real* danger. Nonetheless, it made it very clear how little say she had in anything.

Any choices were taken away. All the shots were determined by armed men in suits who, to be honest, barely said more than a few words to her at any given time. And when they did speak, it was mostly to throw orders they expected her to follow.

Without argument.

Like earlier when Lev demanded they take her back to the hotel and keep her there. *She* didn't like that idea—and knew it wasn't practical when the next forty-eight hours would be spent in a rush of final preparations to walk the runway in the Delavange show.

Did that matter to these men?

Absolutely not.

Gigi simmered in her anger silently for the rest of the drive to the hotel. It wasn't like venting her frustrations would do anything good for her or the men tasked with watching her. By the time they got through traffic and pulled under the hotel's entrance to park, thirty minutes had passed. She had a good mind to snatch her phone right out of Todd's hand when he stood outside the SUV, holding the door open to let her out.

The smart part of her brain said that wasn't a good idea and to just do what she was told until they were at least in the privacy of her hotel suite.

"Thought you said Glen would be ready when we arrived?" the man who had been driving asked as he rounded the front of the SUV. "Where the fuck is he? At least there are no goddamn paps this time. Fucking stupid we can't use the side entrance today. The next couple of days are going to be crazy."

Todd shrugged as he directed Gigi toward the revolving entrance doors with a hand high on her back. "Don't know about Glen, man. Maybe he's at the front desk because there weren't any paps out here to take care of. Let's just get her inside, yeah?"

"Swear to God I'm gonna cut him if he fucked off again. The boss isn't going to stand for that shit if he keeps it up. And it looks bad on *me*."

"Quit bitching. It's all you ever do."

"Yeah, fuck you, too, asshole."

That was probably the *most* Gigi had ever heard the two men talk before.

The other vehicle—full of security from her agency—had arrived behind them as well. Those men, all of which she did know their names and who were more liable to allow her a choice and say when possible, filed out of their vehicle but for the one driving. They were quick to get in line behind Gigi and the two enforcers walking her into the hotel.

Without a word otherwise, too.

Like her, the security from her agency simply got in line when it came to the Marcello mafia's enforcers. They had zero patience and no problem with letting anyone know it in a violent way if need be. When Lev had said her team wouldn't have much of a choice about the mob detail, he hadn't been exaggerating.

Not in the slightest.

As was standard whenever they entered the hotel from the front instead of the side or rear entrances, they headed for the bank of elevators to the right of the check-in desk. Todd stepped away to speak to the receptionist, passing over a thick, white envelope that she suspected held cash but didn't have the guts to ask.

Not that they would have told her anyway.

The silence leading up to Gigi's floor during the elevator trip only added to her growing frustration and the unanswered questions poking at the back of her mind. She knew *nothing*; not what had happened back in that parking lot to bring this on, what might happen now, or what she could do about it.

No, she was just *moved*. From one place to the next. Like a doll without a mind of her own.

Lev was going to get a piece of her mind the first second

she had her phone back in her hand, or he was standing in front of her. Whichever came first, she wasn't picky.

Lost in her swirling, angry thoughts, Gigi barely registered the elevator coming to a stop on her floor. She didn't even think before stepping out behind the enforcers who always headed the team of security now. Running on autopilot, she simply *followed*. Because that's what she was supposed to do.

"*See*," the guy to Todd's left muttered. "Glen fucked off. Just like I said."

Though it was hard to see beyond the broad shoulders of the enforcers ahead of her, Gigi could tell that Glen—the enforcer they kept running off at the mouth about—wasn't standing post at the door. If he wasn't downstairs, then he should have been up here waiting.

"Has anybody talked to my mom since we left?" Gigi asked.

The enforcer who stayed posted at the hotel checked in every twenty minutes with the rest of the team. Had he mentioned her mom leaving, maybe to grab lunch? Was that why he wasn't standing at his usual post?

Todd shot her a look over his shoulder. "Job is you, kid."

Kid.

Like she said to her fans.

It didn't feel the same.

Gigi bristled. "I'm not a k—"

"That's blood."

"What?"

"*Blood*—on the fucking door, Todd, look!"

The words were barely out of the man's mouth before another man on the team grabbed Gigi by the collar of her jacket. He wasn't kind about the way he yanked her backward, making her stumble over her own two feet. At the same time, the men up ahead pulled guns from the holsters beneath their blazers, barrels pointed straight at the door of her hotel suite when they both stepped forward together.

It was then that she saw what they did.

The thick streak of crimson that coated the doorknob and keypad entry to the room. How the blood had been smeared on the doorjamb and even dripped down to make a pool on the floor underneath the handle.

That was *a lot* of blood.

"*My mom*," Gigi said, gasping the words out because her throat tightened like a noose was choking her silent. She tried to go forward despite her heart screaming for her to stay back. Not that it mattered. Her bodyguards just pulled her backward as if she was a child throwing a tantrum and not a grown woman spiraling into the worst panic attack of her life. "My mom! *Where is my mother?* Let me go!"

Her fear came out in rapid-fire questions and broken shouts. Each one sent more tears spilling down her cheeks when silence answered her back. They said nothing and opened the door. The bloody body just beyond the threshold was plainly visible.

That's when everything went black for Gigi.

• • •

Gigi finally had her phone back.

It didn't help.

The man she kept trying to call and text—Lev—wasn't answering her back. Nothing beyond a simple *I'm sorry* when her messages became progressively more panicked that he wasn't picking up the phone for her calls.

That didn't stop Gigi from staring at the screen of the phone, her reflection looking back in the black glass, while a police detective sat across from her hard waiting room chair on his own. Up until that moment, the man had been patient with her silence and shock. He didn't push for more of a statement than she was willing to give; he was able to give her a better update on her mother's current situation than even her assistant or the rest of her team when they finally arrived at the hospital.

The detective was also starting to get annoyed. Gigi could tell by the way he rapped a beat with the tip of his pen against the face of his watch. Though he wasn't verbally telling her to speed it up, he also didn't have to for her to get the point.

"I don't know what you want me to say," Gigi said, her

voice a croak from having cried for *hours*. Just when she thought she was out of tears, more started to fill her eyes and spill down her cheeks. "I told you everything I know."

"Did you?"

Scrubbing her palms down her face, Gigi could still see the detective eyeing her through her fingers. His previous sympathy, especially after a nurse had brought a Valium and water for Gigi to take, was practically non-existent.

"You're telling me *honestly*," the detective continued, "that you don't know why your hotel room was broken into today; why one of your bodyguards was found dead; why your mother was battered, gagged, hog-tied, and left in the bathroom? Where, by the way, one of the assailants specifically wrote to *you* in blood on the mirror that you were next?"

Gigi opened her mouth to speak but the man raised a single hand high, stopping her so he could say, "We're quite aware the man who was killed today has connections to the Marcello organization. Considering your relationship with another Marcello associate—Pink, the enforcer for Andino Marcello, the boss of the operation—"

"I know him as Lev."

And that was all she wanted to know.

The detective clicked his tongue, dismissing her statement when he continued on with, "Nonetheless, I'm not willing to believe you're as ignorant about what happened today as you want me to believe, Miss Parker."

She blinked, the knot in her throat swelling to an impossible size. "Are you blaming *me*?"

"I didn't—"

"It kind of sounds like you think I *know* who it was, and I don't. My agency can provide you with an entire list of stalkers they have on their radar. The same list is given to my security team that they keep updated because they have to. Most of them are harmless. It can't be said for all of them, though. As public as I am … trust that I have my fair share of crazies that could cause problems."

"So much so that you need a hoard of mob enforcers—*criminals*—added to your security team?" the detective asked sharply, his brow arching high. "Because the rest I could get in line with … right up until we come back around to that little detail. You've been in the media a lot lately, haven't you? And your … boyfriend."

She didn't like the way he twisted the word *criminal* as if there was more to it than he was saying. It also bothered her more than she could explain that the man simply labeled the enforcers as criminals like that was *all* they were. Lev was an enforcer, too, but he was also so much more than just that title.

"*And?*" she asked, no longer willing to pretend with this man.

She gave her statement.

She knew nothing.

It wouldn't change.

What were they doing at this point?

Setting his pad of paper and pen aside, the detective leaned forward on his chair, resting his clasped hands over his knees. Maybe in an attempt to revert back to his previously friendly, sympathetic demeanor. It didn't make a difference to her when he had already made his position perfectly clear about what he thought regarding her and the attack at her hotel suite.

"Do you need help?" he asked. "We can help you. Whatever you need … I'm not sure what's gotten you tangled in the mob, Miss Parker, but you *do* have options. Just say the word and I can make it happen."

Her brow dipped as she considered what he told her.

Did she need help?

Yes.

But not from him.

"I've given my statement," she replied, "and now I would like to sit with my mother. *Please.*"

The detective let out a hard breath, sitting straight in his chair once more. Nodding, he snatched up the pad and pen, not bothering to give her another look when he said, "I'm sure you'll find a nurse to take you to her room. Good luck. I hear you have a big day happening, don't you? I'm sure the two of us will be seeing each other again."

She certainly hoped not.

Not that she would be so lucky.

By the time Gigi did get to her mother's room, the hospital announced over the speaker system that visiting hours were ending. One of the two people waiting outside her mother's room had Gigi grateful for the announcement.

Kayla offered her a small smile and a warm hug that Gigi took happily, saying, "Didn't want to head out before I could say goodbye. Don't worry. I'll have all the changes in the schedule handled. I've already got a new suite—a whole floor, actually—booked and ready at The Plaza. Just worry about your mom tonight, okay?"

"Thanks. For everything. You've always got it under control even when everything is blowing up around me, Kayla."

"Seems as though that's happening a lot lately, doesn't it?" asked the woman to Kayla's left.

It was the first time Gigi had seen Marla since the women flew in. Her agent wore the same white power suit she always preferred, and the cold attitude that could burn anyone who got too close hadn't changed, either.

Nothing new to see here.

"Marla," Gigi said, offering nothing else.

Not a hug.

Her hand.

Or a fuck, either.

"I sincerely hope this latest issue isn't going to affect your walk in the Delavange show in two days, Gigi. It's too late to consider changing the headliner now. Delavange won't be pleased, and you can bet you won't wear another of his garments let alone walk in Fashion Week again if you pull out now."

That's what she cared about?

"I haven't even seen my mother yet, and you're already barking at me about my *runway walk*," Gigi said. "I don't even know if she's awake in there or—"

"She is," Kayla spoke up, shooting Marla a frown. "Or she was when I talked to her. She said the water tasted like crap, so I ran down to the vending machines and got her a bottle that she likes instead. She looks worse than she is, I promise. The doctor said she would be out of here in a few days. They just want to see the swelling go down and make sure there's no infection in the wound on her head."

Bile rose to the back of Gigi's tongue. They found her mother in the bathtub, unconscious. The detective was right in how he made her feel—this was partly her fault. She just wasn't clear on all the damn details.

The guilt would kill her.

"And she was asking for you ... a lot," Kayla added.

Perfect.

That just made Gigi's heart hurt worse.

"Yes, unfortunate your mother was hurt today," Marla said, lifting her hand to inspect the French manicure on her nails as she spoke. "Seems bad things tend to happen when you're not where you're supposed to be, Gigi. A shame, that."

"What does that mean?"

Marla shrugged, her steely brown gaze drifting from Gigi to a spot over her shoulder when she replied, "Well, had you been at our meeting during lunch, then you and the entire security team would have been at the hotel, yes? Something to consider. And do not think for one second that this little issue of your mother being in the hospital will stop your responsibilities. You're still expected to show up for the run-through with the rest of the models for tomorrow as well as the—"

"Marla," Kayla muttered.

"One thing at a time, then." The woman lifted her hands high at Gigi's glare. "I'm just saying. It wasn't like the team needed another mess piled on top of the mountain you've already created for us during this trip, Gigi. You used to be so much better at just doing what you were told ... we had much less problems then."

She was not doing this.

Not tonight.

"That's quite enough," Gigi muttered, over the entire day. She had more questions than answers. A mother that needed her. A runway walk coming up that she couldn't *not* do but no longer really gave a shit about. And a man who still wasn't answering her calls. The last thing she was going to do was stand here with Marla and let the bitch tear her down more than she already was, even if only emotionally. "Visiting hours are over. Make sure the car is here in the morning—I'll be in the backseat on time, ready for the day. Are we clear?"

Marla tipped her head up, her gaze colder than ever when she replied, "I'm not sure there's very much that's clear in your world right now, Gigi."

How could she respond to that?

Gigi didn't even bother.

The lights to her mother's hospital room were dimmed when Gigi stepped inside the sterile-smelling space, and she didn't bother to turn them brighter. It wasn't like she needed more light to clearly see the state of her mother's battered body and face tucked into the stark-white hospital-issued sheets.

Blackened eyes. Kimie's top and bottom lip had been split something terrible, the swelling making it far more horrifying. And probably sore. Bruises colored her mother's skin everywhere. They seemed to have no start or end. A bandage on the side Kimie's head covered the wound Kayla had mentioned.

Gigi wasn't even getting the full picture because a quick glance at the note board on the bottom of the bed said her mother also suffered a cracked rib, sprained wrist, and more but she had to stop reading.

She *hurt* looking at her mom. Kimie seemed *so small* in the bed, attached to an IV and leads monitoring her vitals. The soft beeps of the machines weren't enough to cover the sniffles escaping Gigi as she moved to the side of her mother's bed.

As if Kimie felt her presence, her bruised eyes peeked open. Though swollen, she still found Gigi standing there. She tried to smile. It just made Gigi cry harder.

"I'm sorry, Mom," she whispered, bending down to kiss her mother's tender cheek. Her fingers wrapped tightly around Kimie's hand, and her mother grabbed back. "I'm so sorry."

"*Gigi* ... don't cry, my baby. It's okay."

Every word had to hurt.

It sure sounded like it.

"It's not okay. This shouldn't have happened, Mom."

Kimie let out an exhale that rattled. "What have you gotten yourself mixed up with here, Gigi?"

Pain and guilt clogged up her throat.

She didn't have an answer.

Certainly not the right one.

• • •

It was well over an entire day later—*hours* before her runway walk—when Lev finally showed up. Between the manicurist doing her nails, the woman touching up her spray tan, a waxer who fit in a quick appointment before the hairstylist would arrive to add the extensions into her hair along with a color to finally remove what remained of the faded pink in the ends, Lev arrived. Amidst the chaos of her team bouncing between phone calls and last-minute changes for many details regarding the day in the new Plaza suite, he strolled right in like he owned the place. Like it was a perfect time.

Gigi didn't know whether to be impressed by his arrogance.

Or *pissed*.

Despite her repeated attempts to contact him, either on her own or through one of the several enforcers still on her post, he had been radio silent. *Entirely.*

At his approach, she stood from the chair facing the bay windows of the hotel suite; windows that had been allowing the manicurist better natural lighting while giving Gigi something to stare at as people continued touching her.

All of her.

Her hair.

Hands.

Limbs.

Face.

Everywhere.

She couldn't breathe without a new set of hands finding

her body. Add that on top of the fact she hadn't been able to talk to her mother—who was still in the hospital—for more than a few minutes that day and then Lev's sudden presence with no warning, and Gigi's nerves hit their limit.

"*Where have you been?*"

She could count on one hand the number of times she raised her voice on an event day. Not because she worried about losing her voice as that didn't really matter. No, because she liked as much calm as possible in an already overstimulating, chaotic environment.

Lev didn't even wince at her anger, his gaze taking in the scene of her team rushing through the room and barely giving him any thought at all. They had their own jobs to do, after all, and if they didn't do it, then she couldn't do hers.

The countdown was on.

"Busy, isn't it?" he asked, offering her a slight grin.

"Is this *funny* to you?" She took a step toward him, vaguely aware of the quiet noise the manicurist made behind her at the scene. "Do you know what I've had to do over the last day? The interviews with *police* ... the hospital, my *mom*. You left me to do it alone. How dare you leave me here to do that *alone*?"

Finally, the rest of the room seemed to take notice of Gigi's anger and how high her voice raised because of it. The movement all around them slowly came to a stop as several pairs of eyes turned on the two.

"Gigi," the assistant who helped Kayla on event days tried to soothe from his spot at the wet bar, "Do you want a drink, honey?"

"*No.*"

"You sound like you might."

"Get back to work!" She spun to the side, glaring at other members of the team also gawking and now doing nothing. "Stop standing there—*work!*"

This wasn't like her.

Even she knew it.

The trembling in her hands had Gigi trying to hide them so no one else would notice. They already thought she had fucked everything up anyway, thanks to Marla and the woman's constant need to undermine *everything* Gigi did with the team. She didn't need to prove them right.

Lev noticed it, however. "Bedroom, *now*."

Gigi's gaze snapped to his, defiant and disbelieving. "What did you just say to me? "

"Get to the bedroom, babe. We can talk. Or you're going to snap, and I don't think that's what you want to do. *Go*. Right now."

She should have told him to fuck off. He would have deserved it. Instead, like her body was on autopilot, she turned and headed for the French doors across the suite that led into the master bedroom. Lev followed behind.

She went quietly. Until the bedroom doors closed.

TWENTY-FIVE

GIGI WAS seconds away from a nervous breakdown. Lev could tell, and he didn't need her to say it to confirm his suspicions, either. He imagined this wasn't the first time she had been put under an immense amount of pressure and stress.

Her entire career *was* pressure and stress.

He didn't think for a second that she had been put in the kind of situation she was currently facing, however, and it *showed*. He doubted she wanted that which was why he suggested—or demanded, rather—the bedroom for privacy if she wanted to scream her feelings out at him.

She was due.

He wouldn't deny it.

The second the French doors closed behind them, everything Gigi had been trying to hide came spilling out of her like a tornado intent on destruction. He couldn't remember seeing her *so angry* before. Not mad enough to rip a framed picture from the wall. Or to sweep the bottles of perfume and decorations from the dresser.

She moved from one thing to the next. Yanked sheets from the bed. Kicked a purse across the room. Screamed into her fists until she was gasping for air.

Again and again, until the floor became a wasteland of her pain and rage, and there was nothing left for her to destroy. All the while, Lev stood back in the corner, silent until she finally came to a stop in the middle of the room where, without warning, she dropped to the floor.

Sitting cross-legged on the silver blanket with black detailing that she'd ripped from the bed, Gigi's shoulders heaved as her panting breaths turned to aching sobs. Each one sent a splinter straight into Lev's heart, cracking the organ open until it felt like he was bleeding pain and regret into his chest cavity with every beat.

He didn't think she wanted him near her.

He also couldn't stop himself.

Crossing the floor before he could convince himself that it was a bad idea, Lev kneeled down to get Gigi's tear-streaked face in his hands. One cupped her cheek, the other rested on top of the pulse point in her throat where he could feel her heart racing like the wings of a hummingbird. She stared up at him, still so hesitant, her silk letterman jacket vibrating from how she still shook like a little leaf. The light from the window filtered through the crack in the gray shades, spilling through the room to color the space in soft tones that belied the destruction around them.

For a second, it was just him and her.

Nothing else.

"Where were you?" she asked, chin quivering.

"I'm sorry." He wanted to say that first. She deserved to hear it more than anything else he had to say. "Did you see the hoard of paparazzi outside the hospital while you were there?"

The confusion in her stare said she didn't. Frankly, the updates he had received from her guards were enough to know, for the most part, Gigi hadn't been clued into the reality around her for the last couple of days. She was just ... doing what she had to.

Very little else.

"I had to get Arely out of town," he explained, "and by the time I got back, the media was a fucking circus all over the city. *I* was being followed. News reports were blasted about it. It's not just tabloids this time, babe. There's too much attention. Police pulled in every made man they could for interviews all over the city. I would have only made it worse coming and going so I laid low until things were a little better."

But not by fucking much.

Outside The Plaza was a goddamn shitshow of photographers and fans waiting behind metal barriers the police had needed to come and set up. He managed to sneak in through a side entrance when an enforcer came down to let him in, but he doubted his escape would be as clean. Not that it mattered. He needed to be here.

"You didn't even *call*," she whispered, her voice breaking at the end. "Just a stupid text that didn't tell me anything, Lev."

Leaning down lower, his palms slipped under her jaw to tip her head higher. His mouth pressed to her trembling lips, tasting the salt of her tears while his thumbs dragged soothing lines back and forth across her silken skin. He was patient, each caress of his lips across hers encouraging and tender until she was finally kissing him back. He didn't pull away until she was gasping for breath all over again.

"I'm sorry," he murmured against her lips.

A hiccup answered him back.

His poor girl.

She seemed so strong.

She *was*.

Sometimes, she was also so very weak. He didn't mind being the person who gave her the safe space to show that weakness, though. The rest of the world could see what they wanted from Gigi Rey but to him … he would hold together the pieces of what was left.

"I'm gonna be there today," he promised, "watching you, so nothing is going to happen. You do what *you do*—do it well, okay? Don't worry about the rest."

"I don't *know* what the rest even is!"

He kissed her again.

Harder that time.

"We're still figuring that out ourselves," he muttered, not at all happy about it, "but once this day is over, and they stop watching us like they are, I'll fix everything. I will, Gigi. It'll all go away."

"But will it?"

"I promise. I don't break those."

Her small hands reached back for him, fisting into his blazer and pulling him down for a third kiss that was nothing like the first two. While one had been soft and the second, harder, this kiss lit a flame inside his chest that exploded inside his very veins. Her tongue clashed with his before her teeth scraped along his lower lip.

Her intention was clear. Especially when she pulled him down to the floor with her. They were a mess of rushed hands, tangled limbs, and breathless kisses in the pile of her destruction. He found his way out of his clothes before he knew what happened and hers quickly followed. It was clear in the way her teeth found his jaw and her fingernails scored hard into the backs of his shoulders that she didn't want *easy*.

Should he leave marks on her body?

Today of all days?

"*Fuck me*," she begged, arching under his weight until her tits pressed to his chest, and her thighs spread wide for him to grind his hardening cock against the heat of her sex. His fingers flexed tightly at her sides, the need to own her and show the rest of the world exactly who this woman belonged to. They only thought it was them. The truth was so much more raw for him. She was *his*. Every single inch of her. "Fuck me until it goes away—I need to breathe again. Make it go away."

He didn't know what *it* was.

Him.

Her.

The whole world.

He could do what she asked, though. And he could do it well.

One of her hands slipped between them, finding his cock in a tight grip that had him choking out a groan of her name. Thick on his tongue, the sound didn't feel like him and yet it was. Her thumb smeared the drop of precum that had gathered at the tip of his dick, and her hips rocked along the underside of his length at the same time. Between the fleshy lips of her pussy, her slick wetness coated the sensitive skin of his cock with every tilt of her hips.

Her breaths came out faster. Those emerald orbs of hers watched him through dark, long lashes. A slight shift of his hips, and the head of his cock found the wet heat of her slit. His first thrust took her hard, sending Gigi falling hard against the floor and grasping for something to steady her.

"*Lev!*"

"That's right—pray my fucking name. Let them all hear it. If they can hear you rage it, they can hear you scream it too, babe. Fucking give it to me. *All of it.*"

One of his hands caught hers and held them high above her head. His other found the underside of her jaw, squeezing just enough to make her whimper. She gave it back just as hard, every flex of his hips meeting hers while her heels dug hard into his spine, and her teeth caught the tips of his fingers when he ghosted them along her quivering lips.

If she was only cracking before, he was shattering her now. Every slap of their bodies mixing in with her keening moans and his filthy promises.

Every single *take that dick* and *you're gonna walk that runway with my cum in your cunt* only added to the harshness of their fucking. Primal and raw, the sight of her unraveling beneath him when he knew in only a few short hours she would be presented to the world as a perfect doll ready to smile on cue ... well, that did things to him that he couldn't explain.

She came once.

"*Again,*" Gigi demanded.

He had her bent over the bed and gagged with the silk tie from her robe before she had even finished shaking her way through the first orgasm. She came like that, too. A little steadier; still just as chaotic, but clear-eyed and *ready.*

Good.

That's what she needed to be.

He spilled his cum as deep as he could manage, and then smeared what remained on his dick all over her ass when he was done.

She finally looked ... better.

Happier, maybe.

Lev hoped it wasn't a lie.

• • •

Lev stayed safely hidden behind the tinted windows of a rented BMW while he watched Gigi be led through the hoard

273

of photogs waiting outside The Plaza. With large sunglasses hiding her face and an army of guards surrounding her and the team, they certainly didn't get a picture worth taking let alone an answer to their questions. The screaming fans shoving magazines beyond the gates of the metal barriers didn't seem bothered that their icon hadn't paid them any mind as she was directed past their spot.

As fast as she came out of the hotel, she was shoved into the back of a black limo before the others piled in right behind her. By the time the car sped off, less than two minutes had passed.

Well done, he thought. The less time she spent outside four walls right then, the better. Or rather, the *safer* she would be.

In his ear, a familiar voice spoke, confirming something he had been waiting for all day. "Marco is not engaging. The last message I received from him came through this afternoon to my *uncle*—because that wouldn't piss me off at all—and only said he had washed his hands of *this mess*."

Lev considered that, but it only left him with more questions when he asked his boss, "What mess is that exactly? Because I would say his hand has been just fine stirring this damn pot up until now. What, two days ago he was willing to reach out and today he's decided to fuck off? Something isn't right, Andino. Something is—"

"Wrong," Andino interjected coolly. "That's become painfully obvious."

"Did we wait too long? Are we beyond a point of no return here where we can stop whatever he's planning to do, or is this just going to become another waiting game now?"

A loud sigh crackled through the speakers.

Lev knew that feeling too well.

A thought that had stayed with him from the moment he knew Gigi's mother had been attacked in the hotel room came back to the surface, bothering him more than ever. "It's not what it seems on the surface—this is personal. You don't do what they've done and then blame it on someone being pissed about *business*. This is beyond a failed partnership."

"I would be inclined to agree."

"I'm glad we're on the same page. That also does

absolutely fuck all to help—"

"Because it's one hour to the next right now, Pink," his boss said, the no-nonsense tone reminding him that at the end of the day, he still had a job to do and a man to answer to. "And today you're making sure the men get Gigi through her runway walk, then we get her the fuck out of the city."

"Oh, she's going to *love* that."

Sarcasm was still his friend.

Andino chuckled dryly. "Sometimes, women just ... have to make it difficult. Nonetheless, once she is out of the way and safe, we'll move to the next stage."

"He looked at her like he *bought* her. Like something he owned."

"Who?"

"Jensen," Lev muttered. "And the way your ex-partner is acting up in Cali right now, it makes me think washing his hands might just mean protecting him."

"This is hard to deal with when we have a spotlight shining on us, you know? We have to consider every move we make. We cannot rush into anything without knowing that each hit we make will land on the target."

"So help me fucking God, Andino, if Jensen Todrey—or someone from Marco's side of things—steps out of line tonight, I don't care who watches. I will *murder* him."

"It's a terrible thing, isn't it?"

"What?"

"How they always seem to go after our women. Instead of *us*, the people who can answer them back. No, they go after the links they see as the weakest."

"She is anything but *weak*."

Only with him.

Only if she needed to be.

Andino hummed under his breath, adding, "Every move you make will have a consequence if it's not done properly."

"And yet?" Lev asked.

"You know I don't actually enjoy making enemies in my business, right?"

"*Andino.*"

"If I don't get a response to my requests for a phone call by tonight, then tomorrow we go after Jensen first."

A pressure released in Lev's chest.

One night.

That was it.

He just had to get Gigi through the night and like he promised, it would all start to go away.

"Even if the world is watching?" Lev asked.

Andino didn't hesitate. "Even then. Do you love her?"

Yes.

More than the sky and sea and everything within it combined. He loved his daughter in the same way he needed air to breathe. His love for Gigi came from a different place. How could he not love *her*—she reminded him of who he was before he was Pink ... when he was just a man and nothing and nobody owned him by their will. She did, though.

She owned him.

He was hers.

Freely.

He planned on telling her exactly that. But the *when* was just a matter of time because he wouldn't do it while it felt like the rest of the world was watching. He didn't belong to the world. Neither did his love for her.

To his boss, however, Lev simply replied, "Of course, I do."

"I'll make a call. Check up on John and his wife. See how Arely is doing with them out of state."

"Thank you."

"It's almost over, Pink."

But was it?

Why didn't it feel like it?

• • •

Not knowing what to expect during a runway show for Fashion Week—seeing as how Lev's life had *only* intersected with that business through Gigi—the shock of the rather large crowd for the Delavange event put him off-balance.

It wasn't a good place to be, and the longer he sat in the front row seat off to the left at the end of the long runway stage, the worse his agitation became. That he couldn't see her; that the show had yet to start; that it felt like he didn't know *anything*.

Gigi hadn't lied.

They couldn't get backstage. Only *her* team was permitted access and even then, not for long. The stylists and teams working on the models needed room to move and then more room again just in case, apparently. The only reason they were even inside the building was that the Marcello organization pulled weight in the city.

Or just the Marcello name did.

Hence Haven Marcello currently sitting next to Lev in the front row. Her name had been more than enough to get him and the other enforcers tickets. Problem was, once they were inside the venue waiting for the show to start, they were seated and expected to *stay there*. Especially because they were in the front row, and the show was being recorded to be televised at a later date.

Because that wasn't problematic *at all*.

"Phones *on mute*," a man from down the way in a black tuxedo barked at Haven when her cell dinged in her lap again.

To her benefit, she didn't even blink a lash before she raised one perfectly manicured, red stiletto fingernail high. Her middle finger. The guy's jaw dropped as he stiffened, grunted under his breath, and then spun on his heel to head for the men at the far end of the seats with comms in their ears.

"Don't get us kicked out," Lev said under his breath.

She only laughed. "Right. Little late for that. Show's about to start."

Was it?

Lev couldn't tell.

The flashing blue and pink lights overhead moved in time with the music pumping through the place. At the far end of the runway, shimmery drapery hung in heavy piles, spilling to the floor like glimmering puddles. The same material had been strung across the ceiling overhead, connecting overtop the middle of the runway where a chandelier hung down that was the size of a small car.

He only needed to glance at the faces in the front row seats to get a good culture shock. Never in his life had he seen so many celebrities in the same place together, let alone this close to him. Not that he cared *who* they were or that they were there.

It was just ... different.

A whole new world.

As a man stepped out on the runway at the far end, a microphone in hand, Lev moved a bit to the left so that he could meet the gaze of one of the enforcers across the way from him. The seat next to the man was empty making Lev raise his brow in silent question. Todd answered back with a tap to his left temple and then pointed toward the bathrooms.

"Seriously?"

Todd shook his head, mouthing, "Doing a walk around."

Huh.

Well, at least one of them was able to do *something*. That was fucking better than nothing.

During the exchange, Lev managed to miss the announcements made by the man with the microphone. He caught on soon enough when the start of the show was made abundantly clear by the famous singer that came rushing through the piles of shimmering fabric, belting out her latest single that was constantly played on the radio. In towering heels and a white leather ensemble that showed more skin than it covered, the singer twirled and whirled her way closer to the middle of the runway while singing all at the same time.

The lights changed, spinning faster.

Lev's attention snapped back and forth between the singer, the lights driving him crazy overhead, and the fabric at the far end of the runway where Gigi would soon come through to *really* start the show.

"*Opening the Delavange show for the season,*" came a voice through the speaker system, "*is Miss Gigi Rey!*"

Lev's stare locked on the end of the runway, beyond the singer and the crowd and *everything* ... because this felt important for Gigi. In fact, he knew it was. Despite everything else going wrong in her life, this was a moment she had worked hard for and deserved.

She came out of the piles looking like a complex in heels. Ethereal in a white and silver bra and panty set with matching garter, and yet fierce in every sense of the word as she stepped forward.

She was godly, even.

He didn't want to say angelic. That wasn't even good enough to describe the massive glittering wings that loomed high from her back, spread wide on either side of her thin frame. She took two steps, legs gleaming straight down to the silver, diamond-encrusted six-inch heels on her feet. The extra ten inches of length in her blonde hair had been set in large curls that framed her face. A face painted to perfection with red lips and smoked out eyes stared out toward the end of the runway without fear.

Ready, he knew.

He didn't know if it was standard or normal for the crowd to be on their feet at the opening model, but they were. *Clapping.* He joined in with Haven standing next to him at the same time he noticed the other enforcer returning to his seat with a security guard—not one of Gigi's, but for the event—at his side.

There seemed to be a note or beat Gigi was waiting for and once the singer hit it, she started her walk. Every step hit the runway hard with confidence. Her hips swayed with the beat, and her walk until she came to the middle of the runway where the singer was belting out the chorus. She stopped to do a little spin with the singer, hand in hand, the wings on her back fluttering open from the air catching under the feathers.

And then she was right back on it.

All the way down the runway.

She didn't look his way.

He didn't need her to.

At the end of the stage, her hands met her hips for one pose, and then a second. Her left hand popped up to give the crowd the peace sign, earning another round of applause before she spun around just as fast and headed back down the runway.

"Well done, Gigi," Andino's wife said at Lev's side.

"She's ... the most amazing thing I've ever seen."

Haven only nodded in response.

Before he knew what happened, Gigi was at the start of the runway again and then she disappeared off to the side. Another model came out through the drops of shimmering fabric but Lev didn't care to watch anyone else.

He counted down the minutes.

Nearly an hour until the last model had made her final walk, the singer had sung her way through every hit she had in the last five years, and it was Gigi's turn to come out again to close the show as she had opened it.

Except the last model disappeared off to the side like every other one, but Gigi didn't burst through the shimmering wall of fabric like she had before. Ten seconds passed.

Then another few.

Murmurs passed through the crowd. The singer at the middle of the runway even glanced back over her shoulder as she started to close in on the end of her song, clearly knowing something wasn't right.

Lev didn't wait to leave his seat. He wouldn't wait another ten seconds when his heart and soul already knew ... *everything was wrong*. There was no way Gigi would miss her mark.

He could feel it. Deep in the pit of his stomach. Echoing within his chest. Flooding his veins with every beat of his heart.

It felt like emptiness.

Propelled by a force that wasn't his own down the aisle of chairs, past people with faces he had only seen on television before that moment, he made a beeline for the section where men in black suits stood shoulder to shoulder like a wall.

"Lev!" someone called behind him.

To his left, the models started walking out in a long line. One after the other. The official *end* to the show, but it wasn't right.

It just wasn't.

Where was Gigi?

"Sir, you can't go back—"

The man in the suit with the comm in his ear didn't even get to finish his sentence before Lev's fist met the man's face.

The guy hit the floor.

Before anyone could grab him, Lev stepped over the groaning, bleeding man and headed backstage. He heard the yells behind him, felt the arms reaching for him, but he just kept moving. One step after another. Each one had his heart feeling more and more hollow.

The security backstage moved a lot faster than the ones he'd passed earlier. And he quickly found out why, too.

"Gigi is gone," someone said. He didn't know who. Did it matter? "Nobody can find her."

Red tinted his vision.

The rage swelled.

And then Lev was taken to the floor from behind. It took three security guards to keep him down, and he made sure they fucking worked for it, too.

The assholes.

TWENTY-SIX

SOMETIMES, THE whys couldn't be answered. Although Gigi had certainly learned that lesson more than once over her lifetime, it didn't make it any easier when once again, she found herself asking *why*.

Why her?

Why this?

Why me?

Why?

She couldn't remember when she woke up or how exactly she realized that she had been blindfolded and bound with her wrists tied at her back. It took entirely too long for her to understand the swaying movement around her, rocking her against something hard at her left and something softer at her back meant she was probably in the back of a vehicle.

A backseat.

Though it hurt to do—*everything* fucking hurt—and it took way too much energy, Gigi clenched her fingers, her nails dragging across the seat. Supple. *Soft*. Expensive. It was enough to tell her the seats were leather. What good that did for her? Nothing, really.

But at least she knew something.

It was better than knowing nothing.

That was also the moment Gigi came to another horrifying realization—her mind was starting to *clear*. The hazy confusion that she had come to consciousness with was drifting away with each rock of the vehicle. At first, she thought it was a dream. A terrifying nightmare she couldn't wake up from. Now she knew she *was* awake.

And it was still a nightmare.

She just didn't know what kind.

Did it matter?

The clawing panic digging into her chest had Gigi panting out breaths that came in bursts faster than she knew was healthy and yet, she couldn't stop. *Not right. This isn't right.* Her thoughts screamed, the terror an echoing cry that became louder with her racing heartbeats. She tried to let the sound out; to get the screams out of her mind and into the air.

She needed help.

Somebody help me!

And yet, opening her mouth only made the dryness coating her tongue and throat worse as if she was choking on the scratchiness and gagging from the putrid taste of old vomit. Had she thrown up? Getting her mouth open didn't help, either, because she couldn't make a sound. As if everything else wasn't confusing and bad enough, being unable to talk or scream or even *beg* shot her fear sky-fucking-high.

Was what wrong with her?

What was happening?

Every question that she didn't have an answer to only made her terror spiral faster and darker, coiling around her heart and lungs until the organs ached from the stress of it all. The only good thing Gigi could currently do was *move*.

Because she couldn't at first.

Now, it seemed she could. Her limbs were less heavy and dead; the weight that had kept her immobile while the quiet vehicle drove her to ... *wherever* ... started to lift. Like the fog clearing in her brain, allowing her to think and *know* she was in a bad place, it was also letting go of the hold it had on her body.

She used that.

Jerking against the restraints, struggling to get her legs high enough to kick whatever was in front of her. A seat, likely. Before she realized it, Gigi was having a full physical meltdown—or maybe her *fight* instinct had finally kicked in. Either way, her trashing, and silent screams seemed to fall on deaf ears.

At first.

The tears that managed to slip down from beneath the blindfold found her dry lips that she licked away with her next gasping breath. The salty wetness on her tongue was the only relief she found at that moment.

It was the amused chuckle from her right, so close that he had to be in the seat next to her, chilled Gigi to the bone. She froze all over, her fight coming to a stop when she heard the unmistakable voice of Jensen Todrey.

"Stop that nonsense, my silly girl, before you make another mess on yourself."

My silly girl.

How the man could sound both affectionate but also terrifying at the same time, Gigi didn't know. The sudden swell of panic that came on like a wave, however, didn't give her much time to consider it when the vomit came up fast and violent.

Someone swore.

Someone that wasn't Jensen.

"Well, Jesus," Jensen muttered, his voice slightly farther away than it had been. The smell of her sickness was thick with her next breath, pulling another gag from her throat. "Quite enough of that, dolly. Let me put you back to sleep."

"*What—*"

It was the first word Gigi had been able to form.

It was also the last one.

A prick of something sharp hit her in the side of the neck, and in the next seconds she was drifting again. Slipping away into warm darkness that felt like someone had brought a thick quilt to wrap around her entire body. She found nothingness in that blank, black place.

Except she remembered now, too. It was the needle that brought the memory on. The needle Jensen stabbed into her neck the same way he had done at the show when she had slipped behind the dressing curtain after getting her wings removed so that she could easily slip into the final outfit for the night.

He'd been waiting there like it was ... planned. A security guard from the event helped him subdue her with a hand clapped over her mouth and an arm around her throat.

"*You'll just look wasted when we leave,*" he had said, his laugh a taunt when he pulled the needle out. "*Another wasted model fucking up her life, Gigi. They won't even know the difference.*"

She remembered everything.
She wished she didn't.

• • •

The next time Gigi came to some sense of awareness, she
knew two things for certain.

The car had stopped moving, and her blindfold had slipped
down. She was also face down along the backseat in a
position that had her chin propped up on the leather so that
when she opened her eyes, the first thing she saw was
directly outside the vehicle.

Someone had left the backdoor open.

Did she consider running?

Hell.

Gigi couldn't move to run.

She didn't know how long she had been out for the second
time but some things were different enough to say it had
been a while. Long enough for someone to clean the car as it
no longer smelled like her vomit. Or maybe that was just
because the door was open and fresh air rushed in that she
gulped down as much as she could.

If she had been cleaned, Gigi couldn't tell.

All of that was also secondary to the sight right in front of
her face. Beyond the opened door of the vehicle, she watched
Jensen and another man—the same security guard from the
show who had helped him take Gigi—argue until the two of
them were face to face, hands waving wildly and spittle flying
with every shout between them.

Their words sounded funny.

Muffled.

That couldn't be right.

Despite the sensation of being underwater, Gigi caught a
few things thrown between the men.

"I didn't sign up for *that*," the guard snapped.

Jensen barked a laugh, coming forward at the man like a
bull ready to run him over. "*What*—you thought this was
going to be a fun day trip with her?"

Was he mad she had been sick?

Or something else?

"I'm not going to drive you around while you molest her in the backseat. Whatever the fuck you do when I drop you off, that's up to you. But I'm not going to sit there and listen to it *or* watch it, Todrey. You fucking hear me?"

"Oh, you have *morals* now. That's a rich take."

Nausea swelled in Gigi.

Had he been touching her?

Was he—

"Fuck *this*," the guard hissed, pointing a finger at Jensen as he added, "I am *done*. Drive yourself the rest of the way. I'm not going any further."

The man started to walk away.

Jensen was laughing again.

It was such a morbid sound. Evil, but *pleased*. Like he had nothing left to lose. The gun he pulled out from beneath his suit jacket said he didn't care at all.

Gigi choked back a sob, her dry, cracked lips parting to warn the guard walking away because even if he had helped to do this ... weren't his words enough to say the man had some sort of conscience?

Nothing came out.

She still couldn't talk.

Jensen didn't hesitate, the gun in his hand snapping back hard when he pulled the trigger. As if the world wasn't already moving too slow around Gigi, it came to a crawl as she saw the bullet plug into the back of the guard's head.

Blood sprayed.

Gigi coughed on bile.

He hit the ground face first.

She didn't even have time to process what was happening before Jensen wiped the gun on his sleeve, tucked it away beneath his jacket, and turned back for the car. Maybe had she been in her right mind, she could have pretended that she was still passed out.

Instead, she just watched him walk toward her. Each step was more ominous than the last as his angry expression changed to something far more sinister.

"Awake, are you?" he asked.

Gigi didn't reply.

Didn't even try.

Kneeling right outside the car's open door, Jensen came eye-level with Gigi. Tremors rocked her from head to toe, and the tears had started falling again. Silent tears because she had a feeling this man would enjoy the sounds of her cries far too much.

"Do you want to know what I'm going to do with you?" he asked.

She still said nothing.

Jensen grinned, the glint in his eye turning darker as he reached out to stroke her cheek with two fingers. The *soft* touch quickly turned harsh when his grip dug into her cheek and jaw, and he pushed her head back into an awkward position as he stood up. It forced her to stare up at him. Something she didn't want to do at all.

"Doesn't matter," he said. "It'll all be the same to you, but you'll learn to like it. They all did, my girl. They all learned, but I got bored ... I got bored of the same shit, the same *girls*. They all did the same things; heads full of air but they'd do what they were told. I finally got to pick one of my own. *You.* See, that's why you're special. I picked you."

She didn't want to be picked.

Whatever that meant.

Gigi yanked her face out of his hand with what little bit of energy she had left, doing her best to muster up a sneer even through her hot tears. "Don't *touch* me."

The words came out dry.

They scraped out of her throat.

Jensen only laughed at her plight before he slapped her hard enough to make Gigi see stars. Then, his hand was right back on her face, squeezing tight enough to make her whimper and her jaw ache. He shook her head, the strands of messy hair falling into her eyes, but it didn't hide the sight of his other hand reaching for the zipper on his pants.

"Should have learned by now to just *do what you're told*, Gigi. When you become a problem, people don't mind getting rid of you, and that's exactly what they did. See, now you're my thing to play with because you couldn't behave for someone else."

Ice filled her veins.

Did he mean her—

"I don't mind the time it'll take to teach you," he said. "Now open your fucking mouth."

His zipper came down.

She wouldn't do what he said.

"*Open your mouth.*"

She still wouldn't.

He just forced it open.

TWENTY-SEVEN

"I WENT on a boat yesterday, Daddy!"

Arely's excitement on the phone had Lev smiling despite the emptiness in his heart. He didn't know how the rage that constantly kept him company over the last two days could leave him feeling empty, and yet it did.

"That's great, baby," he replied. "I'm glad you're having fun with John and Siena."

He would forever be grateful to Andino's cousin and the man's wife for taking Arely out of state with a handful of bodyguards just in case when Nessa hadn't been able to do it. While he knew the best place for his daughter was far away from New York, it didn't make it any easier to be separated from her.

Especially *now*.

Turning away from the man eyeing him at the other side of the metal table for a better sense of privacy as he talked to Arely, Lev told his daughter, "So hey, Daddy loves you. I know you asked John when you could come home ... but it might be a little longer, okay? Sometimes, we have to do this."

"But why?"

That wasn't an easy answer. And not one she could understand. Lev didn't even try to simplify it for his child, he simply replied, "Because that's what's best right now. You understand?"

Arely sighed loudly on the other end of the phone. "I *guess*. John wouldn't let me watch Gigi on the TV, Daddy. I saw her on it. How come she was on the TV?"

"*Why*," he corrected, the habit impossible to break. "And because that's part of her job sometimes."

It was all bullshit.

He knew exactly what Arely was referring to because he had already been filled in by the man who had come to visit him in jail and also brought a cell phone along for him to make a safe, secure call to his daughter that wouldn't be recorded like on the payphones here. The bullshit charges the cops leveled on him after the show for the punch he threw were apparently going to stick if the officials had anything to say about it. Whatever they could do to get a Marcello associate behind bars.

Little did they know this was the *last* place he needed to be. Not that he thought the cops cared or even understood what was happening outside of the jailhouse. Even Lev didn't know everything but what he did know ... well it was enough to make him want to get *out*.

Now.

Yesterday.

As soon as fucking possible.

Video of Gigi leaving the show with Jensen Todrey—and a security guard who was later found dead on a dirt road that led off from the freeway—through a rear entrance looking out of her mind, totally wasted, had been released to the public the very next day. Statements made by Gigi's agency and management team made it seem like they didn't have any idea why she did what she did by leaving the show early or the reason for her obvious intoxication. Photos of that first lunch date between her and Jensen had also been released, making it seem like there had been some kind of relationship between the two that explained their ... disappearance together.

It was almost like Gigi's team *wanted* her gone, and they were willing to say whatever the public needed to hear to justify behavior that didn't match up to her character or previous actions.

Lev just needed to get out of this fucking jail. That was it. Then he would go through each and every single stupid *fuck* that he needed to in order to get to Gigi. Wherever she was.

I'm coming, babe. I am.

"Daddy?"

Arely's soft call for him dragged Lev from his thoughts. A place that had become a prison of sorts for him lately. It was a bad thing when a man like him had nothing to do *except* think. He knew every failure he made that led to this. He understood how this was his fault. They hadn't done enough; hadn't planned for everything. He fucked up.

And look what happened.

"Yeah?" he asked, swallowing the lump in his throat.

"John says I have to get off the phone. Lunch is ready. I'm having poutine."

He laughed, as weak as it was. "What's that?"

"I don't know but it looks *messy*. Love you, Daddy. Say hi to Gigi."

God.

That hit even harder.

Still, he told his baby, "I will. I promise."

He'd broken one of those already. One he made to Gigi. He wouldn't break another.

"I love you. Be a good girl. I will see you soon."

"Okay, Daddy. Bye!"

Hanging up the call, Lev set the phone to the middle of the metal table and slid it across to the other side with one finger. The lawyer quickly snatched the device away and hid it in the bag he already had opened on his lap.

"Mr. Marcello wanted me to let you know they expect you to be out by tomorrow morning, and if that is the case—"

"Not sooner?"

The lawyer Andino hired sighed, lifting one shoulder. "Red tape. Publicity is all bad. We're *trying*, Lev."

Lev rolled his eyes. "Right, I get it."

"Nonetheless, despite who Andino Marcello is in this city, he can't always get everything he wants as soon as he snaps his fingers."

"Have him tell it and you wouldn't think that was the case."

The lawyer grunted a noncommittal reply before adding louder, "I was told to let you know that if we do get you out in the morning, that you should be ready."

That had Lev meeting the man's gaze. "For what?"

"A meeting with a Californian. Not by his choice; not even sure he's aware it'll be happening. Apparently, he intends to leave the country tomorrow after a stop in Vermont. Just close enough for Andino to get a little bit of work done so that the plane stays grounded until we can get on it, too. And if you can't join the meeting ... the boss wants you to know it will still go ahead as planned. He gave you his word that this would be finished. He will see it through, Lev."

While the lawyer was careful about each word that left his mouth as to not be too specific for anyone who might be listening in around the jail, Lev heard and understood more than enough.

"Call me Pink," he told the lawyer, not missing a beat, "everybody else does. And make sure I'm out of here by tomorrow. No *ifs*, just do."

Because there was no fucking way he would miss that *meeting*. Not a single chance in hell.

• • •

Andino kept his word.

By the time morning arrived, Lev stepped out the jail with one of two charges dropped, and a black town car idling at the side of the street, waiting for him. Just like his boss who was currently leaning against the driver's side of the vehicle.

The folder in Andino's hand caught Lev's eye first.

"What's that?" he asked as he approached.

Tapping the folder against his palm, Andino smirked. "Good morning to you, too. You're welcome that your ass is able to see the sunshine today firsthand instead of out of a cell window."

"They gave me an hour of time outside. This isn't special."

That had his boss laughing hard.

Even Lev grinned.

It didn't last long.

Andino handed the folder over. "A brief for you to look over on your way to the meeting today."

"Yeah, about that—"

"Les and Corrado will explain whatever you need on the way as well as provide you with any tactical gear you might need to join their little excursion. Been a while since they were out, apparently, so today should be fun for all of you."

"Les and—"

"Been a while, Pink," came a new voice from Lev's right.

A little further down the street stood two familiar men, waiting in front of a black Hummer that idled on the curb as well. It had been a while since he had a run-in with Corrado Guzzi or the man's lover, Alessio Sorrento. Assassins for hire, as far as he understood it, Lev could certainly understand how these two men would be beneficial to them for today's meeting—and beyond, possibly, if that was the plan—but some people just rubbed him wrong.

The man on the left—Alessio—was one of those. He took great pleasure out of poking at Lev in whatever way he could whenever the two of them were in the same vicinity. He sincerely hoped that wasn't going to be the case this time around because he didn't have the patience for it. Nor could he promise mercy for Alessio with his current mood.

"It could have been a while more," Lev replied.

"Don't be like that," Alessio replied, grinning just a bit. "You know we like your stupid ass, right?"

Lev gave Andino a look, that his boss did his very best to ignore by staring down the street. Andino *knew* the fucking hell Alessio gave Lev all too well. "Really, you had to call them in for this?"

"Best men for the job, Pink. And we need the best."

"But are they?"

"Must be," Corrado added at his lover's side down the street, "if Andi's willing to pay our freelance fee for retrievals on this job."

"They were also *available*," Andino added, his tone sharper than before, "and on very short notice. Say thank you and be done with it. I'm keeping my word, right?"

Beggars can't be choosers.

He knew that too well.

Right now, they didn't have the time to go with another route. As it was, Jensen Todrey, and possibly his partner, Marco, were days ahead of them.

With Gigi.

"And just how much is that, anyway?" he asked Andino.

His boss cleared his throat, shifting his weight from one

foot to the other when he replied, "The fee?"

"How much will this cost you—or *them*, how much for them?"

Corrado was the one who spoke up at that time. "Quite a bit to keep it under the radar of *our* bosses. Which is always the important part when dealing with New York, eh, Andino?"

Andino's jaw clenched when he muttered, "Usually."

Yeah.

So, maybe Lev wasn't the only one who had an issue with the men. While Alessio could give him hell, Corrado was the bane of Andino's existence. Ever since Corrado's other spouse, Ginevra, was passed between the New York boss to the assassin pair after his arranged marriage with her failed to be seen through. Yeah, Corrado and Alessio weren't just a twosome; they also shared a woman between them

But none of that mattered.

To the men down the way, Lev asked, "What's the rate of success on retrievals if you have a confirmed location?"

Not that they did.

But they might once they had the meeting with Marco. Lev was still convinced the asshole from Cali had somehow protected Jensen either by way of business, money, or connections. Somehow, he *helped* this to happen. Lev needed to know how.

Corrado arched a brow. "Dead or alive?"

Lev winced. "Never mind. Don't answer."

"Fair enough."

Andino checked his watch, saying quietly, "Cutting it close, boys. And I have a breakfast date with my mother."

"You're not coming?" Lev asked.

Not that he was shocked.

Or offended.

The boss *rarely* got his hands dirty. Then again, it wasn't a great thing for the head of a criminal organization to put his life at risk when he did his best work *alive*.

"You don't need me for this," Andino replied, "and at this point, we both know I've done all that I can. The rest is up to the three of you."

A low whistle came from Alessio before the man said, "*Yup*. Get that file open and get your ass in the Hummer. We're already running late, Pink."

He didn't need to be told again. It meant he was one step closer to getting Gigi back.

Maybe.

• • •

The drive to a private airstrip in Vermont where Marco Farginpane's jet waited before it would head out of country went by quicker than Lev expected it to. He spent that time familiarizing himself with the contents of the file Andino had provided.

Not that there was much.

Some details of Marco's current business dealings and what they knew of his schedule. Times for flights that had been put through air control in Vermont. An updated list of security on Marco's team that typically traveled alongside him. *More.*

It never failed to amaze Lev just how much Andino could pull together on short notice when the man was inspired.

"Ready?" Corrado asked.

The three of them stood at the back of the Hummer already dressed in their tactical gear, each with a semi-auto rifle in their grip. Alessio, who had already pulled the black ski mask down over his face, shrugged in response to his lover's question.

"Whenever you two are," Lev said.

A phone was passed over by Corrado, and the number already programmed into the device stared back at Lev, waiting for him to hit the green call button. At the back of the hangar where Marco's plane was being readied to return to the tarmac for takeoff, the three men had arrived and prepped with minutes to spare and without trouble.

At least something was going right.

Lev hit the call button, putting the call on speakerphone so Alessio and Corrado were able to hear the conversation as well. Like the rest of the information in the file that laid out the basics of their plan for the day, Marco's personal phone number had also been included.

The man picked up on the third ring.

"Hello?"

"Marco," Lev greeted, not unkindly though he would rather rip the man's throat out than pretend to be *friendly*, "how are things?"

"Who is—"

"Pink. Or Lev, depending on how well you know me. Andino sends his regards ... and *me*. See, in exactly twenty seconds, we're going to storm the hangar you're currently inside. It'll take us less than sixty seconds to be inside your private jet. At that point, we're going to sit down and discuss Jensen Todrey and what exactly he's done with Gigi Parker. How does that sound?"

Marco didn't even hesitate to reply, "You're aware that we have—"

"Three armed men, and a fourth personal guard who we've already removed from the equation outside here. Go ahead, take a moment to ask your men if their man outside has checked in recently. I'll wait."

A crackle sounded on the phone, followed by dark, muffled words he couldn't really understand. It took all of a few seconds before the man was back on the phone.

"If you come inside—"

"There's a bomb on the plane," Lev interjected before the man could say more. "Placed by a friend of a friend—he's *quite* good with both breaking and entering buildings with shitty security *and* wiring bombs. He placed it shortly after you departed the property after landing. Or, that's what this little file I have tells me about our meeting today. All I have to do is make a call, and this entire building is going to go *boom* in a big way. Which would you rather? A simple meeting with us, or ... death? Your choice."

Marco choked out a sound. "*What meeting?*"

"The one we're about to have. So again, I will see you in approximately sixty seconds. We expect full cooperation while we enter and board the jet. As long as that happens, you will be allowed to resume *your* plans for the day once we're satisfied we have what we've come for. Fair?"

"I hope your boss is happy," Marco snapped, hatred coating his every word. "All he needed to do was mind his own fucking business. We could have avoided all of this."

"Fascinating," Lev drawled. "Again, see you in a moment."

Thankfully, Marco did make it easy to enter the hangar and board the jet. They only needed to kill *two* of his men. The remaining guard waited inside the plane with a gun already pointed at the three men in ski masks as they came inside the plane.

A lot of good it did.

Alessio laughed at the sight. "Put it away. Just ... put it away."

Even Corrado chuckled.

Lev didn't care for theatrics, and he wasn't at all amused by their current situation. Nor was he pleased with the man sitting in the leather seat currently cutting the end off a cigar like he wasn't at all bothered by the chaos around him.

"Marco," Lev greeted, pulling up his mask.

On the plane, there were no cameras.

"There isn't a bomb, is there?" Marco asked, raising a brow.

Lev shrugged. "No, there isn't. You couldn't say for sure, though. After all, we found you. We had enough information to get here and do *this* ... would you take the risk that I was lying about the bomb, too?"

The man didn't reply.

Instead, he glanced out the port window to his left where the bodies of his security rested in puddles of blood. Clean shots right to the head. All compliments of Lev's gun and not Corrado or Alessio's. He might not be the brains running operations or making plans, but he was one hell of a fucking shot when he needed to be.

"Maybe I should thank you. I did need new guards. I was getting bored with those ones. Have a seat."

Lev lowered his weapon slightly but didn't move from his position. "No, thank you. This can be hard or easy depending on how you want it to go from here. I'm really not in the mood to fuck around at this point, Marco. Your little friend has had more than enough time to do that with Gigi while I was in a jail cell. Forgive my impatience."

Placing the cigar into the corner of his smirking lips, Marco nodded while he patted at the pockets of his blazer before finally finding the lighter he wanted. While he worked to light the thick cigar, he muttered, "I told Andino that I washed my hands of Jensen. I meant that. He would have been good business, but he was also a fucking *problem*. As you've clearly figured out."

A wisp of confusion drifted through Lev when he replied, "And yet, the only person we could tie back to him that might have been able to help the asshole do what he's done is *you*. Sure, he's got cash and contacts, but you've got more. A way to get him out of the country. A bigger hand in the criminal sector of business."

"Foolish," the man said under his breath. "You think you know everything, but you know *nothing*. Shame you've done this. A waste of time, really."

What?

Lev's gaze narrowed. "You even came to New York to sit down with the Marcello boss with him *at your side*, Marco. Did you seriously think we wouldn't come to you when Gigi was taken for answers? You're the only one who has them."

"It was Jensen's demand he attend that meeting, not mine. Pissy man—stuck in his fucking feelings about *you* and that woman. With the chance of a deal still being on the table with him, I was willing to entertain what he asked for. I was there for my business with Andino, nothing else. I was clear about my position. I didn't like what your boss did, and he needed to understand that. Andino's choice to cut ties with me was—"

That was enough for Lev.

He wasn't here to have a *real* conversation with the man. He didn't give a single flying fuck about Marco's feelings or excuses for what brought them here. The fact was, *here they were*. And that was enough for Lev.

Despite the man with the gun pointed at him that stood behind Marco's seat, Lev still rushed forward to make his position perfectly clear. Not that he was worried about the guard. Alessio or Corrado would easily handle that fuck if needed.

Lev wasn't fucking around when the barrel of his rifle met Marco's forehead, still warm from the last bullets to leave the chamber.

"*Where is he?*" Lev growled.

Or she, he held back from adding.

"I don't know."

That answer was enough to make Lev shove the gun harder against the man's head until it would surely leave a red ring behind like a bullseye. The problem was Marco didn't flinch. Not at Lev's actions, the threat he faced, or when the words came out of his mouth.

And that's how Lev knew.

Marco was telling the truth.

"You're stuck on the wrong thing," Marco murmured, meeting Lev's gaze up above without fear. *Dead men tell no lies*—wasn't that how the saying went? At this point, Marco had nothing to lose ... no reason to lie. "I can fill in the blanks, but I don't have all the answers."

Lev's heart thundered, his grip flexing on the gun and his finger twitchy on the fucking trigger. He didn't *want* to listen to the man, but it seemed like Marco wasn't going to give him a choice.

"Saw the news," the Cali man stated, shrugging indifferently. "He took her right out of a show, huh? Managed to get backstage. Security even helped. Shit, I'm getting ahead of myself, though." He twirled one finger in the air, adding, "Reverse back ... to the lunch your boss had you sit in. The first time I laid eyes on Gigi Rey in person."

Lev jammed the gun harder, forcing Marco's head back into the seat to the point it must have been painful. The guy didn't even *swallow.*

He just kept talking.

"Are you getting it yet? What you *missed*?" Marco asked.

Lev's jaw ached from how hard he was clenching his teeth, the words spitting from his mouth in a mutter because of it when he said, "That was for *work.*"

"So was the show. And who gets access to those? Who has

access to Gigi Rey in such a way that they can literally *provide* her? Her schedule. Her private matters. Her time. *Her person.* Think about it."

He didn't want to.

The suggestion was *abhorrent.*

"She's not even the fifth model he's had like a ... *toy,*" Marco added quieter. "Go back, *look for it.* It's all there. If he can buy her time for lunch, then what stopped them from selling her for anything else he wanted?"

It was as though cement had been poured into Lev's shoes keeping him stuck right where he stood. The ice in his heart was the killer, though.

The *worst.*

"How long?" Lev managed to ask. "How long has the modeling agency been selling girls?"

"You're asking the wrong man, and the one you need to ask ... well, the last I heard from him, he was asking for a connection to a friend in Mexico."

"You said you didn't know—"

Marco sneered, interjecting coldly, "I don't have *details.* Anybody can buy those ... or your current case, trade them for something else."

"Which is what?"

Because right then, Lev would do *anything* to get the information he needed that would lead him to Gigi. Absolutely anything.

"Business continues with Andino Marcello," Marco said. "Look at it like we hit a restart; go back to our previous agreements before Jensen came along. See, your boss has made it very difficult for me to get anything done lately. He's pulled weight all over the continent ... from Chicago to Canada. The Marcellos really have a reach, don't they?"

Fuck.

Lev couldn't make that promise.

He wasn't the boss.

And still, he said, "Done."

"I'll need my phone. To make some calls, of course. It'll only take a few minutes."

Lev didn't lower his gun. "So, tell your man to get the

fucking phone."

Marco waved two fingers, and that was enough for the guard behind him to follow the silent order. Staring down the barrel of Lev's rifle, the man met his gaze, still calm and unbothered. "There is one other thing you should know ... consider it a professional courtesy since I'll be working with your boss again and that's basically like being friends. *Of sorts.*"

Jesus Christ.

"What?" Lev hissed, still unable to get the tension out of his flexing jaw.

"If you find her alive, I suggest you have someone on hand to help the woman."

"Help how?" Corrado asked from behind Lev.

He hadn't wanted to ask. His heart hurt enough, and he was already struggling to keep it hidden.

"In every way imaginable." Marco didn't look away from Lev when he added, "I got the impression from Jensen that girls rarely lasted more than a few days with him when they were ... the disposable type. And if he *has* bought and paid for her, then I suspect he doesn't plan on her going back, does he? She certainly won't need to be returned in a condition good enough to be presented to the public. Again, a professional courtesy. Do with it what you will."

"*Fucking hell,*" he heard Alessio mutter.

The phone dropped from the guard's hand to Marco's waiting palm.

Lev only said, "Make your calls. And make it fast."

They were running out of time.

He could feel it in his soul.

A soul that was *dying.*

TWENTY-EIGHT

GIGI WASN'T sure what woke her up, but the bright glare of sunlight made her squeeze her eyes shut the second she dared to crack them open. The confusion that had become her constant companion since being taken had finally waned enough that when she woke up now, the only thing she felt was fear.

About what was waiting; what might happen.

Everything.

This time was no exception, but Gigi had become better at hiding it over the past couple of days. Especially after waking in the night to find Jensen looming in the doorway of the bedroom that she was told would be hers until she was deemed *suitable*. Whatever in the fuck that was supposed to mean.

Compliant?

Willing to be raped regularly?

Capable of taking a beating?

That's what it meant to Jensen if she was to trust his actions since kidnapping her to be what he planned to continue to do. The only thing he hadn't done to Gigi since their arrival at the massive, Roman-style estate hidden deep within a Mexican bay? Threatened to kill her. Apparently, because he intended to keep her.

That was even more terrifying.

Except the asshole liked her fear; fed off it, even. She refused to give him anything to urge on his more violent or sadistic nature, not when it meant suffering far worse consequences and *not* when it meant he liked it.

Fuck him.

He wanted a doll. A beautiful, broken *doll* willing to be abused at his demand that he could put back on the shelf—or a locked *room*, in her current case—whenever he became bored or had something else to do.

Gigi's current nightmare was far too real for her to play whatever game of make-believe Jensen had tried to set up for them both at this place. So, while she refused to show him the constant terror he caused with just his presence alone, she also *couldn't* go along with the game he had started.

No, she fought.

Every rape.

Every hit.

Every time.

He liked that a lot less.

The armed guards posted on the property, or the few she had seen during her times outside of the bedroom she had been confined to a lot during the day, were seemingly fine to help Jensen. No doubt, the pay for their compliance in hiding and controlling Gigi when necessary, or turning their cheeks to what was going on, made it worth it for the men.

There was no reprieve.

No help.

She was alone. Entirely, utterly alone in a terrible hell, one she couldn't have imagined even in her worst nightmares. Yet, her nightmare was Jensen's dream come true.

Monsters really did exist.

They wore tailored suits, had too much money and smiled like humans.

They were real.

And she didn't know how she was going to escape hers, but the small spark of hope that *someone*—God, anyone—would make this all go away hadn't left her yet. She prayed that someone was coming even if it had been made clear to Gigi time and time again by Jensen that *no one* was looking for her despite who she was and the circumstances of her disappearance. Because she didn't have a reason to believe otherwise, there was a small part of her that thought he might be telling the truth.

Another part refused to accept that. *Someone* was looking for her. Lev; she just knew it. It hurt her heart to think about the man and his little girl that had tried so hard to keep her safe back in New York, but it was also the only ray of happiness she had.

Just the thought of him gave her hope.

So she kept dreaming.

Until she woke up again.

"Breakfast is about to be served," came the voice of her captor from the bedroom doorway.

She hadn't heard his approach; she hadn't bothered to open her eyes after clamping them shut to block out the bright light from windows that had no covers. Like most of the windows in the estate. Had he been watching her sleep again? *That* bothered her more than even his assaults for reasons she couldn't explain.

It was only the slap of loafers against the marble floor that had Gigi opening her eyes to watch Jensen loom over her. Keys in hand for the shackles that kept her stuck in the corner of the room, chained to a wall by the links connected between her wrists and ankles, he leaned down with a smile that seemed friendly but chilled her to the bone.

His kindness was a lie.

She trusted nothing.

"Your guard has your robe ready. After breakfast, you'll be taken to the bathing house and then later, if you *behave*," Jensen continued, his tone cheerful despite the horror he had caused her for days, "then perhaps we'll take a walk around the property. Together, of course. I think you might appreciate the place a bit more if you get the chance to properly see it. I bought it a couple of years back after a good season."

She would have guessed that.

If only because it wasn't as much the shackles he bound her with regularly to keep her confined in the room without a route for escape, but the marks on the wall that bothered her to her very core. The scratches in the same corner where she was chained. The gouges in the yellow plaster where someone else—or maybe more than one—had clawed until ruddy stains were left behind in the scored lines.

Bloodstains.

She wasn't the first to be here.

Would she be the *last*?

Gigi didn't care to ask.

She was only trying to survive.

"Well, *get up*," Jensen snarled when Gigi didn't immediately jump to stand from the floor once he had unlocked the shackles. With the metal in one hand, he used his other to drag her by the hair of her head to her feet. Naked, cold, and still bruised from the night before, every inch of her body protested in pain when she stumbled upright. He nodded, pleased, saying, "That's better. We'll take breakfast in my office. Don't fight the guard, or you'll get the whip again."

At the mere mention of the bullwhip he'd used on her the first night they arrived at the estate, pain flared through Gigi all over again. The welts hadn't faded on her back and ass at all. The one had actually split her skin on the back of her shoulders, but he'd left her to bleed on the floor until a guard hauled her away.

Reaching out to push back the strands of hair in her face, his fingers grazed her skin. Every touch made her want to puke, but the only thing she allowed him to see was the rage burning in her gaze that refused to look away from his. If he was going to hurt her as he did, then he could stand to see what it did to her, too.

"Smile," he murmured. "It's much better when you smile."

Gigi did, but then she spat in his face, too. He didn't even wipe her saliva from his cheek before his fist connected with the side of her head and stars bloomed behind her eyes.

Just another day in hell.

• • •

By the time Gigi was deemed suitable to join Jensen in the large office with an open veranda that overlooked the bay, her jaw was swollen, and she wasn't even sure how she would *eat*. And yet, at the sight of her standing in the doorway in a sheer robe that did nothing to hide her nakedness underneath, Jensen grinned with twisted pleasure.

He liked seeing her beaten.

Bruised.

But bloody was better.

"Feeling better?" he asked.

Gigi fought the urge to fold her arms over her chest to stop his gaze from lingering on her breasts under the robe, but knew better than to do so. She refused to engage his need to discuss his abuse because he liked that. Instead, she opted to say, "I hadn't realized how large this place is."

Pushing away from the edge of an ostentatious desk that looked more suited to be in a museum of sorts, Jensen gestured at the food waiting on a cart filled with silver dishes. "Fill a plate and *mine*. We'll eat on the veranda. And yes, about thirty acres in total. The team has used the place for a few parties. They've done a couple of movie shoots here as well. Devlin King borrowed the place for his wedding last year. I'm sure you know him—took home three Grammys last year for his recent album."

She watched his back retreat toward the stone doorway that led out to the veranda and wondered ... was he trying to *impress* her by name dropping someone famous? If anything it only opened Gigi's eyes even more to the darkness of the world around her. There was no way all those people around this man didn't know *what he was*.

It wasn't possible.

"Don't make me tell you again," Jensen called over his shoulder. "Hurry up, Gigi."

She didn't need to ask what he meant when there was only one thing he had told her to do. Since she wasn't in the mood for the rest of her face to suffer from the same pain in her jaw, she went ahead and readied two plates from the cart of food.

Eggs.

Fresh bread.

Sliced fruit.

A choice in breakfast meats.

Despite putting only a few things on her plate—soft items that would be easy to chew—Gigi had little to no appetite. The last thing she wanted to do was join Jensen at the table on the veranda, but it was that or a worse fate for disobeying. He had the nerve to thank her when she placed his plate in front of him, but didn't wait for a reply before pointing to the chair directly beside his at the head of the table for her to sit.

Gigi had only made it through a couple of bites of scrambled eggs and a half of a banana when she stared out at the bay ahead of them and the bright blue, cloudless sky overhead. The high cliffs of the bay surrounded them and then jutted out along the bay to the water beyond where she could see.

A part of her wondered ... could she swim that far?

Would she survive if she got away?

As if Jensen could read her mind, he said at her side, "It would take an army to get you away from here, silly girl ... and I assure you there isn't an army on this earth that thinks you're worth the effort currently."

She turned to glance at him as he reached for a folded magazine sitting off to his right on the table. Slapping the glossy paper in front of her plate, the magazine opened to show a picture of both of them on the cover. Walking out of the show, actually. She did look wasted—her eyes barely open, hair a mess, and Jensen holding tight to her as if he was keeping her standing.

The headline was a gut punch.

GIGI REY RUINS DELAVANGE SHOW.

The smaller print below was the knife after the hit.

Agent says supermodel Gigi Rey will be stepping away from all upcoming projects to focus on her health—sources confirm drug abuse, read more on page 12.

"It really helps to spin the story the way we want when you made so little effort to tell the story your way, doesn't it?" Jensen chuckled, the edge of his mouth tilting upward in his twisted happiness. "I always enjoyed working with Marla. She provides the best of the best every single time."

Of course, her agent had a hand in this. Why wouldn't she? The only time that woman had ever been satisfied with Gigi was when she did exactly as she was told to do with no deviation. Hell, it had been Marla who set up that first lunch date between Jensen and Gigi.

She pushed the ball.

Circumstances kept it rolling.

Fucking Marla.

"Nothing to say?" Jensen asked, holding his fork speared with a sausage up to his lips.

She dragged in a quick breath, replying simply, "No."

What could she say?

Nothing he would want to hear.

Besides, just because her physical presence was forced to be there with Jensen didn't mean her mind and heart had to be. So, when he went back to his plate, leaving the magazine in front of her to stare at, Gigi's thoughts drifted to a better place.

Back to Lev.

And little Arely.

To a townhouse, she had only visited once but would give anything to step inside one more time and never leave, if she so chose. A warm bed. The strong arms of a man that didn't hurt her. All the sparkly, pretty things that made five-year-old girls smile.

It was a happy place.

It was *love*, she knew.

Jensen could do many things to Gigi while she was his captive, but he couldn't take *that* away. He could make the world hate her; make the industry turn their back on a model they saw as a problem. He could even ruin her reputation, break her body, and then discard her to a grave when he was finished.

But he couldn't take away what she found before he brought her here. After all, she spent years pretending to be the embodiment of happiness and love for the world ... finally gaining those things without false pretenses was something she would have in her heart forever.

"Perhaps next time, you can eat alone if all you're going to do is sit there and stare at nothing," Jensen muttered at her side.

Annoyed that she couldn't even be *quiet* and do it right, Gigi opened her mouth to snap back a reply that would undoubtedly earn her a punishment. Not that her body could really afford to take another one.

Before she could, though, a ringing phone inside the office sent Jensen up out of his chair and heading beyond the flapping curtains of the veranda doorway. He didn't immediately come back with the phone in hand, his voice slightly muffled as he picked up the call with a sharp greeting past her view.

"What do you mean?" he demanded suddenly.

Gigi might have been interested in whatever conversation—or problem—had come up, but something else caught her attention instead. The choppy *woosh-woosh-woosh* of something approaching overhead. Though she couldn't see beyond the roof of the veranda, she *did* recognize that sound and how fast it came in.

It was a helicopter.

"*And you only saw it now?*" Jensen roared in the office.

Gigi didn't know what propelled her to her feet, but it was something … and she didn't question it. The piercing screech of a wailing siren cut through the air, overtaking even the sound of the chopper as it came closer.

"Every fucking man on the grounds, *right now*," Jensen barked, his voice coming closer to the veranda again.

Was it someone coming for her?

Gigi raced for the stone railing of the veranda, her hair blowing wildly around her shoulders as she leaned out over the side to see what waited below.

Rushing water.

Too deep.

Probably too cold.

Not at all safe.

Overhead, a black chopper came into view before cutting fast to the side and out of her sight. Not before she caught what looked to be someone with a gun at the wide-open door, though.

Could it possibly be—

"Where do you think you're going, you fucking little bitch?"

Gigi glanced over her shoulder, the sight of Jensen coming back through the veranda doorway with a gun in his one hand and the phone in his other sent her heart leaping into her chest. She had no way out and nowhere to run *here*. That much was clear.

But he wouldn't touch her again.

She didn't care what she had to do to make sure of it. He wouldn't lay another finger on her; he wouldn't stick his cock into one of her holes while she cried and bled.

She wouldn't let him.

And if the distraction overhead was her one chance to keep that from happening again, then she was going to take it. Even if it meant jumping.

But jumping to what?

Freedom?

Death?

What if they were one and the same?

"Don't you fucking *dare*," Jensen snarled.

She didn't look back as she drained every ounce of strength she had to climb up onto the railing, the sheer robe whipping around her naked figure from the wind. She hadn't even noticed the black boat that cut through the water from the mouth of the bay, coming straight for her, before she jumped.

The water greeted her body cruelly.

And yet, still *kindly*.

TWENTY-NINE

HAVING FRIENDS in high places paid off sometimes. Lev was never more grateful for the reach of his boss than when they had a location for Gigi and Jensen, and all he had to do was make a call to Andino. In a day, the man had a *team* ready to provide whatever his man and the two assassins needed. A chopper. Even a fucking boat once they had satellite pictures showing the Mexican estate was situated deep within a bay surrounded by rocky cliffs.

But still *accessible.*

In three ways.

One, the water.

Two, the sky.

Three, a road. The road, however, was the last resort that hadn't even been on the table when Corrado, Alessio, and Lev made their plan. It was the most obvious route to get into the estate, and undoubtedly armed to the fucking *teeth.*

"Ten seconds to landing," a voice chirped in his ear.

The chopper pilot.

Next to him, leaning out of the open door of the chopper to peer at the roof of the mansion below where they would soon land, Alessio hissed air through his teeth in disapproval. "Fuck, knew this was gonna be bad. Counted ten guards already that I can see, man. Should have got a bigger team for this."

"Not optional," Lev muttered.

"Right," the guy replied, stepping back away from the door as the chopper made a quick descent. "Because Andino's trying to keep this all *under control.* Fucking Marcellos."

That had Lev shooting the man a heated glance. "One of those fucking Marcellos is the only reason I might get Gigi out of here *alive.* So how about you deal with your feelings another time, huh?"

If she even still was alive …

God.

The agony ripped through his chest without mercy, and Lev was the bitch's willing victim. He felt it was an appropriate punishment for his thoughts that felt like a betrayal to the hope he had refused to let go of over the past days.

Lev didn't really have time to consider his pity party because in the next second, the chopper hit the roof in a rough landing that sent both men in the rear stumbling with the guns in their hands. Not for long, though, because they didn't have the time to fuck up, either.

They weren't even out of the chopper before shots fired. Bullets peppered the side of the helicopter, making the pilot cuss loudly in the comms, nearly blocking out the sound of Corrado in the background telling them, *"In the bay, boys."*

Alessio was out of the chopper first; Lev followed right behind. Coming around the back as the machine started to lift into the air again—the pilot was unwilling to stay on the roof longer than it took to get the men out of the back—both men had their semi-auto rifles high and aimed in the direction of the spray of bullets.

If Lev was a hell of a shot, Alessio Sorrento was a fucking *king*. Alessio came around the rear of the rising chopper, eye to the sights of his gun, and he didn't even hesitate before his finger pulled back the trigger in quick succession.

Once.

Twice.

A third time.

Each bullet hit its intended target—the three men coming up onto the roof of the estate where it looked like a mix between a garden and sitting area. The wind from the chopper's blades had cut down vines and a bush, and sent a wicker table set spinning across the roof. The pilot would continue to circle the estate and bay, only coming back once Lev and Alessio were on the roof.

Or if he saw smoke.

Whichever came first.

Lev might have his feelings about Alessio, sure. There was tension between the man and his lover regarding Lev's boss, but his pride wasn't *that* big of a thing that he couldn't admit certain things. Like this wouldn't have been possible without them.

At all.

Maybe after this—if everything went well—then they might finally be able to bury the hatchet between the four of them. But who the hell knew?

And now wasn't the time.

"*Clear,*" Alessio grunted, not lowering his gun for a second. "Down we go."

They headed off the roof, taking the stone steps as fast as they could until another two men in black gear came around the corner at the bottom with guns drawn. Lev hit those ones, seeing them before Alessio did because the man was trying to hear Corrado on the comms.

"*Ba-bay ... she's ... bay ... Les ...*"

"Fuck," Alessio muttered when Lev passed him by on the stairs, rounding the corner where the bodies of two dead men now rested in puddles of blood, "what's he saying?"

"Something about the bay, yeah?"

"Better not be *in* the fucking bay."

Lev heard the tension in Alessio's voice—the worry he didn't show in his no-nonsense demeanor as he continued on with the job. "Comms wouldn't work. Probably in a spot where the connection isn't cl—"

"*Are you off the fucking roof yet?*"

Corrado's voice came through all at once then. Perfectly clear, too. It sounded like Alessio wasn't the only one who had been worried.

Pressing the comm in his ear, Alessio replied, "Yeah, about to hit the house from the s—"

"*Get her! Get her out of the fucking water! Get her, you stupid fuck!*"

Lev knew that voice.

He knew it too well.

While it wasn't the brightest idea he ever had, Lev rushed far ahead of Alessio to enter the house where a door had been left open by the earlier men. He could have taken a bullet to the head right then, stupidly, because he didn't think it through. And yet, he didn't consider that at all when he heard Jensen Todrey shouting about a *her* like the man was losing his most valuable possession.

If he was talking about Gigi, then Lev bet the man *did* believe she was the most precious thing he owned. Except she wasn't Jensen's ... and Lev planned on making sure the asshole never had the chance to even look at Gigi again after today.

He just had to get to him.

And her.

"Lev!"

Alessio's shout hit his back as the comm crackled in his ear with Corrado's severe *fuck* before the man in the boat told them something that about stopped Lev's heart.

"She's in the water. Gigi is in the fucking water, Les."

"Get her out," Alessio snapped. "Get her in the goddamn boat. *What happened?*"

Lev darted through unfamiliar halls with Alessio close on his heels. He didn't bother to join in the conversation, not when his gun was up ready to blow, he was looking for his next target to get it, and he was so close to ending this that he could practically taste it coming on the tip of his tongue.

Then, Corrado had to go and scare Lev more when the man muttered through the comms, *"I think she jumped from the veranda up top—almost to her, but she's not moving."*

Lev expected *far* more guards inside the house than what they encountered in the maze of stone hallways. The one that did pop around the corner as he followed the sound of Jensen's shouts was easily taken out, and he barely even aimed to do it.

It was only as they came through a kitchen where a chef hid behind an island—the man pointing at the doorways off to the right like he was trying to *help* Lev and Alessio—that the two of them split up. Lev went through the arched doorway on the right, and Alessio took the left side when the man directed him to do as much. The yelling was louder and *clearer* but coming from both directions.

"Can't you fucking shoot?" Jensen raged. "Give me that fucking gun—don't let that asshole grab her. She's *mine*."

What the fuck was going on?

"If we trust the pictures we found of the inside of the place," Alessio said through the comm in his ear, *"then this hallway circles around to the office at the rear—the one facing the bay."*

Right.

Where Corrado was. And where Gigi had apparently jumped from, if Corrado was correct.

For the first time since they landed on the roof, Lev hit the button on the comm in his ear, daring to ask, "Is she alive?"

He wasn't sure he wanted an answer.

He also *needed* one.

The same way he needed to make it out of here alive because he had a daughter waiting for him at home. Just like he needed Gigi safe and happy again *with him* because he could no longer imagine a world where she wasn't in it. There was no possible way he could return to his child and tell her that Gigi would no longer be in their lives. Not when they just found her.

All Corrado replied, the sound of a boat's engine gunning hard in the background, was, *"She's in a bad way. Real bad. Fuck, it's bad."*

But that wasn't dead, and that's what counted. Lev could help Gigi deal with the rest if she was alive to do it.

"Hospital bad?" he heard Alessio ask.

Lev was rounding the corner at the end of the hallway, his jog slowing to a crawl as he realized just how close he was to Jensen and the rest of the man's guards in the house when their voices echoed around the corner.

Right there.

He was just feet away.

"Yeah, man," Corrado replied. *"That kind of bad."*

Lev didn't hesitate to hit the comm in his ear and say, "Then get her to a hospital."

They could deal with the consequences later.

Surely.

And then he rounded the corner.

Lev didn't have time to consider the scene in front of him when he entered the office. Nothing beyond the guards in the office and Jensen further out on the veranda where he was shouted over the railing at something—or someone—down below. Lev was only one man with one gun facing three guards dressed in black with guns of their own. Two had their backs turned. One stared right at him.

He took that asshole out first. His second spray of shots hit another one of the guards. He jerked back out of view of the doorway, his spine cracking against the stone wall when the third started firing his way. Bullets hit the wall in spatters, making stone and plaster spray Lev a little too close for comfort.

"*Holy fuck*," he grunted.

Yeah.

Way too damn close.

Not willing to put his body in the line of fire, even if he did have a bulletproof vest strapped to his chest, Lev stuck his gun around the corner and pulled back the trigger until he'd emptied the clip. Yanking the gun back, he knew he didn't hit the asshole when footsteps approached as he dropped the used magazine and reached for the spare at the strap on his back. He barely had time to slam the new one into the gun and raise the riffle when the asshole came around the corner with his own weapon raised.

Lev's rifle met the guard's forehead, the spray of blood arching up the wall and even hitting him in the face when he pulled back the trigger. He could taste the splatters of blood on his lips when he rushed the office, the gun high to his shoulder and ready to fire all over again.

Except there stood Jensen with a pistol aimed right at Lev.

The two men said nothing, their weapons not at all equal in size or power, but both able to kill. There was an almost psychotic gleam in Jensen's eye as the man grinned at the sight of Lev, like he hadn't expected anything different.

"Should have just let the bitch *go*," the man said.

"Not likely."

"She's not worth much now—not after I've had my way with her. She's certainly not going to be like she *was*. I can't say I'm very sorry about that. It was worth *everything*. Every dollar. Every bit of bullshit. All of it."

Lev's jaw worked to release the tension in his clenching teeth, but it was the only show he gave to Jensen that his words had any impact. "Your life, too?"

Jensen barked out a laugh. "Oh, you don't seriously think *you're* making it out of here alive, do you?"

Yes.

He absolutely did.

During their conversation, the two men had started to circle one another. It continued until it was Lev's back facing the veranda, and Jensen on the other side of the office. Not daring to glance over his shoulder, Lev took a step backward and then another, keeping his gun trained on the asshole across the way.

Where was Alessio?

Why hadn't Corrado checked in again?

The screeching of an alarm overhead started without warning. It had first gone off when they hit the roof, but then it stopped. The sudden distraction had Lev foolishly looking away from the biggest threat he faced, and he knew his error the second he made it.

A bullet plugged into his chest. The pain was instant. It spread wide and *fast,* taking his breath with it. The force sent him flying back a step. His back hit the railing and knocked him off balance so that he was falling backward, *over* it. Jensen's smile was the last thing he saw ... and Alessio behind the man, his gun aimed.

More blood sprayed when Alessio took the shot.

Then it was the sky overhead.

His back hit the water below.

Everything went black.

THIRTY

IT WAS soft, rhythmic beeping in the back of Gigi's sleepy mind that drew her from the deep slumber. She didn't know where she was when she first cracked open her eyes, the dryness behind her lids making the action slightly uncomfortable.

Not that she felt much of anything at all as she blinked, again and again, trying to discern the dimly lit room around her and the vaguely familiar scent she pulled into her lungs with every deep breath. It took her an entire minute to understand two things.

Important things.

She was staring at a hospital room.

And she was *high.*

Really fucking high.

That's why she wasn't feeling anything, even when she lifted her arm to see the IV lines—more than one—sticking out of her arm. There was a dull, sharp sensation poking at the edges of her senses. Stabbing into the numbness like it was trying to break the barrier of whatever pain medication was being fed into her body.

It couldn't get through.

Part of her was grateful. Another wished she could think *clearly.* Or even, to think at all.

Because now, Gigi had no clear understanding of anything. Not where she was—or rather, *what* hospital. Not how she got here. And even her last memory, one she dug hard for in her foggy brain, was of water.

So much water.

Other flashes popped into her head, pictures snapping behind her eyelids when she clenched them shut to slow the rush of memories that suddenly didn't want to stop. The beeping in the room picked up at the same time her heart began to pound so hard in her chest that it felt like the organ might lift her right off the thin mattress of the hospital bed.

"Hey, now," came a new—dark and masculine—voice from the end of Gigi's bed. "Calm down, we don't need them all rushing in here like something's wrong, do we?"

Her eyes snapped wide.

There, standing at the end of her bed in a black three-piece suit with a blazer tossed carelessly over his arm, was a man she didn't recognize. Even though the tunnel of her vision, compliments of whatever pain killers she had in her system, she locked eyes with the unfamiliar man, ready to scream.

Hadn't a man hurt her enough?

What was this one here to do?

"Andino Marcello," he greeted, not moving a muscle, "I'm sorry it's taken this long for me to properly meet you, Gigi Parker. Pink has only said ... *very* kind things about you. His daughter, too. Arely says hello, but I hope you understand why she isn't here with me. This is not a situation for a child. Certainly not one she can comprehend. As for your mother, well, she's still healing but I promise she will be around as soon as she can make it."

She swallowed hard, the words trying to form around the knot in her scratchy throat. Nothing came out but a croaky squeak which only made the man at the end of the bed frown.

"Water?" he asked.

She was still putting together *who* he was. Lev's boss, right?

The *mafia* boss.

"Are you going to kill me?" she managed to ask, her voice raspy.

That had him looking offended.

"But why?" he returned.

She didn't know.

It just felt right to ask.

Andino sighed, stepping around the side of the bed and coming to her right where a table waited with a cup and a bendy straw. Without asking her again if she wanted a drink, he simply picked up the cup and held the straw steady for her when he brought it close enough to her lips that she could take a sip. Cool liquid hit her tongue and throat with total relief. She easily sucked back a quarter of the cup before Andino pulled it away with a chuckle.

"Not too fast," he said, "as it might come back up with the amount of oxy they're pumping into you right now, and they want to wait a bit for your stomach to settle after how much water they pumped out of it. Seems you've got a bit of an allergy to morphine, huh?"

Did she?

Gigi's throat flexed with her swallows, the muscles loosening enough that she felt almost comfortable to talk and not sound like a two-pack-a-day smoker. "Why do you call him that?"

"Pardon?"

"*Pink*. He's ... Lev."

Andino smiled slightly. "To *you*. And that's okay, he can be whatever you need him to be if he continues being what I need him to be, too. No worries," he added at her dipped brow, "I don't expect you to understand."

"But ... *why*?" The man didn't seem to understand what she was trying to ask. Maybe it was because she was high, but Gigi just had to know ... she never asked before now. "Why that name—*Pink*?"

"He's never told you?"

"I didn't ask."

Andino grinned, the severely sharp lines of his face that made him seem handsome but *terrifying*, softening enough that she found humanness behind the facade he clearly kept at the forefront. "Laundry error—he came to work in a pink shirt. An associate gave him the moniker and in business, it just stuck."

She shouldn't laugh.

It wasn't the right time.

And yet ... "That's cute."

"You really are *very* high," Andino muttered, shaking his head as he replaced the cup to the table with a chuckle. "I'm not sure this is the best time for a visit, but I don't think I'll have another chance and since my cousin is working tonight in the hospital ... well, unfortunately, this is the only time I might have to do this before the police begin to flood in here, and I won't be able to come again. Do you think you can listen for a moment? *Hear me*, and really understand?"

She did.

Sort of.

"Police?" she asked.

"Expect *a lot* of police attention," he replied.

Huh.

Then, Andino added quieter, "You were recognized at the hospital in Mexico where you were taken after Corrado was able to get you *and* Lev to shore and call for help."

"Corrado?"

The man waved a hand. "Not important. Focus on the bigger picture, not the minor details. Your high-profile nature meant there really wasn't a chance for us to keep you under the radar, but you needed help. You were in a very bad way when they took you from Jensen's estate in the bay. Three days ago, once they had stabilized you enough, they transferred you back to the states. *Here*, at this hospital."

She remembered none of that.

Not a single thing.

"You nearly drowned when you jumped into the water," Andino explained. "You were already injured, probably had little to no energy to fight the water ... by the time Corrado pulled you into the boat, you weren't breathing. No doubt, him having to turn back for Lev didn't help, either."

She stared back at him, her memories fuzzy though some things still managed to break through the barriers in her mind. Nothing that she liked. Everything that left her scarred with horrors she wouldn't be able to forget.

"I'm sorry for what he did to you while you were there," Andino told her, his voice quiet and *kind*. "I'm so very sorry that I didn't take the threat of Jensen seriously enough to think he was worth more effort than I had already put forth to keep him at bay. I'm sorry you were the sacrifice made for it. There might not be anyone else who tells you those things, and because I do try to be a *good* man, I will be the one to do it now."

Gigi didn't move.

Didn't speak.

A single tear escaped her eye and slid down her cheek in a warm, wet trail. She didn't bother to try and wipe it away.

Drawing in a breath, Andino added, "I have called in as many favors as I can to begin moving things to my—*Lev's*— benefit as a lot has changed since you were returned to the states and public caught wind of it. I don't have time to explain all of it right now, but just know it's not good, and I have just about run out of favors to call in, Gigi. I really only have one question for you and then I can go and you can begin to get better. Because you're going to need to do that. Get better—*be strong*."

"What question?"

"Do you love him?"

She knew who he meant without asking.

Lev.

The answer was easy, obvious, and clear in her mind: *yes*. She loved him more than even the breath in her lungs and the beat of her heart. After all, a part of her just knew that without Lev, she wouldn't still have air to breathe and a heart to beat.

Although, that wasn't *why* she loved him.

"He tried to save me," she whispered, "didn't he?"

"No," Andino replied. "He *succeeded*."

Right.

"And you didn't answer me," the man said.

"I haven't even told him. Why on earth would I tell *you*?"

Andino smiled, fleeting and amused. Nodding, he replied, "Fair enough. I need you to remember that you love him. In the coming days ... weeks, maybe even months. When they hammer you, when they're relentless, and when it hurts and you're alone and you think it's not going to get better ... remember that you love him."

"Why?"

"Because if you do want the chance to tell him face to face and not behind a set of bars and Plexiglas, they will *all* need to believe it, too."

Gigi had a million questions.

Believe what?

Where was Lev?

Arely?

Andino reached for the cup, saying, "One more sip, but then I have to go, and you need to get better. My wife will also be hounding me for an update. A *huge* fan of yours. She would like the chance to meet you someday. She isn't the only one. Okay?"

Well ...

"Okay," she agreed.

Even if absolutely nothing was okay.

THIRTY-ONE

LEV FOUND himself back in jail the second his feet touched American soil—arrested on more charges than he cared to think about. Not to mention the time he could possibly face should he be found guilty.

Some of the charges related to his previous arrest before they went after Jensen; they had proof he left America when he wasn't even supposed to leave the states until that was cleared up. Other charges came from suspicion of his involvement in Gigi's disappearance and attack when she showed up nearly dead in a Mexican hospital.

They even tacked on some interesting charges relating to the strange disappearance of Revver's owner, Jensen Todrey, after the Mexican officials worked with the American side of things to hand over information on the estate in the bay that had burned to the ground.

Along with the bodies inside of it. *Good riddance to trash*, he thought.

Lev wasn't saying anything.

Neither were his lawyers.

If he didn't admit guilt—not to even one of the charges—then he couldn't give them something to use for anything else, either. He had never needed to play this game with law enforcement before. Despite his connections to the mob, he hadn't faced more than a couple of nights in jail for beating the hell out of someone on Andino's demand.

This was not the same.

He was looking at *life*.

Lev wasn't entirely sure how a plan that seemed entirely rock-solid ended up collapsing out from under his very feet, but one good thing *had* come out of the mess. Gigi was alive. *Safe*. That had been the most important thing from the start even if now that seemed like a distant memory.

They could deal with the rest.

Somehow.

Not that he knew how. Because he didn't have the first fucking clue.

Rubbing at the sore spot in the middle of his chest where he'd taken a slug to his vest, Lev listened to the sound of footsteps approaching the outside of his cell. Nearly two weeks since his back hit the water, and it was only now that the bruising in the center of his chest had finally faded to a yellow tint. The bitch still hurt, though.

Or maybe the memory did.

"How are you doing?" the familiar guard asked, coming to stand at the cell's doors.

He passed the guy a look, shrugging from where he sat on the metal bed. The thin mattress and indestructible sheet they provided for him to use couldn't really be considered anything comfortable, so it was basically like he slept on a hard slab. Or sat. *Read.* Ate, even.

All in this fucking cell.

For a man that appreciated his freedom, being locked away like an animal wasn't exactly his idea of a good time. The longer he was kept in jail, the worse his irritation became. Stir-crazy wasn't a good enough word for the constant restlessness that chased his days and nights. He barely slept a wink. The food was garbage. And if one more jailhouse priest stopped by to ask if he had anything to confess or talk about, well, he was going to *blow.*

Lev wanted only a few things.

His daughter.

Gigi.

Home.

And all of it had been taken away. He took some sense of comfort in the fact that he had people working on his side to make sure some things were handled in a way the police, or *others*, couldn't touch. Like Arely. Who, as far as he understood, was in the custody of Nessa until her father was released—*if* he was released. He had Andino to thank for that, and the team of lawyers that immediately stepped in to protect his daughter from the media storm and child services.

The guard passed the food on the tray at the door a look. Lev had left it there, mostly untouched, other than the apple he ate, and the small bottle of water he cracked open and downed. He didn't care for the egg sandwich that smelled like it had seen better days, or the soup that he couldn't quite place. It didn't look like any kind of soup he had ever eaten before, and he didn't plan on putting in his mouth on this day.

He bet the only thing worse than being in jail was being in jail with food poisoning. Nah, he'd rather starve.

"Maybe later, I can get you something better to eat," the guard said. "We'll see how my next break goes."

"You don't have to do that."

The man shrugged. "Don't I, *Pink*?"

The nickname had Lev meeting the man's gaze, an understanding dawning on him that Andino had more people looking out for him than he previously realized. Even in this hellhole. The guard only smiled back.

"You have a visitor, by the way. I'll accompany you down to the conference room. Arms outside of the bars so I can put your shackles on, please."

Lev stood from the bed, asking, "More interviews with cops?"

Hadn't he done enough?

Or hadn't he been silent enough?

The guard only shrugged.

Well ...

Whatever—or whoever—waited for him was better than sitting in this cell for the next several hours until someone decided to take him outside for a walk like he was a puppy.

Right?

• • •

Lev was surprised to see his boss sitting at the end of a long conference table where it would usually be a detective or one of his lawyers in the chair. Up until that second, Andino had done his best to stay away from the jail to keep the media circus at a bearable level. Not that *any* of it was bearable currently.

Nonetheless, if the mafia boss the media kept connecting Lev to in all the papers and reports wasn't around ... then they couldn't prove he *was* affiliated to the man during the period of his lockup. Or that's what the lawyers explained the last time he asked about Andino when they came for a chat.

"Boss," Lev greeted, stepping inside the room.

"Are you leaving the shackles?" Andino asked the guard behind Lev.

"Better not push it in case someone does come around. You've got fifteen minutes ... *safely*," the guard replied. "One is doing his walk on the block. The other is downstairs fucking the clerk like he does every Saturday afternoon. You both should be good but not for too long. Don't push it."

"Understood. Thank you."

"Not a problem."

Once the guard stepped out and closed the door behind him, Andino waved at the chair at the far end of the table. A to-go cup of coffee waited there for him, and Lev couldn't help but be grateful for the familiar logo turned in his direction.

"Coffee from my favorite shop?"

"Right down the street from your place, yeah," Andino replied. "Figured they probably weren't giving you shit in here that was even worth putting in your mouth. It's not been long enough for me to forget how jail treats a man like us, huh?"

Grunting his agreement, Lev dropped into the chair and grabbed for the to-go cup with shackled hands. The coffee wasn't *hot*—barely even warm, actually—but he gulped that shit down because it was the best thing to have touched his lips in weeks.

"You made a deal with Marco that I didn't approve ... that I wouldn't *ever* approve."

Lev swallowed hard, setting the cup down in front of him on the table as he met Andino's sharp gaze across the way. "I did."

"Why?"

"You told me once to do what I needed to do for Gigi,

remember? I needed the info."

"I don't work with skin traffickers, Pink."

"I got the impression he would even be satisfied if you pulled your hand out of his many pots so that he could resume working ... elsewhere even," Lev said carefully.

Andino's jaw worked a tic that just wouldn't let up. A sure sign of his irritation if there ever was one. "You put me in a bad position. In more ways than one."

"I'm not really sorry about it."

"Mmm, because you got what you needed."

"And you would have done the same."

Andino sighed harshly, muttering, "Can't argue with that, can I?"

"Did you come down here and bribe a guard just to tell me you're pissed off at me? Because I'm sure you could have done that over a phone call. The lawyers would have passed the message along like they have every other time."

"Funny," his boss said.

"What is?"

"How even in jail you manage to catch an attitude that drives me crazy. Remember when I first offered you a job? What did I say I wanted?" Andino ticked a finger in the air, saying, "Ah, yes. A man who did his job and didn't give me any attitude while he did it."

Lev couldn't help but grin. "Look how well *that* turned out."

"If you could cause me less headaches when all of this is over, then I would *really* appreciate it, Pink."

"Is it?"

"What?"

"Going to be over?" Lev shrugged, adding, "Because from where I sit, all I see is a fucking mess I can't get out of, Andino. I haven't talked to my kid in a week and the last time I did, she asked why my picture was in the newspaper. Why the police had handcuffs on me. How the fuck is she even seeing that shit?"

Andino grunted under his breath. "Have to ask your little friend—Nessa—that question. Maybe she had something sitting somewhere and didn't think about it. I'm sure it was a mistake."

"I want to see my kid. Get Nessa on that. *Soon*."

"In jail?"

Fuck.

"Don't be a prick," Lev returned.

Andino frowned. "I'm not ... just trying to make you see things with a bit more sense. *Everyone* is staying low and quiet right now. We're not giving the media anything more to talk about than what they already have. Public opinion is going to make a major difference here when shit eventually reaches the breaking point."

"*What* breaking point? I've already fucking *broke*!"

The man across the table didn't even flinch at Lev's outburst. And that was why, he knew, Andino sat in the position he did ... and Lev had his. They were two very different men with completely opposite purposes and personalities in this life.

What seemed cold about Andino on the outside was just a means of protection. Nothing more and nothing less.

"I'm sorry ... I'll have the lawyers work out a longer phone call next time," Andino said. "Will that help with Arely?"

"Not like having her home would be."

"She is at home. With Ness—"

"*I'm* her home, man. *Me*."

Her *dad*.

Didn't he get that?

"I'm all she's got," Lev muttered.

"I'm working on it. I am." Andino shifted in the chair a bit, reaching beneath his jacket to pull an item out of the pocket. His phone, actually. As he activated the screen and his thumbs moved over the glass, the man said, "Besides, even if she doesn't have *you*, she will be getting one more person she's been asking for tonight."

"What?"

Turning his phone around and setting it to the table where Lev could plainly see the video playing out on the screen, Andino said nothing. No, he simply allowed the video to speak for him.

And shit, did it *ever*.

It took Lev a second to discern the figure being directed through a crowd of flashing lights and shouting people. He read the name on the building behind her—the *hospital*—and recognized the Marcello enforcer with his hand at her back and fist in the face of anyone who dared step within an inch of Gigi.

"*Gigi*," shouted one photog, "*give us a statement!*"

"*Do you have anything to say about the arrest of Lev Arsov in connection to your disappearance and—*"

Another guy jumped ahead of the last, asking, "*Gigi, is it true you've refused to speak to police about what happened in Mexico?*"

Finally, she stopped.

Head up.

Eyes clear.

Face *healed*.

Lev breathed a bit easier, finding the strength and conviction Gigi held in her gaze as she looked right at the cameras and reporters. "Lev didn't hurt me. He's never hurt me, and he shouldn't be in jail. He should be with *me*—he should be at home with his child. If all the police want to hear from me is the story *they* want me to tell, then they're going to wait a long time for it. If you want a real story, start looking into the agents selling their models to the highest bidders. At least *that's* got some truth to it."

Then, Gigi looked right into one of the cameras, saying, "Right, Marla?"

The video cut off.

Andino tipped his chin up, his smile not at all condescending but also still *pleased*. "Public opinion always counts, and everyone loves a good old American darling, don't they? She certainly knows how to play the part. If they get nothing from her, you're not saying shit, there's nothing left in Mexico to tie you to Jensen, then at most you're looking at the earlier charge and leaving American soil *if* they can make that one stick. It's a waiting game, Pink. We're *waiting*."

His heart ached.

"Don't put her on a stage right now, Andino," Lev said.

"Don't do that to her. She's been through enough."

Didn't she deserve time?

Privacy?

She needed to heal.

She needed ... *him*.

"I did nothing, Pink. This one's all on her. Shit, who do you think called in the reporters to tip them off on the time when she was released from the hospital today? Looks like your woman knows how to play the game. If she's going to do the work, who are we stop her? The rest of us need to get in line. Including you."

THIRTY-TWO

IT SEEMED strange to Gigi that there had once been a time when she could step outside into the public sphere and *not* feel like everything around her was a threat. Or danger was lurking right around the corner to drag her back to hell. It made even the simplest of things—like running down to the corner store for late-night snacks—a whole *event.*

Gigi hated it and wished so hard she could feel normal again.

She wouldn't.

Ever.

"Gigi, watch me!"

From her spot on the bench, Gigi had a clear view of Arely swinging from one monkey bar to the next. Fearless and having the time of her life, the girl had no idea about the constant swell of panic Gigi was forced to swallow down during their outing to the park.

"Perfect! That's great," Gigi called back to Arely.

The girl beamed when she landed with both feet onto the wooden platform at the end of the row of bars. With twenty other children rushing from one end of the playground to the other, and their parents all around, it was just ... *a lot.*

A lot of movement.

Too many strangers.

All the *unknowns.*

Gigi forced down the anxious ripple that tried to escape in her voice when she called back to Arely, but she wasn't sure she succeeded. The woman—or one of them—sitting beside her said that she hadn't hid it at all.

"Do we need a second to do our grounding?" the redhead to her left asked.

Cara Guzzi was her name.

Therapist.

Mother.

Mob wife.

Gigi's new best friend, apparently.

She had knocked on the door one morning with a kind smile, a short introduction that explained the Marcellos asked her to come, and then they were off to the races. Gigi hadn't realized that she needed someone to come in and fix her *head* before the rest of her might start to feel healed, too.

Instead of answering Cara's question with a simple yes or no, Gigi started listing off all the things around her that made her *safe*. "Enforcer in the parking lot. One at each entrance."

A throat cleared behind her, and Gigi smiled.

"Todd is always behind me," she added.

The man in question chuckled, saying quietly, "Not going anywhere, Miss Gigi."

"There's a gun in my bag," Gigi continued. "I started self-defense classes. There is a *very* low chance of something happening in broad daylight in a public space like this. I am *okay*."

"Are you?"

She glanced over at Cara who hadn't asked the question with any sort of malice or sarcasm. It was just an honest, *genuine* question. One that made Gigi consider all the things she had listed that meant she was currently safe to help the panic die down.

"I am," she returned.

"Good," Cara said.

On Gigi's right, her mother, Kimie, openly frowned at the exchange. She could see the concern warring in her mother's eyes—the constant battle she fought ever since Gigi's return to New York. She swung like a pendulum, back and forth between telling her daughter she would be safe if she just got away from the same people who she thought were the catalyst to her kidnapping and assaults, and also letting Gigi do what she wanted and needed to do.

Which was stay.

Help Lev be free.

Get back to happiness.

At least, her mother was getting far better about keeping

her thoughts to herself. Despite the occasional slipups that left the two shouting at one another, she was glad her mother was there in New York with her. *Helping* her. The more people she had around her, the better Gigi felt. She was still on the world's stage—now more than ever as the public chased answers to all their questions—but it wasn't a real connection. Not like the people she kept close every day.

Thousands of comments constantly flooded her social media feeds. Especially after she had dared to take back control of her accounts and then proceeded to post pictures of her injuries—without context other than to write, *they know what they did to me.*

She refused to name an attacker. Wouldn't confirm the details of Mexico. Claimed to *not* remember. All things the police either couldn't make her do or couldn't prove she was lying about at the end of the day.

If there wasn't a clear crime to find justice for, while she teased the threat of ruining the careers of *many* in the industry that had once launched her to superstardom, well ... what were the police still doing holding Lev behind bars?

That was the question.

She had no answers.

"Well," Cara said, standing from the bench with a soft smile, "I think that's about it for me today. Next week, Gigi?"

She nodded. "Absolutely. I'll see you then."

"Don't hesitate to call if—"

"I'll call earlier if I need you, of course."

"Good. See you then."

It was only once Cara left the park that another presence joined Gigi and her mother on the bench. Nessa, that was. Technically, Arely's current guardian until her father was finally released from police custody. The girl had basically taken over Lev's Manhattan townhouse until further notice because she didn't want to upset Arely's life and schedule any more than it already had been. What was more surprising was how easily and quickly the woman invited Gigi into their home without a second thought.

No, she didn't need a hotel.

She had a bed.

Lev's.

Nessa offered friendship and companionship in such a frank, open way that it was hard for Gigi to say no. She hadn't realized how much of that had been missing in her life. That she really *didn't* have friends outside the industry. Not ones that expected nothing from her except *her* willing friendship in return.

"I think Arely's about ready for a nap," Nessa said with a laugh when she fell into the bench beside Gigi. "And if Lev calls to talk to her tonight, then she'll be *so* much better to get to bed after, you know?"

"Totally," Gigi agreed.

She hadn't been able to get on the phone with Lev. The offer was on the table every time he called, either through his lawyers or when he used the jail's phone. She just didn't know what to say to him yet.

I love you was most obvious. But *I'm not okay* would soon follow.

She couldn't do that to him.

Not now.

"Wanna get going?" Nessa asked her, no judgment staring back from the younger woman at the question. "You looked about ready to puke a few minutes ago. Don't you have that interview with the detective later? *You* probably need a nap before that, too."

Gigi laughed.

So did her mom and Nessa.

"We *all* need naps," Gigi muttered, pushing up from the bench. "But yeah, let's get her home. I'm kind of hungry, too."

And lonely.

Missing Lev.

Ready for it to be over.

Nessa and Kimie were quick to stand and join her. Behind the women, Todd the enforcer decided to make himself known when he cracked his knuckles and said, "Time to play *break your face* with any fucking paps waiting at the house. My favorite game."

So, maybe she couldn't *be* normal. Even when everything

335

was almost perfect again. She could, however, have a new normal. If the rest of the world would *let her*.

• • •

"You're a very busy woman, Miss ... would you prefer I use *Rey*, your stage name, or Parker?" the man across the table asked.

Fixing the wool shawl on her shoulders, Gigi didn't even allow the man the respect of her gaze when she replied, "You can call me whatever you want as long as I don't have to be brought down here to do this nonsense again."

"Is that what you want to call the disappearance of a man, not to mention ... your obvious kidnapping and attack?"

Finally, Gigi lifted her stare to meet the man at the other end of the table. She was supposed to be having an interview with yet another detective. Instead, she had shown up to find the district attorney waiting with a smile.

A kind smile, sure.

Didn't make a difference to her.

They had two different goals, and she wouldn't allow herself to forget it even if it meant telling the truth might finally help her in some way. His goal was to keep Lev behind bars—whether on charges relating to her or otherwise—and hers was to get the love of her life back where he belonged.

With her.

And his child.

"Other than the bodies found outside of the Mexican estate," the man said, opening a folder to spread out a row of pictures across the table, "the home itself and whatever—or *whoever*—was inside was lost to a fire."

She didn't even glance at the glossy photographs. As it was, she had already seen them one too many times. The shots of her leaving the show with Jensen. The burnt-out estate that left the officials with little to no evidence but for a handful of bodies outside.

"I don't know that place," she said, shrugging. "I've never seen that house before in my life. And if I have, I can't remember it. Did you find something that proves I was inside?"

Her innocent question had the man's jaw clenching, but he quickly replaced it with another one of those kind smiles.

"Gigi, I understand you're attempting to protect—"

"I'm attempting to get on with my life after a very difficult few weeks, actually. Weeks that, as I have told *many* people and so have my doctors, I can't remember. A bit of brain damage from my apparent drowning, you know? Or that's what I was told. But I can't move on because between the police hounding me for answers I don't have and the media that won't leave me alone, I'm forced to do this repeatedly."

"Andino Marcello—"

"I have no idea who that is," she lied.

She was sure the DA had introduced himself as Smith Gerdson, but she honestly didn't care to use his name or see him as anything other than another roadblock to Lev's freedom.

Because the thing was, Gigi knew how this would end ... if she admitted to *anything* that happened inside the Mexican estate during her captivity, even if it was to name her rapist and what he had done, then she had to explain how she was freed, too. And *that* was where things became tricky.

Because Lev wasn't supposed to leave the states when he was still facing charges from an incident at the Fashion Week show. Sure, it would clear any suspicion they had regarding his involvement in the state she had been found, but it would only cause more problems for every other legal issue he faced.

And she wouldn't do that.

The District Attorney leaned into the table, clasping his hands together as he eyed her speculatively. It took him an entire thirty seconds before he spoke again. "You understand that I find it very hard to believe the story you're trying to sell us when ... outside of these walls, you've been saying *very* different things. In fact, I have a half of a dozen social media posts from you that suggest you know a great deal more than you're sharing."

"And what would it matter?"

"Pardon?"

Gigi smiled thinly, saying, "The story I have to tell—what does it matter? It won't match the one you have laid out for the courts. It won't fit the narrative your team of people has been feeding the media since this all began. It *certainly* won't help me."

"You're a victim. The only thing we want to do here is help—"

"A victim of what, exactly?" The man opened his mouth to reply, but Gigi was quick to interject with, "Oh, you mean what the medical records say? I suppose those will be the only things you'll have in a trial to collaborate any evidence because you sure as hell won't have me, sir. What are you going to do? *Force* a victim on the stand? To say what—that man you're trying to put away for life didn't beat or rape me? Because that is what I'll say. It's the truth."

"So, you do remember—"

"Off the record," Gigi said, pointing at the recording device he had placed on the table when they first began this shitshow. Her lawyer at her left reached over and hit the red button to pause the recording before she continued speaking. "I will if you put me on the stand. I will be your absolute worst nightmare. If you think I can't control the way the public sees this play out, then you haven't been paying close enough attention to what I already have been doing."

"Is that a threat? You realize we're capable of charging you with obstruction of justice, don't you?"

Gigi laughed, tired and over this entire thing. "Prove it. You can't *make* me say what you want. The same way every post I've made on social media, and each statement I've given to reporters or tabloids all had a purpose. You don't make a narrative for me. I have *my own*. Trust me when I say, Mr. Gerdson, that you are not the first to learn this about me. I'm not a puppet. Not for the media. Not for my agency. And certainly not for police who are trying to ruin the life of an innocent man who only ever *loved* me. Do you have any other questions?"

"No, but you might find it interesting," the man replied, "that your most recent social media post about your previous agent, Marla, has started an investigation into her business affairs in Paris. Of course, we're not privy to—"

"*Questions*," Gigi interrupted sharply. "I asked if you had any more of those."

She didn't care about Marla. That trash would take itself out. Andino said so—one way or another. Since the man really hadn't given her a reason to distrust him, then she took him at his word.

"Back on the record," the DA said, nodding at the lawyer to start the recording again. Then, to Gigi, he explained, "Whether or not you comply with the investigation is inconsequential at this point, Miss Parker. We will proceed with what we have. I am giving you the option to fill in some blanks."

His threats were hot air.

Pointless.

"Good luck with that," Gigi replied, "because as far as I understand it, even the Mexican officials aren't going to proceed with any extradition or charges because they have nothing, can't tie anyone to the house except the dead bodies they found, and they can't even put enough evidence on the table to point a finger at Lev. The only reason *you* have him where he is, is because you're using charges from before to keep him locked up. This entire thing is starting to look very ... *unstable*. Isn't it?"

"Why are you doing this?"

"I love him," she said simply. "What it really boils down to is putting a man attached to a criminal figure in prison. None of this is about you helping me find justice for what was done to me. Because don't you see?" She waved at the photos spread out on the table, her voice quieter when she added, "Someone already did that. And it wasn't you."

• • •

"An offer slid into my email today," Kayla said, her voice distorted by the wind in the background of the call. "If you're at all interested in hearing it."

Gigi fiddled with the edge of the comforter on the bed, considering her assistant's words. Despite putting as much distance as she could between her old team—and their connection to Marla—she had kept Kayla for a couple of different reasons. Long before shit went bad, Kayla had helped Gigi time and time again. She had not proven herself untrustworthy, and in fact, had stuck her neck out more than she needed to. And when Gigi needed access to the media under the radar, Kayla was the one with the contacts to get it done.

"For what?" Gigi settled on asking.

"A shoot and interview. They're willing to let you have total say on what's published and—"

"Tell them thanks, but I'm not interested."

The silence that answered Gigi back wasn't all that surprising. While her contracts had run out through the agency and the management team had essentially washed their hands of Gigi Rey in the industry, that didn't mean the industry was entirely done with her. In a lot of cases, it seemed like Gigi was wanted even more.

She just wasn't up for it.

Any of it.

"Did you hear that Marla's offices were stormed this morning in Paris?" Kayla asked.

"First I've heard of it."

All she knew was what the DA had told her days earlier. She decided not to follow along with Marla's downfall anymore than she needed to. If someone came knocking to ask her questions, then she might consider talking. As of right then, no one had.

"Yeah, I guess it's ... a mess. And hey," Kayla added quieter, "I wanted to say sorry."

"For what?"

"I think I might have unintentionally been the one who fed Marla information about you and Lev. Like that bar and the photos that came out after? I needed to make sure it would be okay for us to use the car and driver without security ... I didn't even think about it until—"

Jesus.

Gigi let out a shuddering breath, stopping her assistant from saying anything more when she told the woman, "Why wouldn't you trust her? Why wouldn't *I*? Thank you for telling me, though."

"Gigi?"

"Yeah?"

"Are you ever coming back—is Gigi Rey still a *thing*?"

At the same time Kayla asked the question, a little pop of curly black hair peeked in the doorway of the master bedroom. While the townhouse was quiet, and it was *way* too late for Arely to still be awake, sometimes the girl surprised her by crawling into Lev's bed. Gigi never said anything one way or another.

Nessa never asked about it in the morning.

She figured ... Arely was just trying to get close to her dad in whatever way she could. She asked about him constantly; he was always on her mind. It was hard to hide everything from her but especially when the kid was so intuitive as it was. She picked up on a lot whether they told her or not.

"Gi?" Kayla pressed.

"Gigi Rey is dead," she replied, thinking, *or whoever that was*, "and I'm fine with that."

She didn't linger on the call for much longer. The second she had discarded the phone to the bedside table, Arely leaned in the doorway a little more, her big blue eyes wide and silently pleading to be right where Gigi currently was.

They didn't need to tell Arely something was wrong when it came to her dad. The girl knew; it was so painfully obvious that there was a giant Lev-shaped hole in her tiny heart. Nessa had even found three of Lev's shirts hidden under Arely's pillow, and the girl had gone as far as stealing photos of her dad from around the house to hoard in her bedroom.

At least, she had finally stopped asking when Lev would be back or other questions that neither Gigi nor Nessa could answer. Not without needing to delve into deeper discussions that a girl of her age couldn't possibly understand.

"You wanna sleep in Daddy's bed again?" Gigi asked.

Arely nodded. "Yeah."

"Come here, then."

She didn't need to be told again. Gigi swore Arely's bare feet barely touched the floor three times between the doorway and the end of the bed before she was up on the mattress and crawling across the comforter. She already had the blanket pulled back for the girl to slip under and hide away from the rest of the world.

Gigi needed that, too.

Tucked beneath the blanket, Arely peeked over at Gigi with a little grin as she said, "I don't want *you* to miss Daddy, too. Right?"

She blinked.

Oh.

Maybe it wasn't just about Lev.

Kids.

They were the purest of souls. The sweetest of hearts. Especially this one.

"Right," Gigi whispered, reaching over to push the dark curls out of Arely's eyes. "You're so right, kiddo."

While the time Gigi had spent with Arely compared to Lev was much less significant in measurement, it didn't matter. She was just as much a part of Gigi's heart as her father, and she couldn't imagine that ever changing. She loved the girl— in a different way than she loved her father, sure, but *still*. It was there.

Constant.

Growing.

Real.

Arely wasn't her biological child, but she found that didn't make a difference when the girl *needed* her. Because she needed her, too.

"But I do," Arely said, sighing. "Miss him."

Gigi swallowed hard. "Me, too."

"You won't leave, right? You're not leaving, are you?"

It was a new thing.

Every time Nessa left the house, or Gigi, then Arely was suddenly in a panic that they weren't ever coming back. Part of her knew it was because the girl believed her father wouldn't come home, either. That killed her.

Snuggling down beneath the blanket, Gigi smiled when Arely pushed closer to her in the bed until the two of them were arm in arm and hiding away from the world. She pressed a kiss to the top of Arely's head, settled and happy. *For now.*

"I'm not leaving. *Ever.* I promise."

And that was that.

THIRTY-THREE

TWO.

Two months in lockup while the officials played keep-away with Lev's freedom. He had started to believe that the games of the police would never end despite the hard fight his lawyers put up every step of the way.

But then it did.

The case they attempted to build against Lev started to fall apart one single charge at a time—starting with the catalyst charges from the night he punched a security guard who, for some reason, decided to drop all charges. That might have had something to do with the bribe Andino paid out to the guard, but Lev couldn't say.

Either way, everything else quickly went to shit for the officials after that. If they had no charges stemming from the show, then they couldn't hold him for illegally leaving the country when he wasn't supposed to so, either.

As far as anything related to Gigi? They had a victim who said there wasn't a crime. The mess in Mexico? The officials from down there weren't going forward with charges for something they couldn't physically tie him to.

What was left? That's what his lawyers asked when they were given a seat in front of a judge to demand someone *look* at what was happening to him. What were they doing? That's what the judge demanded after the hearing.

Lev was released within forty-eight hours of that meeting between the DA, his lawyers, and the judge. The judge who was a good man, Andino had said a couple of weeks earlier, that would be willing to help them on this little issue.

For a price.

Everything came with a price. That had never been more obvious to Lev until now.

The waiting game had come to an end and as he stood on the steps of a jail that had housed him for months with no reprieve, it all felt a little … surreal. In a suit that had been brought in by his lawyers for him to wear, he shoved his hands in the pockets of the slacks and stared up at the bright blue, winter sky overhead.

He didn't have a coat.

It should have been cold.

Lev felt none of it.

"Enjoy it," came a familiar voice from down the steps of the jail, "because if we all get our way, you'll never feel like this again."

Lev smiled, his gaze coming to settle on the man who leaned against an idling, black BMW. Andino, that was. "And what is this feeling?"

His boss smiled.

"Relief isn't a good enough word, is it?" Andino asked.

Lev shook his head. "Not even close."

"I don't have a better one."

And yet, Lev also understood what the man had meant by never wanting to feel this way again. Because if he was capable, then he was never going to sit inside a jail cell again with his future on the line.

That was a promise.

"Who do I thank," Lev asked, coming down the steps slowly, "for keeping the media away today?"

"The jail likely. Even I didn't get a call about your time of release until the last minute. I think they want to … like the rest of the fucks in this city … sweep all of this under the rug. Pretend like it didn't happen."

Lick their wounds, Lev bet.

As they should.

This had been a travesty. It could have been worse.

By the time Lev reached the end of the cement steps, Andino had thrust his hand forward to catch his in a tight grasp. Then, he used that same hold to yank Lev close enough that he could give him a one-armed hug with a hard smack to the shoulder.

"That was too close," Andino muttered, letting him go.

Lev grinned. "It *really* was."

"Let's not do a repeat, huh?"

Well ...

"That's fair," he told his boss.

Andino grunted under his breath, shooting one last look at the jailhouse that he had avoided other than the one visit. A lot like everyone else. He understood and wasn't about to get in his feelings because of it. The less attention and stories they gave the media while they handled his situation, the better it would be for all of them.

After all, it wasn't just the officials that needed the spotlight to go away ... no doubt, Andino's criminal organization had a broom ready to get the dirt under the rug *fast*.

"How much?" he asked Andino.

"Hmm?"

"All of this. How much did it cost you?"

Andino lifted one shoulder, stepping away from the car to smack Lev on the shoulder again with a chuckle before he waved at the car. "Doesn't matter, get in. I hear there's a couple of girls who are *really* looking forward to seeing you today."

Yeah.

His little Arely.

And hopefully Gigi, too.

Every call he was able to have with Arely was *just* with her. Sometimes, he heard Gigi in the background. He'd been told she was staying at his townhouse, too. Sleeping in *his* bed. But for whatever reason, she couldn't get on the phone.

Maybe it hurt too much.

Maybe she was scared.

God knew he had been.

Sitting in the passenger seat of the BMW, he turned to his boss to say, "Shit, look at this."

Andino glanced his way, pulling off the curb. "What?"

"*You* are driving *me*."

That had them laughing.

It felt *good*.

Real.

Then, Lev said, "I feel like I should ask again, though. How much? I owe you and—"

"One can't put a price on true friendship."

"And that's what I am—a *friend*?"

His boss had said it before. Lev still wondered if the man might someday say enough was enough. But apparently, not.

Andino smirked. "One of my best, one of my first *I* chose."

"That can't be true."

"More than you know, Pink."

No, he knew.

It was exactly why he *was* Pink for Andino.

And always would be.

• • •

The drive home was quiet, but Lev didn't mind. It gave him a moment to think and while he certainly had more than enough time for that in jail, this was different. Then, he had been thinking about all the things he was going to lose. Everything he had yet to do. Now, the only thing on his mind was what he wanted.

Home.

Love.

His girls.

Lev barely took a step out onto the quiet street before the front door of the townhouse was thrown open with enough force to knock into the flowerpot off to the side. The first person out of the house was Arely.

Arms wide open.

Smiling huge.

Crying already.

"*Daddy, Daddy, Daddy!*"

He barely had time to consider the other women who slipped out of the house because—they would understand—he had to deal with the most important thing first. The very idea that his child thought he somehow abandoned or forgot about her during his time away absolutely gutted him. He would spend the rest of his life making sure Arely knew he wasn't going anywhere.

Ever again.

Her feet hit the paved walkway with hard smacks, bringing

her closer and closer to his open arms until he had her wrapped in them. Nothing had ever felt better than lifting his daughter from the ground, hugging her tight enough that even God himself wouldn't rip the child from his arms, and forgetting everything else.

None of it mattered.

Just *that* moment.

"I'm sorry, I'm so sorry," he told her.

Over and over.

I love you.

I'm not going anywhere again.

Daddy's here, baby.

He kept saying those things. Again, and again. As much as she needed to hear them. Because each time he said it again, Arely cried a little harder. He rained kisses over her wet eyelids, on her pinked cheeks, and even a peck on her now-smiling lips. Her heartbeat raced—beating as fast as hummingbird wings against his own chest.

Face to face ...

Eye to eye ...

He stared at his daughter, and *everything* was right again in the world.

Or almost.

In his haste to get his daughter back where she belonged in his arms, Lev had spun to face the road and his boss leaning against the BMW. Turning back to the house, he stopped at the sight of the two women standing side by side, their arms locked together as they smiled at the sight in front of them.

Nessa and Gigi.

"We told you, Arely," Nessa said. "See, we weren't lying."

Arely sniffled. "I know but—"

"No buts," he told his girl, pressing a kiss to the side of her head. "Daddy's home, right?"

She nodded fiercely. "*Right.*"

Nessa broke away from Gigi's side with a grin before she came close enough for Lev to grab her by the arm. Pulling the girl who had always been like the little sister he never asked for into a one-armed hug, Nessa's laughter filled the yard.

"Thank you," he told her. "For putting shit on hold ...

looking out for her ... *everything*."

Nessa smiled, whispering, "Of course, Lev."

Only one left, he thought.

As if Nessa could read his mind, or maybe she had just noticed where his stare traveled over her shoulder, she reached for Arely. Helping to pull the girl from his grasp, without *too* much fight, thankfully, she had the situation handled and stepped aside with his daughter. With a coat in hand for Arely, she managed to wrangle the girl into the jacket to help with the cold.

Lev finally had his hands free. And a full view of a *very* nervous Gigi.

Wringing her hands together, Gigi shifted from foot to foot when their gazes met, and he took one step forward. Then another. *And another.*

"I'm sorry I couldn't talk when you called," she said. "I just didn't know what to say. It feels like all I've done is *talk*, but not to the person I wanted to, you know? And—"

"*Gigi.*"

Her rambling came to a stop all at once. In the next breath, Lev was in front of her, close enough that his chest molded against hers, and his hands were able to slip under her jaw to hold tight. He didn't care about who watched. He didn't give a shit if the neighborhood was recording them.

"I love you," he told her.

Gigi trembling lips stretched wide with a beautiful smile. "Yeah?"

"I'm sorry I didn't tell you before."

She answered that with a shake of her head before she pushed up to her tiptoes, those grinning lips of hers finding his with a slow, soft kiss that told him everything was going to be okay. It might take time but that was fine, too. They had so much to figure out. So many things to talk about.

But that kiss, the languid sweeps of his lips against hers that coaxed her mouth open for him, felt like a restart. A single second in time where the two of them could just *be*. Nothing else had to matter.

"I love you, too," she whispered against his lips as her fingertips grazed his cheekbone. "Before ... *after*. Forever."

That was all he wanted.

This woman.

His child.

The life they could have *together*.

Now, everything was right. His world was perfect again. What more could he ask for?

They could figure out the rest later.

EPILOGUE

"COME ON, you're going to be late," Lev said, rushing his already annoyed daughter to the front door. Arely even had the nerve to stomp her feet and give him one of her signature glares when he didn't let her slip on her boots and coat, opting to just do it himself to save time. Standing straight, he arched a brow at her attitude, but it didn't concern her in the least. "Are you quite done?"

She put her hands to her hips, saying, "No. Are *you*?"

If it was any other morning, then he might have laughed. But they were *both* running late, he had another issue to deal with upstairs, and this little girl had to get going because he was not in any mood to deal with yet another letter from the fucking school about tardiness.

"Arely Dawn Marks-Arsov," Lev drawled, taking his time with her full name, so she knew he was serious this time. "Do you want to try that again?"

She pursed her lips. "Maybe."

Maybe?

Maybe!

Where did this kid come from?

Oh, yeah.

Him.

"I love you, Daddy," Arely said, "but sometimes you make me *very* angry. Especially when you rush me. I just wanted—"

"You can't wear makeup to school. You might be almost six, but that doesn't mean *sixteen*. And that wasn't even your makeup. That was Gigi's makeup you were playing in. Try again."

She sighed.

Another foot stomp came after.

351

Lev just waited it out.

"*Fine!*"

That was that.

Lev pulled open the front door to expose the man already standing at the bottom of the stoop, waiting for Arely. Todd, that was. The enforcer stayed on Lev's post to do with what he wanted. Usually, the man handled taking Arely to and from school, a bit of driving and errands, and looking out for Gigi when needed.

He counted him as a friend.

Arely stomped out of the house, shouting over her shoulder, "But I *do* love you!"

Todd shot Lev a look.

He only shrugged back.

"Love you, too, kid," he called.

"Hard morning?" Todd asked.

Lev heaved a breath. "Man, you have *no* idea."

And yet, he wouldn't give it up for the world.

Now ...

The problem waiting upstairs.

• • •

Lev tapped his knuckles to the bathroom door, listening for a confirmation inside that he could enter. At first, he heard nothing. The second rap of his hand to the door, however, and Gigi's quiet voice came through the wood when she said, "What?"

That wasn't an *okay*.

It was still good enough for him.

Twisting the knob and stepping inside the bathroom, he was entirely unsurprised to find Gigi naked, the steam in the bathroom wrapping around her freckled skin as she stood over the sink, hands curved at the edge of the bowl, while she stared at herself in the mirror.

"You okay?" he asked.

She passed a look his way, and her next exhale came out shaky when she whispered, "I don't know if I can do it, Lev. I thought I could but now I know the car is going to be here in ten minutes to pick me up and all I can think is ... like, what are people going to say when they see the scars or—"

Her words cut off when she choked out a soft cry, her head dropping low as the wet strands of her hair fell over her shoulders. There was nothing that killed him more than when this amazing, *strong* woman had moments where she felt anything but those things. He blamed a dead man for the fight Gigi still dealt with constantly, the scars on her heart and in her mind invisible to the rest of the world but so very apparent to him.

"*Hey, hey, hey ...*"

He didn't really have time on his schedule to handle a mental breakdown when he was supposed to be at Andino's restaurant in less than an hour to sit down at an important meeting between his boss and other made men, but some shit couldn't be helped.

"Come here," he murmured, crossing the space between them and slipping in behind her. In a second, he had her warm, wet form pressed against his. Wrapping his arms around her chest the way she liked because she said it felt *safe* and *good* and *right* ... he held here there, dropping soft kisses across the six-inch scar between her shoulder blades. A whip, she told him one night when he asked.

He didn't push a lot.

She didn't offer details.

He was fine to do whatever she wanted.

Whenever she wanted.

While some things had been so easy for them after everything happened, others were not. She found solace when he loved her, and monsters in her dreams beside him. He could take her away from the world with sex and affection, but he couldn't save her from the war in her mind.

But she kept fighting.

And he helped when he could.

Like now.

With his lips at the back of her neck, he murmured, "Do you want me to get your phone—have Kayla call off the interview and shoot?"

Her first in *months.*

It wasn't even one she was being paid for but rather, a campaign she had chosen to join to bring awareness to violence against women. Because as a survivor, and as more and more things became publicly known about the horrible things happening to women in her industry, she felt like she owed it to the world to say, *if it can happen to me, it can happen to anyone.*

He didn't think she owed anybody shit.

Not even him.

When Gigi didn't reply, Lev was quick to add, "You know it doesn't matter to us, right? Me and Arely, I mean. We don't care if you're in magazines. We don't care how many people know your face or if your name is in lights ... you're ours regardless, Gigi. You're just *ours.*"

Because he knew that was the thing ...

She feared the camera; the very idea that a lens would start to capture the parts of her that were not the same. The scars left behind. The darkness that sometimes shone through in her bright green eyes. Any of it.

All of it.

That scared her.

He understood why.

"And we love you no matter who you are or what you do," he said against the shell of her ear, his hold flexing tighter around her until he started feeling that tension drifting away. "Always. Tomorrow. Whenever you need us. We love you."

The truth won.

Every single time.

He kept telling her those truths until she finally heard them. *Really* heard them. She eventually turned in his hold, and her trembling hands wrapped around his neck to pull him in for a kiss that set his heart off like fireworks. It wasn't like he needed to be reminded that he was already running *way* too late, but the buzzing phone in his pocket did exactly that.

Not that it did *anything.*

This woman was still his wettest, wildest dream come true. And she reminded him why he was willing to risk his boss's wrath for being late when she let him lift her to the bathroom counter. Her intentions and wants were clear in the rushed, chaotic movements of her hands as she yanked open the button of his pants and then pulled the zipper down.

Sometimes, she wanted slow and sweet. Other times, she wanted to be fucked until she couldn't breathe. There was no rhyme or reason to the whys of the ways they loved but he adored it, nonetheless. Right then, she only seemed to want the same thing he did.

For him to be *with* her.

Inside her.

They found heaven together.

Something better.

Sweeter.

A life worth living; one worth *keeping*.

And when they did finally come together with him deep inside her, and her thighs spread wide; his lips had found hers again so that there was no possible way he could be closer when she told him, "I love you, Lev. You make me *better*."

She did, too, for him.

He was a better man for her.

That would never change.

BIO

Bethany-Kris is a Canadian author, lover of much, and mother to four young sons, three cats, and four dogs. A small town in Eastern Canada where she was born and raised is where she has always called home. With her boys under her feet, a snuggling cat, barking dogs, and a spouse calling over his shoulder, she is nearly always writing something ... when she can find the time.

Find all the places to stalk Bethany-Kris on her website at www.bethanykris.com.

OTHER BOOKS

Cross + Catherine

Always
Revere
Unruly
The Companion
Naz & Roz
The Naz & Roz Chronicles

DeLuca Duet

Waste of Worth: Part One
Worth of Waste: Part Two

Standalone Titles

Pink
Pretty Lies
Dirty Pool
Effortless
Inflict (**permanently free**)
Cozen
Captivated
Dishonored

Donati Bloodlines

Thin Lies
Thin Lines
Thin Lives
Behind the Bloodlines
The Complete Trilogy

Gun Moll Trilogy

Gun Moll
Gangster Moll
Madame Moll

Filthy Marcellos

Antony
Lucian
Giovanni
Dante
Legacy
A Very Marcello Christmas
The Complete Collection

Seasons of Betrayal

Where the Sun Hides
Where the Snow Falls
Where the Wind Whispers
Seasons: The Complete Seasons of Betrayal Series

The Chicago War

Deathless & Divided
Reckless & Ruined
Scarless & Sacred
Breathless & Bloodstained
The Complete Series
Maldives & Mistletoe

The Russian Guns

The Arrangement (**permanently free**)
The Life
The Score
Demyan & Ana
Shattered
The Jersey Vignettes

Fantasy Romance

The Hunted

Find more on Bethany-Kris's website at www.bethanykris.com.

www.ingramcontent.com/pod-product-compliance
Lightning Source LLC
Chambersburg PA
CBHW072025020726
47501CB00006B/1959